THE RELUCTANT NUDIST

To Andy
thanks for all your
help. Much
appreciated
Alan
16 Oct 20??

THE
RELUCTANT
NUDIST

A W Palmer

PRUDENCE BOOKS

First published in Great Britain in 2005 by
Prudence Books

Copyright © A W Palmer 2005

ISBN 1-933570-39-3

Typeset by Hewer Text UK Ltd, Edinburgh
Printed and bound by Cox & Wyman Ltd, Reading, Berkshire

www.reluctantnudist.com

Thanks to Kathy Parsons, David Boughton
(no relation to our hero), John Loden, Susie Green,
Robert Packham, Clive Underhill, Andy Spark, Garry Cheek,
and all others who've given me their help, time and
encouragement in completing this novel.

DAY ONE

1

It wasn't what you'd call a great start to a holiday. By even the most elastic stretch of the imagination. What had begun as a straightforward drive down to the empty roads of deepest rural South West France had ended here. Stopped in the dead centre of nowhere. At one a.m. on a steamy hot August night.

'Well, where the hell are we?' asked an exasperated Nick. 'You've had the road atlas in your lap for the last half hour. It might just as well be the complete works of Walt Disney for all the good it's done us.'

'Please don't shout,' said Ros. 'Map reading isn't one of my stronger points.'

'You amaze me.'

'I'm just as anxious as you not to be lost. To the best of my judgment I think we're here,' Ros said, pointing at a tiny D-route on the map. 'Or again we might be here,' indicating a spot at least five inches to the left.

'This is hopeless! At this rate, by the time we get there,

Phillip and Kathy will be tucked up in bed – if they're not already. I'll ring them.'

Nick picked up his mobile, checked a piece of paper and called the number. Nothing happened. He looked at the phone. No signal.

'Oh great. Just what we needed.'

'Look Nick, we're both tired. We don't know where we are. And we're not even sure how to get to the gîte. Phillip did say it was hard to find. Let alone in the middle of the bloody night. So let's get somewhere to stay and start again tomorrow. Please, love?' She put her hand on his arm.

'OK,' Nick sighed, putting the car into gear and moving off. 'But I can tell you, the chances of finding somewhere around here are about the same as discovering intelligent life on Kiss FM.'

Just as he said this, they rounded a bend and there, on the left hand side of the road, a red neon sign glowed over a large gateway. It simply read 'Le Paradis'.

'Is that a camp site?' asked Ros, and answered her own question, 'Yes, it is.'

'Perfect. But for one small detail.'

'Which is?'

'We don't have a tent.'

As Nick slowed the car, lettering below the neon sign came into view. Ros interpreted, ' "Cabines à louer", cabins to rent.'

'In the middle of August? I very much doubt it.'

'Come on. Let's give it a try. What can we lose.'

Nick turned into the entrance roadway. To their right was a reception building with, unexpectedly, the lights on.

They pulled into a parking space and Nick switched off the engine. 'Wait here. I'll see if they've got a vacancy.'

Nick got out. The night sky was pitch black, illuminated only by pinpoints of stars. The only sounds were the slight ticking noises from his cooling engine and the insistent croaking of crickets or tree frogs. Even this early in the morning, it was ridiculously hot.

Nick climbed the steps to the reception glass door. Beyond it he could see a high wooden counter behind which stood a middle-aged man. Only his bare-chested top half was in view. Nick entered and was struck by a wave of heat, even more oppressive than outside.

The receptionist smiled in welcome, 'Bon soir, m'sieur.'

'Er, bon soir. Um, avez vous une cabine pour la nuit?' Nick managed to utter. French had never been his strongest subject.

The man smiled. 'We don't usually have any vacancies in August but today must be your lucky day.'

'You're English!'

'You're not wrong. We do actually have a cabin. Late cancellation. It's forty euros, including linen. There's a fridge, basic cooking facilities and, of course, bed.' He smiled. 'How long you planning on staying?'

'Just the one night.'

'Would you like to see it first?'

'No, we'll take it,' said a very relieved Nick.

'Could you fill in this registration.' The receptionist passed a card over the high counter. 'And I'll need your passport.'

Nick completed the registration card, produced his passport from the top pocket of his short-sleeved shirt and handed both over. As the receptionist took them, Nick walked over to the door to give Ros the thumbs-up. As he turned back to the counter, the receptionist had already returned with the key.

'There you go. Cabin 12. I'll tell you where it is. I'd like to show you but I'm the only one on duty. You go round the perimeter road outside to the right. Follow the road round the bend and then take the very first left – Avenue A. Number 12 is six down on the right. OK.'

'Sixth cabin on right. Avenue A. Thanks a lot.'

'The restaurant's open in the morning for breakfast. Or you can buy food here at the site supermarket.' The receptionist indicated a darkened building opposite. 'Opens at eight.'

'Thanks all the same but I think we'll be on our way pretty early tomorrow, er, today.'

Nick left the reception building and returned to the car, displaying the cabin key through the front windscreen to a very relieved-looking Ros

Nick got in and started the car. The faint light coming from the office illuminated the trees that presumably screened the rest of the camp site from the road.

The driveway continued for another hundred metres or so and turned sharp left. Another twenty, and the headlights illuminated a wooden sign with the legend 'Avenue A' painted roughly on it.

They found cabin 12 and pulled into the parking space out front. It was one of a long line which wouldn't have looked out of place at Butlins Skegness, circa 1955. In fact, these very buildings may well have started life in a British seaside resort, retiring here in their declining years to enjoy some well-earned sunshine.

Separated from its identical companions by about six foot of space either side, cabin 12 had a small beach hut-like front verandah reached by three wooden steps. A central door was flanked by two small windows. Even in the gloom, the whole edifice seemed to be pleading for a refreshing coat of paint.

Nick climbed out of the car and handed the cabin door key to Ros. Careful not to wake sleeping neighbours, he whispered, 'Go ahead.'

Quietly removing their two bags from the boot, he followed Ros into the cabin.

It was bigger than it looked from the outside. But it was still no Tardis. The door opened onto a combined living, kitchen and dining space. There was a sofa bed, in that nice shade of shag-pile brown that the French do so well. A rickety table, two chairs and a primitive, possibly illegal, gas ring kept it company. Below the hob was a small fridge, open and unplugged.

A beaded curtain led through to the bedroom. A double bed was made up with fresh clean sheets. Badly self-assembled bedside cabinets flanked the bed, wall-mounted lights above. A dressing table and stool completed the ensemble. Another window opened onto the side alleyway between their cabin and next doors'.

At the far end of the cabin was an en suite bathroom. Perhaps that was too ambitious a term for a room which contained a cracked tiled cubicle with a plastic shower curtain – stencilled with large dolphins – a hand basin, bathroom cabinet, wc and bidet.

'Well, it won't win any style awards but it seems reasonably clean', Nick said, putting the bags down on the bed. 'Fancy a night cap?'.

He pulled out a bottle of red wine, bought on the ferry "duty free", which could be translated as "three times the price of a similar bottle in France".

'Why not.'

Nick went into the kitchen, and found a waiter's friend corkscrew which he applied to the claret. 'Any glasses around?'

Ros went into the bathroom and emerged with two cheap glass tumblers, holding them up as if for Nick's approval and putting them down on the work surface by the sink.

Popping the cork, Nick filled both glasses and handed one to Ros. 'Here's to a really great holiday,' he said as they clinked glasses, 'and let's hope it runs a bit more smoothly than it has so far.'

Ros took her drink into the bedroom and sat on the bed, taking a sip and placing the glass on her bedside cabinet. 'That's good.'

Nick sipped from his tumbler as he followed her into the bedroom. It was their first drink since the wine which had accompanied their less-than-average late dinner while waiting for the car to be repaired. Nick would kill Tony when he got back. He was supposed to have checked the hoses.

Sitting on the rather lumpy bed in this dingy hut, feeling sweat gathering on his brow and under his armpits, and drinking tepid wine from cheap tumblers wasn't quite the romantic scenario Nick had conjured up when the idea of a holiday in France had first been discussed.

Phillip and Kathy were older friends in their early fifties. When they'd suggested Ros and Nick spend a stress-free holiday with them in their gîte in France it had seemed ideal.

Time to unwind and spend lazy days by the pool. With a couple, most importantly to Nick, at ease in each other's company. Attributes which Nick hoped would rub off on his relationship with Ros. Or distract attention from the fact that they didn't seem to be getting along as well as they used to.

Although they'd been together for over six years, or perhaps *because* they'd been together for over six years, the magic, if not totally worn off, was a trifle threadbare. They didn't seem to have such good times together. Or such good sex. If any sex. But perhaps that was inevitable in a relationship. Especially when you reached the age of 34.

God, did he ever dream he'd be this ancient. If he'd been born in his father's generation he would almost certainly have been a parent by now. His youngest child would be, what, at least ten – probably much older.

Maybe that was part of the problem. Ros had been dropping lead-lined hints that the time was well overdue for the pitter patter of tiny feet. And she didn't mean, as W C Fields once famously remarked, wanting to employ a midget butler.

No, child-rearing was firmly on her agenda and he wasn't at all sure he wanted to be part of it. Nor the loss of freedom and the commitment involved. Don't get him wrong, Nick loved Ros in his own way but had a sneaking suspicion that there might be something a bit better round the corner. Options needed to be kept open.

'Is there a drop more,' said Ros, interrupting Nick's thoughts.

'Er? Oh yes, sure.' Nick picked up the bottle and filled Ros's empty glass. 'Not bad is it? Do I detect a hint of pineapple and disinfectant?'

Ros smiled. She sluiced the liquid round in her glass, savouring the rich bouquet and looking straight ahead in an unfocused fashion. 'Do you think they'll worry about us? You know, wonder what's happened?'

'Phillip and Kathy? Probably think we've stopped off somewhere on the way. Which is exactly what we have done. I'll ring them in the morning and let them know what time we might arrive. Always assuming we can find the bloody place.' Nick looked around him. 'Where is my phone, by the way?'

'Did you leave it in the car?'

'Better go and look. Anyway I need to pick up my shoulder bag.'

Nick knew that the chance of his mobile being ripped off in the middle of the French countryside was similar to that of bears in the woods developing alternative toilet arrangements. Even so, urban London survival habits were hard to shake. Having perhaps had a touch too much, too quickly, of the claret, he stumbled out of the cabin into the silky suffocating heat of the night.

Opening the car, he found the phone, put it into his shoulder bag, hefted bag out of car, and activated the locks behind him.

As he walked back to the cabin, he heard a short but piercing scream — probably a fox or other wild animal. It seemed to come from the bushes and trees at the back of the cabin. Investigating the noise, Nick took a few paces into the shadows and tripped over a dustbin, perfectly camouflaged in the dark.

Stumbling and trying to regain his balance, the bag fell from his hands.

'Fuck!' seemed the most appropriate utterance as he went down on hands and knees to retrieve his camera and phone, both of which had leaped out as if of their own volition. They seemed unharmed, unlike their owner.

He got to his feet, brushed himself down and went back into the cabin.

'What was that noise?' Ros asked.

'Me falling over a bloody dustbin.'

'You OK?'

'Yeah just bruised my leg,' Nick rubbed his shin. 'Any more of that wine left?'

Ros topped up his glass and her own. 'What time do you want to leave?'

'Not early. It can't be that far to the gîte. And it'll seem so much better in the morning. Perhaps we will have breakfast here after all.'

It was hot. Very hot. Impossibly hot. Too hot for sleep. Or anything strenuous.

Getting into bed after finishing the wine, Nick and Ros lay damply, clammily naked and chastely apart under the thin cheap cotton sheet.

Not a breath of wind blew through the open side window. The only sound was the noise of insects. If central casting had added jungle drums, Nick and Ros could have easily been lulled into believing they were in sub-Saharan Africa instead of rural France.

While Ros had a knack of falling asleep immediately her head hit the pillow – which she duly did – sleep for Nick, even in the most favourable conditions, didn't come easily.

Closing his eyes, he could see endless French roads unrolling steadily past, legacy of the long drive down. Was it only this morning they'd set off? It didn't seem possible.

Having finally descended into fitful sleep, Nick came awake suddenly. He thought he heard sounds, maybe voices. So close they could have been in the bathroom. Just as he gained full consciousness, the noises stopped.

Nick drifted off. Once more he woke. Was it much later? It was hard to tell. He thought he heard the sound of a car door opening and softly being closed. It was another response to habitual urban living. Sometimes in London he wondered whether the noise of a car door opening and engine starting in the street outside was that of his own car – being stolen. He really did need a break from all that, perhaps more badly than he'd realized.

Nick looked at his watch in the dark. The glowing hands told him it was four o'clock. He could clearly hear a car engine ticking over. The good news was that it wasn't his. It was outside the next door cabin.

Taking a sip of water, he tried not to disturb Ros. Should he take a piss now or later? Well, as he was awake.

He inched his way to the bathroom, feeling in the dark for the handle. As he stood there, light from the car's headlamps briefly illuminated the cracked tiles of the shower. Tyres crunched on gravel as the car moved off. Nick craned his head to get a better view from the window but couldn't see anything. Finishing, he returned to bed and, eventually, to sleep.

2

It was light when he next surfaced. Ros was still asleep, her dark shoulder-length hair partially covering her face, her arms wrapped round a pillow. She looked younger than her thirty three years – or was it thirty four. Nick got out of bed and noticed a large bruise on his right leg. How the hell did that happen??? He remembered. Falling over and items spilling from his shoulder bag. He'd retrieved his phone, but what else might he have missed? Best check.

Nick pulled on a pair of boxers and went quietly through the beaded curtain into the next room. Opening the front door, he peered out. It was still fairly early. As no-one seemed to be about, he stepped out onto the verandah and leant on the rail. The sun already felt hot on shoulders still rather pale from the usual grey English summer they'd left behind.

Now it was daylight, he had a clearer view of their surroundings. And very pleasant they were too. He could see lots of shady trees facing onto the hard gravel surface of

Avenue A. Opposite were identical cabins, most with cars parked outside.

There was absolutely no sign of life. Nothing moved. Birds twittered. Sun shone. A perfectly peaceful scene. He glanced at the cabin to his left. He was sure a car had been parked there last night. Must have been the one he'd heard drive off. The cabin on the right did have a car outside. A rather ancient red Peugeot 309. Complete with English number plate and GB sign, it was in desperate need of a good wash.

Remembering why he'd come out in the first place, Nick was about to step down the stairs when his attention was drawn by a strange noise. Coming from the direction of the camp's front entrance, it got progressively louder until an ancient pushbike hove into view, pedals slowly turning, wheels and bike chain squeaking from lack of oil.

Its rider was a man, probably in his early sixties, with baguette protruding from under left arm. Nothing too remarkable in that, thought Nick, he's obviously just been to the site's supermarket. He was also wearing a beret. Again, fairly much par for the course for, presumably, a Frenchman in a French camp site. No, what Nick's early morning brain found slightly hard to process was the fact that the man appeared not to be wearing much. Let's re-examine that, thought Nick. He appears not to be wearing anything at all.

As the rider got closer his suspicion was confirmed. Yes, apart from the beret, he was stark naked. The bicyclist greeted him with a cheery 'Bonjour, m'sieur' and disappeared from sight, the squeak receding to nothing. Nick feebly raised his hand in greeting, fully thirty seconds after man and bicycle had gone. Nick tried to take in what he'd just seen. Was the man wearing something and he hadn't noticed? No, the evidence of his eyes told him that the man really had been nude.

Before his brain had time to assimilate this information, he caught the sound of a handle being turned. It came from the cabin beside theirs – the one which boasted, if that was the right word, the dirty English Peugeot. As he looked, a middle-aged, very tanned man appeared. Instinctively, as this man was also nude, Nick looked away to give the man a chance to dart back into the cabin. Nick's reasoning was that he obviously thought nobody was about at this hour of the morning and had decided to see what the day had to offer.

When Nick looked back, the man had not only *not* gone back into the cabin, he was now leaning against the railing very close to him.

'Good morning, nice day isn't it?'

'Er, yes,' was all Nick could manage. Master of the art of conversation.

'Martin. Martin Pike,' said the man offering his hand.

Churlish not to take it, Nick proffered his own and they shook hands above the void between the two cabins. 'Nick Boughton'.

'Just arrived, I see?'

'Oh what? The pale skin. Yes bit of a give-away isn't it,' said Nick, thinking that he was acting terribly well in the circumstances, talking to the second naked person he'd seen – in what, two minutes – as if to the manner born.

Martin Pike was shorter than Nick, around five ten and wore old-fashioned tortoiseshell glasses. Slightly pot-bellied, he looked as if he'd never done much in the way of exercise. His flesh was soft. Muscles remained undefined. Even below his brown skin he had an unhealthy pallor, as if he'd just emerged after spending too many years indoors. His bright blue eyes, magnified by the lenses of his prescription specs, glittered at Nick.

'No I didn't mean the skin. I meant those,' said Pike indicating Nick's boxers. 'They won't like those.'

Perhaps he was still asleep and this was a dream. He seemed

to be having a conversation with a nude man about underpants. What did Pike mean? Who is it that wouldn't like his choice of nether garments? And why wouldn't they?

'Sorry?'

'It *is* obligatory you know.'

'Sorry? What is? Look, er, Mr Pike . . .'

'Please call me Martin.'

'Er, Martin. Forgive me, but I'm not sure I understand what you're saying?'

'Nudity,' Pike explained patiently as if to a particularly backward, or even wilful, schoolchild. 'It's compulsory you know.'

'Compulsory?'

'Yes, that means that you're obliged to be nude. Not wear any clothes?'

Nick was still not sure he was hearing this and decided to have one more try.

'Are you saying that I'm somehow breaking the law by wearing this pair of underpants?'

'Well, I wouldn't put it quite like that. You're not breaking any, if not all, of the French Napoleonic, civil or even criminal laws. But you are most certainly flouting the rules of Le Paradis.'

The penny finally clunked into a slot in Nick's brain. 'You mean that this site . . . where we're staying . . . is . . . is a nudist colony?'

'Not a nudist colony. We don't use that antiquated term these days. But yes, Le Paradis is a naturist resort. You must have known that when you checked in?'

'No we didn't. We . . .' Nick's voice trailed off.

'Well, don't worry about it. Just enjoy the freedom. You'll soon get used to it. You'll love it.'

I certainly won't, thought Nick. He'd always felt ill at ease in communal dressing rooms. Like many men who never engaged in team sports he'd never got used to the idea or sensation of being around naked men.

In the flesh he'd probably seen more nude females, particularly when photographing models at fashion shows. And he'd rather it stayed that way. Except that he'd already added two more naked men to his tally this morning. And if Martin Pike was right, and wasn't an escaped lunatic, he was surrounded by many, many more. Getting used to it wasn't an option. And thankfully didn't have to be.

'Erm, well, unfortunately we won't be able to. We're leaving this morning.'

'That's a shame. Well, I can safely say you don't know what you're missing.'

'Well that's probably our loss. Now if you'll excuse me, we need to get packing.'

'Right-o', said Martin Pike. 'Nice talking to you.' With that, he stepped down from his verandah and headed off. 'Have a safe journey'. Nick stared after Pike's leanish bare flanks, also nicely brown — if more than slightly wrinkled — as he walked up the Avenue.

Shaking his head as if to dispel the image, Nick turned and entered the cabin. The conversation with Pike had driven totally out of his head why he'd come out on the verandah in the first place.

'Nick?' came Ros's voice from the bedroom.

Going through the curtain he found her propped up on one elbow in bed, one hand pushing her dark thick hair away from her eyes and at the same time exposing a still firm, large, well-shaped breast, with small attractive dark nipple. She didn't look that different from the young intern he'd taken on winter afternoons, during the early stages of their relationship, to a friend's flat behind Tottenham Court Road. She still retained her curvy figure with its slim waist and shapely legs.

He sat down on the bed and gave her a kiss on the forehead. Something he hadn't expected to do and she hadn't expected to receive.

'Hi, it's a lovely day out there', said Nick.

She smiled, as much at the unexpected kiss as his comment. 'What's the place like?'

'Seems very pleasant. But for one slight, well, not problem, but issue.'

'Which is?'

'How can I put this? Well, nobody appears to be wearing any clothes.'

Ros sat bolt upright in bed, the sheet falling to expose her other equally perfectly formed breast. 'You're not serious?'

'Absolutely. And I've just had a riveting conversation with our nude male next-door neighbour to confirm it.'

'Let me get this straight. What you're saying is that we are currently booked into a nudist colony?'

'Please, that's so antiquated. It's a naturist resort', said Nick, echoing the words of Martin Pike.

'OK a "naturist resort". So there's little point in my getting dressed, is there?', Ros said provocatively leaning forward.

'Actually, no. You could go out exactly as you are and nobody would take the blindest bit of notice.'

'Right then. I will', said Ros, getting out of bed and running her hands through her hair.

Before Nick could do or say anything else, she pushed through the beaded curtains, strode straight to the rail on the verandah and looked out. So sudden was her appearance, that another elderly nude man riding past on his bike, wobbled and nearly fell off at the sight of her ample bosom hoving into view.

'You're right! How about that!'

'Er, shouldn't you put something on? You know, cover yourself up?'

Ros turned to face him, leaning her rear against the rail. 'And what would be the point of that? Seeing as everyone here is nude?'

'Well', said Nick, feeling slightly uncomfortable, 'it's only right, isn't it. I mean, you know, it's, well, it's . . .'

'Yes?'

'Well, not natural,' Nick finally exclaimed.

'You always were unhappy about nudity, weren't you? Do you remember that beach in Greece a few years back? Miles from anywhere and yet you still kept your bathers on, "in case anyone came along." It's not as if you have anything to be ashamed of', said Ros, coquettishly, lifting her right foot and tickling her toes under Nick's boxer shorts.

'Erm yes, well, er don't you think we should be going before anybody else comes along?'

'Didn't you mention that there's somewhere we could get breakfast? Let's go and find it. Oh, but please do take off those undies first. They're so antiquated', said Ros.

'OK. Joke over,' said Nick primly. 'I think we'd better be making a move. Let's find a café for breakfast. *Outside* the grounds of this place. Remember? Phillip and Kathy? Gîte? Holiday?'

'Yes, but you must admit it's not everyone who can say they booked into a nudist camp by mistake.'

It was already stifling in the cabin as they got dressed and packed. It was going to be another hot day. Best to get going as early as possible. With any luck, thought Nick, by lunchtime he would be lounging in Phillip and Kathy's pool with a cold kir to hand.

Nick followed Ros out to the car and opened the boot. Putting in the bags he suddenly remembered why he'd originally come out onto the verandah.

'I've just got to check I didn't drop anything else last night. Won't be a minute,' said Nick.

He peered into the shadows, and yes, there was his Swiss pocket knife. As he stooped to pick it up he noticed something sticking out round the back of next door's cabin. It was pink and motionless. In fact, it looked very much like a foot.

He straightened up and took a few cautious steps forward until he could see that the reason it looked like a foot was because it was one. And what's more it was attached to a person.

And that person appeared to be male, nude, face down, very still. Looking towards the head, Nick saw a mass of red surrounded by buzzing flies. That's when he stumbled back to Ros.

'What's up?' said Ros.

'There! At the back of the cabin,' Nick blurted out, shakily pointing an arm to indicate – unnecessarily, as it happens – where the back of the cabin was.

'What on earth's wrong?'

'A body. I think it's dead.'

Ros decided to take matters into her own hands and strode round the back of the cabin. She gasped as she saw the nude man. She could tell even without touching him that he was dead, but checked his pulse anyway. His head was turned to one side and he had nasty dents in his skull. His scalp was matted in clotted blood which had spilled down the side of his face and onto his lower jaw and chin. From what she could see, Ros thought he was in his late fifties with a healthy-looking tan – healthy-looking had he been alive, of course.

Ros quickly walked back to Nick.

'You're right. He is dead. I suddenly have a feeling we're not going to get to Phillip and Kathy's quite as early as we thought.'

3

Ros's words were prophetic. While she stood near the body, Nick drove, fully dressed, to Reception – figuring nudity was not obligatory where an emergency was concerned.

Hurrying in, he saw that the male receptionist had been replaced behind the counter by an attractive young blonde woman. As she was shorter than last night's receptionist, all Nick could see of her body were shapely brown shoulders and finely-defined collar bones.

In front of the desk, a middle-aged woman engaged the receptionist in rapid French, her only accoutrements a pair of high-heeled sling back sandals and a bored looking poodle on a lead. Trying not to look at the woman's nude rear quarters – where was the right place to look in a naturist resort? – he turned his gaze to the poodle, which looked up at him and wagged its tail in greeting.

Conversation or query finished, the rather ample woman turned suddenly, looked disapprovingly at Nick's clothed state and left with a sour 'M'sieur'.

Moving closer to the counter Nick had a clearer view of the receptionist. And very pleasant it was, too. In her early twenties, she had fashionably short bobbed hair, pert nose and light blue eyes. She also had a slim, almost boyish, tanned figure and, he couldn't fail to notice, shapely, nicely formed breasts. She also appeared to be nude, but her bottom half was hidden below the counter and it seemed impolite to check out his hunches — or should that be her haunches.

So taken was he with the sight, that he almost forgot why he'd gone there in the first place. Was this what it would be like in a naturist resort? You not only lost your clothes but your short-term memory as well.

'M'sieur?' She smiled at him.

'Erm, parlez vous Anglais?' asked Nick.

'No but I speak fluent Oz!' Came the reply in a broad Australian accent and a pearly white grin.

'Thank goodness! Look we're staying in cabin 12 and well, we've found a dead man!' Nick blurted out.

'What! You having me on?'

'No, I'm absolutely serious.'

'Hang on a minute. You been drinking?'

'Certainly not'

'How do you know he's dead?'

'My partner's a doctor. She knows a dead body when she sees one.'

'Well . . .', the receptionist still sounded doubtful. 'Perhaps I'd better check for myself. Wait there.'

She disappeared for a moment and re-appeared with a key in her hand. Lifting a portion of the counter she stepped through into the main office.

Nick's heart rate rose dramatically as he noted that her bottom half was not only as naked as the top but perfectly in proportion, with slim hips and shapely legs. She didn't seem to be the slightest bit concerned that she wasn't wearing a stitch of clothing and that he was fully dressed.

'Let's go take a look,' she said locking the reception door and hanging the key round her neck by its string so that it nestled snugly between her breasts.

It appeared to be even hotter outside the reception area than it was before, but perhaps that had more to do with Nick's increased pulse rate rather than the ambient temperature.

'Er, I've got my car here,' said Nick.

'OK then let's go', said the receptionist, getting into the passenger seat.

Nick felt a strange dislocation. Had he really discovered a dead body just five minutes ago? And was there an attractive young woman sitting in his car? Stark naked. And totally unfazed by the fact?

The last time he'd had anybody nude in a car, the woman in question had been his girlfriend and they'd been in the back seat of his old Rover in a small cul-de-sac in suburban North London. That had been many years' ago but he could still remember the cold clamminess of those leather seats on his rear . . .

'Are we going or what?'

Her words jolted him back to the present. 'Right', said Nick starting the car and wondering how Ros would react to him coming back with a naked companion.

They drove the short distance to the cabin in silence and got out. Ros looked at the receptionist and then at Nick. Nick gave her a shrug and a look that said ''what can I do''. Even so, Ros did not look at all happy.

'So where is this body?'

'Round here', said Ros, leading the way.

The receptionist gave a small shriek, raising her hands instinctively to her face. 'You sure he's dead?' she said, now sounding distinctly less blasé.

'Absolutely.'

'Christ. Right I'll go call the cops. Don't worry, I'll walk back. Stay here and keep watch. And don't mention a word to anyone.'

So saying, she disappeared across the road and through the trees – a short cut that took her back to Reception.

'Well,' said Nick, for want of something to say.

Ros looked even more displeased, with arms folded over her t-shirt in the style of Norah Batty. 'I let you out of my sight for a few minutes and the next time I see you is with a naked woman.'

'Come on, Ros! Be reasonable! What should I have done? Tell her to get dressed. This is a nudist resort, for God's sake. Everyone's nude – except us. We're the weirdos in this scenario.'

'Well, let's hope that we can get all this sorted out quickly and be on our way.'

'Christ, yes. I'd almost forgotten. Phillip and Kathy. They must be really worried by now.'

Nick tried his phone. Still no signal. He had the feeling that it was going to be just one of those days.

4

The police had arrived promptly. An official car had deposited four uniformed gendarmes outside the administration block. A second unmarked large black Renault unloaded two plain-clothed officials – an inspector and a forensic doctor.

Two of the gendarmes had immediately taken control of the gate with orders not to let anybody leave or enter. The other two accompanied the inspector and doctor to reception.

Here, they had been greeted by Jack Webster, the man who'd checked-in Nick. With him was the young Australian receptionist, whose name turned out .to be Shareen.

With gendarmes and doctor in tow, the plainclothes inspector, who'd introduced himself as Raymond Lagardère, had accompanied Jack and Shareen to the body which was being "minded" by Nick and Ros.

Nick was pleased to see that both Jack and Shareen were now clothed. Shareen was wearing a sleeveless top and shorts that were ever so slightly too short – and too tight. Nick was reminded of a younger Kylie Minogue. But far more attractive.

When he found that Nick had discovered the body, the inspector asked in perfect English for all of them to go to the reception area and wait for him. Which is where they now found themselves. In an office at the back. In chairs around an old battered large wooden table, which doubled as a desk. An ancient floor-standing fan, which wouldn't have looked out of place in a 'thirties movie, reluctantly wheezed around the increasingly hot air.

Still, things were looking up. Marginally. Ros and Nick had eaten breakfast. Croissants bought by Shareen with coffee made by Jack.

'Must have been a bit of a shock for you, Nick, falling over a body and all?', said Jack.

'Not the way I'd have chosen to start a day, no,' Nick replied. 'Does anyone know who he is, I mean, was? You know. The body?'

'Not yet,' said Shareen. 'Mind you I didn't look too closely. And with his head all bashed in, it makes him a bit hard to recognize. This time of the year, we probably have around a thousand people in the resort? Hard to know who's who in that little lot?'

Nick noted that Shareen had that irritating way of making every statement sound like a question by raising the intonation of her voice towards the end of a sentence. The only saving grace was that she was Australian and they all did it. They knew no better. No excuse in his mind for people in Britain who increasingly adopted this affectation. He blamed 'Neighbours' and, what was that other programme? Oh yes. 'Home and Away'.

'And nobody's been to the office to say they're missing a friend or relative so far this morning,' said Jack. 'Mind you, it's still early.'

Nick looked at his watch. Unbelievably, it was only half past nine.

'He might have been here on his own', said Shareen, examining her rather attractive red nails, 'which means it could take even longer to find out who he is. Was. Poor bastard.'

'Must be difficult to identify someone if they've got no clothes on. You know. No driving licence, papers, that sort of thing,' Nick said.

'What about a key?' This from Ros, who'd been idly gazing out the office window. An instant image of the Reception door key nestling between Shareen's breasts came instantly and unbidden into Nick's mind. 'He must have had one for his cabin.'

'Didn't see one round his neck,' said Nick, hoping his pink face was mistaken as a side effect of the heat. Ros gave him a funny look.

'Besides, we don't know that he had a cabin,' said Jack. 'The only cabins are the ones where you are. Most people have caravans, tents or camper-vans. And there's little enough crime. No reason to lock things up. Specially at dead of night.'

Nick hadn't paid much attention to Jack last night, but now he had a chance to get a better view. In his fifties, Jack had greying hair, pulled back in a pony tail, framing a slightly gaunt face and wiry body. A bit like an ageing hippy. If Nick had had to describe him to someone, the closest he would have got was Neil in ''The Young Ones'' – but thirty years on.

Jack got slowly to his feet. The two gendarmes and the inspector were coming through Reception. As they walked into the room the inspector asked Jack something in rapid French, to which he replied. Jack then left with the gendarmes.

Inspector Lagardère was 45 or so, around 5'10", with grey crew-cut hair which gave him a slightly military appearance. He was wearing a white short-sleeved shirt, with blue tie, beige chino trousers and smart deck shoes. Putting his soft leather briefcase on the table, he took the chair previously occupied by Jack.

'It's very hot today. No wonder so many people seem to have taken their clothes off,' was his opening remark.

'No, that's because this is a nat . . .' Nick started to say and realized that Lagardère was making a joke. 'Right. I see. Very good.'

'OK. Let's get down to business,' said Lagardère. 'I need to take your names and statements for the record. So perhaps I can start with the person who found the body?'

'That's me,' said Nick.

'Right.' Lagardère turned to Ros and Shareen. 'Would you please wait outside while I take the statement.'

Closing the door after them, Lagardère sat down opposite Nick.

'Your name and address please.' Nick obliged. 'And your occupation?'

'Photographer.'

'And you arrived when?'

'Last night. No, sorry, this morning.'

'At what time?'

'About one.'

'And you went straight to your cabin?'

'Yes, the one next to where I found the body.'

'And did you leave your cabin at all during the night?'

'No, but I did wake a couple of times and heard noises.'

'Go on.'

'It was very hot and I'd been driving all day. Made it difficult to sleep. Around about three, three-thirty, I can't be more exact, I thought I heard some noise.'

'What sort of noise?'

'Perhaps raised voices, I'm not really sure,' said Nick. 'I

drifted off to sleep and woke up again at four. I heard the sound of a car starting and driving off.'

'Did you see the driver?'

'No. I didn't even see the car.'

'And then?'

'Well, I went back to sleep.'

'Tell me about discovering the body.'

Nick told Lagardère exactly what had happened when he'd got up.

'Did you recognize the deceased at all?'

'No, he was a complete stranger.'

'Then how do you account for this?' Lagardère took a clear polythene snap bag from his briefcase and held it up for Nick to see.

At first Nick couldn't determine what was in it, but as he peered more closely it looked familiar. In fact it was . . . 'One of my business cards!' exclaimed Nick.

'And do you know where we found this?'

'Probably on the ground. I did fall over and spill stuff out of my bag last night.'

'No, Mister Boughton. We found this card grasped in the dead man's hand.'

'That proves nothing,' said Nick. 'He could have picked it up and, and . . .' Even to him it sounded a bit unlikely, '. . . and before he could rise from the ground he was, well, attacked and killed.'

'What about the noises you say you heard? The raised voices? If the deceased was one of those, why would he have been holding your card in his hand? Unless of course he was arguing with you.'

'Well . . .' Nick had run out of suggestions.

'Let me paint another picture for you. Perhaps this man arrived in your car with you and your wife . . .'

'Partner,' Nick corrected Lagardère, although he didn't know why.

'. . . partner. Then you had a little disagreement in the middle of the night, maybe over your "partner". You then went outside, argued and you killed him.'

'But that's absurd!' exclaimed Nick. 'Why would I then discover and report the body in the morning?'

'A perfect alibi. A smokescreen.'

'And what about his clothes and belongings? And murder weapon?'

'We're already carrying out a search for those around the site perimeter. But we'll also need to check your car.'

Nick suddenly felt that things were getting a touch out of hand. Yesterday he'd been looking forward to a relaxing holiday by a pool in France. Today he was looking at a charge of murder or, if he was extremely lucky, merely manslaughter. Did they still have the guillotine in France?, he wondered.

'Wait a minute! What about the car I heard leave. If anybody was the murderer it's more likely to be him – or her – than me,' said Nick.

'Yes, Mr Webster, checked-out the man next door last night . . .' Lagardère looked down at his notes. '. . . about four fifteen. That part of your story tallies. That man was also English, a Mr Parker. He told Mr Webster that one of his relatives was ill and that he wanted to start the long drive back to England early to avoid the heat. We've got an alert out to stop him.'

'Well, there you are. It was probably what's his name, Parker, that did it. After all, you must admit it's a bit suspicious leaving the next door hut the same morning a corpse is found.'

'Maybe. Maybe not. We have started our enquiries in Le Paradis. Discreetly of course. We don't want to upset the guests or alert the killer,' Lagardère said, 'but until they are completed, I must ask you and your partner to remain here in the resort.'

'You're putting us under arrest?' asked Nick incredulously.

'Of course not, Mister Boughton. We are going to keep *everyone* here on site until we've completed our enquiries.'

'But that could take, what, days.'

'Absolutely. But why are you concerned. The weather is glorious. You are staying in a nice place. Just relax and enjoy yourself. And don't try to leave as our gendarmes have orders to shoot on sight.'

'What!' said Nick shocked, and then gave a weak smile, realising that Lagardère was making a joke again.

The inspector got to his feet. 'Right Mr Boughton, please would you send in your partner and I'll take her statement. Thank you for your co-operation. And enjoy your stay in Paradise.'

5

Nick and Ros walked back to the cabin. It was even hotter and there were more people about than before. Unlike the weather, the stares they got from the many naked campers they passed were distinctly frosty.

'I guess they were right about the resort's compulsory nudity clause,' said Nick glumly as they reached the steps of the cabin. 'I think I'll just stay indoors until we leave.'

'Don't be ridiculous. You'll just have to put up with it. If it doesn't bother anyone else why should it bother you? You've got basically the same equipment as half the population of this camp. So why worry?'

Before he had a chance to reply, a gendarme emerged from the cabin carrying an attaché case and a couple of small plastic bags. He reached into his pocket and returned Nick's car keys. Saluting the couple, he disappeared down the steps heading in the general direction of reception. The only sign that anything untoward had occurred was some French police tape sealing off the area between the two cabins.

Nick and Ros entered their cabin, which looked even more spartan in the hard glare of the day.

'Well, if we are staying, we'd better make ourselves as comfortable as possible. I'll get the bags,' said Nick.

'I don't think we'll be needing much in the way of clothing though,' Ros couldn't resist adding, sitting in front of the dressing table and addressing herself to her make-up.

Refusing to rise to the bait, Nick went out and was removing the bags when a voice called to him. It was neighbour Martin Pike, sitting in a beach towel-covered canvas chair on his terrace.

'Hello there! I don't know what you've done but I can't remember more activity in this place ever. Body being removed under a sheet. Gendarmes swarming all over your cabin. Great excitement.'

'Yes, well never a dull moment when we're around,' retorted Nick, non-wittily.

By this time, Martin Pike had got up from his chair and was again leaning against the railing, looking down at him. Nick had a good view of his genitals from eye level and it wasn't a particularly pleasant sight.

'So you've decided to stay?' Pike said.

'Been ordered to, I'm afraid. Confined to barracks by the gendarmes.'

'Well, there are a lot worse places you could be. Just think. You're marooned in a virtual oasis of freedom. Free of clothing. Free of restrictions. Free of rules and cares. Experiencing nature as it was intended to be enjoyed. Unencumbered by clothes or convention. I just know you'll have a really great time.'

Determined to alter his viewpoint of Pike as quickly as possible, Nick climbed the steps to their own verandah.

Nick put the cases down. 'So what is there to do here?' he asked Pike.

'Oh, loads of great activities! The main leisure part of Le Paradis is over there,' said Pike pointing in the opposite direction from the entrance. 'You'll find a road that runs right down the middle of the resort. It's called the Champs-Elysses. I think it's a French attempt at a joke. Anyway, follow it southwards and you'll find a bar, restaurant, swimming pool and the lake.'

'Lake?' Nick was slightly taken aback. 'There's a lake?'

'Oh yes. You can take out small boats and even do a bit of wind-surfing. It's very pleasant.'

'It's a lot bigger than I thought', said Nick and suddenly regretted his choice of words. 'I mean, I, we'll have to investigate further.'

'Yes, but make sure you get dressed first,' said Martin pointing at Nick's clothes. 'Don't want to frighten the natives, eh?'

Nick gave him a weak smile.

'Oh, and don't forget your towel. Very important the towel,' added Martin.

'Towel?'

How was it that everything that happened in Le Paradis seemed so surreal? On top of everything else, here was Martin Pike talking about towels. It rang a distant bell in his subconscious. Wasn't a towel an indispensable item of baggage for inter-planetary travellers in 'Hitchhikers Guide to the Galaxy'? But that was fiction. What relevance could it possibly have to life in Le Paradis?

Seeing his confused look, Martin Pike decided to enlighten him. 'Sorry, forgot you're new to naturism. I've got a special section on towels in the Naked Guide.'

Again, Nick had a feeling of being way out of his depth. Prince of repartee he could only repeat 'Naked Guide?'

'Yes. I'm writing a book. It's called "Naturism. The Naked Guide." Of course it's still in draft form but progressing remarkably well. It's a first, you know. A total guide to the world of nude living. Bound to be a best seller. Well, we can but hope.'

The Naked Guide has this to say about the towel:

The humble towel, in all its forms — from hand through bath to beach and sheet — plays an essential role in the life of the naturist, forming as it does the only necessary textile [see under 'T' for 'textile' in index] item in a naturist's wardrobe.

Its primary purpose is not as an item to be worn but to be used as a barrier between the naturist's nether regions and surfaces upon which the naturist sits or lies — such as seats, sofas, chaise longues, loungers, deck chairs and so forth.

It's an accepted part of nudist etiquette to always carry a towel around to put on a surface before sitting on it. Not to mention other essential uses, such as covering oneself when venturing into non-naturist areas. As a last resort, it can also be used to dry oneself after taking a shower, bath or welcome dip in sea or pool.

The generic term 'towel' can also be stretched — if you will pardon the pun — to include any piece of material that's big enough to sit on so that the naturist's body doesn't come into direct contact with the surface being sat or lain upon.

So whilst naturists wear nothing and are unencumbered by clothing, ironically all still normally carry around a piece of cloth with them, draped over or round shoulders, under the arm, in a bag or carried in the hand.

Having been well and truly enlightened about towels, Nick finally bade farewell to Martin Pike, carried the bags back into the cabin and sat abruptly down onto the bed. He just couldn't believe this was happening to him. Perhaps he was suffering delayed shock.

'You might be suffering delayed shock,' said Ros, sitting solicitously beside him and putting her arm around him. 'After all, it's the first dead body you've ever seen isn't it.'

'And also please don't forget that I'm the prime suspect around here. That doesn't do a lot for my peace of mind, either.'

'Yes, well I know you didn't do it.'

'That's comforting. Just go and tell Lagardère and let's get out of here.'

Ros suddenly stood up. 'Well, I for one am not going to skulk in this hot, pokey cabin all day. You can do what you like, but I'm going to unpack and go for an explore. Find a nice spot, read my book and soak up some sun. And if that means wearing no clothes then so be it.'

With that, she hoisted her case onto the bed and unpacked what she saw as the essentials. These included toiletries, books, a scarf, money, sunglasses and a beach towel.

'Oh good. You've remembered your towel,' said Nick.

Ros gave him a strange look as she pulled her t-shirt over her head exposing her breasts beneath. 'I don't know what's got into you. You're being very difficult you know. This is our holiday. We are supposed to be having fun.'

'Having fun? We break down in the middle of France. End up in a nudist colony. Discover a dead body. And get put under house arrest. If this is fun, then I demand an instant re-definition of the word from the ruling body of the Oxford English Dictionary!'

Ignoring his rant, Ros continued undressing until she stood stark naked in front of Nick, not amused at what she saw as his churlishness.

'It's probably only going to be for a few days at the most so please stop complaining.'

'You're not actually going out like that are you?'

'Of course not. I'm going to put something on.'

'Thank God.'

'My factor 8. Here make yourself useful. Rub this into my back would you,' said Ros, handing Nick a bottle of sun lotion.

Nick obeyed and as he rubbed cream into her shoulders continued, 'I mean, you really are going out totally nude?'

'Of course. We're only talking bodies here. I see most parts of them each day in the surgery. There's nothing to worry about,' said Ros, although she didn't feel as certain about the whole venture as she sounded.

In fact, she had butterflies in the pit of her stomach at the thought of walking around amongst other people in the nude. She decided to keep such misgivings to herself.

Finishing applying sun lotion to the rest of her body, she turned to Nick. 'There, how do I look?'

'Great! If you were getting ready for bed. But a little under-dressed for promenading around a camp site in front of hundreds of strange men.'

Ros gathered up book, sunglasses, lotion and purse and dropped them into her large canvas shoulder bag. Adding her novel and some euros, she slung her folded beach towel round her neck, so it hung down slightly covering her breasts, and stepped into her flip-flops.

'Are you coming with me or are you staying here all day?'

The prospect of remaining alone in the hot cabin without food and drink was not one that appealed terribly to Nick. If he was being honest, his thoughts also turned to the Australian receptionist, Shareen. She was possibly out there somewhere and probably also not wearing a great deal – if anything at all. It would be nice to see all of her again. And casually chat over the morning's events like old friends.

'Well . . . just to keep you company. Make sure nothing happens to you.'

Nick reluctantly pulled his t-shirt over his head. Bare-chested, he undid and removed his shorts and pants and stood nude in front of Ros. If they'd been monitoring his pulse rate or heart beat, he was sure both would have gone off the scale by now.

'There that's not so bad is it? Let me put on some sun stuff for you,' said Ros, picking the lotion from her bag and applying it to Nick's back. He held his hand out and she squeezed some into it for application to his front.

'Do you think you need extra protection factor for your, well, you know, er, John Thomas?' he asked.

'I don't think so. It's just another part of the body after all.'

'But one that just might be a tiny bit painful if sun-burnt,' said Nick, rubbing sun lotion, for the first time ever, he noted, onto his genitals.

He had a broad white band where he'd been wearing his shorts in the garden on the odd nice weekend. The rest of his body was, well, not tanned but a little less white. He had a bit of a paunch developing around his middle which was usually not so noticeable. He must join a gym or take more exercise he thought. Still, he wasn't grossly overweight or obese. Just slightly cuddlier than he had been ten years ago.

'There. You're ready to go,' said Ros, wiping surplus cream from her hands down her thighs. 'Let's explore life in the nude.'

'You sound like one of those naturist films they used to show years ago,' said Nick looking into the dressing table mirror. Was he really going to set foot outside the door like this? His heart started pounding again. In fact, it hadn't stopped from the time he'd removed his shorts. But what was there to worry about? After all, everyone he'd see from that point on would be equally naked. Somehow he didn't find that the slightest bit comforting. And what was it that most men worried about when going nude in company for the first time?

'What about erection problems?' he blurted out to Ros.

'I didn't think you ever had any of those. At least not while we've been together.'

'That's just my point. What if I get an erection? How embarrassing is that going to be?'

'Look you'll have your towel with you, won't you? Just hold it in front of you if you feel the . . . well, urge coming on.'

Ah yes, the towel. Nick grabbed his beach towel as a drowning man to a plank of driftwood. Putting it over his arm, very much as a waiter would a napkin, he peered into the mirror. The towel now screened his genitals from general view. It was something, but not quite enough.

'What about my arse?'

'It looks very nice.'

'No I mean, it's uncovered! People walking behind me can see it!'

'Nick, I am now really losing my patience. Everyone here is nude. Nobody is going to be looking particularly at your bum or any other part of your anatomy. For God's sake! You will get used to it. I promise.'

With a final 'Right', Ros set out for the cabin door, looking more determined and confident than she actually felt.

Instead of bounding outside as playfully as she had earlier, she opened the door and peeped out. It was very quiet, and very hot.

Nick hesitated behind Ros's rather nice behind. Taking a deep breath he followed her into Avenue A.

It was a weird feeling. A bit like being in a dream. His heart continued to pound. Try as he might, he couldn't stop that feeling of panic. It was just like those phobias people experience. Like fear of spiders or of great heights.

He also made sure he held his towel in front of him. He hoped that this looked dead casual to anyone who happened to be looking. But he still felt distinctly uneasy about his nude backside.

They reached the "Champs" and enjoyed their first mass sighting of the inhabitants of Le Paradis. On each side of the road were caravans – many of which looked permanently tethered – tented caravan awnings, tents of various shapes and sizes, camper vans and larger recreational vehicles. Each had its own plot under shading trees.

In and around them, people were going about their everyday pursuits. Peeling potatoes for lunchtime frites. Watering plants. Cleaning the car. Drinking coffee. Chatting. Arguing. Or just sitting. And every single person naked. What seemed just as strange to Nick was, that if news of the murder had travelled this far, nobody seemed the slightest bit concerned.

He also noted, with some relief, that few people appeared to pay the slightest attention to them, apart from the odd 'bonjour', probably aimed more at Ros who, Nick thought, looked pretty sexy in her sunglasses and flip-flops. It was a view literally shared by some of the Frenchmen who rested their gaze upon her just a fraction longer than was probably polite. If she noticed, she didn't say anything. In fact, Ros was trying not to look anywhere but straight ahead and control a slightly fast-beating heart.

After a few hundred metres, the trees ahead thinned out and the Champs ended where it met the orbital road which ran around the circumference of the camping area of the site. This was known, a painted board informed them, as "La Périphérique". Yet another example of rib-tickling French humour, thought Nick.

On the other side of La Périphérique were pedestrian and bike paths leading southwards across a large parched grass lawn, which sloped down to a fair-sized lake. Woods at the far end gave a bucolic, picturesque setting.

Noise from their right came from a large open air pool, glittering blue in the morning heat. Well, not from the pool itself but from the many brown holidaymakers and their children. And set back from the pool was a bar, doors open at the front, facing towards the lake.

To the left was a restaurant, with tables and chairs under a long, candy-striped awning. Two waitresses were cleaning tables and setting up for lunch. He noted that they were actually wearing clothes – shorts and t-shirts. Must be for hygiene reasons he thought. Or safety. Spilled moules down naked breasts couldn't be that enjoyable, but then again . . .

'It all looks quite attractive,' said Ros, interrupting his thoughts. 'Right, I'm grabbing a lounger. Coming?'

'I think I'll get a beer first.' He needed something to steady his nerves. Perhaps a liberal amount of alcohol might ease his stress levels. 'Wonder if you need to get dressed to go into the bar?', he asked, more in hope than expectation.

'I hardly think so. Get me a fresh orange juice if they've got one, will you please, love. I'll be somewhere over there,' Ros indicated a quiet spot to the back of the pool area. 'Here, you'll need these,' she said, taking out some euro notes and pressing them into his free hand.

Nick nodded and watched Ros's attractive rear end man-oeuvre between the various sunbathers. He turned towards the bar and, feeling extremely uneasy, walked up to its open façade. Never in his wildest dreams, or should that be night-mares, did Nick ever think he'd visit a bar naked. It sounded like one of those jokes. You know, "a man goes into a pub in the nude and the barman says . . ."

Plucking up courage, Nick stepped over the threshold, his eyes slowly adjusting to the dim interior. There appeared to be only two drinkers inside, both propped up on high stools at the typically French zinc-topped bar. And both, yes, as predicted by Martin Pike's "Naked Guide", sitting on towels. Otherwise, they were most definitely totally nude.

One of the men was very hairy, bearing a marked resemblance to a silver-backed gorilla, although a lot thinner, and sporting an unkempt beard. Probably in his sixties, he seemed to have just too much hair, covering every surface from shoulders to feet. On a very strict interpretation of Le Paradis' rules he could almost be said to be clothed.

The other drinker was younger, probably about Nick's age but very much larger, with buttocks spread over his stool. He had a fashionable skin-head crop which didn't do a lot for a round face which, like the rest of his body, had a reddish hue from too much sun. Proud possessor of a large beer gut, which would have protruded over his swimming shorts had he been wearing any, he was sitting slouched forward and puffing on a cigarette.

Both men presented a not particularly pleasant sight, thought Nick. But then much he'd seen this morning had left a great deal to be desired. Whatever the pros and cons of wearing clothes, he was rapidly coming to the conclusion that garments improved the appearance of virtually every human — including himself.

This theory was instantly disproved as a slim, attractive figure emerged from a door at the back of the bar. It was Shareen, carrying a tea towel and drying a beer glass. Shareen spotted him. 'Nick! Hi! Come on over. I've just been talking about this morning with these two reprobates.'

'Charming!' said the large red man, laughing as he did so, and coughing as smoke went down the wrong way.

Nick approached the bar, trying as best as possible to keep his towel between the eye-line of Shareen and his privates.

Once the comparative safety of the overhang of the bar had been reached, he spread his towel on the bar stool next to silver-back and sat down. Then, as nonchalantly as possible, he wrapped the towel casually over his thighs, in order to protect his parts from general view.

Shareen introduced him. 'Nick, this is Hamish,' indicating the silver-back.

Hamish turned and muttered a 'Hello' with a pronounced Scottish accent. He then re-focused his attention forwards to the glass of, what in France passed as bitter, which was resting between his hands on the bar — keeping a whisky chaser company.

'And this is Garry.'

'Wotcha!' said Garry, in a Cockney accent, leaning across Hamish and offering his multi-gold-ringed hand to be shaken. Nick obliged. 'Shareen's just been telling us all about you. France's most wanted, eh?'

'Er, sort of,' was all Nick could reply.

'Don't tease him, Gaz. He's had a very tough morning, haven't you pet?' said Shareen. 'What'll you have to drink. Let me get you one on the house.'

'Ello. You're well away there my son. Been here nearly a week and haven't had as much as a sniff of a free glass of water,' said Garry, good-humouredly.

Nick smiled weakly. 'A draught lager would be good,' he said, leaning his elbows on the bar. 'Thanks.'

Nick's blood pressure rose even higher as Shareen reached up to lift down a glass. Luckily nothing else about his person seemed to rise. Amazing what you could do with a little will power, he thought, or was it just social mores? He must talk about the issue with Ros, but without mentioning Shareen, of course. He realized that Garry was saying something to him. 'Sorry?'

'The body? Must 'ave been a bit of a shock for you, eh?'

A welcome, foaming glass of ice-cold lager was put in front of Nick. He picked it up, with slightly shaking hand, and raised the glass to his lips for a careful sip. As he tilted his head to drink, he took a surreptitious peer – or more accurately – leer, at Shareen's breasts.

He turned to Garry, taking in Hamish with his glance. 'Er, yes. Terrible shock. I almost fell over him. And it wasn't as if it was the only surprise I'd had this morning.'

'The other being?' asked Garry.

'Well, to be frank,' said Nick, suddenly, for some unknown reason, feeling the need to come clean, 'that we'd checked into a nudist colony – I mean, naturist resort.'

The Naked Guide has much to impart about the term "nudist colony":

'Nudist colony' is used by non-naturists to describe resorts, holiday villages or indeed any settlement of buildings, tents or other structures – permanent or otherwise – which are home to those who enjoy social and leisure activities in the nude.

But why colony? Imperialist nations have colonies. Ants and termites live in colonies. Then how is it that naturists are described as inhabiting a colony?

Does the word 'colony' mean that naturists live in enclaves where rules are subsumed by a greater, almost colonial, power which allows social nudity providing it's under the thumb of the established government? Many naturists believe this to be the case, including those activists who think they should be allowed to wander naked at will in general society, as freely as those wearing clothes.

Or is colony meant to denote, like the ant pile, a mass of mindless drone-like toilers with no personality or individuality?

Surely the time is overdue when the term 'nudist colony' becomes as unacceptable as other racist or derogatory descriptions.

Shareen looked at him with raised eyebrows. 'Say that again! You didn't know you'd checked into a naturist resort? That's perfect! And you've never stayed at one before? This is your first time?' she asked incredulously.

'Well, yes,' replied Nick, looking down at his drink and feeling slightly defensive. He wished he hadn't mentioned it now. It didn't make him sound too cool. 'We were only looking for somewhere to stay the night and now, well, who knows when we'll be able to leave.'

'You couldn't have chosen a better place', said Hamish, putting down his beer and turning to Nick. 'I've been coming here for twenty years now. Regular as clockwork. Every August.'

'Tows his van up from Spain, don't you Hamish. Costa del Crime, that's his home these days. Prefers it to life in the Gorbals', added Garry.

'Pah!' said Hamish, unimpressed but not too annoyed, either. 'Do they know what the poor chap died of?'

'Not sunstroke, that's for sure.' Garry couldn't resist commenting, firing up another cigarette with a gold Dupont lighter.

'The inspector told Jack he'd suffered several blows to the head. But there were other injuries,' said Shareen.

'Other injuries? I didn't see any,' Nick said.

'Well, not real injuries but marks, you know, on both ankles and wrists? As if he'd been tied up?'

'So he could have been restrained somewhere else, then killed and dumped outside the cabin?' said Nick sounding more animated. 'In which case that means I could have been nowhere near the man when he was alive.'

'Aren't you forgetting something?' Shareen said.

'What?'

'The fact that they found your business card in his hand. You could have tied him up and brought him in the boot of your car, lifted him out and untied him?'

'Why would I do that? Why not just dump him in a wood or somewhere on the way?' Nick felt his spirits fall again. 'Well, there's still that person who checked out in the night, Parker.'

Shareen looked at him quizzically. 'You didn't do it, did you, Nick?'

'Of course not. Why would I kill someone I'd never seen before?'

'Only got your word for that my son,' said Garry, tipping ash into a glass ashtray in front of him. 'But you seem kosher enough to me. How about another beer? I'll get them in. Same again please Shareen.'

Nick drained his glass. He was feeling a bit calmer. The alcohol must be helping. And, being stationary, it was easier to forget that he was in a public place separated from his clothes by many hundreds of metres.

'Cheers!' Nick raised his refreshed glass to Garry who returned the gesture. He had a nagging feeling in the back of his mind that there was something he should have done but hadn't.

6

Looking more confident and relaxed than she actually felt, Ros walked down the long side of the swimming pool towards the vacant sun loungers and umbrellas at the far end.

Fifty or more men, women and children were in and around the pool, indulging in pool-type activities. Such as talking, gesticulating, reading, smoking, dive bombing, throwing balls or idly scratching balls (men only). Needless to say, none was clothed and none seemed the slightest bit bothered.

Ros moved a lounger out of the likely path of running children, spread her towel over the sunbed, lay down and took a paperback from her bag.

Feeling less conspicuous, Ros took a closer look at her surroundings. A sign on the wall announced how much a day Le Paradis residents had to pay to use the sunbeds and umbrellas. Although nobody was around to take her money.

Looking down towards the lake, she saw a group of twenty or so children on the parched grass. Ranging in age from about three to twelve, they were playing a game which involved pitching rings over posts, as well as much shouting and screaming.

Keeping control was a dark-haired, extremely tanned, young woman who couldn't have been more than eighteen herself. She was obviously employed by the resort to look after the kids, some of whose mothers were sitting on benches, sunning themselves and chatting amiably – happy to let the minder get on with it.

Ros was drawn to one particular blonde little girl. Probably not yet four, she was being shown a point of the game by the kneeling young woman. Ros thought the little girl was gorgeous with her blue eyes and tanned skin. It made her realize how much she yearned for a child of her own.

After all, she was "not getting any younger", as her mother un-originally kept reminding her when they went down to visit – as if she wasn't acutely aware of the statistics about age and diminishing female fertility.

She didn't want to end up like the Roy Lichtenstein-like comic book drawing of a career woman she'd once seen in the Guardian. Holding her hand up to her face and looking startled, the caption speech bubble from her mouth read "Oh! I forgot to have a baby!"

Ros didn't want this to happen to her. Nick, on the other hand, would be quite happy if she *did* forget to have a baby. Kids were definitely not on his agenda. This was the issue that created most friction whenever it was raised – usually by Ros.

Nick wanted to wait. To build his career. To really establish himself as a fashion and advertising photographer.

If you asked him on a good day, Nick would have described his progress in this competitive field as stop-start. Over the past couple of years, however, increasing numbers of magazines and agencies were using him. The fact that picture editors, in the main a female bunch, seemed to find his six foot frame and dark features attractive, also did no harm at all.

Children, he told Ros, would get in the way of that. In fact, with Ros's demanding job, she knew that Nick probably suspected that he'd end up as baby sitter and house husband.

It was OK for her, Nick argued. She had a right to feel she'd arrived. After years as a junior doctor, she'd recently secured a position as general practitioner, albeit junior, in a London practice. She had a solid foot on the career ladder.

Nick had a habit of referring to children in general, and those of friends in particular, as "ankle binders". Ros had once picked him up on this and asked whether he really meant "ankle biters".

'No,' Nick had replied, 'I call them "ankle binders" because it's an accurate description of what they do. Children bind your ankles, restrict your freedom of movement and action. And they don't only bind your ankles physically, i.e. you can't go to the cinema, pub, restaurant or, in fact, anywhere without elaborate preparations to get them looked after, but they also bind your ankles emotionally, psychologically and financially.'

'Haven't you missed something out in that list?' Ros had asked sarcastically and, just a touch, irritably.

Nick addressed her point seriously and continued with his one-person argument: 'Oh yes. And geographically as well. They bind you to one spot for years while they're being educated. And . . .' Nick really getting into his stride now, '. . . it's not as if they ever get to a point where they stop being ankle binders. Look at John and Vicky's sons. 26 and 28 and still at home binding their parents' ankles. Restricting their freedom of action.'

Yes, it was a touchy subject. Ros hoped Nick would change his mind. But she'd been hoping that for a good few years now. She considered the options.

Option One: Leave him and find someone else to father her child or children. That would be difficult, because she loved almost everything else about him. Yes, he could be irascible and moody, but then that applied to most men in her limited experience. But on the whole they did get on well. But, to be honest, not that well of late.

Option Two: Get pregnant anyway and confront him with a "fait accompli". Bit risky this. She might discover that Nick really was serious about not having children. He might go off and leave her. As she couldn't imagine having a termination, she'd then be a single mother with all the problems that entailed.

Option Three: Gradually wear him down. This hadn't worked so far, but it might be the only way. There didn't seem too much else on offer.

Her musings were interrupted by a man's voice close by. 'Ma'm'selle?'

She looked up. A tall, dark, archetypal Frenchman stood looking down at her. He was in his early twenties, lithe body and slim hips, with black hair flopping over one eye, and handsome features.

This was as much as Ros noticed in her first pass. A second glance yielded other information. Deep brown eyes, smooth hairless chest, leading down to dark curly hair above what appeared to be a reasonably-sized penis.

'Er?' was all Ros could muster in reply.

'Cinque euros, s'il vous plait'.

Ros looked blankly at him. Noticing her English paperback, he translated: 'Five euros please. For the bed and parasol'.

'Oh! Right!' said Ros, reaching sideways away from him into her bag on the floor for some money. Whilst fishing in her bag, she sensed that his eyes were roving over her body as more of her buttocks became exposed to view. Or had she been reading too many bonkbusters?

Finding a five euro note she handed it to the attendant who took it with a 'merci ma'm'selle' and placed it into a cash belt strapped around his waist – the only item of clothing he was wearing.

He was just about to turn away from her when he stopped – which was a pity for Ros as she was looking forward to seeing if his rear was as attractive as the rest of the package.

'Don't forget. Twelve o'clock,' he said. Was this an assignation only between themselves?

'Pardon?'

'Twelve o'clock at the, how do you say, not so deep end of the pool.'

'The shallow end?'

'Yes, the shallow end. Aquarobics. I take a session every day. Good for your circulation . . .' This last word pronounced in the French way with five syllables. '. . . and health.'

'Right. I'll be there. Sounds fun,' added Ros, with more enthusiasm than she felt.

He smiled, turned and walked away from her. And yes, the back view *was* as nice as she'd hoped.

She found it hard to get back to her book. Her mouth was suddenly very dry. She liked to think that it was the heat, which was now building and making sweat stand out on her arms, stomach and below her breasts. She suddenly remembered she'd asked Nick to bring her an orange juice. Where the hell was he? And where was her drink?

'Jean Luc's quite a looker, isn't he?', a cockney voice piped up.

Ros started guiltily, thinking her innermost thoughts about the Frenchman had been not only read and analysed but turned into a thesis on lust.

Turning towards the direction of the comment, Ros saw a shortish plump woman hauling herself out of the pool. She flopped, Ros thought, like a well-fed brown seal on the concrete next to her, squeezing water from her hair. Seals, however, at least on the David Attenborough programmes Ros had watched, did not have gold rings through their nipples, if they had nipples at all.

Wrenching her eyes away from the woman's breasts to her face, Ros felt she ought to make some reply. 'Yes, he is rather, well, attractive, isn't he.'

The woman raised herself upright with some difficulty, grabbed a towel from an adjacent sun-lounger and started to dry herself. 'He's the resort's Red Coat. They call them "animateurs" here. Arrange activities to keep the camp's inmates occupied.'

Ros thought irreverently that Jean-Luc could most certainly keep her occupied. Animate her in a big way.

'Just got here, have you?' the woman asked, nodding at Ros's pale skin.

'Yes, only this morning actually.'

'Well be careful you don't burn. It's very fierce, this sun.'

'I'll be careful.'

'My name's Sam, short for Samantha. Those are my two over there.' She indicated two unattractive and overweight boys, probably about eight and ten, taking it in turns to dive bomb into an inflatable ring in the pool. 'Little buggers.'

'Ros'. Ros introduced herself whilst watching the kids. Maybe Nick had a point after all, she thought as she watched the two boys splashing and shouting.

Her attention returned to Sam who was asking: 'You're not here on your own, are you, Ros? Attractive woman like you? If you don't mind me saying so.'

'Thanks. No. I'm with my partner. Last I saw of him he was heading towards the bar.'

'Just the same as my Garry. Men eh?' She then totally

changed the subject. 'Here, have you heard about the dead body they found this morning? What a terrible shock, eh?'

'Heard about it. Nick, my partner, was the one who found him.'

'He never!', said Sam, dragging her sun-lounger, to Ros's dismay, much closer to hers. 'Well go on! Tell me about it!'

So Ros found herself talking to Sam about the events of that morning, as if talking to a nude woman with nipple rings about a murdered man whose body they'd discovered was something that she did every day of the year.

When she'd finished, Sam asked, 'They found out who he was?'

'They've got no idea. But until they do find out, we're all stuck here. And that means everyone in Le Paradis.'

'Can think of worse places,' said Sam. Her eyes instinctively switched to the pool. 'Oi Gareth! Leave Mason alone!', she called to her two sons, adding 'Little buggers.'

7

About halfway down his second beer, Nick suddenly realized what had been nagging at the back of his mind.

Bloody hell! Ros's orange juice! How long had he been in here? He looked at his watch. Only half an hour or so. Well, three quarters maybe. That wasn't too long to wait, was it? Must be quite hot out there, though. And Ros was probably getting a trifle parched.

The dilemma was this. Nick was feeling relatively at home in the bar, well as at home as you could be with your privates only partly covered by a towel. Taking an orange juice to Ros would mean getting up, leaving the bar and letting all and sundry, particularly Shareen, get a good view of his rear — and more. Perhaps better to stay put for a while.

'. . . so the geezer says "No, I'm only here for a choc ice"!' Garry was delivering the punch-line to a slightly risqué joke to which Hamish, a man of few words — many of them undecipherable – gave a non-committal grunt, and Shareen a polite small laugh.

Nick drained the rest of his glass. His conscience got the better of him. He couldn't really sit here all day.

'Another beer for Nick, Shareen,' said Garry, indicating his empty glass.

'Not for me, Garry, thanks. I promised Ros I'd get her an orange juice. Better get back. She'll be wondering where I've got to.'

'Let me get it for her,' offered Garry. Nick protested but Garry insisted.

'Freshly squeezed?' asked Shareen of Nick. Why did everything have double entendre connotations in this place. He suddenly imagined freshly squeezing Shareen, but quickly put the thought to the back of his mind as he remembered he had to go outside very shortly. He doubted if Captain Oates had found it as difficult to get up and leave as he was finding it.

'Please. If you've got it.'

Shareen poured orange juice from a container she'd taken from the fridge. 'Only made this morning,' she explained, putting the glass down in front of him. 'There you go.'

"Thanks. And cheers, Garry.' Nick raised the glass of orange juice in acknowledgement towards Garry and got up from the stool. He soon realized that holding the glass in his hand before getting up was a big mistake. He now had to manoeuvre the towel from underneath him, one-handed, seriously restricting his ability to cover himself. He nearly fell as he got his feet caught in the towel, which dropped to the floor. He saved the orange juice from following suit, slopping some over his hand.

'Whoops! Just how many drinks have you had, my son?,' laughed Garry.

Nick rested the orange juice back on the counter and bent to retrieve his towel, feeling very foolish in front of Shareen – and very exposed.

Wiping his sticky hand on the towel – another use for Martin Pike to note in his book – Nick searched his vocabulary for a witty response. There wasn't one. All he could do was smile weakly as he re-positioned towel over arm, hoping it gave some strategic cover to his genitals.

This naturist lark was not only playing havoc with his heart rate, it was also having a dramatic effect on his personality. Usually he liked to think of himself as confident, sociable and on the extrovert side. But since getting here he seemed to have shed his personality along with his clothes. If clothes really did "a man maketh", then Nick had come totally unstitched.

'Right. See you later, all,' was the only line he could manage as he lifted the glass with his free hand, took a deep breath, turned away from the bar and walked outside.

Leaving the darkness of the interior, he stepped into the blinding light and heat of the noon-day sun. Squinting around, he tried to locate Ros. Not seeing her, he set out in the general direction she'd last been heading.

As he reached the far end of the pool, a drum and bass beat became louder and more insistent. The sound was coming from a large portable boogie box by the poolside. Beside it a nude man was jumping up and down. Below him in the water, it looked like feeding time at a piranha farm.

On closer inspection, the splashing was being made by a group of, mainly, women, leaping up and down, imitating the movements of the man by the poolside. And there in the middle of them was an attractive dark-haired woman who looked just like, but it couldn't be, but it was! Ros! Giving her best impression of a salmon heading upstream to its spawning grounds.

'You Nick?', a very brown woman on a nearby lounger enquired.

'Er, yes?' Nick noticed this woman had pierced nipples with gold rings through them. How painful must that have been, he thought.

'Ros's lounger is just 'ere,' Sam said, indicating the adjacent sunbed. 'I recognized you by the orange juice.'

'Oh? Right!' Mr Woody Allen.

Nick put the orange juice on a small low plastic table and looked around for another sunbed for himself.

'You'd find it easier if you put your towel down,' said Sam, examining him over the top of her sunglasses. 'Ros told me you're a reluctant nudist. There's nothing to be ashamed of you know.'

Well, thanks a lot Ros, Nick thought. You can't even keep your neuroses hidden in this place. Finding a spare lounger he put his towel over it and lay down.

'Is my Garry still in the bar?'

'Yes.' If Nick had felt uncomfortable in the relatively dim and covered interior of the bar, here he felt really exposed in the bright sunlight talking to a slightly overweight nude woman. He determined that the best approach was to look directly into her eyes.

The Naked Guide has this to say about the direction of gaze in a naturist resort:

In spite of the fact that you may think naturists would be the one group in Society not to worry too much about others seeing their naked bodies, it is in fact considered extremely rude to look overtly at the breasts and privates of your fellow naturists.

The direction of gaze must be restricted to shoulder height and above. 'Fairly and squarely in the eye' is the safest rule of thumb. It avoids embarrassment, misunderstanding and any charge of voyeur-

ism. In any circumstance, except in an emergency, do not lower your
point of vision to below shoulder height.

'I take it you must be . . .' Nick racked his memory and a name
mentioned by Garry popped up. '. . . Sam. Good to meet
you.'

'And you, Nick. Your Ros is really getting into the swim of
things,' Sam said nodding towards the pool.

It was strange, thought Nick, how nudity was affecting Ros.
Normally cautious, down-to-earth and slightly introverted,
Ros seemed to have become more sociable the less she wore.
Almost as if she'd shed her protective shell and inhibitions along
with her clothes. In fact, the direct opposite of Nick, who had
seemed to have acquired a whole cabin trunk-load of inhibitions.

The music ceased. There was much laughter and an exaggerated bow from the man at the side of the pool. He put
down a hand to help lift one of the women out of the pool.
Hang on. It was Ros. She giggled at him as he lifted her up,
holding onto his arm, it seemed to Nick, a touch too long as her
feet made contact with the poolside. She spoke a few words to
him and turned towards Nick and the lounger, pushing her hair
back from her face as she did so. Seeing him, she waved in
acknowledgment and walked over – the animateur having a
great view of her arse as she did so.

Taking her towel off the lounger, Ros began vigorously to
dry herself. Spotting the orange juice on the table, she greedily
picked it up. Instead of complaining about the time it'd taken to
arrive, she said to Nick: 'Fresh orange juice. Great!' And
downed half the glass in one go.

'Er, sorry, it took slightly longer than planned. I got a bit
held up,' Nick offered.

'Been talking to my Garry', explained Sam to Ros. 'Garry

has that effect on people. Could talk all day, every day. But lovely with it.'

Ros seemed to be completely at home – totally unconcerned by the fact that she was wearing not a stitch. She asked Nick to re-apply sun cream to her back, whilst chatting with Sam about the toughness of the work-out she'd just been through. All this from someone who wouldn't even say "boo" to a goose, even at a "Say boo to a goose" party.

Having finished, Nick lay back on his lounger. By this time the effect of a couple of early beverages, the broken sleep of last night and the overall tension of being in this unnatural habitat began to tell. His eyes closed and off he went into a deep, deep slumber.

8

'Nick . . . Nick . . .' Someone was shaking his arm. He opened his eyes. It was Ros. 'Are you asleep?'

'Not now I'm not!' he said irritably.

'Good. Because I could do with something to eat.'

'What time is it?'

'Gone one. You've been asleep for an hour or so. I thought we could go to the restaurant for lunch.'

Nick had now fully come to. He looked around. No, it hadn't been a nightmare. He really was lying there nude, amongst other nude sunbathers, in a nudist resort. Oh yes. And he was still suspect number one in an on-going murder enquiry.

Sam had disappeared. Ros told Nick she'd gone back to their caravan with the kids and presumably Garry to cook lunch.

It was now seriously hot and Nick felt a slight "zizziness" about his body. He looked down and the white bits round his midriff looked distinctly pinker than he remembered them. Just as well Ros had woken him otherwise he may have spent the holiday in the third degree burns unit – which on reflection may have been preferable to his current situation.

Steeling himself, towel over arm, he got up. Ros almost too casually put her towel around her neck and slung her beach bag over one shoulder. She even waved to the animateur chap who was over the far side of the pool talking to two elderly women. Nick didn't like the way he smiled and waved back.

They set off along the now relatively deserted poolside to the open air restaurant. About thirty or so people were sitting at tables under the shady awning.

'M'sieur?' a waitress asked.

'Pour deux,' Ros replied before Nick could open his mouth, and they were both ushered to a table at the far end.

No sooner had Nick placed his towel on the seat and applied his posterior to it than he heard a familiar male voice: 'I don't believe it!!! Is it really you two?'

Ros and Nick turned in unison towards the direction of the voice, which came from a table behind them. My God! This was getting too much to bear – or should that be bare.

Sitting no further than six feet away were next-door-but-one neighbours from their street in Stoke Newington. Geoff and Lynne Russell. But Geoff and Lynne as they'd obviously never seen them before. Unencumbered by clothing. Totally nude. Well, much the same as themselves, actually.

'What a coincidence! Fancy bumping into you here. Come and join us', added Lynne, rising slightly to move two chairs out at their table in invitation and exposing even more tanned flesh.

Ready to move heaven and earth several times over not to rise and expose himself fully nude to Geoff and Lynne, Nick looked pleadingly at Ros. It was too late.

Getting up from the table and grabbing her towel, but not, he noted, to cover any specific part of her body, Ros called back, 'Love to!'

With that she was off. Reaching the table she proffered kisses to Lynne and Geoff and looked back at Nick, who was reluctantly rising from his seat, covering himself as best he could.

When he reached the table, Lynne proffered her cheek to be kissed, which he dutifully did, muttering a 'Hi there.'

Nick quickly took his place across the table from Lynne. Was it his imagination or did she look amused at his discomfort. And did she take more than a disinterested glance downwards as his nether regions disappeared from sight.

Slightly older than Nick and Ros, the Russells had seemed – up to a nano-second ago – to lead fairly dull and conventional lives. Geoff was a partner in a quantity surveying firm – whatever that was – and Lynne was a counsellor in some form of therapy. Yet here they were, sitting in an open air restaurant, stark naked and greeting them as naturally as if they'd met in the checkout queue at Waitrose.

Just how embarrassing could this whole holiday get? Geoff and Lynne! Naturists!. Whatever next. Bumping into perhaps Ros's parents? Or his own? After this, nothing would surprise him.

Having only seen Geoff and Lynne socially back in London, Nick naturally had never seen Lynne naked. He'd always thought she'd had a nice figure and, in idle moments, had speculated on what she would look like nude – don't all men, he thought, defensively? And here she was. And from what he could see of her top half, he liked what he saw. Small breasts that had nicely uptilted nipples.

A bit on the skinny side with almost boyish figure, Lynne had an androgynous appearance which wasn't made any more feminine by a short haircut which could almost be described as vintage pudding basin. He'd once mentioned to Ros that it looked as if it had been cut and sanctioned by the Stoke

Newington Health Police, right-on leftish-wingers that made up the majority of Lynne and Geoff's friends — and a fair proportion of their own, come to think of it.

Despite all this, the overall package, particularly with its rather fetching tan, looked pretty good from where Nick was sitting. Perhaps not as attractive as Shareen or Ros, but definitely — as Garry might have said, if he'd been there, — "it had a bit of form."

He'd always thought that Lynne had a soft spot for him. At the odd party or social gathering, she'd always been slightly too attentive, always laughed a bit too much at his jokes, always stood a fraction closer than was polite — or strictly necessary.

In contrast to Lynne, Geoff was overweight, bearded and with a slightly receding hairline. As tall as Nick, he was probably some five stone heavier. And in a naturist resort, Nick observed, it really did all hang out.

'You never mentioned to us you were naturists', said Geoff over the top of his menu, in a comment aimed, Nick thought, too interestedly, at Ros. 'We always had you marked down as textiles.'

'Textiles?' queried Nick.

According to the Naked Guide:

In naturist circles the word 'textiles' is not used to describe bolts of cloth or items manufactured in mills located largely in the northern regions of the United Kingdom, but mainly as a derogatory term.

'Textiles' are those who keep their clothes on when bathing, sunbathing or engaged in other outdoor activities where it is natural, if not proper, to remove all items of clothing.

On a beach, therefore, those who retain the smallest item of clothing — towels excepted, of course — are referred to as 'textiles'.

The term can also be used as an adjective. Hence any beach

*which bans nudity is referred to as a 'textile-only' beach. Or any
area which forbids nudity is a 'textile-only' area.*

*While textiles make up the majority of the population of the
world, inroads are currently being made, both in the increasing
number of beaches being made available to the naturist and in the
increasing number of resorts catering for naked holidaymakers.*

'Actually we're not really naturists. To be totally honest, this is
our first time in a nudist resort', said Ros.

'So what made you take the plunge?' asked Lynne.

'Total accident,' Ros continued, going on to explain their
disrupted holiday plans, their arrival and how they'd discovered
their error this morning.

Lynne and Geoff smiled at her description.

'But if you're supposed to be staying with your friends, how
come you're still here?' Geoff asked, reasonably enough.

This entailed a longer explanation of the discovery of the
dead man and their "house arrest", a tale listened to almost
disbelievingly by Lynne and Geoff with the odd exclamation
such as 'No!', 'Really?' 'That's unreal!', 'You're not serious!'
and similar.

When Ros had finished, Lynne said, 'That must explain
why a gendarme came round to our camper-van just now. He
had a Polaroid photo of a man and was asking whether we
knew him. At least that's what I think he was asking. My
French is a bit rusty. And I couldn't help noticing he seemed
more interested in looking at my tits than in listening to our
reply.'

This last sentence was delivered with an accompanying
thrust forward of her bosom to illustrate the point.

'Please!' said Geoff, somewhat prudishly, either at her use of
the word 'tits' or her gesture – possibly both.

'A photo?' Nick couldn't resist asking – although he too was literally, as well as metaphorically, sharing the view of the randy gendarme. 'Er, how did they get a photo of him?'

'He was hardly in a position to refuse to pose, was he now?', said Ros. 'Mind you, he wouldn't have been able to smile or say "cheese". Or anything else, come to think of it.'

'Oh, yes, I see what you mean,' Nick added meekly. My God, if he spent one more day here he'd be rendered totally speechless, like one of those poor stroke victims. Able to understand and appreciate all that was happening around him but unable to utter a single meaningful word.

'And *did* you recognize him?' Ros asked Lynne.

'Well I think so,' Geoff answered for her. 'He looked very much like a chap that we used to see in the bar. He was staying on his own in one of the cabins – probably close to you two, actually. I mentioned it to the gendarme and he presumably went off to check. Haven't heard any more since.'

A waitress arrived to take their order. With all the chat, none of them had given the menus serious consideration. Geoff consulted the others and ordered carafes of red and white and 'fizzy water' to be going on with, while they made up their mind as to what they were going to eat.

'Cheers. Lovely surprise!' Lynne toasted the others as soon as the wine had arrived and been poured. They all dutifully clinked glasses and Lynne gave Nick a small smile as her glass touched his.

Once they'd finally ordered, conversation naturally enough turned to Le Paradis.

'We've been to other places, of course, mainly in France but also in Spain, but like you this is the first time we've been here. Unlike you though we did actually mean to come', Geoff laughed at his feeble joke.

Nick was not amused. He seemed to have undergone a sense of humour by-pass with everything else.

'How long have you been here?' Ros enquired of Lynne.

'Just a week so far,' Lynne replied. 'Got another week and then home.'

'So what have you been doing?' My God! Nick found he'd been able to string an almost coherent sentence together.

'We've played a bit of tennis. The courts are over to the right hand side of the lake there.' Geoff indicated the general direction.

Visions of Geoff's portly naked body running around the tennis court came unbidden and unwelcome to Nick's mind. Now Lynne on the other hand . . .

His thoughts were interrupted by Lynne herself. 'We've taken out a dinghy on the lake, that was good fun. You ought to try it Nick. I'll show you the ropes if you like.'

What did she mean by that, thought Nick. Maybe she actually would like to show me the ropes. But not any that Francis Chichester may have been familiar with.

'Apart from that, we've been pretty inactive. Just swimming, sunbathing and enjoying this fantastic weather,' added Geoff.

'We've also been to the night club once. It's on the far side of the lake, so as not to disturb the natives. It might be nice if we all went together perhaps,' Lynne finished, again looking at Nick.

'Not sure if we'll be here that long. I mean, we could be free to leave the resort this evening for all we know,' Nick protested.

His mind had already taken in too much today. Even thinking about the implications of a night club in a naturist resort might, if he gave it more than fleeting thought, cause serious short-circuiting of brain synapses – even permanent insanity.

There was a brief lull in the conversation as the salades niçoises, omelettes, frites and bread arrived. They got stuck in.

'What about the people here?' Ros asked.

'Nice bunch,' said Geoff, taking a sip of wine. 'We've met quite a few English of course. Friendly lot your naturists. Removing your clothes also seems to remove barriers between people and classes. Doesn't matter whether you're a lord or a, or a . . .'

Nick helped him finish the sentence: 'Lavatory cleaner?'

'Precisely. Thanks Nick. Whether you're a lord or a lavatory cleaner, in a naturist resort you're all equal. And we all get on well together.'

'Oh yes, I can just imagine Sid the dustman discussing the finer points of inheritance tax with Lord Snooty over a plate of moules marinières', Nick said. My God! It just goes to show that it took someone as pedantic and pompous as Geoff to restore his power of speech.

Ros kicked him lightly under the table. 'So have you met any lords or, um, lavatory cleaners?'

Lynne, smiling perhaps at Nick's previous comments, took up the baton. 'Well, we've met a very interesting English couple who are staying just a bit down from us. You just wouldn't believe it, Ros. I know that piercings are all the rage these days, but this couple have piercings in places, well, it makes me blush to even think about.'

'Tell me more,' said Ros, sounding far too interested for Nick's liking.

Lynne leaned forwards, as if conspiratorially, towards Ros and Nick. 'Well, not that I make a habit of looking at these things, but they've got so many studs, chains and what-have-you about their lower regions it's a wonder they don't trigger a full scale terrorist alert every time they go near an airport x-ray machine.'

'Such as?' Ros also leaned forward, prompting, Nick noted, a slight raise of eyebrows from Geoff, as he got a better and closer view of her breasts looming across the table at him.

'He's got a ring through the end of his penis and studs and chains through his balls. I don't suppose they're actually through his balls, but you know through the scrotum,' said Lynne, actually looking slightly embarrassed as if suddenly regretting starting this conversation.

'And she not only has pierced nipples, which is not that uncommon here, but also breast implants and . . .' here Lynne hesitated again. 'and . . . er . . . a ring through her, well, labia type regions.'

Ros involuntarily raised her hand to her mouth, eyes wide. 'No! And she walks around like this? Nude?'

'Absolutely!'

'This couple. What are their names?' asked Nick, wanting to join in the conversation, but sounding remarkably like a Nazi camp commandant.

'Janet and John,' Geoff answered, as he downed a substantial gulp of wine.

'Janet and John?', said Nick in disbelief. 'Now you are winding us up.'

'No, they really are called Janet and John. God knows what else they get up to. But they're very pleasant company. He's an Inland Revenue tax inspector and she's a primary school teacher. Both live in Orpington,' added Lynne. 'In fact, you can meet them yourself. We're having dinner here with them this evening. Eight thirty. Why don't you join us?'

'That sounds fun. We'd love to, wouldn't we Nick?' said Ros.

Nick felt a further panic attack. He was not sure whether he could actually have dinner with Geoff and Lynne in the nude, let alone a man with ironmongery attached to his balls and a woman with breast implants. Well, he wasn't being totally honest about that. Yes, he would quite like to have dinner with a woman with breast implants. But even so . . .

'Well, we may not be here by this evening,' Nick said.

'Of course we will. They're not going to sort this out by then,' said Ros. 'Yes we'd love to meet for dinner, if it's OK with Janet and John, of course?'

They were promised that there would be no problem and Nick found himself the odd man out. He'd just have to go along with it. Maybe he'd get lucky and break a leg on the way back to the cabin. He took a further swig of wine and tried to put the thought of the forthcoming evening out of his mind. I mean, just how worse could it all really get?

9

Nick and Ros were walking back up the Champs to their cabin after lunch. Nick was feeling only slightly less anxious than before, aided no doubt by the couple of carafes of wine he'd helped Geoff consume. He'd need a hogshead to get totally used to the idea of communal public nudity. His heart was still beating faster than it should. And he couldn't shake the idea that any minute someone would come along and arrest him for indecently exposing himself in a public, or should that be pubic, place.

On top of all this, he was still concerned that he'd experience a sudden erection, although that seemed unlikely as his penis had stayed put for both Shareen and Lynne.

Turning his attention to Lynne, he thought how unlikely it was that someone as fussy about the dangers of everyday living, diet and skin cancer could be a naturist.

'Lynne and bloody Geoff bloody Russell!' exclaimed Nick. 'Of all the people to run into. Who would have believed it. Nudists! Wait 'til I tell the guys down the pub.'

'Aren't you forgetting something?' asked Ros.

'Like what?'

'Your friends down the Prince of Wales may ask how exactly you know they're nudists. And what you were wearing yourself at the time you were carrying out these observations.'

Nick executed a mental handbrake about-turn any joyrider would have been proud of. 'Ah. Well, perhaps it is best if we keep totally quiet about their holidaying preferences after all.' He thought he might be able to take a certain amount of "joshing" about his nudist idyll from his friends, but he didn't want to become the butt – unfortunate choice of words – of their jokes from here 'til last orders do us part.

Reaching the door of the cabin, Ros looked in her beach bag for the key, which of course had slipped right to the bottom. Finding it, she opened the door into the stuffy interior.

With some relief Nick threw his protective towel onto the bed. 'This is all turning into a total bloody nightmare. I don't think I really can go out again undressed like this. What were you thinking, agreeing to go to dinner with the Russells, let alone two strangers with an interest in making as many holes as possible in their bodies?'

'It seemed a good idea at the time,' Ros said, casually fishing around in her bag for her hairbrush. 'Anyway it's too late now. You should have said something. You'll just have to put up with it.'

'On top of everything, I think I've caught the sun a bit,' Nick added, as he tried to look at his bum.

'You need to watch that. Don't want it to burn. After all it probably hasn't seen the light of day for the past thirty years. Like other parts of you,' said Ros, giving his testicles a gentle squeeze. 'Wonder what you'd look like with a ring through your balls.'

Nick flinched away, both from her grasp and at the thought

of someone sticking a red-hot needle – or whatever the hell they do – through his testicles.

'It's not funny Ros. I don't know how you can just happily swan around without a stitch on, seemingly without a care in the world. I'd never have dreamed it if I hadn't seen it with my own eyes.'

It was something Ros had been asking herself. She was feeling fairly relaxed about the nudity. Yes, it felt a little strange, open air whistling around parts that hadn't previously had open air whistle round them. In a way it felt naughty and daring. She quite liked the total freedom and the glances she received from the male populace. And one in particular.

The image of Jean-Luc conducting his aquarobics class came unbidden to her mind. From where she was standing in the pool, she had a very good view of his slim, almost boyish body, unlike a particular certain other part of him. She found herself wondering whether Jean-Luc was a "grower" or a "show-er".

This was the, admittedly not very scientific, theory of Ros's friend Ruth. Ruth felt that men fell into two categories as regarding penis size. There was the "what you see when it's flaccid is virtually what you get when it's erect" category, which she named the "show-ers". Then there were the "doesn't look too promising to start with and then, my God!" category. The "growers". Ros didn't think this theory would stand up to close inspection, ho-ho, but it made speculating more interesting.

This train of thought was interrupted by Nick before she could develop the imagery further and consider how it applied to Jean-Luc. 'Do you think it's all right to drink the tap water, Doctor?'

'My diagnosis would be best not.'

'I'm parched. Must be the heat.'

And the litre or so of wine, thought Ros. 'Well, let's go and get some bottled water at the supermarket. If we are staying here the night, as looks likely, then we'll need some basics anyway. Coffee, milk, orange juice, that sort of thing.'

'Isn't that a bit of a waste? I mean, we'll probably be away in the morning.'

'Then we can take the stuff to Kathy and Phillip,' said Ros, fishing her purse out of her beach bag.

'Bloody hell! Kathy and Phillip. We still haven't rung them.' Nick grabbed his mobile. Still no signal.

'There's a phone in the reception building. I'm sure we can use that.'

'Good perhaps you could call them. Oh and while you're there, don't forget to get us some beers and wine for later.'

'What do you mean "while you're there"? I'm not going to carry all the shopping back on my own. Come on. Get dressed. This seems to suit you sir,' said Ros, picking up Nick's towel and holding it up in front of him so he could look at himself in the mirror.

Taking the towel he almost groaned. 'Not exactly Paul Smith, is it.'

'Don't make such a fuss. It's not far, and I doubt there are many people about. It's the French equivalent of siesta time after all.'

Ros took the key and her purse and looked round for her own towel. What the hell! She wasn't going to sit down anywhere. They were only doing the shopping. 'Come on, then. Let's go.'

'You've forgotten your towel.'

'No need for it. Less to carry,' said Ros as she walked out the door. Actually carrying small things was something of a problem. The only handbag she'd brought with her had been chosen to go with a smart dress in the evenings and would definitely have looked rather inappropriate when matched with a nude body. There was also, of course, a lack of pockets. She took with her the beach bag, which was OK for shopping but a bit large for everyday wear.

Nick followed her onto the verandah. Ros was right. There were very few people about – and no sign of Martin Pike.

They took the short-cut path Shareen had taken this morning which brought them to the supermarket. As they approached the door, they stopped for two nude young men to exit, who thanked them with a double 'merci'.

The supermarket was not exactly huge but well stocked. It was noticeably cooler inside. At the end of the first aisle was a large vertical chilled food cabinet into which a young French housewife was leaning for a four-pack of yogurt. The only thing she was wearing was a sun-visor. She spotted Ros looking her way and gave a friendly quick smile before moving on to the cheeses.

What a strange dreamlike experience this was, thought Ros as she picked up a basket and walked down the first aisle, Nick reluctantly flip-flopping at her heels. She tried to imagine the reaction of Mr and Mrs Shah if she attempted to repeat this trip round her local convenience store in Green Lanes. It would almost be worth trying just to see their faces. Almost.

The Naked Guide has this to say about nudity and dreams.

Many of us have had dreams where we have been naked when all around have been fully clothed. In 'The Interpretation of Dreams' Freud concluded that being naked or scantily clad in the presence of strangers only demanded our attention when shame and embarrassment are felt.

Interestingly, Freud observes that the persons before whom one is ashamed are almost always strangers – yet those strangers are normally totally indifferent to your nude state.

Freud says that memories of the dreamer's earliest childhood lies at the heart of the dream – a time when we are not ashamed of our nakedness. This age of childhood, in which a sense of shame is

unknown, seems a paradise when we look back upon it later. In
paradise men are naked and unashamed, until the moment arrives
when shame and fear awaken. Expulsion follows and sexual life and
cultural development begin.

Freud says that it is into this paradise that dreams can take us
back.

Loading up with coffee, milk and orange juice for tomorrow's breakfast — the store seemed to be out of fresh bread and croissants — Ros added wine to her basket while Nick chose some beers and a multi-pack of water.

As they approached the checkout, Ros noticed a selection of small bags just big enough to contain a paperback book together with notes and coins. She added a nice leather one to her basket.

The clothed middle-aged woman at the checkout put down her crossword magazine to ring up their purchases. And bade them 'au revoir' and 'bon journée' in that sing-song way the French do, as they emerged into the heat of the afternoon.

'Why don't you go across to reception and phone. I'll wait here,' said Ros.

Nick crossed the Champs, glancing longingly at the gate which was guarded by two bored-looking gendarmes in white plastic chairs.

Reaching Reception, he tried the glass door. Locked. And then noticed a sign. Damn. Closed for lunch. A very long lunch it seemed.

He turned to come back and noticed a phone call box just by the side of the supermarket. Getting some euro coins from Ros, Nick padded across to the booth, which was as hot as a stolen Hackney mobile phone.

He listened to the unfamiliar French ringing tone from Phillip and Kathy's phone. No answer. Probably out by the pool. He let it ring at least 20 times. No answer. No answering machine. He gave up. And hung up.

As he emerged from the phone booth, sweat standing out on his forehead and chest, he put his towel to alternative use and gave himself a good mop down. God it was hot!

Ros remained standing under a tree, seemingly totally untroubled by the nude world round her, surrounded by plastic shopping bags. He was about to walk over when he heard a 'Nick! Hi!' It was Jack poking his head out of the reception door. 'I've got some news.'

Nick indicated to Ros that he was going over to Reception. She found a concrete bench in the shade and sat down. Sod the towel rule in this instance, she thought rebelliously.

Nick walked over to Jack. 'Thought you were closed.'

'Just got back. I don't know whether you've heard but they've caught the fugitive! You know, the guy that checked out this morning? The one you said you heard leave? Parker. They stopped him on the autoroute a few hours back. Inspector Lagardère has gone off to interview him.'

'That's great! That should put us in the clear.' Nick found himself talking like a character in a bad American B-movie. He could at last see the possible end of this nightmare existence.

Forget Le Paradis, this was more like Hell. After all, there seemed little difference. In both places you were stark naked, sweating in ferocious heat with a bunch of complete strangers. But at least to gain admission to Hell you had to commit some dreadful sin. All he'd done was trust Ros with the map-reading.

'When's Lagardère back?' Nick asked. He and Jack were both standing out of the fierce sun under the overhanging roof at the front of reception.

'Later this afternoon. Until then, we're confined to quarters. Especially you! Inspector's orders.'

'Any idea who the murdered man was yet?'

'They're still checking. I've given them a list of all the people I think are here on their own – at least according to what they told me when they checked in. Two gendarmes are going round the resort to see if anyone's missing. Could take awhile.'

'We heard that they've taken a photo of the dead man and have been showing it around the place.'

'Photographed him in the back of the supermarket.'

'Sorry?'

'Yeah. They were waiting for the ambulance and asked if there was anywhere cool to store the body. I said not, until I remembered an old chest freezer in the storeroom. So we switched it on and laid him out in the freezer. They cleaned the blood off his face and took the photos.'

'I hope you took the frozen peas out first,' said Nick.

Jack was slow on the uptake, thinking Nick was serious for a minute. 'Oh right! No, it's not in use. We were going to throw it out this winter anyway. I expect we'll hear more when Lagadere gets back.'

Nick excused himself. 'Better get back myself,' Nick replied, setting off with a slightly raised hand in goodbye to Jack, who returned the gesture and went back into reception.

'What was all that about?' Ros asked. Nick filled her in on the detail as they walked back to the cabin.

'So if this Parker turns out to be the murderer, we're free to go?' said Ros, opening the cabin door.

'I bloody hope so. I don't think I could stand it here much longer.'

The interior of the cabin was hotter than ever as they put away the items in the small fridge, Nick helping himself to a huge swig of water in the process.

Ros walked through to the bedroom and flopped back down on the bed, legs slightly apart, hands behind her head. She was, if truth be told, quite frisky. A mixture of the heat, walking around nude and thinking about Jean-Luc had left her, well, not to put too fine a point upon it, feeling like a good seeing-to.

'Come and lie down for a while,' said Ros. 'I think you could do with a little rest and recreation.'

'Right.' Nick came into the room and lay down beside her.

She snuggled up seductively against him. One advantage of being in a naturist resort, she thought, was that you didn't have straps, underwear, shoes, socks or other encumberances to remove. Once you lay down next to someone you were as good as having sex.

'As good as' being the operative words, as the minute Nick lay down he was off. Fast asleep. Delayed reaction from lack of sleep, the wine and stress. And snoring lightly with it. Not one of his most endearing features at the best of times. And definitely not at all welcome at the present.

For a moment it crossed Ros's mind to continue without him, but it didn't have the same appeal. She didn't feel at all tired. Frustrated, yes. Tired, no.

She got up and ran her hand through her hair looking into the mirror. How did she really feel about all this? Quite excited. A bit apprehensive. But about what? Jean-Luc? Nick's possible arrest? The uncertainty? It was hard to pin down. All she did know was that she couldn't stay here for the afternoon.

She looked at her watch. Half past three. She decided to return to the pool. It would be nice to take a refreshing dip and maybe, just possibly, bump into Jean-Luc. She had after all paid for her sun-lounger for the day. Why not get her money's worth?

Putting her towel into her beach bag, and the bag over her shoulder, she quietly opened and then closed the door after her, leaving both the cabin and Nick slumbering in the heat of the French August afternoon.

10

Ros quickly discovered that going out alone in a naturist resort was a very different experience from accompanying Nick.

She immediately felt more vulnerable and more exposed – if that were possible. As she walked down the Champs towards the lake, she was extremely uneasy. Le Paradis had fallen into a post-prandial stupor. Very few people seemed to be about. Yet she had the irrational feeling that she was being watched. She even turned once or twice to look behind her. Nobody in sight. The only human beings she saw were either chatting quietly under awnings, sleeping or just relaxing in the shade.

Get a grip, she told herself. Nothing's going to happen. It's only the fact that you've never been nude in a public place before, until today that is. Even so, Ros was relieved when she reached the end of the tree-lined Champs and emerged into the open, in front of the swimming pool. The lake shimmered attractively in the afternoon sunlight, boats moving slowly on its surface in the lightest of breezes.

The restaurant was shut and deserted. In front of the bar a few people sat under umbrellas, enjoying either a late lunch-time, or early evening, tipple.

As she was passing the bar, Shareen emerged from its shady interior carrying a round metal tray on which stood two foaming glasses of beer. These she expertly unloaded onto a table in front of a very large, and extremely brown, couple. 'Danke schoen,' said the man, as the glass was put in front of him.

Shareen turned away and spotted Ros. 'Hi Ros! How's it going?'

Ros had no option but to go across to Shareen, who stood with now-empty tray clasped to her bosom, clearly wanting a chat.

'Well, not too bad, considering,' said Ros, pushing hair away from her forehead.

'Oh yeah. Nick shared with me that this was your first time at a nudist resort.'

Thanks a lot, thought Ros, forgetting she'd told Sam about Nick's "nudophobia". She wondered what else Shareen and Nick had "shared".

'Here. Thought you'd like to know. They found out who the dead guy was. We just heard. It was a great shock!' Shareen continued.

'Oh. Why?'

'Because he was one of our regulars. Giles Curtis. Really good bloke. English.'

'So how come you didn't recognize him this morning?'

'Well, he was rather, well, bloody and battered. And face down like that, one nude guy looks very much like another, doesn't he?'

Thinking of men in her surgery she was examining for prostate problems or piles, Ros could see what Shareen meant.

But then again, wasn't it a bit unusual that she hadn't identified him? He was a regular after all, by Shareen's own admission. 'How did they find out who he was?'

'The cops got a lead from some English couple.'

That could have been Lynne and Geoff, thought Ros, remembering their story over lunch.

'Went to his place and found it like the Marie Celeste? That ship, you know?' Shareen continued. 'As if freshly abandoned? Glass of Scotch, half-drunk. Bedside lamp still on. Bit creepy, eh? And such a shame. Such a popular guy.'

'Well, who was he? I mean, what did he do?'

'Didn't give much away. Seemed to know all the poms, sorry, English in the camp. Nobody's quite sure exactly what job he had. Or used to have. All I knew was that he lived in London, took early retirement and was here on an extended holiday. Not that extended though was it? Poor bastard.'

At this point, a Scottish voice called from somewhere inside the bar, 'Shop! There's a man dying of thirst in here!'

Shareen turned her head towards the direction of the voice and shouted back, 'OK! Keep your sporran on!' And to Ros, 'Gotta go. Catch up with you later. And regards to that man of yours.'

With that, Shareen turned and was off back into the bar, giving Ros a view of a pert wiggling backside which she immediately hated.

She was suddenly filled with an irrational suspicion. Did Shareen have designs on Nick? Or he on her? Grow up, she thought. We've been here less than 24 hours. Nothing ever develops that quickly. Conveniently forgetting her earlier lustful thoughts for Jean-Luc.

She re-adjusted her beach bag over her shoulder and repeated her walk of this morning, down the side of the pool to the far end and her sun lounger.

There were almost as many people as this morning, but most seemed to be more somnolent, as if knocked out by the heat. People were dozing under parasols. Even the few children about were only half-heartedly bombing each other in the pool.

Her lounger was still free. And beside it, under their own parasol to protect them from the fierce sun, lay Sam on a lounger next to a new arrival, a rather large man who she assumed was Garry, asleep on his back, gently snoring, on an adjacent sunbed.

Sam looked up from reading her own holiday book. 'Hallo love. Didn't know if you were going to be back, but I kept your lounger for you anyway.'

'Thanks,' said Ros, putting her bag down besides the lounger and spreading her beach towel over it. 'It's so hot. I've just got to have a dip.'

So saying, she dived into the pool, gasping at the sudden chill of the water. She'd swum in a girlfriend's parents' pool naked many years ago and was reminded how liberating it was. The feel of the water on your bare skin. She briskly swam front crawl ten lengths of the pool, feeling that it would be good for her, take her mind off other things. Their current situation in general and Jean-Luc in particular – of whom there seemed to be absolutely no sign.

Ros returned to her lounger and started drying herself. Sam, with an effort, pulled herself into a sitting position and took a swig of what looked like Coca Cola. She sat up, with legs over the side of her lounger, facing Ros.

'Have you heard they've identified the bloke what was killed?' Sam said.

'Yes,' Ros said, tilting her head to one side to get water out of her ear. 'Shareen, you know, the woman behind the bar, she told me. Apparently it was a bit of a surprise?'

'You can say that again. He was a really smashing bloke, Giles. Kids liked him as well. Used to play with them endlessly in the pool. They'll be upset when they hear. Good mates with Garry and all,' Sam said, inclining her head backwards to indicate her still supine partner. 'Used to go out drinking late together many nights. Liked a drink, did Giles. Wondered why we hadn't seen him around today. Thought he must be hungover. Now we know.'

'Shareen was telling me he'd made lots of friends?' Ros said, applying some sun lotion to her shoulders and breasts.

'And clearly an enemy,' said Sam. 'A very vicious one, by the sounds of it. I hope they catch the bastard soon.'

'What bastard's that love?' asked Garry, now awake and struggling to sit upright. Catching sight of Ros, who was at that point spreading sun cream over her stomach and thighs, he said 'Oh, 'allo.'

'The bastard that killed Giles,' answered Sam. 'This is Ros, by the way, Nick's partner. And this is Garry.'

'Pleased to meet you.' Ros said, and for something to say added, 'I hear you knew Giles well?'

'Not that well,' said Garry a bit defensively. 'We had a few beers together. Nice bloke. Bit secretive though. Never really knew what he was thinking.'

'Well someone must have taken exception to him,' said Ros, laying down on her lounger and putting on her sunglasses.

'Yeah. Suppose you're right,' Garry said, appearing to Ros to take a little too long looking at her body. 'Come on. Let's go in for a swim and play with the kids. They look as if they need livening up,' Garry said to Sam.

Ros looked across the pool where the two rather plump boys were sitting on the side of the pool, idly kicking their feet in the water.

*   *   *

Left alone, Ros picked up her book and tried to concentrate on the story. Louise, Sir Jonathan's wife, was just deciding whether to reveal her clandestine sultry affair with the head groom to Jonathan when suddenly he appeared at her elbow.

'Bonjour, ma'm'selle.'

Ros gave a start and looked up from the page. Jean-Luc smiled down at her, wearing even less than this morning in that he'd removed his money-storing belt.

'Hi!' said Ros, her heart beating quickly, not from the prose in the book she was reading, that was for sure.

'It's very hot this afternoon. You should be careful not to burn your skin,' said Jean-Luc, gently but chastely touching her shoulder as if to demonstrate.

Ros shivered, very much like Louise might have done, at his touch. 'No I've just put on some cream', was the best she could manage in reply.

Jean-Luc squatted down beside her lounger so that his eyes were level with hers. He pushed back a forelock of dark hair from his forehead. 'If you don't mind me saying so, your breasts, might also be getting a little over-exposed to the sun.'

Ros was reminded of an earlier passage in her romantic novel where the head footman "undressed Louise with his eyes". If she hadn't already been stark naked, this would have been precisely the feeling that Ros had.

'Er no, yes, thanks, I'll be careful,' she replied.

'It looks as if you don't normally go to a naturist resort?'

'No, it's my first time, actually,' said Ros.

'I'm sure you will enjoy the experience,' Jean-Luc smiled, adding 'My name is Jean-Luc', a piece of information Ros had already learned from Sam. He held out a hand for Ros to shake.

When she did, she found it disappointingly limp. She had expected a far stronger, he-man grip.

'Ros.'

'I'm just going to take a sailing class, over at the far side of the lake. Have you ever sailed, Ros?' asked Jean-Luc, releasing her hand but still crouching by her lounger and looking into her eyes.

'Er, no, not really. I once went out on a thirty-foot yacht for a weekend and well, to be honest, found it all rather boring. We left port, sailed up the coast, anchored in some dismal dank creek for the night, slept in the claustrophobic pointy end of the boat and came back in freezing rain and gale force winds thirty six hours later. Ended up cold, wet through and miserable. Thought it a total waste of time, actually,' blurted out Ros, in a stream of consciousness monologue. Why was she saying all this?

Jean-Luc just smiled and said, 'You need to go sailing with the right person and in the right boat. This is a small dinghy. Much more fun. Come with me.'

He stood up, turned and looked across the lake, hand raised to brow in "I see no ships" pose, to cut out the glare of sunlight on the water. It was a pose which either incidentally or deliberately gave Ros a clear opportunity to view his sizeable and, she noted, from a professional viewpoint only, you understand, uncircumcised male member which was also silhouetted against the bright lake.

'I can see my class gathering at the jetty. Come on. I'll show you how it's done,' said Jean-Luc.

'I don't know. I mean . . .' Ros couldn't really think of an excuse not to go. Well, why not? It was something to do. What possible harm could come from it? 'All right. Let's go!' she added, wondering what on earth she was agreeing to.

She stood, put her book in her bag, bag over shoulder and towel around neck and smiled at Jean-Luc. He smiled back and then he set off in the direction of the far side of the lake, Ros by his side.

As she left the pool she happened to glance across to the far side to see Sam, raising her hand in farewell and smiling as if to say 'good on yer girl!' Ros waved limply back.

The path down to the lake took them past some tennis courts on the right. And, oh no! There were Geoff and Lynne engaged in a singles match. Bizarrely, but she supposed sensibly, both were wearing socks, tennis shoes and sun caps – protection against the fierce heat bouncing off the red clay court. But that was all they were wearing. To Ros it looked slightly obscene – as if they were just taking a quick break from shooting a porn movie before getting down to business again.

She looked away a little too late as Geoff spotted her and gave a cheery wave as he was about to serve. Lynne looked around, with a quizzical expression on her face, as she saw Ros's companion. Again, Ros limply acknowledged Geoff's wave. She was getting good at waving limply, she thought. Is there a career in this? Well the Queen had made a living out of it for many years, so it must be possible.

Moving on, they walked round the lake. Ros couldn't think of much to say. Jean-Luc seemed quite comfortable not speaking, so they progressed in companionable silence, not unlike, Ros thought, an old married couple – or, more recently, Nick and herself.

As they approached the end of the lake, the side farthest from the resort, trees shaded their approach to a small jetty. At the far end two anglers, seated on fold-up stools, patiently dangled rods into the water. Static in the heat, they looked much like brown garden gnomes, just waiting for a touch of paint before being put up for sale.

A small motor boat and dinghy were tied up to the near end of the jetty. On the narrow sandy foreshore were a number of other dinghies, lined up in front of a large wooden boathouse, which had several windsurf boards and sails leaning against it.

Above the large central open doors of the boathouse, a small balcony jutted out over the shore. Behind the balcony were French windows, presumably leading into an interior first floor room.

Waiting by the jetty, under the welcome shade of the trees, was Jean-Luc's class. It was a mixed bunch comprising a boy of about eleven or twelve, a very brown slightly overweight couple in their early fifties and a thin, tanned teenage girl. Probably nearer Jean-Luc's age than her own, this girl instantly made Ros feel pale, old and fat – and all at the same time.

It was a beginners' class so Jean-Luc took them, in English, through the basics of sailing. He demonstrated, on the boat tethered to the jetty, how sails, rigging and rudder operate. Each of the pupils tried out individually the various moves in the boat, starting with the young boy and working through to the thin teenaged girl, who happened to be Dutch.

When it came to Ros's turn, Jean-Luc helped her from the jetty into the boat. She was conscious of him sitting very close to her. As he literally showed her the ropes, he gave a running commentary to the other class members who were standing on the jetty.

During this instruction, Ros was acutely aware of the touch of his thighs, accidental or otherwise, on the sides of hers. Whilst Jean-Luc seemed not to notice, it distracted her so much that she mixed up her 'tacking' with her 'going about' to the amusement of the class. Why didn't sailors give orders in English rather than in some arcane language?

Despite the proximity of Jean-Luc, Ros still found the whole procedure extremely tiresome, reinforcing her opinion of sailing as one of the dullest occupations around. At least most sailors did it out of sight of land, sparing everyone else the tedium.

Having been indoctrinated, albeit briefly, the time had come for the pupils to put what they'd learned to the test. Instead of creating a hazard for the ducks and other lake users by giving each pupil their own boat, Jean-Luc opted for one-on-one tuition.

First he took out the Dutch girl, generating in Ros a feeling that she could put down, well, to downright jealousy. As she sat on the jetty under the shade of the tree, she watched Jean-Luc sitting next to the Dutch girl, putting his arm chastely round her to show her how to pull the rigging – or whatever the hell the ropes were called. She was feeling irrationally irritated, when a voice next to her asked: 'I say, have you done much sailing before?'

Ros turned. The voice was that of the middle class, middle aged, slightly overweight English woman – her fellow classmate. Without waiting for a reply, the woman plonked herself down next to Ros on the jetty, legs dangling. Her accent and tone of voice were uncannily similar to Linda Snell in the Archers, thought Ros. The woman's husband stood beside her, looking out over the lake.

Remembering how she'd "gone off on one" when last asked this sailing question, Ros restricted herself to the far shorter 'Only once, on a bigger boat, on the North Sea.'

Seeming to ignore this answer, as if she'd only asked the question as an opening conversational gambit, the woman continued, 'My name is Camilla, by the way.'

'Ros.'

Camilla indicated upwards with her thumb. 'And this chap beside me is my husband Charles.'

Ros turned to look at Camilla to see if she was being serious.

'I know,' sighed Camilla, 'Charles and Camilla. Our life's been a total misery since those two got together. But we were first. And, despite the slings and arrows, etcetera, we've been happily married since 1980. Haven't we, darling?'

The last remark was addressed up at Charles, who appeared to be more interested in watching the boat. Whether he was admiring the way it was being sailed or the shapely form of the Dutch girl under instruction was uncertain.

'Ehmmmmm?!', was Charles's reply. Ros wasn't sure if it was a statement or a question. It didn't matter anyway, because Camilla simply continued.

'Haven't seen you around the place before?' she said to Ros.

'No, we only arrived this morning and since then, well, everything seems to have been a bit of a disaster.'

'Ah!' Camilla said, lowering her voice – although there was absolutely nobody other than her husband within earshot, 'You must mean the Giles Curtis business.'

'You know about that?'

'Yes, news travels fast amongst the British community in this place. There's so few of us that we tend to get to meet one another over the days. You know, familiar friendly voices in the bar. Rivalry in getting the only copy of the Daily Mail and Telegraph when they arrive each morning at the supermarket. That sort of thing.'

Ros couldn't imagine fighting over who gets to buy a Daily Mail – The Guardian or Independent, maybe.

'Anyway,' Camilla continued, 'it was an awful shock. We were only having dinner with him last night. We own a rather large caravan and awning, with all the facilities you know, so it seems a shame not to use them. He came round bright as ever and we had a terribly jolly evening. To think that he's now dead. It's dreadful, absolutely dreadful. I hope the French police are doing all they can to apprehend his murderer – or murderers.'

'My partner, Nick, was the one who found him,' added Ros when she could get a word in edgeways, or any other ways.

'Really? Do tell.'

So, yet again, Ros recounted the events of that morning. She was feeling like one of those eye witnesses to a terrible event who become word perfect through sheer repetition.

'So your partner . . . ?'

'Nick,' prompted Ros.

'Nick, yes, found poor Giles by your cabin. Where would that be exactly?'

'Avenue A.'

'That's would make sense,' said Camilla, staring across the lake at nothing in particular.

'Why?'

'Because Giles also had a cabin on Avenue A.'

'So you know where he lives? I mean lived? Here on the site that is?' Ros asked.

'Oh yes. It wasn't a great secret. Charles and I have been back there on a couple of occasions for late nightcaps. Nice chap. Very well-educated for a civil servant. Very keen naturist as well.'

'Civil servant?' asked Ros, ignoring the other question that sprung to her mind as to what a "keen naturist" was.

'Well, retired civil servant. Or something in the Government. He wasn't very specific. One got the impression that it was all a bit hush-hush. One didn't like to pry too much.'

'Do you know where he lived – in England, I mean? It might help the police track down his next of kin?'

'Somewhere in London, I think,' answered Camilla. That narrowed the search down.

'So, if he was with you last night, you may have been the last to see him alive. Have you reported this to the police?'

'Do you think we ought?'

'Yes I do. It might help them catch his killer. What time did he leave you?'

'Oh about eleven, something like that. We assumed he was

going straight back to his cabin. If he wasn't, he didn't mention to us that he was going anywhere else.'

Before Ros had a chance to ask any more questions, Jean-Luc was helping the Dutch girl out of the boat, very much as he had helped Ros out of the pool that morning. She felt that old irrational jealousy return.

Coming back up the jetty, Jean-Luc smiled at them both, bidding the Dutch girl goodbye with a quick Gallic peck on both cheeks. Lesson over, Dutch girl couldn't quite decide what to do next. So she opted for sitting on one of the upturned dinghies outside the boathouse, where she sat idly twirling a lock of her hair in her fingers. As if waiting for a bus. Or, more likely, for Jean-Luc, when free, to give her a different form of one-on-one tuition.

By the time that Ros had looked back, Jean-Luc had taken the young boy out.

Camilla resumed her conversation, which was more of a monologue. She and Charles lived most of the year in Portugal, inland from the Algarve coast, although they did have a tiny pied-à-terre in Chelsea. On further enquiry, this turned out to be a three-bedroom flat near Sloane Square. Camilla dabbled in property development and interior design, while Charles, who retained his silent air of detachment throughout, seemed to be an antiques and art dealer.

While she was talking, Ros took the opportunity to look at Charles and Camilla more closely. Like many of the naturists in Le Paradis, Charles and Camilla were overweight. Not obese but they could each have done with losing several pounds.

Charles was not as tall as Nick but looked as if he could have handled himself in his youth. And probably still could. He retained large arms and sturdy legs, spoiled only by a medium sized paunch. He was wearing an expensive Rolex gold watch, which Ros presumed was the genuine article, and a gold chain that would have looked more at home on a Hackney crack dealer.

It was Charles's turn next for tuition, although Camilla hardly noticed as she droned on. Ros found it quite restful in a way, not having to pay all that much attention. She found the odd 'really?' or 'that's interesting' did the trick.

Camilla had blondish hair done in a style which could only be described as Sloane Ranger circa 1980. Shoulder length, middle parting and culminating in a fringe which was slightly too long and too young for her. All it needed was an alice band to complete the effect.

What was most noticeable was the amount of expensive jewellery about her person. She was wearing a gold, presumably water-proof, watch, several diamond and gold rings, gold bracelets on both arms, a gold necklace and even a thin gold chain worn round a not-too-thin ankle.

Portuguese interior design was clearly a lucrative field to practice in. Or maybe it was old money. It was hard to tell. Ros had often wondered about people like Camilla and Charles. Where did they get their money? And how did they keep it, let alone make it multiply? It was all a bit of a mystery.

Peace finally descended on the jetty as Camilla took her turn in the boat. Charles took Camilla's place next to Ros on the jetty.

He was as quiet as Camilla was voluble. Ros felt him looking at her with his pale grey eyes, maybe a bit too intently, as if eyeing an old master or piece of porcelain at an auction. Perhaps gauging its worth and deciding whether to make a bid.

To avert his gaze and à propos of conversation, she asked him about Giles. 'Camilla said you knew Giles well?'

'Yes. Bad business.'

'You were probably the last to see him alive, Camilla tells me.'

'No, the murderer was.'

'Of course, I didn't mean to suggest that you had . . .' Ros petered out. And so did any further conversation. They silently sat and watched Camilla struggle with ropes and rigging, not helped by the lightness of the wind on the lake.

At last, the boat returned to the jetty and Jean-Luc returned her to where Ros and Charles were sitting. Ros got to her feet.

'That was most exhilarating,' said Camilla. 'We must come again, mustn't we darling? When it's a bit windier perhaps. Thank you so much Jean-Luc. We'll see you again soon I hope.' So saying she proffered a cheek to Jean-Luc and made an mmm-mmm noise as he kissed each in turn.

'Don't be a stranger, Ros. Bring that partner of yours over to see us some time. We're on Avenue E. Look for the parked Daimler. That's where you'll find us.'

So saying, she and Charles departed. Apart from the fishing gnomes, Ros was now alone on the jetty with Jean-Luc. Again she felt her pulse quicken. Was it a coincidence she was the last one left? She looked towards the boathouse. Not quite last. The Dutch girl was still there, seemingly engrossed in a novel.

'OK. Ros, are you ready?'

'As ready as I'll ever be,' Ros replied.

Jean-Luc smiled at her, brushing back a stray lock of hair. As he did so, he stepped down into the dinghy. Perhaps he was more intent on looking at Ros than where he was going. The next thing Ros saw was his foot slip off the side of the boat and he fell heavily against the jetty.

He quickly recovered and got both feet on the boat, feeling the back of his thigh.

'Are you all right?' Ros called down.

'I think so,' said Jean-Luc. 'I think I may have something in my leg.' He turned away from Ros giving her a good view of his rear. What she saw was a large splinter of wood about three or four inches long embedded in his leg. Blood was already beginning to seep from the wound. It would shortly become a flow, thought Ros.

'You've got a splinter,' called Ros, as Jean-Luc gingerly felt the wound and looked at the blood on his fingers. 'Let's get that out and dress the wound.'

Jean-Luc winced as he climbed back onto the jetty. 'It's nothing.'

Suddenly Ros was aware of another person on the jetty. It was the Dutch girl. She'd seen the accident and had come to stand with them. She looked concerned. 'Are you all right?'

Ros replied on his behalf. 'It's not too bad. But we'd better get it cleaned up.' Ros, transformed into efficient ER doctor-mode. 'Do you have any first aid stuff here?'

'In the boathouse,' said Jean-Luc, wincing slightly as he put weight on his leg.

'Right, let's see what we can do.'

'Are you trained in first aid?' asked Dutch girl, clearly concerned about what might happen to her favourite instructor.

'Yes, I'm a doctor,' replied Ros. Dutch girl looked surprised at the news, as in fact did Jean-Luc, 'and the less help I have the better. I can handle this. Why don't you run along.' She hated herself for saying it, but Dutch girl was really beginning to irritate her.

'Yes, Lorna, I'll be alright. I'll see you later,' said Jean-Luc giving Dutch girl a rather unnecessarily long kiss on each cheek. Reluctantly, Lorna left them, taking her book and bag with her.

Ros, Jean-Luc limping beside her, entered the boathouse. It was hot and stuffy inside, with a heady mix of smells. She identified varnish and petrol, along with damp and decay.

Sails, rope, tools and unidentifiable cans — wearing French labels — all fought for space on shelves lining two sides of the boathouse. In the gloom, she also spotted chosen tools of the art of the animateur – boxes of ping-pong balls, a pile of boules (if that's the right collective noun, thought Ros), nets, a few broken tennis rackets and, bizzarely, a clown costume.

'The first aid kit is over there.' Jean-Luc indicated a large white wooden box with red cross, mounted on the wall by the far corner.

Ros took down the box and found it well-stocked, including the tweezers, antiseptic and bandages she needed. Looking round the place, she failed to find anywhere she could ''operate''.

Jean-Luc guessed the problem. 'It's best if we go upstairs. It's lighter and there's somewhere to sit.'

He indicated a flight of rickety wooden open tread stairs almost invisible in the dark at the back of the boathouse. He led the way and, with some difficulty, climbed the stairs in front of her. This gave her a chance to see that the splinter wound wasn't too deep, but there was a fair amount of blood running in a rivulet down the back of his leg.

At the top of the stairs a door opened on to a large room, with French windows at the far end leading onto the balcony that Ros had spotted when they had first approached the boathouse. She suddenly realized, with a tiny shiver – must be the change in temperature – that this was the room he occupied in the resort. Let's be more precise, she thought, this is Jean-Luc's bedroom.

Her gaze took in a double bed with crumpled sheets and bolster-type French pillow. There was no wardrobe but a chest of drawers on top of which were hard cover books and a few A4 loose-leaf folders, biros and pencils. On a separate table a portable cd player was linked to a pair of speakers. Nearby were a jumble of CDs, some out of their cases.

In the corner, a pair of worn blue Levis hung over a chair, on which were two or three t-shirts neatly folded, as if freshly ironed. If there were any other clothes they could have been in the chest of drawers. But given the nature of the resort, Ros guessed, probably correctly, that they were clothes-free.

Jean-Luc, for some reason, seemed slightly embarrassed about the room. Maybe because it was messy. Or maybe that she had him at something of a disadvantage, given his wounded condition. 'The balcony is lighter,' he said.

'No, it's best if you lay on the bed. Face down. I need to remove that splinter.' Doctor Ros again.

Jean-Luc lay on the bed, his naked lithe body looking even browner and more attractive against the white of the cotton. Ros felt her throat dry, her hand shake slightly, as she swabbed the wound with cotton wool and surgical spirit.

'This might be a bit painful,' she said, as she attempted to get a good grip with the tweezers on the splinter, trying not to be distracted by the slightest haze of dark hair on his buttocks.

Jean-Luc winced as the splinter reluctantly gave up its hold in his flesh. Ros now got a good look at the wound. It wasn't too bad. Not bad enough for stitches, she thought. A few butterfly pieces of plaster with a small dressing should do the trick.

When she'd completed the task, Ros stood back and admired the finished result – and she was not just admiring the neatness of the dressing. 'There. Try not to get the bandage wet. It'll be sore but bearable.'

She resisted the urge to give his rump a gentle tap with her hand, as if to say "finished". Although she was sorely tempted.

Jean-Luc got to his feet slowly. Patched up, he seemed to regain his confidence. He now appeared perfectly happy to be alone with Ros in his room.

Suddenly Ros realized the seriousness of the situation in which she now found herself. God, here she was totally nude with a similarly non-attired young, rather handsome French-man, in his bedroom. She remembered her musing earlier in the day about how easy it would be to have sex without the bother of layers of clothing to remove. What on earth was happening? How had this come about?

'Thank you very much, Ros. It was very professional,' said Jean-Luc, looking into her eyes.

'Right, yes,' Ros replied, slightly flustered, and pushing back her hair from her forehead. 'Um, is that the balcony out there?'

Before he had time to answer, she walked out through the French windows. There was a small metal table and two canvas film director-style chairs. Ros noted, with some jealousy, two empty wine glasses. Who could have been here drinking with Jean-Luc? Was it that anorexic Dutch girl? There was also a half-melted-down candle in a French red wine bottle. And remains of what looked suspiciously like a couple of joints in the ashtray.

She walked over to the edge of the balcony. There was a great view back over the lake. She could see the swimming pool at the far left and the nearby bar and restaurant buildings. The main camp, shaded by trees, completed the scene.

'Fabulous view,' said Ros, as Jean-Luc joined her at the balcony rail.

'Yes, it's particularly pretty at night when the lights from the restaurant and bar reflect in the lake. You must come up and see it sometime,' said Jean-Luc, much, thought Ros, in the style of Mae West. Although in this situation a quick glance downwards would tell Ros whether Jean-Luc was pleased to see her or not. She did just that. She appeared to be safe in that department for the time being.

'Yes, that would be nice,' said Ros, and part of her thought it would be rather more than nice. Instead she said 'I'd better be getting back.'

'Sorry we never went in the boat together. Maybe later in the week? When my leg has recovered.'

'Maybe.' Ros hesitated and, almost for something to do, looked at her watch. My God! It was nearly 6 o'clock. What on earth would Nick be thinking? 'Can I leave you to put the stuff back in the First Aid kit?'

'Of course,' said Jean-Luc, who seemed to have moved even closer to her.

'Don't see me down, I'll find my own way,' said Ros, and gave Jean-Luc a goodbye kiss on each cheek, surprising herself as well as him.

Before he could react, she was back through the bedroom and making her way down the stairs. She heard a faint 'au revoir' behind her as she descended into the gloom of the boathouse, picking up her bag and hurrying out into the hot early evening. Before, she thought, she had the chance to change her mind.

11

Nick woke abruptly. It was hot, but not as hot as earlier in the day. As it was still light outside, he presumed it was the same day. A very slight breeze came through the window. He looked around. He could see into the open bathroom by way of the reflection in the dressing table mirror. No Ros. He looked at his watch. It was five thirty. He felt a bit muzzy from the heat and maybe the wine he'd drunk at lunchtime. But what was it that had woken him?

His question was soon answered by an insistent rapping on the wooden door of the cabin. He blearily got to his feet and called 'Just a minute'.

Grabbing his towel and wrapping it securely round his middle – well he was in his own cabin after all, they couldn't make nudity obligatory in his own home – he went through the bead curtain, through the kitchen and opened the door. Standing there was Inspector Lagardère.

'Sorry to disturb you, Mr Boughton, but would it be convenient to have a word?'

'Yes. Of course. Come in,' replied Nick.

'Is your partner in?'

That was a good question, thought Nick. Where the hell was she?

'No, I don't think so. I mean, no.'

'You don't seem too sure.'

'I was asleep. I think she's gone out to, er, explore?' was all he could think of. He needed something to quench his thirst. 'Would you like some water? A beer?' Nick asked, opening the fridge.

'Thank you. Yes, a beer would be good,' replied Lagardère, sitting himself on the shag brown sofa. He was looking a little more crumpled than this morning, with slight sweat stains round the armpits of his shirt and concertina creases in his chinos. 'I've had a busy day.'

'So I hear.' Nick handed him a bottle of French beer and washed the glasses they'd used for their wine the night before. Handing one to Lagardère, he took a beer himself and poured it into his own glass. 'Santé'.

Lagardère returned the toast and, leaning back on the sofa, sipped his drink. Nick, feeling more at home in his make-shift towel sarong, sat on the rickety kitchen chair and waited for Lagardère to speak.

'I think you ought to know that we caught up with our suspect, Mr Parker.'

'Yes, I did hear that from Jack – the receptionist.'

'We stopped him on the autoroute just north of Toulouse. He was very surprised to be surrounded by three police cars.'

'I bet. So he's now safely in custody? And we're all free to leave? To get on our way?' Damn! He was doing that Australian questioning thing himself now!

'No. We have eliminated him from our enquiries.'

Nick almost spat out a mouthful of beer at this news. 'What!!! But surely he must have done it?'

'But why, Mr Boughton?'

'Well, I heard noises . . . voices . . . in the night. Shortly after that I heard his car leave. Therefore, he must be guilty. Q.E.D.'

'Not quite. First of all we only have your word on whether there were voices.' Lagardère ticked the point off on his hand, having rested his beer precariously on the arm of the sofa. He held his hand up as Nick was about to interject. 'Second, we can't really establish the exact time of death until we get full forensic. Mr Parker could have left while Giles Curtis was still alive. '

'What!!!' said Nick again. He was once again getting monosyllabic, despite the comfort of wearing a towel.

Lagardère ignored his exclamation and continued. 'And third . . .' still ticking off the points on his fingers '. . . Mr Parker happens to be a 75-year old English High Court judge.'

Nick had read about people being dumbstruck, or totally lost for words, but thought it a fictional construct. He was now, well, not to put too fine a point on it, totally gobsmacked. All he could manage was an open-mouthed gaze at Lagardère who seemed to be enjoying his discomfort, peering at Nick over the glass of beer which he'd now picked up and raised to his mouth.

'But . . . but . . .' Nick eventually managed to get out a short sentence. 'Are you sure?'

'Absolutely. We checked it out with the English authorities. Exchanged photos and details and there is not the slightest doubt of his identity.'

'But he could still have done it, couldn't he?' Even to Nick this sounded a bit weak.

Lagardère gave Nick a typically Gallic shrug. 'What motive can he possibly have had? Sexual jealousy? A 75-year old judge? Maybe a homosexual argument? In France they say that most Englishmen are, what is the word, ''gay''?

'Yes,' said Nick and, realising what he'd answered to,

quickly corrected himself. 'I mean no. Well that is, I mean 'gay' is the word, but most Englishmen aren't gay . . .' The sentence didn't so much peter out as fall off the edge of a cliff.

'Anyway, when Mr Parker, or should I say "His Honour Lord Justice Parker" left Le Paradis, it is possible that our victim was very much alive and kicking.'

Nick very much needed another drink. He went over to the fridge and separated another small beer bottle from its cardboard packaging. Lifting it towards Lagardère, who shook his head, he twisted the cap off the bottle and re-filled his glass, sitting back on his chair.

'So what happens now?'

'Well, we agreed to keep our apprehending of the judge quiet. Not just for our sake, you understand, but for his as well. If people in Britain thought one of their judges was a naturist, well, as a race you're still not completely comfortable with the concept of public nudity, are you?'

Lagardère fixed Nick in his gaze at this point so much so that Nick involuntarily crossed his legs – making sure he did it discreetly of course, lest he give Lagardère a "Basic Instinct" moment. 'Our judge was anxious not to have his holiday preferences become public knowledge, you understand.'

'Yes, I can see the tabloids now – "Naked pervert judge in murder scandal". Or similar.' That wasn't too bad. Must be the second beer.

Lagardère didn't reply, looking extremely relaxed on the sofa. He raised his now empty glass. 'I think I will have that beer after all, if that's OK.'

Nick obliged, and watched Lagardère pour it. 'We also know the identity of the murdered man.'

'Who was he?'

'Does the name Curtis mean anything to you, Mr Boughton? Giles Curtis?'

Nick thought for a moment. 'No, doesn't ring any bells.'

'Tell me? You live in London, don't you?'

'Yes.'

'In postal district N16, I seem to recall?'

'Yes.' Lagardère either had a very good memory or, for some reason, had looked his address up from Nick's statement.

'And you've never heard of the name Giles Curtis?'

'No. Look inspector. London is a huge place with millions of inhabitants. Why would you think I'd know this person?'

'Apart from the fact that he had your business card in his hand?'

'Well, yes, apart from that.' Nick had momentarily forgotten this tiny detail.

'We've talked to reception and the card Mr Curtis completed when he checked in gave his address as a road in Tottenham. And that's in N15!' Lagardère added.

Nick looked puzzled. 'So? That's in the next borough. It may be next to N16 but there are a few hundred thousand people in each place. Twice as big say as the population of, er,' Nick thought of the nearest place he could remember in France, 'Perpignan.'

Lagardère frowned. Nick thought he may just have got one over on the inspector. It didn't last for long.

'Even so, it is possible you were acquainted. You live within, what, a few miles of each other in London. He's found here in the middle of "La France profonde" with your card in his hand. Next door to your cabin. A lot of coincidences there, don't you think?'

'But what connection could we possibly have had?'

'That's precisely what we're trying to discover. It seems Curtis has been here for a week. He may have checked in and agreed to meet you for some reason.' Lagardère continued. 'Anyway, we've reported the murder to New Scotland Yard and they're carrying out investigations into next of kin and so on. They hope to get back to us some time tomorrow.'

'Some time tomorrow!' Nick exclaimed. 'Does that mean you'll be expecting us to stay until then?'

Again a shrug from Lagardère. 'But of course. You want to help us find the murderer don't you?'

'Of course,' Nick replied in turn. Not mentioning that it was only so they could get the hell out of this place and wear some clothes again. Freedom? Huh! Nick had never felt so restricted in his movements – both around the resort and around the people in it.

'Now that we know the murdered man was English, we are tracing and interviewing all those here in Le Paradis who may have met him in the last week. And more importantly we need to find out what Mr Curtis was doing yesterday – up to the point of his death. Who he was with. Who he spoke to. That sort of thing. And our starting point are the English,' said Lagardère.

'Why?

'Because as an Englishman he would have been likely only to talk to other English people – you know how good your countrymen are at speaking other languages. So we will be interviewing all the English people in the resort to see if we can find any grudge, or motive, for his murder.'

'But that could take days!' Nick protested.

'Perhaps not that long,' Lagardère gave yet another shrug, 'but we have to be thorough, you understand. It's always difficult when a national of another country gets killed. We need to demonstrate that we've done all we can to catch the murderer.'

Lagardère finished his beer and stood up, putting the glass and bottle on the drainer by the small kitchen sink. 'Many thanks for the beer. And my regards to your "partner", wherever she may be. Have you looked round the back of the cabin?'

'What for . . .' said Nick, and realized once more he was having his leg pulled by Lagardère. 'I don't think that's in very good taste in the circumstances.'

'You're right. I'm sorry.' Lagardère apologized.

It suddenly occurred to Nick that the murderer may not have specifically targeted Giles Curtis at all. He, or even she, may be a homicidal maniac just starting on a campaign of terror around the resort. Maybe Giles was just the first of many.

He shared the thought with Lagardère. 'Have you considered that this may have been a random killing. For all you know, there might be a serial killer roaming loose on the camp site.'

Lagardère paused as he was about to leave the cabin. 'Yes, that has occurred to me. I think it unlikely, but we are maintaining a discreet police presence. I would say 'undercover' but, in this instance, a clothed police officer might be a bit of a give-away. We won't know whether he – or she – is a serial killer unless, and until, they strike again.'

'That's comforting,' replied Nick. 'But if it is a random murder, then the murderer is just as likely to be French. Or German. Or whatever. Not just English.'

'Also possible.' Any other thoughts, Lagardère was clearly keeping to himself. 'Well, au revoir, Mr Boughton,' said Lagardère. No doubt we'll be seeing quite a bit of each other in the next few days. And I think I'll be seeing a lot more of you than you will be of me.' He added, nodding his head in the general direction of Nick's be-towelled mid-riff, before leaving the cabin.

Nick sat down on the sofa which Lagardère had just vacated. He wished he hadn't suddenly thought of the 'maniac on the loose' theory. If there was one, then he/she could strike again. Any time. Any place. Any where. As the old Martini commercial used to say. And if so, Ros herself could now be lying in a pool of blood . . . Mustn't let his imagination run away with him. Even so, he had to admit that he didn't like the idea of her wandering alone around the camp site – particularly naked.

So where the hell was she? He wondered what time she'd left. And where she had gone. Probably back to the pool to work on her tan.

The news from Lagardère hadn't put him in too good a mood, either. It now looked as if they were in for a longer stay than they'd bargained for. With all the naked horror that involved.

He needed a shower. It was still oppressively hot and he felt sweaty. Whether it was at the thought of a longer stay in the resort, or a possible maniac on the prowl, wasn't clear.

Say what you will about nudity, Nick thought, one advantage was that it made taking a shower a piece of piss – as, incidentally, did taking a piss become a piece of piss. A quick pull at the towel and, hey presto, he was ready to go.

The down side of this was that, by discarding his towel, he was not only ready to relieve or lather himself but also, coincidentally, dressed for dinner later that evening. In the resort's restaurant. With Geoff and Lynne. And two pierced people. All of which filled him with complete dread.

As he stepped out of the shower and was drying himself, he thought he heard the door of the cabin close. He stood stock still. Was it an intruder? Maybe the murderer? He quickly moved and hid behind the door as footsteps came towards the bathroom. It was not a good time to be totally naked with only a bar of Knight's Castile to hand. Could you kill someone with a bar of soap?

12

'What the hell are you doing hiding behind the door!?' Ros cried, instinctively raising both hands to her throat. 'You gave me a real fright.'

'I thought you were, er, well . . . er, doesn't matter,' said Nick. Recovering his composure, he went on the attack. 'And where have you been all afternoon? I've been worried sick.' Which was a slight exaggeration as he had actually spent most of the time fast asleep.

Ros turned and walked out of the bathroom, back into the bedroom. Nick followed her, instinctively wrapping the bath towel round his waist as he did so.

Ros picked up her brush from the dresser and sat in front of the mirror brushing her hair. Nick couldn't help but admire her breasts as they were lifted by the movement of her brushing arm.

'Can't think why. I've just been to the pool. Swimming, tanning, talking to Sam and Garry,' Ros said, in a non-committal way.

'No aquarobics by any chance?'

Ros turned to face him. 'What are you on about?'

'Aquarobics? You know. Leaping up and down with elderly women. Attended to by young French guy?'

'Jean-Luc, you mean. No, but I have seen him this afternoon as it happens. As I had nothing better to do.' She looked at him accusingly, remembering his sudden slump into sleep. 'I walked round to the other side of the lake and saw Jean-Luc about to take a sailing lesson. So he invited me to join in,' said Ros, bending the truth ever so lightly.

'You hate sailing.'

'In big boats, yes. But I thought it might be different in small dinghies. Anyway it passed the time.'

'I bet it did. I think he fancies you.'

'Don't be silly, Nick. And don't worry about me. I'm certainly not into cradle-snatching,' said Ros, protesting slightly too vehemently, thought Nick.

He watched as she examined her skin. Ros always tanned easily and, after just a few hours here, was on the way to acquiring a good base coat. Unlike Nick, who took ages to go brown. His middle section had gone a bit pink. Lucky he hadn't spent too long in the sun today.

'Actually, it was just as well I *was* there as he had an accident,' said Ros.

'Nothing trivial, I hope?'

Ros stopped brushing to fix Nick with one of her hospital matron stares. 'Rather a nasty splinter in his leg, if you must know. I removed it and dressed the wound. So you'll be delighted to hear that he won't be aquarobing, or whatever the word is, for a few days yet.'

Nick knew it was irrational, as well as unusual, to feel jealous of Ros. It must be something to do with the unsettling sight of her wandering about in the nude. Maybe it was proprietorial.

Perhaps it was a primeval urge in men to keep their females literally under wraps and away from the prying eyes of other males. Whatever the reason, he was beginning to see not just a nude Ros, but a new Ros. Someone who he'd begun to take for granted and now, well, realized was an attractive young woman desired by other – and younger – males of the species.

He sat on the bed and watched her in the mirror. 'Lagardère came round this afternoon,' Nick said, diplomatically changing the subject.

'What did he want?'

'To let me know that they not only caught the suspect but instantly let him go again. And that we've got to stay here until they get a lead on the real culprit.'

'What?' said Ros, stopping the brushing she'd just re-started, and looking round at him.

Nick explained that the suspect had turned out to be a judge and that the murdered man was someone called Giles Curtis.

'Oh yeah, I knew the name of the deceased,' said Ros. 'I had a chat with your little Australian friend. You remember, Shareen? Your naked hitchhiker from this morning? It seems the murdered man was extremely popular round the place. Knew everyone apparently. And they all wondered why he wasn't around today.'

Nick was going to ask about Shareen but thought better of it. Ros continued. 'Later, when I was talking to Charles and Camilla . . .'

He looked up at her sharply. Was she all right? Could it be that the heat and stress had got to her? Charles and Camilla? Here in Le Paradis? Taking a naturist holiday? Now that *would* be a paparazzi scoop. You could retire on the proceeds.

Seeing the expression on his face, Ros added 'I know it's unlikely but they're a couple I met down at the boathouse, far side of the lake. Anyway . . .' Oh no! I'm beginning to sound like Camilla herself now, thought Ros. '. . . she told me that Giles had something to do with the government, or used to have. They had dinner with him last night you know.'

'That means this Charles and Camilla could be the murderers,' said Nick, sensing an end in sight to their incarceration. 'Does Lagardère know about this? I mean it's important evidence.'

'I don't think he does. Do you think we ought to tell him? Isn't it a bit sneaky? I mean they don't look the type to bludgeon someone to death.'

'And I do? Because that's what Lagardère thinks. We really ought to tell him.'

Ros got up from the dressing table and stretched her arms above her head. 'If you think so. I'm going for a shower.'

Ros went into the bathroom, leaving Nick in the bedroom. He needed to think more about the situation. Here they were stuck in this nudist resort under camp arrest – an appropriate description given Lagardère's earlier expressed view of British male sexual preferences – with no sign of early release.

Perhaps, and here a vague thought was beginning to search for space in his brain, if they could solve the crime, the murderer would be apprehended and they could get out and resume their lives.

Which reminded him. Bloody hell! Kathy and Phillip! They still hadn't phoned to let them know why they hadn't arrived. Must try again. Maybe before dinner. But not just yet.

Nick consulted his watch. Just gone seven. It was still very light outside. Going through to the kitchen, he helped himself to another French beer and took it onto the verandah to sit at the table and ponder.

No sooner had he sat down and raised the glass to his mouth than a voice very close by said 'Still here, then, I see.'

It was so abrupt an interruption that Nick slopped some of

the contents onto his chest. He was getting quite proficient at spilling drinks. Wiping the liquid away with his free hand, he turned towards the source of the comment. It was next door's verandah. And there, sitting at his own identical table, was Martin Pike. In front of him was a glass containing something that, to Nick's untrained eye, looked like lightly coloured urine.

Seeing Nick's glance, Pike continued. 'Apple juice. Always have one this time of the evening. Very refreshing after a hard day.'

'A hard day doing what, exactly?' Nick couldn't resist asking.

'Well, I always try to get a bit of exercise in the mornings — a bit of a jog round the lake, that sort of thing. Some time in the pool. Back for lunch. Bit of a siesta and work on the book, naturally.'

Nick, by this point, had regretted asking the question.

'And, of course, I've been helping the gendarmes with their enquiries,' said Pike. 'That police inspector has just been around to question me, asking about my movements yesterday and whether I knew the deceased, that sort of thing.'

'And did you?'

'Did I what?'

'Did you know the deceased?'

'Oh yes! Poor Giles. A lovely man.' Pike looked glumly down at his juice. 'He was a seasoned and dedicated naturist of some many years. Absolutely fascinating to talk to. Very well informed on naturism in Britain since the 'sixties. Gave me lots of interesting information and further sources to research. We were going to get together back in Blighty, maybe visit Portland Bill when we got back. Now, alas, not to be. Great shock.'

Nick presumed Portland Bill wasn't a naturist chum of Giles, and used the slight pause to interrupt: 'Leaving the history of naturism alone for the moment, interesting though it may be, did Lagardère tell you how the investigation was going?'

'He didn't mention anything about it to me,' Pike said, taking an almost too dainty sip of his apple juice. 'But I did tell him that Giles and I had lunch yesterday, at this very table as it happens. A nice salade niçoise with a very acceptable bottle of rosé. Quite delicious, even if I say so myself.'

'And what time did he leave?' Nick asked a touch impatiently, before Pike could go into more detail about the composition of the salad dressing or vintage of the wine.

'Must have been, what, about four o'clock, something like that.'

'Did he say where he was going?'

'Yes, he said something about getting a bit of exercise on the lake. I assume he was going sailing or windsurfing or swimming. He was a very active man.'

'And that was the last you saw of him?'

'Alas, it was.' Pike continued to look glumly into his drink. 'Such a waste. All that knowledge gone. A great loss for British naturism.'

The Naked Guide has this to say about naturism in Britain:

Inspired by news of the German naturist movement (see separate entry on origins of modern European naturism) one H C Booth published articles in various magazines in the early part of the twentieth century extolling the virtues of naked living.

His theories were put into practice in 1922 with the formation of the English Gymnosophist Society in Essex.

Throughout the twenties and thirties, British naturism grew slowly. By 1937 the National Sun and Air Association had a membership of over 2,000, with a London office and gymnasium.

During the Second World War, the 'British Sun Bathing

Association' was founded with membership growing steadily. By 1951 there were 51 clubs or groups in the membership. The Central Council for British Naturism (now often called British Naturism) was formed in 1964.

Increasing acceptance of naturism resulted in the public showing of naturist films from 1957, the hire of public baths for naturist swimming from 1965 and the setting aside of public beaches for naturist use from 1978.

Today, it's estimated that there are over a million people in the UK who take some form of relaxation in the nude — on UK or foreign beaches, belonging to naturist clubs or simply enjoying the privacy of their own secluded gardens or terraces. It's a far cry from the attacks on topless (male) bathers carried out in the early thirties on the Welsh Harp reservoir in Hendon.

'What did Giles do for a living?' asked Nick.

'Funny, your inspector chummie asked me that as well.'

'And what did you tell him?'

'All I knew really. That Giles was retired and that he'd worked for the Government.'

'Doing what exactly?'

'He didn't say. Mind you I didn't ask. One doesn't like to pry does one? Although he did say his old job involved investigating villains, fraud, that sort of thing.

'A policeman?'

'Oh no. Giles didn't have many good words to say about "our boys in blue". Thought they were overpaid and incompetent.'

It suddenly occurred to Nick that he knew very little about Martin Pike. Could this mild-mannered, slightly pedantic man be Giles Curtis's killer? Stranger things have happened. And if he was, what motive could he possibly have had? On the plus side, he did seem upset about Giles Curtis's demise. Of course, he could also be a random serial killer and – not too comforting this thought – living within six feet of their cabin.

'Er, I hope you don't think I'm being rude, but what exactly do you do Martin? I mean, in England?'

'Oh, me? I'm on the middle-aged scrapheap. Used to teach geography. Secondary school in Basildon. Offered early retirement so took it. Like poor old Giles really. Two professionals washed-up on the shores of Lake Redundancy. Decided I'd had enough.' Pike stared mournfully into his apple juice.

Suddenly, as if pulling himself together, he brightened up and looked across at Nick. 'Still, every cloud has a silver lining. If I hadn't given up my job I would never have discovered the joys of naturism. I'm a late convert you know. It's joined and really almost totally supplanted all my other interests.'

Nick couldn't stop himself asking 'What other interests?'

'Oh, you know. The usual. Bird watching, metal detecting, rock collecting.' As if everyone in Britain practised these. He indicated his dirty car. 'It was very difficult getting all the equipment in the trusty Peugeot, you know. Telescope, binoculars, birding manuals, metal detector, hammers and such. Still now being a naturist, it's a lot easier.'

Nick again had to ask, 'Why?'

'Because you don't waste space on unnecessary clothes, of course.'

'Of course.' Nick, sensing that Pike was about to launch into a long explanation of one or more of his hobbies, abruptly got up. He still had his towel snugly wrapped round his waist. 'Sorry Martin. Must see how Ros is getting on. We're going to dinner with some friends at the restaurant.'

'You're quick off the mark. Making friends already,' Pike said.

Nick explained the situation. He then raised his hand to bid Pike farewell. 'Expect I'll see you later!'

'I'm sure you will! Enjoy yourself! And don't forget to get dressed!' Pike said, again indicating the towel around Nick's waist, in a reprise of the ''joke'' he'd made that morning.

'OK, right, nice one,' Nick replied, walking into the cabin.

It was now slightly cooler, but that still made it oppressively hot. Hot enough to make wearing clothes unnecessary from a temperature, but not sanity, point of view. Even with the door and windows open, the inside of the hut was extremely stuffy. Ros was sitting once again in front of the dressing table mirror, this time applying her make up.

'Who were you talking to?' she asked.

'Next door neighbour. Martin Pike. He's an ex-teacher, you know. And also a friend of the deceased. Had lunch with him yesterday.'

'Popular lad our Mr Curtis,' said Ros, in a mock Inspector Morse voice, before applying a pale lipstick.

'Why are you getting all dolled up?'

'Mmmmm?' Ros said, moving the lipstick carefully round her lips.

'I mean, we're only meeting Geoff and Lynne.'

'Well, just because I can't wear a sexy little black number and high heels, it doesn't mean I have to let myself go totally. Here, give me a hand with this chain.'

Nick fastened the thin gold chain around Ros's neck, a present he'd given her for her thirtieth. 'I don't know. It just seems, well . . . unnecessary.'

Nick sat on the bed. He didn't like to say that most of the women he'd seen in the few, well not that many, porn films he'd watched with mates, all wore immaculate make-up and not a great deal else – well nothing else, actually. A lot like Ros at this moment.

'Nick, if I'm going out to dinner like this . . .' said Ros, indicating her nude body, '. . . then I've got to have some warpaint to hide behind. Give me confidence.'

Ros reached over to put on her watch. 'It's nearly ten to eight now. You know how Geoff and Lynne are sticklers for being on time. We'd best get a move on.'

'I'd rather get some clothes on,' groaned Nick. 'Look Ros, can't you go on your own. Tell them I've got sunstroke or something. They'll understand.'

Ros stood up and looked down at him, hands on her hips in Northern battleaxe stance. 'If you think I'm going out tonight, undressed like this, on my own – and back in the dark – when there's a killer on the loose, then you're very much mistaken. You agreed to the dinner. You can just bloody well put up with it.'

Nick sighed, raising his hands in surrender. 'OK. Let's get this over with. I suppose I can always drink a bit to ease the embarrassment.' Making it sound like a chore.

'Now what do we need?' Ros put an assortment of items into her new leather shoulder bag. 'Money . . . credit card, if they take them . . . what else, yes the key, when we've locked up.'

Ros slipped into a pair of holiday casual basketwork type mules, with slightly raised heels. Rummaging around in her suitcase, she pulled out one of those beach type sarong brightly coloured pieces of cotton that women wrap round their bikini bottoms for modesty.

'This will be lighter than carrying a great beach towel,' Ros explained, managing to fold it into her new shoulder bag. 'Ready?'

'As I ever will be,' Nick said, transferring his towel waiter-style to his arm.

13

They set off southwards down the Champs. It was now twilight, the sun setting behind the trees as they walked towards the lake. There was the smell of burning wood in the air as barbecues were smokily lit.

Le Paradis people were outside and around their "homes", enjoying an aperitif or getting the evening meal ready. In many instances that involved the menfolk doing something they'd rarely do at home. The cooking. Five thousand years of civilisation and people still felt the need to burn food outdoors, thought Nick.

As Ros and Nick approached the restaurant, they noticed an illuminated sign and entrance in front of them — that is on the wooded, camping side. They hadn't noticed this entrance at lunchtime as they'd approached the restaurant from the pool and lake side. To their right was the long back wall of the bar, so they couldn't see round to the front. Of either the bar or restaurant.

'I guess this is the more formal entrance for the evening,' said Nick. He stood back so Ros could go in first, figuring she'd give him a bit of cover as they made their way to Geoff and Lynne's table.

There was a small entrance hall with a high, pulpit-style desk on which sat a reservations book and behind which stood the Maitre D', dressed in a white shirt, bow tie and black trousers.

'Bon soir, M'sieur, Madame.' He greeted them. 'Vous avez un reservation?'

'Oui,' Ros replied, mentioning the Russells' name.

Checking off the name in the book, he asked them to follow him. He went through a door, turned right then left. They were now in the restaurant. The tables at the back were mainly empty but as they followed the waiter to the front open terrace, an increasing number were occupied.

As they passed the first few occupied tables, there was one fact about the diners that was immediately noticeable.

I just can't believe I'm seeing this, thought Nick. What his brain was desperately trying to take in, was the fact that at first sight − and at second sight too − virtually everyone in the restaurant was dressed.

Men were wearing normal, everyday shirts and slacks. Women wore dresses or skirt and blouses, some admittedly a little skimpy perhaps, but there was absolutely no getting away from the fact that he and Ros appeared to be the only nude people in the entire restaurant.

It was everyone's worst nightmare. One of those anxiety dreams where you're nude in a public place and everyone else is clothed. But unfortunately this wasn't a dream. This was for real. They actually were naked in the middle of a restaurant, where all around them sat fully-clothed diners.

Ros also noticed this at about the same time as Nick and

pulled to a halt in shocked realization. It was all Nick could do to avoid running into her.

'Nick everyone is . . .'

At this point the Maitre D' leading the way sensed they'd stopped, so he turned and requested they follow him.

Now half-way towards the terrace, Nick and Ros had little option but to continue. The next thing that Nick's shocked senses took in was the fact that they were standing in front of a table on the terrace at which a bemused – and clothed – Geoff and Lynne were sitting.

'I say, you're a bit keen aren't you,' said Geoff, getting to his feet and giving Ros a peck on both cheeks.

As Nick stooped to greet Lynne in similar fashion, she added 'Didn't think you'd take to naturism this enthusiastically,' with what Nick took to be a surreptitious glance at his privates.

They sat down as quickly as they could, Ros wrapping her cloth round her bottom half, but still conspicuously sitting at the table topless. Nick also found some small comfort in pulling the towel around his lower half. Fortunately, apart from a string of fairy lights along the front of the terrace, it wasn't as bright as further back in the restaurant.

'Janet and John are always late,' said Geoff, indicating the two spare places at the table. 'Never mind, let me pour you a drink. You look as if you've seen a ghost or something.'

Geoff filled their glasses with white wine and they all joined him in raising and clinking them.

'Ehmmm?' Nick began. 'Er Geoff, forgive me asking this but I can't help noticing that everybody in the restaurant – including you two – is dressed'

'Not everyone, obviously,' said Geoff, nodding his head at Nick and Ros, 'but most people, yes.'

'But why? We thought nudity was obligatory, how do the

rules put it "weather permitting"? It doesn't say "except at night",' added Ros.

'Ah! So that explains why you're, well, sitting there like that,' Lynne said, hardly bothering to suppress a smile.

'Well, yes,' said Nick, a trifle testily. 'But you still haven't explained why this morning, nudity is obligatory but this evening it's not.'

'To be honest, we've no idea,' said Geoff. 'It seems to be the done thing. I suppose people like getting dressed to go out in the evening, so they do. Typically French, don't you think, make one rule and then instantly ignore it when it suits them.'

'You might have told us,' Ros said, shifting slightly uncomfortably in her seat and raising one arm instinctively to cover her breasts as a waiter handed her a menu.

'Sorry, we just didn't think. We assumed you'd know,' said Geoff, looking a little too long in the direction of her bosom than perhaps was polite. 'Anyhow, it's a nice warm evening so no chance of catching a cold on the chest, or anywhere else.' He laughed but soon stopped when rewarded with a look from Ros that could have frozen a fish finger at ten feet.

Nick took a greater slug of his wine than he would normally. 'But if everyone dresses in the evening, are we breaking any rules by, well, by sitting here in the nude?' Nick asked, looking over his menu at Geoff.

'Not at all. You're perfectly entitled to go around nude at night,' Geoff replied. 'Did the Maitre D' turn a hair when you walked in?'

'No. He acted as if it was totally normal,' said Ros.

'There you are. You're not alone either. In fact, there are some naturists here in the resort who believe you *should* remain nude at all times. We call them the naturistas, like guerrillas who have a point to make. In fact, you've got company.

There's a couple of them over at the side of the restaurant. Oh, you can look now, as they're studying their menus.'

Nick turned and looked over in the direction indicated by Geoff. There, at a table for two, were next-door neighbour Martin Pike with hairy Hamish, the abominable Scottish snowman Nick had met earlier in the bar.

Yes, both did appear to be nude and totally unconcerned. As he looked, Martin Pike caught his gaze and raised a thumb in approval – presumably at Nick and Ros's undressed state. Nick acknowledged his greeting and turned back to the table. So when Martin Pike had reminded him to get dressed this evening, he had been serious after all.

'You see, in the evening, you can really suit yourself as to what you wear,' Geoff carried on, warming to the topic. 'Some go around nude, like you two . . .'

'Not by choice!' Ros interjected.

'. . . others get fully dressed to go out to dinner or night club,' continued Geoff, ignoring her, 'and some adopt a sort of half-way house.'

'Half-way house?' asked Ros, holding the menu in front of her and looking over the top of it, as temporary protection from Geoff's possibly prying eyes, although she knew she was getting a touch paranoid about this.

'What Geoff means is that some of the women, and it usually is the women, may get dressed in the evening but many wear very little,' said Lynne.

At this point Nick noticed something he just hadn't spotted before, having been too shell-shocked up to that point. Now accustomed to the low light on the terrace, he looked across at Lynne and discovered that the green blouse she was wearing was virtually transparent. She wasn't wearing a bra and you could see very clearly her pert breasts and firm nipples through the material.

He felt a slight stirring in his loins and was pleased to have the protection of his towel. How was it that he'd sat there at lunch looking at a totally nude Lynne without any problems, but now she was half-dressed he found it a complete turn-on.

Perhaps this was what the French had discovered and why they'd junked the "nudité obligatoire" rule at night. Being partly clothed seemed so much more erotic than total nudity. Not an original theory but one that Nick had now proved to his own satisfaction.

'Er . . . ,' said Nick, raising his eyes perhaps a little too quickly to Lynne's face, 'without being prurient, when you say "wearing very little", you mean?'

Nick's question was instantly answered, not by Geoff or Lynne, but by the arrival of the couple who could only be their missing dinner companions, Janet and John.

Standing by the table, and being kissed on the cheek by Geoff, was a tall shapely attractive woman with long dark hair. Probably in her mid-thirties, she was wearing an extremely short tight red leather skirt and a skimpy, slightly too small, red leather bra, above which protruded a significant amount of implant-enhanced flesh. The whole ensemble was completed by calf-length lace-up Dr Marten red boots, and studded red leather collar and wristbands. Plus of course studs through navel, ears and one nostril. And those in addition to the piercings that weren't on view. Nick decided not to even think about those.

As she bent to be pecked by Geoff, Nick got rather more of a view of her rear than he'd expected. It seemed that Janet had put on her skirt but apparently couldn't find any knickers to wear beneath it. An oversight he was sure.

'Jan, this is Nick and Ros.' Geoff introduced them. 'And this is John.'

Nick had been so engrossed in staring at Janet that he hadn't paid much attention to the man until now. He held out his hand to John who took it in a powerful knuckle-crunching grasp.

'Hi!' said John, and sat down.

John was as tall as Janet, with thick centre-parted shoulder-length black hair, which he swept back from his forehead with both hands as he sat down. He looked no stranger to the gym. An appearance accentuated by the fact that all he was wearing above the waist was an unbuttoned black cowboy type leather waistcoat which wouldn't have looked out of place with a sheriff's star pinned to it. Beneath the vest were perfectly bulging arms, tattooed with some Maori-type patterns and hairless, probably shaved, thought Nick, chest complete with gold nipple rings. How did he get them in there? And what happened if you caught one in something? Nick winced inwardly at the imagined pain.

John's ensemble was completed by a pair of tight black leather shorts and Timberland-style boots with laces undone. It was a look, Nick thought, that was half "YMCA", half World Wrestling Federation. He again resisted the temptation to imagine what was below those shorts – embedded in John's private parts like a veritable Meccano set.

'Sorry we're late. We got rather tied up,' said Janet with a smile, looking over at John.

'No problem,' said Geoff, ignoring any possible trace of double meaning in the comment and doing the honours with the wine. 'I suppose you heard about the murder?'

Nick thought he caught Janet making quick eye contact with John, but couldn't be sure. 'No, what murder?' Janet asked, leaning forward over the table towards Geoff and giving both him and Nick even more of a view of her cleavage than before, if that were possible.

'Nick found a body this morning outside his cabin. Turns out it was someone called . . . what was his name again, Nick?' asked Geoff.

'Giles Curtis.'

'That's it. Curtis, Giles Curtis,' repeated Geoff, a little superfluously, thought Nick.

'It was a terrible shock,' Nick said. 'particularly as he'd been battered to death.'

Janet put her hand up to her mouth involuntarily in shock. 'Battered to death! No! I don't believe it!'

Nick once again thought Janet's eyes had involuntarily looked at John, who was trying not to look surprised by the news.

'Did you know him then?' asked Nick.

'We did, but not all that well,' said Janet, yet again glancing over at John. Leaning back in his chair with his arms crossed, John was giving a passable impression of a drug store wooden display Red Indian. 'We'd seen him around and talked to him occasionally, of course, he seemed a nice guy.'

Nick thought Janet looked particularly worried about the news of Giles Curtis's demise, as if she was being evasive about something. Did they know Giles Curtis more intimately than they were letting on?

'I think you ought to tell the police. It might help them in their investigations,' Lynne said, taking a chunk of French bread and dipping it in olive oil.

'Oh, I'm sure we couldn't add anything. We hardly knew the guy,' added Janet dismissively.

'Where did you find him?' John asked Nick, looking slightly more animated.

Nick recounted his discovery of that morning. As a final flourish, he ended by explaining that the chief suspect — apart from himself, of course — had turned out to be a high court judge. This was not only news to Geoff and Lynne but even got a wry smile from, an up-to-that-point, serious Janet and John.

The dinner progressed at a leisurely pace from course to course as French meals have a habit of doing and conversation meandered taking in London restaurants, work, traffic and organic food along the way.

With his privates not on parade, Nick felt more able to join in the conversation and became quite voluble. Ros by contrast was quieter and more introverted than she had been at lunch.

By the time coffee and cheese arrived, the subject turned to naturist resorts they'd known and loved. A topic about which Nick and Ros had very little to contribute.

This was the first time Janet and John had been to Le Paradis, although they had stayed at many other naturist sites on the continent. This led to a discussion of the relative merits of resorts. Nick didn't mind. It distracted attention from their nudity. Which in reality only they seemed the slightest bit bothered about.

'We went to Cap d'Agde for the first time last year,' said Geoff.

'And the only time!' added Lynne.

'We did find it a bit of a concrete jungle and much too busy. So many people. Very crowded,' Geoff continued.

The Naked Guide says this about Cap d'Agde:

Located on the southern coast of France between Marseilles and Narbonne, Cap d'Agde (pronounced 'dag' with a hard 'g' as in 'dagger') is a modern French holiday resort. Unexceptional in every way bar one. What makes it a beacon for naturists all over the globe is that, next to the textile main town, lies the world's largest naturist resort – in the height of summer, home to around 40,000 naturists.

Covering an area of 90 hectares, the 'Naked City', as it is also sometimes known, includes not only large apartment blocks and villas, a 3,000 place camp site, its own yacht harbour and three kilometres of sandy beach but every facility needed to conduct everyday life in the nude.

There's a naturist hotel, a dozen or so restaurants, bars, night clubs, supermarkets, butchers, bakers and other shops, a service station, hairdressers, bank and doctors.

So the moment you drive or step through the gates of the resort to the moment you leave, you can spend your whole time in the nude.

Purists, however, may quibble with the fact that Cap d'Agde is a totally naturist resort, claiming that these days it's more – that awful description that sends a chill through the soul of the true naturist – 'clothing optional' (see separate entry).

Over the years the obligatory nudity rule has been increasingly ignored, resulting throughout the day in a mix of clothing options, and in the evening in virtually everybody going textile. A far cry from twenty years' ago when to wear even a pair of swimming trunks at any time, night or day, was to risk ridicule or expulsion.

'But the night life at Cap d'Agde is good, isn't it?' Janet added, again looking furtively across at John, as if sharing a secret. 'We found it very mellow. Very laid back. Made loads of new friends and acquaintances. Still see many of them today back home.'

'Well, I wouldn't describe the night life as "good"!' said Lynne, a tad frostily, thought Nick. 'The club we went to was "couples only" and – well! – the things that went on there . . .'

The sentence was left hanging in the air. Nick actually was interested in what went on there and was about to ask for further details but, catching sight of Ros looking at her watch, thought better of it.

Having now finished dinner, Ros was anxious to leave. As the day had worn on – and what a day it had been – she'd become increasingly conscious of her own nudity. What had started as a novel thrill was now beginning to pall – particularly as she was the only woman she could see who was actually topless. Although Lynne was making a passably good attempt at it.

Knowing Lynne from London, Ros would never have guessed she would have been an exhibitionist. Perhaps it was the contrast with wearing nothing that made a see-through blouse appear a conservative and acceptable choice in evening wear. Or perhaps she just did it to look sexy.

Ros was too tired to be interested in following that chain of thought. 'I think we ought to be going.' Ros put her hand on Nick's arm. 'It's been a long day.'

'Oh, right. Of course. I'll ask for the bill,' said Geoff, swivelling round to look for the waiter.

'How long do you think you'll be here for?' Lynne enquired of Nick.

'I really don't know. As short a time as possible I hope. Oh sorry, I didn't mean that to sound as if we want to get away from you. It's just that, well, naturism doesn't quite seem to be our thing.'

'That's what we thought originally,' Lynne said. 'But give it a couple more days and you'll wonder how you ever went on a textile holiday.'

Having endured a day's nudity, he couldn't in his wildest nightmares imagine what another couple of days would be like. Surely Lagardère would make a break-through tomorrow. Hear from the police in England and solve the case. But what if there was no progress? Just the thought was enough to plunge Nick into deepest gloom.

'I think I'll take your word for it,' said Nick, carefully getting up so that his towel was securely wrapped round his waist. 'How much is our share of the bill?'

'Don't worry about that,' Geoff waved his hand magnanimously. 'We'll sort it out tomorrow. We're over on Avenue D, left hand side. Come over and see us for coffee or a drink.

You'll recognize the camper van. I'm sure you'll still be with us then. Unless the killer gets you first, of course.'

Geoff raised his glass in mock toast. Nick managed a weak smile and pecked Lynne on both cheeks in farewell, making sure his eyes didn't stray downwards as he did so.

'Good to meet you,' he said to Janet and John. Ros kissed Geoff and Lynne on the cheeks. It looked as if both couples were settling in over the remains of the carafe of red.

Nick and Ros left by the terrace exit, which meant not having to go through the brightly lit restaurant in full view of the clothed diners.

Nick fleetingly had the uncomforting feeling that they were like insects scuttling away from the light back under the nearest stone.

They decided to take the longer route home around the Peripherique. It was quieter and less crowded, only having tents, caravans and vehicles on the right hand side, the left being bounded by trees, bushes and the perimeter fence of Le Paradis.

It was quiet, save for the insistent noise of cicadas and the occasional sound of radios or televisions. Lights on wooden poles spilled pools of illumination over the hard gravel roadway.

When they reached their own cabin, Martin Pike's was in darkness, not surprisingly as they'd last seen him in the restaurant engrossed in a long conversation with Hamish. The cabin the other side of their own, however, showed light behind the drawn curtains. Clearly somebody had moved into the empty property – the one vacated by the English judge.

Ros reached the door and as usual appeared to be stunned that she didn't seem to have anything in her hand with which to open it. This resulted in much searching in her shoulder bag for a key. While she did so, Nick mused on the past day.

It was still only half past ten. They'd been in Le Paradis for less than 24 hours. Yet it seemed a lifetime ago that they'd turned the corner of the road and spied that red neon sign. They'd entered a world that Nick had never thought even existed. A world where nudity was the norm and clothing the exception. He just couldn't figure out why people did it. And perhaps never would.

DAY TWO

'Why be given a body if you have to keep it shut up in a case like a rare, rare fiddle?'

Katherine Mansfield

14

Birds sang and light streamed through the flimsy curtains as Nick awoke from a deep sleep. He picked up his watch from the bedside table. Eight o'clock. Ros was lying on her side, facing away from him, hair bedraggled.

Taking care not to disturb her, Nick got up and walked into the bathroom. He inspected himself in the three-quarters length mirror.

Yes, the pinker bits looked slightly browner today. He wondered if he needed to put a stronger factor sunscreen on his privates. Although Ros said not, he was still worried that his penis was more likely to get burned than other parts of his body. Must ask Pike next time he saw him. Or not. But, all in all, he was not displeased with the reflection and the progress of his tan. Not so obviously two-tone as yesterday. Oh no! Yesterday!

For starters, it was the first day he'd spent in the nude since – well – ever! Even as a baby he must have worn something at some time during the day – if only a nappie. And it had ended with dinner for six in a restaurant, at which only two of the diners were nude. Unfortunately it happened to be Ros and himself.

He didn't think that he had ever suffered greater embarrassment, though had to admit it must have been worse for Ros, sitting there like a lap dancer asked to join the guests.

Having quietly finished his ablutions, Nick padded back through the cabin and out front to get some air. Even at this hour it was hot. Pausing at the door he looked round for a towel to wrap round himself. Should he or shouldn't he? The hell with it, he thought, as he gently opened and closed the door behind him. Nobody would be around at this time of day.

As he stepped out onto the verandah, he instinctively looked to his right, half expecting Martin Pike to be there. He wasn't. That was a relief. He couldn't bear the thought of a monologue on whichever of his hobbies Pike decided to elaborate on.

Leaning on the rail, Nick looked out musing on their current situation. He wondered when they'd be free to go. And get some clothes on. There was something else nagging at the back of his mind. Christ! They still hadn't phoned Phillip and Kathy! Really must do that this morning.

'Looks like another fine day.'

Nick jumped as a voice spoke to him, not from Martin's cabin but from the verandah of the cabin the other side of theirs.

Nick turned and there, half hidden in the shadow of the porch, was Inspector Lagardère. He was sitting in a canvas-back, director's style chair and holding a mug of what was, presumably, coffee. Unlike Nick, he was fully clothed – if you could call wearing short-sleeved shirt and shorts fully clothed.

All of a sudden Nick's decision not to wear anything seemed not to be the smartest. He instantly regretted being naked in front of the policeman. But there was little he could do about it without looking prudish. Dashing inside to grab a towel would definitely not be cool.

'It does, doesn't it,' Nick agreed, continuing to look ahead over the verandah rail.

The inspector remained seated, like Nick looking in front of him, as if with weightier problems on his mind.

'I've moved in here while the investigation's going on. It's convenient and, most importantly, I can keep an eye on you,' Lagardère said, turning to Nick and nodding his head.

Nick didn't know whether he was joking or serious. It was hard to tell with Lagardère.

'Er, how *is* the investigation going?' Nick asked, turning towards him. 'Made much progress, only we need to get on our way. We're supposed to be staying with our friends? You know, enjoying ourselves?'

'How are you finding life here?' Lagardère asked, totally ignoring Nick's original question. 'It's very peaceful isn't it.'

'Apart from having a homicidal maniac on the loose, it's terribly relaxing, yes.'

'Not sure I'd be happy walking around nude all the time. Though you seem to have taken to it, how do you say, like a duck to water.' He indicated Nick's undressed state with his free hand.

'I don't have much choice,' said Nick, turning slightly away from Lagardère so he was not too full frontal, before realising that Lagardère now had an excellent view of his arse. Lagardère, thankfully, seemed not to be interested and was looking forward again.

'We hope to get a response from Scotland Yard today. I spoke to them last night and they're trying to track down more information on the deceased, next of kin, etcetera. Curtis is not a common name but there are quite a few. Lucky for you he wasn't called Smith, eh? You might have been here all winter, as well.'

'Very amusing, I'm sure. Just how long can you keep us here? You know, under French law. Habeas-corpus and all that?'

'We don't have exactly that law in France,' Lagardère said, somewhat vaguely. 'But if all goes well you should be free to leave in a few days or so. Providing you're innocent, of course. We just need to complete our enquiries. And hopefully apprehend the murderer.'

Nick's heart sank at the thought of spending even one more day in the nude let alone a series of them. He was thinking about this when Lagardère spoke again.

'I enjoyed my time in England. I was there for three years, you know.' This explained Lagardère's excellent English. 'Seconded to the anti-terrorist squad some fifteen years' ago. Place called Croydon. Do you know Croydon, Mr Boughton?'

'No, but I hear it's "très jolie" '.

'It isn't. But you get used to anything don't you,' said Lagardère, again waving his hand in the direction of Nick's naked body. Nick wished people would stop doing that.

Whilst making a welcome change from Pike's proclamations on naturism, Nick was still not in the mood to stand and listen to Lagardère's views on the UK. 'Have you got any fresh leads on the murder?'

'Not at the moment. We still haven't found the murder weapon, either. It's like looking for a needle in a haystack. Hundreds of tents, mobile homes, caravans to search, and looking for what? Probably a length of wood, a wooden club, baseball bat – could even be a stout branch. By now it could have been burned on one of the barbecues. We'd never know.'

'How about questioning the suspects? Establishing the last

movements of the deceased? That sort of thing. Isn't that what you're supposed to do?' Nick said, a touch tetchily.

Lagardère detected the tone in his voice and replied perhaps a bit more sharply than he had meant to.

'Yes, and we now have a very good idea how Curtis spent his brief time in Le Paradis. Who he associated with, who he talked to, what he did. He seemed to have made friends with many of the English people. No French that we know of. So we still believe it was one of the people he knew.'

'Doesn't that eliminate us?' said Nick, in more reasoned tones. It probably wasn't a good idea to rub Lagardère up the wrong way. 'After all, we only arrived the night of the murder.'

'On the contrary, he could have been on his way to see you. It could have been pre-arranged. He did have your card in his hand remember.'

It was irritating that Lagardère kept bringing that up. Nick was just about to say something, when the door behind him opened and Ros walked out onto the verandah.

'I thought I heard voices,' she said.

'You did,' said Nick, nodding towards Lagardère.

'Good morning,' Lagardère said, getting to his feet, Nick suspected, to get a better view of Ros's naked form. 'Looks like it's going to be a scorcher again.'

'Yes,' said Ros, a bit taken aback to find the inspector there.

'Well, must be on my way,' said Lagardère, placing the mug on the table. 'We are questioning those we haven't got round to yet. I'll let you know how we get on.'

Giving a mock salute to Nick and Ros, which looked too much like that given by the French police captain to Humphrey Bogart in Casablanca to be coincidental, he picked up his briefcase from the table beside him and set off in the direction of Reception.

'Don't tell me he's living next door?' Ros said, joining Nick at the rail of the verandah, both studying Lagardère's back as he walked up the road, disappearing from view through the short cut.

'Says it's all the better to keep his eye on us. And I certainly noticed him keeping his eye on you.'

'Did he say how much longer we'd be here?' Ros said, ignoring Nick's comment.

' "Some days" was the best I could get out of him.'

'Oh, no! I don't think I could face all that time without clothes.'

'But you were OK yesterday?'

'That was before last night. That was so humiliating. I can't tell you.'

Nick put a comforting arm round her and she rested her head on his shoulder. 'Well, there's nothing we can do but grin and "bare" it.'

'Ha bloody ha.'

Nick volunteered to get the croissants while Ros attended to the coffee-maker. Grabbing Ros's new small leather bag and making sure it had sufficient euro coinage within, he grabbed and arranged a towel about his person and set off for the shop.

Having braved the supermarket aisles, chill cabinets and checkout person, Nick emerged and decided to try and phone Phillip and Kathy again. The reception office seemed the best bet. You never know, he might bump into Shareen.

Reception seemed to be empty as Nick entered, but he caught sight of Jack in the room beyond.

'Just making some coffee,' Jack called to him, holding up a pack and spoon as if to demonstrate. 'Like some?'

'Please. That'd be good.'

'Come on round.'

Nick joined Jack as he switched on the coffeemaker, which almost immediately started making warming-up, bubbling noises.

Jack was, of course, wearing de rigeur Le Paradis uniform – nothing at all – apart that is from a watch and a pair of rather tatty espadrilles. Nick noticed that Jack looked a lot fitter than he'd first thought. Well-defined shoulders and arms and a fairly flat stomach beneath his deep tan.

'Here, park your bum,' said Jack, clearing some papers off one of the chairs.

'Thanks.'

'Cigarette?' Jack offered a pack of Gauloises Light.

'Don't smoke, thanks. Gave up five years' ago.'

Jack extracted a cigarette and lit up with a red Bic lighter. 'Never quite managed it myself.' Jack exhaled a plume of smoke away from Nick and towards the open window. 'How you enjoying yourself?'

'Well, apart from the fact that I've been unwillingly separated from my clothes, that I'm number one murder suspect – no, correction – the only murder suspect, and that we're supposed to be somewhere else relaxing with friends on holiday, I can't really complain.'

Jack smiled. 'If you didn't do it, you've got nothing to worry about. You didn't do it did you?'

'Of course not!' said Nick indignantly. Why did everyone seem obliged to ask him that question.

'Only kidding. But you got to admit there are a lot worse places to be. Relax. Get some sun on your arse. Enjoy yourself. Go sailing, windsurfing. There's a lot to do. We make sure of that.'

'Sorry, who's "we"?'

'Pasquale, the wife and myself. Saw the place up for sale, what, some twenty years' ago and decided to buy it. Land's gone up fantastically in value since then, of course. You should have seen the state it was in. Had to re-fence it. Dredge the lake. Re-surface the pool. Bloody hard graft. And it doesn't get any easier.'

'Pasquale? Is she French.'

'Yeah. Local girl as well. Born just up the road. She's off visiting her aged mother at the moment in Perpignan.'

The coffeemaker had now dripped through enough coffee. Jack got up and, cigarette dangling from mouth, poured two mugs, bringing them back to the table.

'Help yourself to milk and sugar,' Jack said, indicating an open tetrapak and a bowl of wrapped sugar cubes.

Nick stirred some milk into his coffee. 'Do you live here all year round?'

'We usually stay on site just for the season. We've also got a little place down on the coast. But there's work to do here most of the year. Upkeep and maintenance mainly. Get some of the guys who work the vineyards to help. They've got sod all to do in the winter except drink pastis and sit in bars. They welcome the extra money.'

Jack lit up another cigarette. He was sitting slightly to one side in the chair, one arm resting on the table the other casually over the back of the chair.

'I saw Lagardère this morning,' Nick said. 'He's moved in next door to us.'

'Thought you'd appreciate the company.' Jack smiled. 'How's the investigation going?'

'I hoped you might be able to tell me that.'

'Keeps very much to himself. He's had quite a lot of plain clothes flics around the place, questioning staff, guests, that sort of thing, but doesn't talk to me about what's going on.'

'Isn't it all a bit disturbing for the guests?' Nick asked. 'You know, not being able to leave?'

'To be truthful, not many people have noticed yet. Most of our happy campers usually stay inside the resort and are here for a week or more. The ones who wanted to go out yesterday were politely told that the police are investigating an unspecified incident and asked to stay. Mind you, if the investigation goes on until the end of the week . . .' Jack left the sentence unfinished, clearly thinking about the problems he might have with a resort-load of angry guests confined to quarters.

'I almost forgot. I came in here to see if I can use your phone. My mobile doesn't seem to work.'

'Help yourself.' Jack gestured towards the phone on the counter. 'We're in a bit of a thread-bare mobile reception area. Guests are always complaining.'

'Thanks,' said Nick, getting to his feet and rescuing his towel and shopping bags. 'And thanks for the coffee as well.'

'You're welcome. Drop by any time.'

Nick walked round to the customer side of the counter, picked up the phone and tapped out the number. It rang. And rang. Still no bloody answer. It was now nine o'clock in the morning. Where could they be? Surely not still asleep? Maybe out shopping? He hung up.

'No reply. Thanks again,' Nick called back to Jack, who waved in acknowledgement.

Nick headed back to the cabin. The sun shone from a cloudless blue sky. It was perfect holiday weather, even if this wasn't the perfect holiday. But Jack was right. There were lots worse places they could be. If only he could be re-united with his clothes. But wait a minute. He could. This evening. The time everyone gets dressed. That at least was something to look forward to.

As he approached the cabin, he noticed that Ros had company. She was sitting drinking coffee with . . . Oh, no!

Bloody Martin Pike! This time he'd migrated to their verandah. Give him another couple of days and he'd probably be living with them.

'Hello!' Pike called out to him. 'Been shopping I see.'

'Very observant,' replied Nick, putting the croissants down on the table and pulling up a chair.

'You've been a while,' said Ros, pointedly, to Nick.

'Sorry. Went to call Phillip and Kathy and had a chat with Jack at Reception.' Nick helped himself to some coffee.

'If there's a drop more . . .' Martin held his cup out and Nick re-filled it.

'How were they?' asked Ros.

'There was no reply,' said Nick.

'Ros was telling me that you're a photographer? That must be interesting work?' Martin Pike continued.

'Yes, it is,' Nick replied, begrudgingly.

'I hear photographers specialise in one thing or another. What do you photograph mainly?'

'People, fashion models for magazine features and ads, that sort of thing.'

'You'd be quickly out of work round here then.' Martin smiled.

Ros seemed to be glad Nick was taking over the conversational burden and was sitting, leaning forwards, elbows on table, cupping her mug between her hands as if warming them, whilst staring into the middle distance.

'Have you got your camera with you?'

'I have.'

'Well I would advise you not to use it here in Le Paradis.'

'Why on earth not?' asked Nick.

'Naturists are very touchy about that sort of thing. They don't like being photographed in the nude.'

'But surely they don't mind others seeing them naked?

Otherwise they wouldn't be here in the first place?' Nick
protested.

'Ah but being nude doesn't mean that you can't have
privacy. That's what they're trying to protect. You never
know where your photo might end up. Maybe on a website or
in a magazine.'

Nick nibbled on a croissant while Martin continued talking,
warming to his subject.

'Let me give you an example. A man gave his wife some
holiday brochures from which to choose a holiday and left them
with her while he went off to work. On returning, he found his
wife in a very bad mood. When asked why, she showed him a
photo in one of the brochures of a couple lying on a beach,
pointing out that it was him – and the woman he was lying next
to clearly wasn't the good lady wife.

'The man admitted that it did look like him but, of course,
it couldn't be. Why then, the wife replied, is he lying on our
beach towel? To which of course he had no answer. He'd
been snapped on a so-called business trip with his secretary.
So you see, that's why photography is banned in naturist
resorts.'

Pike folded his arms and raised his chin, suddenly reminding
Nick of Mussolini, having made an extremely important point.
Nick was about to challenge the non-sequitur of Martin Pike's
argument but didn't have the energy.

'I'll bear that in mind,' was all he could manage.

'Well, thank you very much for the coffee,' said Pike,
getting up and moving his towel from under him. 'I'd best be
off. Need to get to the pool before the kiddies start dive-
bombing and splashing. Have to get in my thirty lengths, you
know.'

'Right. Good bye,' said Ros, coming out of her reverie.

'See you later,' replied Pike, as he headed off, presumably to the pool, his thin brown haunches and skinny legs moving briskly away from them.

'I hope not,' Nick said under his breath.

'God, I thought he'd never go,' said Ros, 'I bet the kids in his school celebrated the day he retired.'

Nick took a sip of his coffee. 'So what do you think of the holiday so far?'

Resisting the urge to be flippant, Ros considered her answer. 'I've had less stressful times in A & E. It's strange isn't it. I don't think I could get used to being a nudist. It's supposed to be free and liberating, yet there are many more rules, regulations and conventions than on an ordinary holiday. What not to wear. What to wear and when. Where to look when talking to people. Carrying something around to sit on all the time. They seem to have replaced the restrictions of clothing with restrictions of not wearing clothing.'

'Do I take it that you're finding it a bit of a strain?'

Ros smiled. 'Oh I suppose it's not that bad. I just wish that we could get on with the holiday we planned.'

Nick got up from the table and started clearing away the breakfast things. 'So what do you want to do today?' he called, as he went inside to the kitchen.

Ros thought about this. If she was honest with herself she would most have liked to see Jean-Luc, maybe with the excuse of seeing how his wound was healing. She felt herself get hot as she thought about examining his thighs and upwards to his firm buttocks . . .

'Well?' Nick called from inside.

'Erm, nothing really. I think I might stay here and read a book or something,' was all Ros could think of saying.

Nick returned to the table with a cup and tea-towel in hand. 'I thought I might explore the camp. Didn't really see much of it yesterday.' And his exploration might well include a visit to the bar to get better acquainted with Shareen.

'You go. I'll stay here.'

'You sure you're going to be all right on your own?'

Ros smiled and gave him a small peck on the cheek. 'Of course. I'm a big girl remember.'

'What was that for?'

'Does there have to be a reason?' Ros was feeling what? Maternal? About Nick? Surely not.

Nick walked back inside to get ready. 'Well, if you can face it, let's meet up for lunch. At least at that time of the day we're guaranteed that *everyone* will be nude.'

Ros smiled and looked up at him. 'OK, shall we say one o'clock?'

'Right, you've got a date.'

15

Having applied high factor sunscreen to his body – and higher still factor sunscreen to his, erstwhile, private parts – Nick kissed Ros goodbye. He set off towards the centre of the resort armed with just shoulder bag, money and towel.

Nick really had been in too much of a daze to take in the size or layout of the place the day before. Today, feeling slightly calmer albeit still extremely uneasy about his naked state, he could look at the place more dispassionately and establish its geography a bit better.

Despite his unenviable status as head murder suspect and without a stitch of clothing, Nick suddenly began to feel the tiniest bit less stressed. He liked the feel of the strengthening sun on his naked body. He really didn't feel as self-conscious as yesterday. After all, nobody appeared to notice, care or pay any attention to his nudity.

The bar seemed the natural first port of call but it was shut. Too early. So he continued on across the grass to the lakeside.

There were people out in boats, although there was little in the way of breeze.

Unbeknown to him, he followed the same route Ros had taken the day before — anti-clockwise round the lake. Arriving at the far end he noted the jetty and boathouse. Apart from two immobile fishermen perched at the end of the jetty, it was strangely quiet and peaceful.

Nick stopped on the jetty, sat down on his towel and dangled his legs over the side. The sun was pleasantly hot on his back and he hoped the sunscreen factors were doing their protection thing. He looked down at his freshly aired genitals and, with mind free-wheeling, mused on the subject of pubic hair.

Yesterday Nick had been too distracted to look closely at his fellow naturists. Now he was feeling just slightly less panicky he'd taken the opportunity to study — discreetly, of course — his fellow inmates' pubic areas on the way over.

He was sure that Pike would have a section in his Guide about the subject of naturists and pubic hair. From Nick's own limited observations he concluded that not having to wear bikinis, the female naturist had no need to be concerned about the modern day problem of the bikini line. Many therefore decided that this was an area best left "au naturel". A view which seemed to be shared by the majority of male naturists, who similarly opted for laissez-faire and luxuriant pubic hair non-styling. A classic example being Hamish the Hairy.

Those women who did pay attention to their bikini lines, presumably because they wore costumes when in gyms or public swimming pools at home, opted for a marginal v-shape. This was the style adopted by Ros, who had never thought it would be on public, or should that be pubic, display.

Less popular, but also prevalent, was the Brazilian wax, favoured by most of the models he photographed. This left a thin 'landing strip' of central pubic hair. This quite appealed to him he decided, having seen it displayed on a number of younger women he'd passed.

But what surprised, and yes, he had to admit it, shocked Nick most was the number of naturists who had no pubic hair at all. Well, obviously they had pubic hair to start with but had decided to eliminate it totally.

He thought the shock came from the child-like state of no pubic hair translated to the distinctly unattractive setting of an 18-stone, middle-aged German male. It didn't seem, well, natural. That word again.

He also noticed a couple of men who he could have sworn were completely bereft of any body hair at all. That included legs and arms. He thought of John's hairless chest last night at dinner and wondered briefly if that extended southwards before deciding that these could be defined as homosexual thoughts. But why did they do it? Was it only exhibitionism? He'd probably never know the answer.

Nick was correct in his first, and earlier, assumption. The Naked Guide does have more than a few enlightening words to deliver on the subject of shaving body hair:

Is it possible to be 'barer than nude'? It is according to the now defunct Smoothie Club of Great Britain. Originally founded to promote the acceptance of what it calls 'the smooth look' within the naturist world, according to the internet it's now been superseded by the World of the Nudest Nudist or WNN for short (or should that be 'short and curlies'!) Their aim is to promote the aesthetic ideal of a smooth and hairless body. This is not a new idea.

Ancient Egyptians believed that a hairless body was the standard of beauty, youth and innocence, so all over Egypt women took care that there was not a single hair on their bodies, using depilatory creams to achieve the result.

The Greeks also adopted this idea of smoothness for women,

demonstrated by sculptures of women which show not a single pubic hair — as opposed to male statues which did. The Romans too preferred their women to be pubic hairless. And even as late as the 16th century, Turks were quoted as considering it 'sinful when a woman lets the hair on her private parts grow'. Public Turkish baths all had special rooms where the ladies could get rid of their hair.

Today there's been a revival in the concept, stretching even to male 'textiles' (see entry under 'T') who have chest and back hair regularly waxed for aesthetic reasons.

Looking down at his own dark pubic hair, like most other non-naturist males, untouched since puberty, Nick wondered if he should give it a trim, spruce it up a bit. After all, just as you wanted to look your best in clothes, surely you should make an effort to make your body look as presentable as possible?

Nick's musings on the subject were interrupted as, from the corner of his eye, he noticed a figure coming out of, what was it, some sort of boathouse, and walking towards him up the jetty.

The figure was female, blonde and smiling at him. Yes, if he wasn't mistaken, it was Shareen.

'Nick, hi!'

She stopped directly in front of him before he had time to move, giving him the chance to notice that Shareen also favoured the bikini line 'V' And that she was a natural blonde unless, of course, she dyed her pubic hair.

'Can I join you?' she said, and without waiting for a reply, sat down carefully on the wooden jetty next to him, dangling her shapely legs over the edge.

'Gotta be careful with the wood on this old jetty. Can be dangerous. You know? Lucky you're sitting on your towel. Don't want splinters in your rear end?'

'Er, yes, I mean, no.' Nick wondered if he'd ever be able to have any type of conversation with Shareen. She must think him a total idiot.

'How are things?' asked Shareen.

'Not too bad.' Almost a complete sentence. Not witty, humorous, flirtatious or amusing but almost a sentence. Who knows, with practice . . .

'On your own again?'

'Sorry?' Nick was so impressed with his last response, he was not listening.

'Well, whenever I see you, you're never with your wife?'

'Partner, actually.'

'OK partner, then. What's her name? Ros?'

'Well, we do see rather a lot of one another in England.' Nick said, a little pompously. 'So on holiday it makes a change if we go our separate ways.' Why was he being so defensive?

'She was going her separate ways down here yesterday, so I hear.'

'Yes, what's his name, Jean something or other. She told me she performed some first aid.'

'That's what she called it?'

Nick didn't quite know how to take that remark. Was it a statement or question? Hard to tell when everything Shareen said sounded like an enquiry. Or was Shareen suggesting something else had happened? And if so, what? He felt a change of subject might be in order. 'You working today?'

'Yeah, but not 'til eleven? Back on bar duty.'

'You worked here long?' Nick asked, thinking at the same time that it was a chat-up line that had been drawing its old age pension even when he was a kid.

'Just for the summer. Wanted to see Europe and needed the money. Same old Aussie story. Saw this job when I was in Narbonne and thought "why not?"'

'But what about the, er, the er . . .' said Nick, indicating her body in similar fashion to Lagardère's glance at his own, a few hours earlier.

'Nudity?' Shareen helped Nick out. 'No worries. Not a problem. Not all "Sheilas" are uptight about that sort of thing, you know?'

Nick hadn't thought they were. Or, rather, hadn't given the concept brain space. 'So what do you do in Australia?' he said, guiding the conversation away from the fact that both of them were sitting next to each other totally naked – making him feel very uneasy on more than one level.

'Just finished my M.A.? You know? Post-grad? University?'

Now there was no way Nick considered himself elitist or a snob. But, he had to admit that this latest piece of information subtly changed his opinion of Shareen.

No longer did he view her as just a rather – all right, *very* – fanciable Kylie look-alike, albeit ten years younger, but as someone with an "-ology". Despite himself, he was impressed.

'What did you study?'

'Existential psychotherapy.'

'Oh,' said Nick, buying time. 'That's, er, really interesting.'

Shareen filled in the silence. 'Yeah, that's the reaction I usually get. If you ask me nicely I'll promise not to tell you all about it.'

'So,' said Nick, ploughing gamely on, 'Is there much demand for existential psychotherapy in Australia?'

Just at that point, Nick's attention was distracted by a sudden flash of sunlight. He looked towards the shore and saw that it had been caused by a movement of glass on the balcony of the room above the boathouse. Someone had opened the French windows. Or perhaps they had simply moved in the breeze.

Shareen also followed his gaze and looked shorewards. She turned back towards Nick and smiled at him. She moved her bottom closer to him and leaned towards him. 'Hope so. Gonna start my own practice when I get back.'

Nick suddenly felt his face get redder. Shareen was now very close and looking into his eyes in an open, and perhaps, inviting way. He had never been good at reading signs in women and wasn't too sure what Shareen was up to – if anything.

'Is that going to be difficult? I mean, Australians aren't noted for their introspection, so I hear'.

'Are you trying to say we're all "thickies", Nick?' said Shareen, playfully touching his shoulder in a mock aggressive manner.

'No, that's not what I meant. I mean. I mean . . .'

'Yes, what do you mean?' Shareen asked, leaning even closer towards him.

'That it's an unlikely occupation, well, for anyone.'

'Let alone an Aussie?' Shareen added, leaning away from him and looking into the water of the lake.

Afraid that he'd somehow annoyed her, Nick explained. 'No, I meant it's a . . .' He'd rather lost the thread of his argument so stopped abruptly and joined her in gazing idly at the lake. Viewed from afar, Nick and Shareen must have now looked like immobile twin companions to the two gnomes at the end of the pier.

'So, using your therapy skills, what would you say Giles Curtis was like?' Nick felt on safer ground talking about a third party, particularly one that was deceased.

'It doesn't quite work like that. We're not experts on human nature you know? While he was outwardly gregarious there was also something closed-in and secretive about him. Even when laughing at one of Garry's terrible jokes, his attention always seemed to be elsewhere. He wasn't really present.

All I learned was that he used to work for the government,

was retired and seemed unmarried. Or at least lived on his own. That was about that.'

'Lagardère tells me that Giles lived in London. An address not far from us actually.'

Shareen turned to him. 'Really? That's interesting.'

Nick instantly regretted mentioning it, as this revelation seemed once again to put him firmly back in the guilty frame. 'Whoever he was, and whatever he did, someone wanted him dead. Lagardère is convinced the murderer was one of the Brits in the camp.'

'Could be right,' said Shareen, brushing back a wisp of hair from her eyes.

'If it was one of the Brits who murdered Giles, which one would you choose?'

She looked up from the lake, turning her blue eyes on him and smiled. 'You'd be pretty high on the list.'

'I do mean apart from me,' said Nick, wearily. He'd got very bored with his "most wanted" role.

Shareen turned her attention back to looking at the lake, giving Nick a good sideways view of her breasts. 'O.K. He seemed to get on well with most people, but he did have a heated argument with Garry on the morning he was murdered.'

'Where was that?'

'In the bar. They were talking at one of the tables and I couldn't really catch what they were saying. Garry seemed pretty angry about something.'

'You told Lagardère about this?'

'You think I should?' said Shareen, looking towards him again.

'It might help,' Nick said, thinking that if Garry was arrested he'd be able to get out of here. Although chatting to an attractive nude young woman, made being trapped in Le

Paradis a much more appealing prospect than it had seemed yesterday. 'What about the others?'

'Hamish, you know, the Scotsman? He seems harmless enough. Always got on well with Giles as far as I could tell. But who knows. Then, of course, there was John . . .'

'Of Janet and John?'

'Yeah. All those studs and things. Yeuch! So tacky!' Shareen pulled a face at the thought and then returned to the subject. 'They seemed to be quite close to Giles. Used to go off together at odd times of the day. God only knows to do what.'

'That's funny. They didn't mention they knew him as well as that when we had dinner with them last night.'

'You had dinner with them? You don't look as if you're into that sort of thing?' Shareen looked at Nick.

'No, it wasn't like that,' he said, hastily, 'they're friends of our neighbours . . . it's a long story.' Nick suddenly remembered Martin Pike. 'The guy next door to us, Martin Pike, he had lunch with Giles on the day of the murder.'

'Oh yeah. I remember him. The one who goes on and on about naturism. If he could wear an anorak in here I'm sure he would. Can't see him bashing someone over the head. Boring them to death, maybe.'

'Ros also mentioned a couple she met. Wealthy. Live in Portugal. Charles and Camilla.'

'You having me on?'

'No, really, that's their names.'

'Can't say I know them,' said Shareen, looking down again into the water.

'Unless the murder was totally random,' said Nick, recalling the madman on the loose theory. 'There's also the question of motive. Why did someone want to kill him?'

As Nick said this, there was another flash of light from the boathouse. Although Shareen seemed not to notice, she turned to Nick smiled and put her arm through his. So unexpected was the touch of her bare flesh, Nick had to stop himself flinching.

'Perhaps we should try and find out,' she said, looking disconcertingly closely into his eyes.

'Er . . .' Nick tried to concentrate. 'What? Carry on our own investigation? Like out of, well, a bad Agatha Christie?'

'Why not? Where would we start if we were doing it for real?'

The words "doing it for real" took Nick's mind off the subject momentarily. He recovered. 'Don't detectives try to piece together what the deceased was doing right up to the moment of his murder and discovery of the body . . .'

'By you.'

'Yes, thanks for reminding me. You know. Who he saw. What he did. That type of thing?'

'Yeah, well we know some of that. He was in the bar with Garry and Hamish that morning, went off for lunch with the Pike fellow and in the afternoon, what?'

'Pike told me he came here to the lake to do some windsurfing,' said Nick.

When he said this, Shareen turned her head to look towards the boathouse balcony. Nick followed her gaze. There was no movement from up there. She turned back to Nick.

'Then what?' she said, a little more seriously.

'Well, we don't know what he did then until the evening when he had dinner with Charles and Camilla. They were the last to see him alive. Perhaps we ought to start with them.'

'Why not just tell Lagardère? He *is* your next-door neighbour after all?'

Yet again a flash of light. Shareen got suddenly to her feet and then, almost as an afterthought, looked at her watch.

Nick followed suit, picking up his towel as he did so and holding it in front of him.

'Hey. Didn't know it was so late. Gotta go and prep the bar,' said Shareen, reaching up and giving Nick a light peck on the cheek. 'See you later, Poirot.'

And with that she was off, back down the jetty, giving Nick a view of the same swaying backside that, had he known it, Ros had found so irritating yesterday.

Strangely enough, this was not the sentiment shared by Nick at that moment, as he watched Shareen walk round the lake and disappear behind the trees.

Nick started walking slowly back along the jetty towards the boathouse.

Now what? What did he feel about Shareen? Yes, he thought she was extremely attractive. But did she fancy him? She was sitting awfully close on the jetty.

What about investigating the murder? Could it be that dangerous? After all, it made him feel he was doing something to get out of this place. Since he'd got here, he'd seemed to lose all control of his life together with his clothes. Stripped of his personality. Stripped of his freedom. What else had he to loose? Well, his life, of course, if there really was a murderer who took amiss to his interfering. But that was the stuff of television dramas. It wasn't likely here in Le Paradis, surely?

And where did Ros fit in all this? Despite the odd temptation over the past six years, he'd been faithful. But things hadn't been good lately. The whole biological time clock thing had been taking its toll. Maybe sex equated in both their minds with babies. Ros realising she wanted one and Nick realising that it could happen if he had sex. He had learned something from Biology GCSE after all.

And being trapped here, naked, hadn't helped. Ironically, when sex couldn't have been easier – after all, both were permanently dressed for it – there seemed to be an inhibition. Why? Because . . .

As these thoughts and more were whirring through Nick's brain, he'd reached the shore. He turned the corner of the boathouse and nearly fell over a figure doing something with a coil of rope. It was the aquarobics man.

Jean-Luc looked up and, stiffly, got up. To Nick, he seemed very young. Using his professional photographer's eye, even Nick could appreciate that he was good-looking – in a rather dark and surly sort of way.

'Oh, terribly sorry!' Nick said.

'No problem,' said Jean-Luc standing up. He was as tall as Nick, but more slightly built. 'If you've come for tuition, you're too early. You need to come back this afternoon.'

The thought of lessons rang a bell with Nick. After all, Giles Curtis had, according to Pike, come to the lake to wind-surf, following their lunch together.

'Are you here every afternoon?'

'Yes, one day we give lessons in windsurfing, the next in sailing,' said Jean-Luc, pushing hair back from his eyes and looking at Nick in, what might be called, a guarded manner.

'What about the day before yesterday?'

'A windsurfing day.'

'The Englishman, Giles Curtis. Did he turn up that afternoon?'

'You mean the one who was killed?'

'Yes. How did you know that?' asked Nick.

'Shareen – the girl you were talking to just now – she told me. I remember an Englishman taking a board out. There was hardly a breath of wind but he seemed determined so . . .' Jean-Luc shrugged.

'This person, if he was Giles Curtis, what time did he bring the board back?'

'Maybe about five. He headed back towards the resort,' said Jean-Luc, indicating the main area of Le Paradis.

'Thanks.'

'Were you a friend of his?'

'No just an innocent bystander really.'

Jean-Luc looked puzzled but either couldn't be bothered to follow the comment up or didn't understand what Nick was saying. 'I need to get back to work if you'll excuse me.'

As he turned away from Nick, the bandage high on the back of his thigh was revealed. Nick tried not to imagine Ros cleaning the wound and putting on the dressing mere inches from the more intimate parts of this young naked Frenchman.

'By the way, how's the leg?' Nick couldn't resist asking.

'Oh, not too bad,' said Jean-Luc, touching the bandage. 'It's still a bit painful. But how do you know?

'My partner, Ros, bandaged it for you.'

At this Jean-Luc appeared to Nick to look extremely shifty, almost guilty. Or was it his imagination?

'Oh. She told you all about it?'

'Why shouldn't she?'

'No reason. But it wasn't that serious.' Was Jean-Luc hinting at something that happened?

'Lucky it wasn't otherwise you'd be out of action for some time.' said Nick, adding a little double entendre of his own. One which he hoped carried the slightest threat of violence.

Jean-Luc didn't seem to notice. 'It'll be fine in a few days.'

'You were lucky she came along at the time, eh?'

'No, she was already here,' said Jean-Luc, vaguely indicating the jetty and boathouse. 'She wanted to learn sailing so we walked across from the pool.'

'The swimming pool?'

'Yes. We came over together. She seemed very keen.'

So Ros hadn't casually passed by and been tempted to take

part in the sailing class. She'd come along with Jean-Luc. Not quite the story she'd told him. How much else hadn't she remembered?

'If you want to learn how to do it properly, come over any afternoon.' Jean-Luc gave a small smile, but behind his smile his eyes looked hostile.'

'I'll remember,' said Nick. 'Au revoir.'

He turned and decided to walk back to the resort. It wasn't yet time for lunch, but suddenly he had a strong desire for a think – and a drink. Whether served by Shareen, or not.

16

After Nick had set off, Ros felt alone and vulnerable. A feeling exacerbated by the heat. Even with the windows and doors open, the cabin was giving a good impression of a sauna with malfunctioning thermostat.

What she wanted was a nice cup of tea. She found a couple of aged tea bags in the kitchen cupboard and put the kettle on. Waiting for it to boil – why were foreign kettles so slow – she thought about their current predicament.

All told, it wasn't that big a deal being stuck here in Le Paradis. Yes, there was the minor inconvenience of not wearing clothes, but she felt she could live with that – even after last night. She still felt that she'd cast her inhibitions adrift with her undergarments. That is, providing she wasn't the only one nude when everyone else was clothed.

But what about Nick? Was he acting strangely? It must be hard for him. He was the textile equivalent of the "naturista" – a "fashionista". He was at one with the world of style, its labels, logos and brands. But perhaps not so happy in his own skin. An appropriate metaphor she felt.

He'd become quieter. More subdued. Less self-confident. In short, not his usual self. Maybe he also had something else on his mind – their relationship perhaps. It hadn't been that great before they'd come on holiday. And, after all, he'd had a deal of stress, what with finding the body and losing his clothes.

Thinking about nudity led naturally to the thighs of Jean-Luc. He was only a kid, really. What was the great attraction? Apart from the sinewy lithe body, great arse, member that looked as if it could be a "grower" with the right level of encouragement. Maybe she ought to pay a visit to the boat-house to see if his dressing needed changing.

This line of thought made her feel even hotter, or was it just the kettle, now emitting clouds of steam. Stirring tea bag with spoon, her mind whirled on.

Kathy and Phillip. What on earth must they be thinking? No sign of guests who were now a day overdue. Would they inform the police? Set up a manhunt for them? Which would be ironic seeing as they were being held captive by the gendarmerie.

Maybe Ros should see if she could phone them herself. They had to be contactable somehow and sometime.

She decided to finish her tea and take a walk over to Reception. She could also get some fresh tea bags and do a bit of shopping. Mind made up, she took bag, purse and flip flops.

Unlike yesterday, she now found herself looking for a beach towel, making sure it covered as much of her as possible. It wasn't much but it was enough she thought to deflect the casual glance.

With the phone booth occupied by a couple of naked giggling teenage girls, Ros decided to do the shopping first.

Halfway round the supermarket, she spotted the rather large figure of a man bending over reaching into the freezer chest. From where she was standing, almost directly behind him, it did not make for a particularly pleasant sight.

Suddenly the figure lurched upright, as if jerked by puppet strings. It looked in her direction. It was Geoff. He smiled and waved her over.

'Do you know they sell frozen moules provençales here? Is that not amazing?'

'Er . . .' Ros couldn't decide whether it was or not. And didn't particularly care.

'On your own?' asked Geoff, picking up a pack of the aforementioned molluscs and putting it into his basket, once again looking her up and down a bit more intently than perhaps he would have done had she been dressed.

'Yes. Nick's gone off for an explore.'

'Oh really?' said a voice at Ros's elbow, giving her a start. It was Lynne, looking better than Ros had ever seen her. Slim and very tanned. Standing next to Geoff she looked positively wraith-like. But then again, thought Ros, so would Vanessa Feltz.

'So our murder suspect is out roaming Le Paradis in search of victims,' Lynne added playfully.

'In search of beer, more like,' added Ros.

'Have you both recovered from last night?' Lynne asked, as if wanting to remind her of their embarrassment.

'Oh yes. Bit of a laugh really,' said Ros.

'Well I think you both took it extremely well.' Why did Ros detect a superior and condescending tone about Lynne?

Geoff moved on up the supermarket aisle.

'I suppose you can get used to anything after a time,' said Ros, looking at Geoff's large and somewhat hairy back disappearing in the direction of the wine racks.

'Sounds as if Nick's also getting used to being nude if he's off on his own,' said Lynne.

Ros suddenly shivered. She wondered why until she realized she had been standing only a foot or two away from the frozen vegetable section of the open freezer chest.

Not fancying frostbite of any part of her anatomy, she moved away and walked along the aisle, Lynne by her side. Geoff seemed to be doing the shopping. Lynne appeared to be there in a consulting role.

Ros added wine, milk and nibbles to the Lipton's tea bags and paid at the checkout. She politely waited while Geoff packed his groceries into plastic bags. As he did so he turned to Ros. 'What are you doing now?'

'Not a lot, really. Got to phone our friends, then nothing.'

'Why not come for a game of boules?' Geoff suggested.

'I've never played before.'

'Doesn't matter. You'll soon pick it up, won't she Lynne?' Geoff asked rhetorically. 'Come on. Get some exercise and sun at the same time. You'll love it.'

'Well, all right then,' said Ros dubiously. 'Where do you play?'

'It's by the tennis courts, remember, where we saw you yesterday?' said Lynne, adding rather unnecessarily, 'With that French chap?'

Lynne looked at Ros as if suspecting her of some impropriety with Jean-Luc.

'Oh yes. I know where you mean,' Ros said, ignoring the tone of Lynne's voice.

'Well, what say we meet there in quarter of an hour or so?' said Geoff.

They all emerged into the bright light of day. The heat was building. Ros put on her sunglasses and adjusted her towel for maximum protection against both the sun and Geoff's gaze. So what if Geoff was looking at her more intently than he should? She ought to be flattered. But it didn't feel that way.

'See you later.' Geoff waved and wobbled off down the road, loaded with plastic bags, Lynne by his side.

The phone booth was now empty. And very hot. Ros dialled Phillip and Kathy's number. Still no reply. Her mind imagined the phone ringing in a cool shady room with dappled light reflected from the swimming pool coming in through partly-drawn shutters. What she would give to be there now. No reply.

Reluctantly, she hung up and stepped out into the searing heat. She was beginning to think that Phillip and Kathy were a figment of their joint imagination. Like a mirage. They didn't really exist. Or, rather, existed in a parallel world which had very little to do with the one Nick and Ros inhabited. A world where people wore clothes. A world where you could come and go as you pleased. A world where your partner wasn't a murder suspect.

Sure enough, the patch of hard earth given over to boules was beside the tennis courts. Partly shaded by trees, it offered some respite from the sun.

Geoff and Lynne were already there when Ros, having dropped off the shopping, finally arrived. Facing away from her, they were in the middle of a game. Geoff was standing hands on hips in a fashion which reminded Ros of a retired colonel watching a polo match.

By his side Lynne was crouched, staring intently forward as she weighed the boule in both hands. Standing up, Lynne carefully took aim and loosed the boule one-handed at those in the distance. The result was a resounding reverberation and clicking as Lynne's boule took Geoff's far away from the jack.

'Good shot!' Geoff said begrudgingly, giving her an exaggerated high fives, before both set off to collect their boules for the next round.

As she watched, Ros realized that one thing she hadn't taken into account when she had accepted Geoff's invitation was that you could not play boules encumbered in any way by a towel. You needed to move freely. Was this why Geoff had invited her? The opportunity to study her totally nude? Again that old paranoia. Yesterday she'd been quite happy having lunch with Geoff and Lynne. Today, what was the matter? She seemed to be less, rather than more, comfortable about her lack of clothes.

Ros thought that she'd just as soon not play. Could she slip away before being spotted? Too late. Lynne and Geoff had reached the other end and were now looking in her direction.

'Ros! Hi!' called Lynne. 'Come on over. We've got a spare set for you.'

Keeping her towel around her shoulders, Ros listened patiently as Geoff explained the rules. They were fairly self-explanatory after all. Just like bowls, you had to get the boule closest to the jack. Unlike bowls, you pitched the boule at the jack in order to overcome the irregular hard dirt surface.

When it came to her turn, Ros, with fast-beating heart, reluctantly cast aside her towel and released her first boule. It fell far short. In fact, the towel went almost as far as the boule.

'Now where you went wrong there,' said Geoff, 'was that you didn't gauge the force correctly. You're not holding the boule in the right way. Here, let me show you.'

Much to Ros's dismay, Geoff stepped behind her and put his arms around her and over her hands to demonstrate how she should hold the boule. She felt his breath on her neck. Fortunately that was all she felt as he was careful to avoid any other bodily contact.

'That's better,' said Geoff, stepping away and looking, she

hoped and presumed, at the boule in her hands. 'Try that and give it a bit more trajectory.'

Regaining her composure, Ros launched the boule into space. It landed way past the jack but was a great improvement. Despite herself she was rather pleased with the effort. And, after a while, she forgot that she was nude and began to enjoy herself.

The sun was bearable, filtered as it was by the trees, and she liked the exercise. It was also one of those mindless occupations which required little thinking, allowing your brain to free-wheel.

Ros thought this a nice quiet part of the resort. They had the boules pitch to themselves – probably too early and hot for any self-respecting Frenchman to play – and the only noise came from the thwack of tennis balls and occasional shouts and calls from the nearby tennis courts. Sounds from the pool could just be heard in the distance. Otherwise it was just birdsong and the click of boule on boule.

There were few people about, as well, with only the odd cyclist or pedestrian using the nearby path which circled the lake. Whilst she was standing next to Lynne, in between shots, a familiar figure came into view on that path, heading back towards the resort.

'Isn't that the barmaid girl?' asked Lynne, squinting some-what into the brightness of the path.

'Shareen? Yes it is.' said Ros. At that moment, Shareen spotted them and waved, uttering what sounded like 'G'd day!' before disappearing past the tennis courts.

'Must be getting ready to open the bar,' said Geoff, looking at his watch and licking his lips. Ros couldn't tell whether the latter action was brought on by the thought of a pint of lager or by Shareen pouring it. Probably both.

More boules were thrown. More tennis balls thwacked. Five

minutes or so later, another familiar figure followed in Shareen's footsteps away from the lake.

'Nick! Hi! Over here!' shouted Lynne.

Nick stopped and looked across. Doing a double-take at seeing them all there, he left the path and walked over.

Lynne offered her cheeks to be kissed, resting her hands briefly on Nick's shoulders as she did so, Ros noticed.

'Come and join us,' Lynne said, brightly. 'How are your boules?'

'Pardon?' said Nick. 'Oh, I see, no not very good actually.'

'Ros didn't know one end of a boule from the other but now she's becoming quite an expert,' Geoff said. 'Who knows, you may have hidden talent.'

'Perhaps some other time. I don't want to interrupt your game with my amateurish efforts. Anyway, I thought I'd go to the bar for a drink.'

'By some strange quirk of coincidence, Shareen just headed that way, said Ros. 'Only a few minutes' ago, in fact.'

'Yes, I bumped into her down at the jetty. You know, the far end of the lake,' Nick replied, defensively.

The jetty instantly conjured up for Ros vivid pictures of the boathouse and Jean-Luc's bedroom . . .

'Your friend was there, too. The one with the bandage,' said Nick, as if reading her mind.

'And how is the patient?' Ros enquired, in her best bedside voice.

'He seemed fine,' said Nick, looking at her, Ros thought, a bit suspiciously.

'Well, why don't we all meet for lunch?' Lynne suggested, looking at her watch. 'Say at twelve thirty – an hour's time?'

'Good idea,' said Geoff, putting his arm round Lynne and almost making her disappear from view in the process.

'Why not,' said Nick.

'And I might see you slightly earlier,' Geoff said to Nick, forefinger tapping side of nose with an exaggerated wink.

Ros watched Nick's departing back. She wondered if his meeting with Shareen had been accidental or planned. And she couldn't say she was thrilled about his visit to the bar on his own.

'Your shot,' called Geoff, and Ros turned with a smile, to continue to play the game.

17

As he made his way up the hot path to the bar, Nick's thoughts turned to Ros.

She had lied when she told him she'd casually come down to the lake. She had actually accompanied Jean-Luc. Sailing! She hated sailing. So Jean-Luc must have provided the attraction. But surely nothing untoward could have occurred?

Then again, how did Jean-Luc receive his injury? Falling out of bed? No, his imagination was working double overtime. Ros may have taken a passing fancy to Jean-Luc but he was sure she wouldn't go any further. Just like him and Shareen, really. Sure, he was sexually attracted to Shareen, just as any man would. Fortunately, women didn't look on men as sex objects, Nick reasoned.

Arriving at the bar, Nick found going inside brought on fewer feelings of panic than yesterday. His eyes rapidly adjusted to the gloom. Propped up on a stool was a figure in a cloud of smoke that could only be Garry. There was nobody serving.

Nick walked across to the bar, whisked his towel onto a stool and sat down by Garry's side.

'Mind if I join you?' Nick enquired.

'Looks as if you already 'ave.' Garry looked at him and laughed, starting a fit of coughing.

'Where is everyone?'

'Dunno. Hamish is usually around at this time. Might be out haggis-shooting for all I know. I hear it's open season.' Again that harsh laugh, more like a cough.

'And how do you get a drink?' Nick asked, noting the absence of Shareen or any bar staff.

'Just ask nicely and uncle Garry will get you one,' said Garry, struggling off his stool and walking round to the other side of the bar, beer belly proudly preceding him.

'You allowed to do that?' enquired Nick, 'After all, I don't need "receiving stolen goods" to be added to my impending charge sheet.'

'Na, Shareen left me in charge. She's gone off to get some cheese and onion crisps or something. Lager OK?' Garry expertly pulled Nick a half litre and plonked it in front of him. 'It's on the house, mate. I'll settle up with Shareen when she gets back.'

Garry refreshed his own glass and returned customer-side. 'Cheers. Your health, Nick.'

'Cheers.' Nick savoured the ice-cold beer. Now might be a good time to find out more about Garry. He looked a bit of a villain, but seemed a nice bloke. His mates probably described him as "salt of the earth". He wouldn't look out of place in the Queen Vic – provided he put some clothes on, of course. Before he could raise the subject, Garry saved him the trouble.

'How they doing on the murder enquiry?'

'Not too sure. I do know that the police inspector has moved in next door. "To keep an eye on me", is how he described it.'

'Yeah, he's a bit of a joker that one – or thinks he is.'

'Why do you say that?'

'He came over last night to question me and Sam. Asked what we knew about Giles, when we last saw him. All that stuff.'

'And what did you tell him?'

'Couldn't really tell him a lot. Giles seemed a nice enough bloke. Got on well with most of us. End of story.'

Garry hunched over his beer, seeming a bit more serious than his normal self. Perhaps, thought Nick, the interview with Lagardère had been a bit more uncomfortable than Garry was making out.

'But you didn't always see eye to eye, did you?' said Nick.

Garry turned to look at him. And it wasn't a pleasant look. 'Why do you say that, Nick?' he said, evenly.

Nick wondered whether to carry on and decided to risk it. 'Well, I know you normally got on quite well with him, and Sam and the kids liked him. But didn't you have a bit of a disagreement on the day he was murdered?'

'And who says so?' Again ice-cool.

This was a bit trickier to answer. Nick didn't want to drop Shareen in it for reporting the argument between Giles and Garry. But, on the other hand, he did need to know whether Garry could have had a motive for the murder.

He decided to fudge the issue. 'Er, well, some of the people in the bar saw you having a bit of an animated talk with Giles. Could have been about football for all I know.'

Garry seemed to relax a bit. He stared forward. 'Yeah. Well it wasn't about football, but he was a Spurs supporter. Bastard.' Garry chuckled to himself at this. Nick had no idea why. 'But no reason for murdering the man. Although some may disagree.' Another chuckle. Another pull on his cigarette. He seemed to have come to a decision. 'No. Just between you and me, Nick, it was about Mason and Gareth.'

Nick looked blankly at Garry.

Garry patiently elaborated. 'Mason and Gareth. My sons?'

'Oh right,' said Nick, wondering where this was going.

'You see, Giles really got on well with the kids. He was always in the pool playing with them. Like a big kid himself really. Never had any of his own. They enjoyed it. They're not too big to join in a bit of splashing and wrestling about. But, you know, you read in the papers about paedophiles and such and, well, I became a bit suspicious that Giles's intentions weren't totally, if you get my meaning, innocent.'

'Did you have any proof?'

'Na. Sam told me not to be so stupid. She said that if Giles was interfering with the boys they'd have let us know. But again, I just wanted to make sure.'

'So you asked him about it?'

'Yeah, that morning. The day before he died. I tried to put it as politely as possible and he went ballistic.'

'Being accused of being a paedophile is not something you'd take lightly.'

'I know. I was a bit heavy-handed. Nothing physical, you understand, but I suppose I was a bit abusive. Threatened that if I ever found he'd been messing about with my boys that, well, that . . .'

'You'd kill him?'

Garry ground out his cigarette in the ashtray. He turned to look at Nick. 'Yeah. Doesn't sound too good, does it. Less than 24 hours later he's brown bread. Gone.'

'Did you tell Lagardère about this?'

'You joking? Don't want to end up sharing a cell on Devil's Island with that bloke, what's is name?'

'Papillon?'

'Yeah, whatever. Swimming's not my strong point.' Garry

indicated this by taking a roll of his belly in his hand. Not an attractive sight.

Nick was inclined to believe Garry. Otherwise why admit the argument? Or perhaps it was a double bluff. Play the innocent. Then why hadn't he told Lagardère? Yes, the French legal system might be summed up as "guilty until proven innocent" but surely Lagardère could check out Garry's story, DNA and such. Maybe Garry did have something to hide after all.

Before Nick could muse further along these lines, a large box of snacks appeared in the doorway behind the bar, topped by a tiny head. Shareen had returned.

'That's all right guys. I can manage,' she said, sarcastically, as she lowered the carton to the floor. 'Christ, I could do with a drink myself after that.' She pulled herself a draught lager while Nick admired her breasts, slight rivulets of sweat between them, imagining she'd been doing something slightly more strenuous – preferably with him. Garry's voice fortunately interrupted that line of thought.

'I owe you for a couple, Shareen,' said Garry putting a five euro note on the counter.

'And while you're at it,' Nick put down a further note, 'could you make it the same again for all three of us.'

'Make that four,' a familiar voice added. Both Nick and Garry turned to find Geoff manoeuvring himself onto the vacant stool next to Nick. Nick suddenly felt as if he'd been trapped between two very large bookends.

'Hi Geoff,' said Nick, 'this is Garry . . .' Garry leaned across to shake Geoff's hand, '. . . and Shareen, who I think you've met before. Another beer please, Shareen.'

Shareen put the beers down in front of the three of them, and busied off to the far end of the bar, loading snacks from the box into a glass counter display, the men idly watching her as she did so. As if appraising a filly in the 3:15 at Catterick whilst sipping their beers in the grandstand bar.

Geoff was the first to break the silence. 'Now there's a sight you don't see in the Prince of Wales.' A reference to Nick and Geoff's local.

'Just as well, really, seeing as how Carole is eighteen stone and due for her bus pass,' replied Nick.

Garry cough-laughed and turned his attention to Geoff. 'You two know each other from back home, then?'

'Total coincidence meeting here. We live virtually next door to one another in Stoke Newington,' replied Geoff, sipping his drink.

'It's a bit poncey, isn't it? Stoke Newington? Don't get me wrong. Got nothing against the place. Only the people who live there. Present company excepted, of course,' Garry continued, smiling.

'Well, I always think it's like that sign you get in shops. You know, "You don't have to be mad to work here but it helps"? The Stokey equivalent is "You don't have to be vegetarian to live here . . ."' said Nick, thinking he'd gradually been recovering the power of joined-up speech. What's more he found himself only thinking about his naked state every other minute, instead of every nano-second.

'We live in Islington. Nice flat on an estate. Family's been there donkey's,' volunteered Garry.

'What do you do?' asked Geoff.

'You know. Bit of this. Bit of that. Used to be a tear-away in my youth. Was a scaffolder for a while and all. Got too much like hard work. I get by.' Garry appeared to draw a line under Geoff's enquiry, as if to say "don't ask me any more questions".

'Do you know what Giles did for a living? Before he retired, of course.' Nick took the opportunity to resume his "investigation".

'Didn't have much to say on that,' said Garry. 'Got the impression that it was something he thought people wouldn't approve of. Like a tax inspector or something. Kept well schtum about it.'

'Perhaps if we knew what he did, we might have a clue as to why he was killed – and who did it,' Nick mused.

'Here, why are you so interested in Giles?' Garry asked. 'If you're kosher, you never even met him – alive that is.'

Nick replied. 'Because if we can find out who murdered him, I can be a free man. Wear clothes again. And get on with our holiday – the authorized, clothed version.'

'So what's wrong with this place?' Geoff asked. 'What more could you want? Sun, healthy exercise, freedom.'

Nick thought Geoff was beginning to sound like Martin Pike. Perhaps that was an occupational hazard of being a naturist. You got really boring about it. 'Well, Geoff. It's free and yet it's not free. There are so many unwritten rules about the place. You know. When to dress. When not to dress. Where to look. Where not to look. No cameras. And so on. No offence. It's just that I wasn't cut out to be a towel-carrying member of the nudist party. That's all.'

Having finally bade farewell to Garry, and waved a reluctant goodbye to Shareen, Nick and Geoff stepped out into the midday glare. It seemed, if anything, hotter than yesterday, the sun beating down vertically from an azure blue sky.

Fortunately, their walk to the restaurant, with its cool awning, was a short one.

Unlike last night, the lunchtime clientele were nude. And in all shapes, sizes and shades of white. From factor 35-protected white skin through to mahogany brown. Nick noticed that he had not seen a black face since he'd been in Le Paradis. He wondered if naturism was popular amongst Afro-Caribbeans.

After all, they'd probably invented it in the first place. Or was that a racist thought? He must ask Pike about it. Then again . . .

Whilst the Naked Guide has little to say about naturism and the Afro-Caribbean — yet! — it does consider nudism and its acceptability through the early years of mankind:

Everyone knows the bible story of Adam and Eve and that nudity was man's original state until the temptation of serpent and apple. But what's less generally known is the prevalence of nudity in ancient civilisations.

As one website has it 'before the Judeo-Christian concept of body shame, most of the tropical and temperate world was one big naturist resort.'

Until loom technology emerged in Asia about 6,000 years ago, clothing wasn't an available option anywhere on the planet unless one was into fur — a bad choice on hot days in the tropics!

Modesty was presumably not a burning issue and the notion that human bodies were obscene could never have been imagined.

Public nudity was common in ancient Egypt. Students in Greece exercised and received instruction whilst unclad. In ancient Greece, 'gymnos' or naked, were how the young athletes competed. And did so until 393 AD when the Christian emperor banned the Olympic Games because he considered them pagan.

Romans wore clothing as necessary or for social functions, but sports and bathing were openly enjoyed while naked.

Ascetics in ancient India practiced nudity as part of their quest for simplicity, with Hindu Gymnosophists (literally 'naked philosophers') using nudity as part of their spiritual practice.

Even certain Christian sects from the second to the fifteenth century practiced public nudity.

Public nude bathing was also common on the beaches of Britain by the 1840s, before Victorian repression clamped down.

And in modern times, the Japanese practiced nude communal bathing until not so many years ago.

It is only now that re-acceptance of social nudity is becoming more widespread. It's likely the time will come when nakedness will be as commonplace as it was in the earliest days of mankind.

Geoff found an empty table, 'towelled' his chair and lowered himself into it. Nick took his place beside him so both had a good view over the lake. There was no sign of Lynne or Ros.

'Wherever they've got to, it's no reason to waste valuable drinking time. What do you say to a carafe of rosé?' Geoff suggested, and without waiting for a reply from Nick, passed on the order to a passing waitress – and in passable French. Although you didn't need much French to order a carafe of rosé, thought Nick.

When it arrived, Geoff did the pouring and helped himself to bread from the accompanying basket.

Geoff toasted Nick. 'Santé!' And then settled back, nibbling contentedly on his bread, and slurping his wine.

Nick had never been really close to Geoff. Sure, they'd been down the pub together, even flung the odd arrow at the dartboard, but never bosom buddies. Geoff was slightly pedantic, a bit of a plodder really, and neither the years nor the pints of bitter had been kind to his waistline.

Nick wondered what Lynne saw in him. You could never tell in any relationship. What did the Chinese say? "Marriage is a closed box." The outsider had no idea what went on. For all Nick knew, Geoff was a demon in the bedroom. But he rather doubted it.

'Here they are,' said Geoff, pointing at two figures making their way from the pool area towards them.

Nick followed Geoff's finger. The women were chatting away, seemingly oblivious to the fact that both were totally nude. Ros appeared to have re-gained some of her confidence, as she now had her towel over one shoulder. Lynne just had a beach bag over hers.

Nick couldn't help but notice the contrast between the thin, almost skinny, physique of Lynne and Ros's fuller, curvier, figure. Both very attractive in their own way.

Geoff partially stood up and waved at them. 'Over here!' he cried, in a voice loud enough to distract a nearby Frenchman from the act of raising an unidentifiable piece of lobster to his mouth. Something he didn't seem too amused about.

Lynne bent down to kiss Nick on both cheeks in greeting. And, in doing so, brushed one of her nipples against his chest. If it was accidental, it still felt good. As she sat down, she looked at him as if to gauge the effect. Nick pretended not to notice, simply raising his glass of rosé to his lips. Lynne looked none too pleased at being ignored.

'What kept you?' Geoff enquired amiably.

'It was so hot we decided to go for a swim,' said Lynne.

'No aquarobics?' Nick enquired innocently of Lynne.

She looked puzzled. 'No. Just a swim.'

Ros shot him an unfriendly look, before explaining to Lynne. 'I think he's referring to Jean-Luc.'

'Oh, he's gorgeous, isn't he?' Lynne continued. 'If I was a few years younger . . .' Geoff looked sulky. '. . . and, of course, if I wasn't married to Geoff . . .' Lynne turned to him and put her arm on his, leaving the sentence unfinished.

Hastily, Ros changed the subject. 'Let's order. I'm starving.'

Lunch progressed smoothly — much as dinner had last night. Salades were crunched. Omelettes consumed. Frites nibbled. Vin drunk. Small talk talked.

Over coffee, conversation turned to murder. It was Geoff

who raised the subject. 'Wonder how the gendarmes are getting on with finding that chap's killer?'

'Wish they'd get a move on,' Nick said. 'An early arrest would be welcome news.'

'Unless it was you that was arrested,' added Geoff, rather unnecessarily, thought Nick.

Lynne decided to give the gathering the benefit of her theory about the murder. 'Has anyone considered that it might have been a crime of passion? Carried out instantly and instinctively? Totally unpremeditated? It may well have been that he annoyed someone in the resort and that person had, well, simply lashed out? Happens.'

Lynne delivered this speech with her ''Hey, I'm a therapist that knows about these things'' serious air. An air slightly at odds with her sitting in a restaurant stark naked. Not that Nick was complaining, you understand.

'Must have been some huge irritation for someone to batter him to death,' Ros added.

Nick wondered whether he should mention his conversation with Garry on the topic. Paedophilia could count as a ''huge irritation''. He decided not to.

'I was talking to a woman, yesterday who told me she thought Giles worked for the Government — ''something hush-hush'' were her words,' Ros continued, hoping Nick wouldn't enquire where she had met this woman.

Instead Lynne asked, 'Do we know her?'

'Her name is Camilla and yes, before you ask, her husband's called Charles,' said Ros. She continued before Geoff could put in his two penn'orth. 'Those two were probably the last to see Giles alive.'

Lynne leaned forward, not doing a lot for Nick's already high blood pressure. 'Really! Then how come they're not prime suspects?'

'We were going to mention it to Lagardère, but . . .' Nick actually couldn't remember why he hadn't. Might have had something to do with trying to cover his arse – in more senses than one – when he'd spoken to the inspector this morning.

'I think you should,' said Geoff. 'At least it might take the pressure off you – for the time being.'

Nick didn't like the addition of "for the time being" at the end of Geoff's comment. 'It seems a bit sneaky, doesn't it? And they could be totally innocent.'

'If they're innocent, then they've got nothing to worry about,' said Lynne. 'Let them sort it out.'

Nick relented. 'OK. Next time I see Lagardère I'll mention it. He may already know, of course. He doesn't give much away.'

So intent were they in discussing the proposed course of action that they didn't spot a figure appear at their table. Nick noticed the smell first. Nina Ricci, if he wasn't mistaken. A very distinctive perfume. He turned, and there by his elbow was a middle-aged, very brown woman in designer sunglasses.

The expensive perfume was accessorised with many thousands of pounds of necklaces, bracelets and rings. What she was wearing was worth more than a whole wardrobe of designer label clothes, thought Nick.

The woman was looking at Ros, who eventually noticed her. 'Oh, hello!' Ros flushed slightly, 'We were just talking about you.'

Camilla, for it was she, smiled tightly. 'Nothing detrimental, I hope?'

A little flustered, Ros smiled back. 'No. We were just discussing the murder. Oh, sorry this is Nick my partner. Geoff and Lynne. Camilla.'

'Nice to meet you all.'

'Would you like to join us. We're just going to have another coffee,' said Geoff, pulling over a chair from an adjacent vacant table and shifting his own chair to make room.

'I couldn't possibly. Oh, all right,' Camilla said, putting a very expensive looking silk wrap down on the plastic chair before resting her ample rear.

Nick wondered how long she'd been standing there. He was pretty sure she hadn't been present when they were talking about shopping her and Charles to the gendarmes.

'It really is a dreadful business,' Camilla continued, as Geoff ordered more coffees. 'He was a lovely man. Sadly missed. And nobody with a clue as to his killer.'

You might have some idea, thought Nick. Or your husband.

'Anyway, the reason I came over to the table was that I saw Ros here. Recognized her from the sailing lesson yesterday . . .'

Nick glanced over at Ros who avoided eye contact.

'. . . and thought she might like to come to a celebration we're having tonight. The celebration of a life. The life of Giles Curtis.'

'You mean a wake?' Geoff corrected her.

'If you must call it that. I prefer to remember Giles for the charming person he was,' Camilla continued. 'We are going to have a barbecue. Nothing too elaborate. Please do say you'll come. All of you are very welcome.'

The thought of half-cooked sausages, charred hamburgers and choking smoke, which always seemed to blow in the direction of where he was standing, didn't seem that appealing to Nick. Before he could turn down the invitation, Geoff accepted for all of them. How come in this place he never got the chance to do what he wanted? Every decision was made by someone else.

'Love to come. Even though we didn't know the man, we'll raise a glass to his memory.'

Too late to do anything else other than follow Geoff's lead, everyone concurred and muttered little acceptance noises: 'Love to', 'Be delighted' and, from Nick, 'OK'.

'You'll be in good company. I've invited all those who knew Giles. It should be quite an occasion,' said Camilla.

Geoff, always the practical one, particularly when free food was on offer, asked 'Where exactly is it going to take place? And when?'

Camilla finished her coffee and reached into a large Dior bag for some euros, presumably to pay, which Geoff waved away. 'Oh, thank you so much. Our place is in Avenue E. Just look for the Daimler outside.' She got up. 'See you about eight? Don't bother bringing any wine or beer or anything. Charles has an extensive stock.'

With this she wrapped the silk round her waist and tottered off on heels that were slightly too high for the terrain.

'Better hold off telling Lagardère for a while, otherwise there'll be no party,' said Geoff smiling. Which made Nick doubly determined to spill the beans on Camilla and Charles as soon as he could.

It was gone three o'clock by the time they left the restaurant. Bidding farewell to Geoff and Lynne – a chaste kiss and no nipple contact on this occasion, as if Lynne was annoyed that Nick had paid her no attention the first time – Nick and Ros set off side-by-side back to their cabin, in a not very companionable silence.

The resort was in similarly quiet mood. It was almost as if someone had released a cloud of nerve gas over Le Paradis. As they passed the various caravans and tents, Nick could see immobile people everywhere. Bodies lay on loungers, in hammocks, on air mattresses, slumped in chairs, under trees and under awnings. Suffering the effects of a good lunch and thirty-plus degree heat. Who knows, some of them could even be new victims of the murderer, thought Nick.

Reaching the cabin, they went inside. Then it began.

Ros put her bag down and went into the bedroom. Nick divested himself of his towel and helped himself to a welcoming draft of water from a bottle in the fridge.

'God it's hot,' he called into the bedroom.

'Come in here. It's slightly cooler with the window open,' Ros called from the other room.

Nick walked through the beads into the bedroom and discovered Ros lying face downwards on the bed, head turned towards him wearing a smile and not a lot else. Well, nothing else, actually. 'Can I interest you in anything, sir?'

Now, normally, the sight of Ros lying on a bed in the nude would have indeed generated a great deal of interest in Nick. It hadn't been that common a sight back home in recent months, but he remembered past times when it had. Here in Le Paradis, though, it failed to raise much, if any, movement.

He didn't know what it was. The heat, maybe. Perhaps it was the fact that he'd seen Ros nude the whole of the past day or so. Not to mention the hundreds of nude bodies around the place wherever you looked. And – this was a scary thought – maybe he was getting immune to the sight of naked female bodies.

Suppose it was like one of those allergies that come on in life? You know. People suddenly get allergic to wheat or dairy products. Maybe he'd become allergic to nude women. No, that couldn't be the case, thought Nick, remembering Shareen. But even that had failed to raise interest in a certain part of his anatomy, he remembered.

'Come on sweetheart. Come and lie next to me,' said Ros in a voice she reserved for seduction.

'Er, I'm not really in the mood.'

'Well, come over here and we'll see if we can't do something about that,' Ros said, rolling over onto her back and putting her arms behind her head in a fair approximation of a Goya 'woman on sofa' painting, albeit a couple of stone lighter.

Even this didn't seem to work for him. Whilst Nick's brain told him that Ros looked very desirable in this position, his heart wasn't in it. 'I'd rather not.'

'Why not?' Ros raised herself on one arm to look at him more closely.

'No reason. I just don't feel like it. That's all.'

'But it's been weeks since the last time. Come on. I'll do all the work. All you have to do is lie back and think of England.'

'Perhaps later.' Nick searched around for a plausible excuse. 'I don't feel that good. Must be the heat.'

'Please, don't insult my intelligence with the "I've got a headache" excuse,' said Ros, now sitting upright and looking none too pleased.

Oh no, thought Nick. His Ros barometer sensed a storm brewing. They didn't often quarrel. Mainly due to the fact that Nick would do all he could to avoid confrontation. Which, of course, practically guaranteed an argument, as Ros felt he wasn't listening and was avoiding her complaints and needs.

Attempting to avert the inevitable, Nick went over to the bed and tried to put his arm round Ros's shoulder to placate her. She shrugged it away.

'Get off! I wouldn't like to inconvenience you in any way. I'm sorry it's too much trouble to make love to me.'

'It's not that, it's just, well . . .'

'Well what? Don't you fancy me anymore?'

'Of course I do.'

'Well you've got a very funny way of showing it.' Ros seemed to be slightly calmer. But that wasn't necessarily a good sign. She didn't particularly relish a fight but sometimes Nick could be so, what were the words she was searching for, oh yes – utterly fucking maddening.

'Look, it's just been a very worrying time for me. The stress of the situation. The murder. I'm sure it'll be all right when we get out of here,' said Nick, injecting just enough reassuring tone, he thought, into the statement.

Unfortunately it didn't work.

'But that could be days' away. I want sex and I want it now,' Ros almost frightened herself at her forthrightness.

Unlike his normal persona, which he felt he'd left outside the gates of Le Paradis, along with his clothes, Nick actually now found himself engaging in the argument. He couldn't stop himself from childishly saying 'Well maybe a certain French teenager might oblige. It seems that you've spent a great deal of time with him already.'

Reddest rag to reddest rag-hating bull. Ros suddenly stood to confront him, so quickly that Nick inadvertently stepped backwards. 'If you're referring to Jean-Luc, he's not a teenager and I haven't been doing anything other than helping dress his wound.'

'Yes,' said Nick, 'and I saw where that wound is. High up on his thigh. Enjoyed dressing that did you. Pity it wasn't a bit higher.'

'Now you are being absolutely infantile,' Ros replied, although flushing at the thought of said French thigh.

Nick knew Ros was right but couldn't resist charging on. 'If it's all so innocent, how come you told me you'd just bumped into him yesterday at the boathouse? I know you went down there with him from the pool.'

Ros suddenly felt on the defensive. It was unusual to have this sort of argument with Nick. Usually it would be game, set and match to Ros by now. By default. With Nick either walking away, shutting up or uttering placatory noises. Not this time. What had got into him?

Feeling slightly guilty – but hey, what reason is that to stop an argument – she resumed her attack. 'Only because I was bored and you were asleep in here having been boozing with that Aussie slut.'

Nick stood his ground and they were now close to one another, not quite shouting but none too quiet either. 'First of all, I was not boozing with her. She was serving the drinks. It is what a bargirl does, by the way. And second, Shareen is not an "Aussie slut". She's highly intelligent.'

'Oh yes?' said Ros. 'Why, has she just managed to work out how much change to give for two litres of lager from a ten euro note?' Good line, she thought.

'If you must know she's a qualified psychotherapist,' said Nick, bending the truth slightly. 'She's just doing this as a getting round Europe job.'

'Well, it certainly seems she's got round you.'

'What's that meant to mean?' said Nick, slightly set on the defensive.

'I saw you following her skinny arse up from the direction of the boathouse this morning. What were you doing down there, eh?' Ros liked this promising line of attack. It also deflected Nick's attention from Jean-Luc.

'It was all totally innocent. I took a walk and she happened to be down there.'

'Little out of her way, wasn't it?' Ros said, taking the offensive.

This stopped Nick momentarily. Was it out of her way? Come to think of it, he'd assumed Shareen lived somewhere up near the reception area in the staff block he'd spotted. What was she doing down there first thing in the morning? Just taking a walk like himself, perhaps.

'Perhaps she was just taking a walk like me. Perfectly innocent. Enjoying the view.' Even to Nick it didn't sound too convincing.

Ros took this brief lull in the argument to get up and go to the dressing table. She felt a vigorous hair-brushing coming on. She stared into the mirror at Nick, standing there looking slightly bemused. Ros took the opportunity to press her advantage. She couldn't resist it.

'If you're too stressed, tired or ill to do anything, why should I be concerned about you and the Aussie slut.' Ros looked into the mirror to see what effect these words would have on Nick. He rarely got red mist angry. And never ever used physical violence. At this moment he seemed at a loss for words.

In fact, Nick was wondering how he'd got this far down an argument. In one way, he'd achieved his objective of deflecting attention from his involuntary inability to service Ros. In another, they'd now strayed onto dangerous territory. What did they say? Never criticise a man's sex drive – or his driving. Nick suddenly felt wearied by the argument.

'If that's what you think, well, then you've got absolutely nothing to worry about, have you? So please, let's drop the subject,' said Nick.

Ros, however, was now in true fighting fettle. She still felt randy. More than ever. Nothing like a good argument to raise blood pressure and stir emotions. She turned from the dressing table to look at Nick. 'So what are you going to do?'

'Sorry? What do you mean?' Nick thought this was a further reference to Shareen. It wasn't.

'Are we going to have sex? Here? Now? Or not?'

If Nick had not felt in the mood before, the argument had done zero for his libido. If it were possible, it had now reached the lowest level since records began.

Ros, took his non-reply as a "no". She put the hairbrush down and moved swiftly to the beaded divide. 'Right. Well, I'm not staying here with you all afternoon. I'll leave you to convalesce. There are some paracetamol in the bathroom. Why don't you take a handful. Don't stint yourself. As for me, I'm going out. And I may be some time.'

With these parting words, she swept out of the cabin, pausing only to pick up her beach bag, and slamming the door after her. Well, on these occasions it was obligatory, wasn't it?

18

Ros stormed down off the verandah and had walked a brisk fifty yards along Avenue A, when she came to a sudden halt. For one thing, she'd slightly calmed down. For another, she was sweating – from split hair-end to painted toenail. My God, it was absolutely boiling. Four o'clock in the afternoon and still around thirty five degrees.

Ros used her towel for a quick mop down and, reluctantly, put it in her beach bag. It was just too hot to have anywhere near her skin. Instead, she sheltered behind her sunglasses, which strangely made her a little bit more confident to wander around nude.

She continued, more slowly this time, under the shade of the trees, towards the pool. As she walked, Ros pondered on the scene that had just played itself out.

Apart from the fact that it was most unlike Nick to argue, the thing that worried her above everything else was simply this. Did Nick still fancy her?

Be logical about it, thought Ros. We've been together now, what, six years. It's inevitable that partners' lust levels would decline. She often came back from the surgery dead beat, wanting only to sit with her feet up watching bad television – 'crapwatch', Nick called it – before retiring in comforting flannel night-dress to sleep. Same with Nick – well, without the flannel night-dress, obviously.

On the other side of the argument, she did look damn sexy. Tanned and lying naked on the bed. Any man would have literally jumped at the chance. But it didn't arouse any interest in Nick. She'd been able to check the evidence with her own eyes. Add to this the fact that it had been weeks since they'd last had sex and it was even more inexplicable.

Let's try to be fair to Nick, she thought charitably. Yes, he has had a stressful couple of days. It's not every holiday you're suspected of murder. Or parted from all your clothes for prolonged periods. Or appear naked in a restaurant when virtually everyone else is clothed. She could see that this could pre-occupy his thoughts and maybe put him off sex.

But what about Shareen? He seemed keen enough to hang around her. With his tongue hanging out. And another part of his anatomy as well, she reminded herself. Surely he couldn't actually be interested in her sexually? Could he?

Even if Nick did fancy Shareen, would she fancy him? She was a fraction of his age. By Shareen's standards, Nick was almost middle-aged. Ros hastily skated over in her mind that this description could easily be applied to her by Jean-Luc. Good-looking though Nick undoubtedly was, he was no spring chicken. But who knew with women? He might appeal to Shareen as a father figure.

At the word "father", Ros's thoughts took a further turn. Maybe that was it. Perhaps the underlying problem was babies. After all, it was the unresolved issue between them. Perhaps in

Nick's mind "sex" meant the outside possibility of "baby" which meant 'responsibility' and ultimately 'trapped'. This would explain the marked reluctance to indulge as often as he used to, or she would have liked, over the past few months. Ridiculous really, because Ros would never fall pregnant and present Nick with a "fait accompli". Maybe it was just the thought that put him off.

She sighed to herself. Like their previously concealed bodies, they really needed to get this problem out in the open. Regardless of where it might lead. But now was just not the time. Once they'd reached Phillip and Kathy's and relaxed some, perhaps.

This chain of thought had taken Ros down the Champs-Elysses as far as the Peripherique. Ahead of her the lake glittered in the sunlight. Beyond that she could see the boat-house. She looked at her watch. About three hours to kill before having to get back for the barbecue-wake. Why not take a stroll around the lake? It was something to do. And a pleasant walk.

Who knows, maybe she would bump into Jean-Luc. There was a very good chance that he would be in or around the boathouse. Would he have finished his lessons for the day? Perhaps she'd offer to look at his wound. Just in case it had gone septic. Change the dressing. And, maybe, while away the time by having a brief chat about this, that and the other.

Her feet automatically left the hard surface of the Peripherique and set off across the parched grass towards the lake. If she did meet Jean-Luc, two questions occurred to her.

Question One. Would Jean-Luc fancy her? Well, he was a good bit younger, but, hey he was a man! If the opportunity for a quick one presented itself to most men, they'd take it. And he'd seemed fairly keen yesterday, once he'd recovered from the shock of the accident.

Question Two. And this was the big one. Could she be unfaithful to Nick? She never had been in all their time together. Sure, she'd been tempted. But she loved Nick. She didn't want to spoil their relationship. Which, she reminded herself, hadn't been that great of late. What harm could come from a "quickie" with Jean-Luc?

Well, quite a lot actually. For a start, if not AIDS, there was the risk of a sexually transmitted disease, which would take some explaining away even given her ability to blind with medical jargon and terminology.

Next, there was the not inconsiderable risk of pregnancy. Ros had prescribed herself off the pill a year or so ago. For health reasons, she told Nick. Suppose a brief liaison brought forth a dark-haired little baby? Well, it could be Nick's — always assuming that sometime in the very near future he deigned to have sex with her.

Then again, there was the real risk of being caught. She was pretty sure he'd not forgive her. But how would he find out? She wouldn't ever tell him. Of course, Jean-Luc might ''fess up'. But she doubted it. Self-preservation made it unlikely that one man would tell another that he'd screwed his partner. And at the moment, Nick was back in the cabin sulking. But was he? Could he have worked out where she was going? Perhaps he'd been following her? She'd been so deep in thought that she wouldn't have noticed.

Ros looked anxiously back over her shoulder. She'd now travelled a fair way round the lake. There was nobody on the path behind her. She relaxed. Only for an instant. Suppose he'd waited in the cabin for ten minutes, say, and *then* set off after her, figuring she'd gone to the boathouse. He would arrive and catch them both at it.

Hang on, thought Ros. Catch them at what? She was only going over to view Jean-Luc's wound after all. Maybe change his dressing. Then why did she feel all hot and bothered? Must be the weather.

The boathouse looked deserted. No eager pupils. No Dutch girl. No Charles and Camilla. Nobody. Except the two fishing gnomes at the end of the jetty. Had they moved since yesterday, Ros wondered?

She hesitated at the door, smelling the heady mix of varnish, rotting wood, dry earth and other odours she couldn't quite identify. Apart from the flies buzzing under the eaves, it was quiet inside the boathouse. And, after the bright sun outside, very dark.

She couldn't see much until she took off her sunglasses. Her eyes slowly adjusted to the light. Her heart beat more quickly. Now was the time to stay or go. She decided to go.

'Hello!' she called into the interior. No reply. There really was nobody around. She felt disappointed and, if she was being totally honest, slightly relieved. She replaced her sunglasses and left the boathouse.

As she was about to set off on the long hot trek back, she heard the sound of running water. It seemed to be coming from the back of the building. A concrete path ran round the perimeter of the boathouse. Ros set off to investigate. If it was water, she could certainly do with a drink.

She turned the corner and there, at the back, was the source of the noise. A shower head set into the wall above a shower tray. Open to the elements. And below it, lathering shampoo into his hair, Jean-Luc. He was facing away from her but she recognized, not only his rear, but the rather wet dressing on the back of his thigh. Not following doctor's orders.

Ros was at a loss as to what to do next. She didn't know whether to say anything. Or just leave. To save making a decision, and just for the want of anything else, she did what virtually any woman in her position would do. She stood and admired the view.

It was an intimate thing to be watching. A male stranger taking a shower. The sun catching the water droplets as they bounced off Jean-Luc's head, turned them into a halo of diamonds. Suddenly, pushing the hair back from his face, he turned and gave a slight start as he saw her standing there.

Shaking water from his face, he smiled at her and turned the shower off. 'Hi Ros. Lovely to see you. Could you pass me the towel.' Jean-Luc gestured to a hook on the wall to Ros's left, though he could well have reached it himself.

She handed it over. 'Thanks,' said Jean-Luc, and proceeded to dry himself. This was also a very intimate sight for Ros. She normally associated this sort of behaviour happening behind locked bathroom doors, not the great outdoors. And with a member of the opposite sex watching.

Jean-Luc finished drying and came over to Ros, giving her a peck on each kiss. Even though totally chaste and innocent, Ros felt even hotter than she had before.

He put the towel over the branch of a nearby tree to dry. Moving quite close to her, his dark eyes looking into hers, Jean-Luc asked, 'What brings you down here, Ros?

'Umm, I had some time to kill, so decided to take a walk. See how your wound is healing.'

'Oh that.' Jean-Luc turned his lithe tanned body slightly so he could look at the wound, enabling Ros to get a better look at him as he did so. 'It's fine. A bit sore, but . . .' he shrugged '. . . I'm sure it will be all right.'

'If you like, I can take a look at it. Make sure it's not infected. Change the dressing,' Ros said casually.

It must have been something in the tone of her voice – or her look – that Jean-Luc picked up on. 'Well, if it's not too much trouble . . .' Leaving the sentence unfinished.

'Not at all,' said Ros, sounding to herself very stiff, formal and British. 'I'll get the first aid box.'

They went inside the boathouse. It was stifling. Ros picked up the box and found Jean-Luc waiting for her at the foot of the stairs leading up to his room. He was waiting for her to go first. There was the outside chance that he was being polite and a gentleman. Ros doubted it. But it made her heart beat faster knowing that Jean-Luc was only a few steps behind her as she walked up the stairs. Enjoying an excellent view of her rear.

Light streamed in from open French windows, the light breeze from the lake made the curtains billow, making it much cooler than downstairs. Apart from that, the room was very much as it had been yesterday.

The sheets were still crumpled and, if she was being picky, a bit grubby. Unlike yesterday, Jean-Luc didn't seem to be so embarrassed about his surroundings. He was quite close and looking at her as if to say, "well you came over here, now it's your move".

Ros played for time. She wandered over to the dresser while Jean-Luc sat himself down on the bed, watching her. She idly picked up a CD case and looked at it. An unknown French singer. 'Is this good?' she asked Jean-Luc, holding it up to him.

'One of my favourites,' said Jean-Luc, still holding her in a gaze which, if she wasn't already naked, Ros would have described as the "undressed me with his eyes" look she'd experienced yesterday by the pool.

This was ridiculous! Let's dress the wound and get out of here! Ros suddenly became decisive. She put down the CD and moved across the room to where Jean-Luc was sitting.

Picking up and opening the first aid box, she metamorphosed from hapless female into efficient medic. 'Right! Now lie on your front, please, and let's see how that leg is healing.'

Jean-Luc smiled and shifted his feet from floor to bed. Lying there for a second looking at her before slowly turning over on his front. A movement which resulted in a veritable swarm, if that was the right word, of butterflies launching into Ros's stomach.

She removed the dressing with a sharp tug, making Jean-Luc wince slightly. 'How does it look?' asked Jean-Luc, peering over his shoulder at her.

Taking some disinfectant and a swab of cotton wool, she cleaned the wound again. It seemed to be healing nicely, with the beginnings of a scab forming. 'I can safely say you'll live.' Ros replied. It was an old line but one, perhaps, a Frenchman hadn't heard before.

She busied herself with applying the clean dressing and was so absorbed doing this she quite forgot where she was. It was almost as if she was back home in her surgery. 'There. Finished. But try not to get it wet. It doesn't help.'

As she smoothed down the last piece of tape on the dressing, inexplicably Ros's hand moved a few inches upwards and gently caressed Jean-Luc's buttock. My God! What had she done? In England you could be struck off the General Medical Register for doing that. But she wasn't in England. She was in France. Naked. In a bedroom. And with a nude young French patient who suddenly looked round at her to see what was happening.

'Ros?' Jean-Luc sounded serious, looking at her with his dark brown eyes.

'Erm?' Ros noticed that her hand was still resting on his buttock and pulled it away, although making no attempt to move from the side of the bed. Jean-Luc turned over and sat up. He took her hand and moved it gently up to his mouth to kiss, first the back, then the palm and finally the wrist.

Ros closed her eyes and felt a bit giddy. That heat again. She sat down on the side of the bed next to Jean-Luc facing away from him, just until she felt capable of standing again, you understand.

As she had shown no sign of objecting so far, he gently caressed her back with his hand, finally reaching her neck which he massaged gently. Ros leant her head back, eyes closed. That felt extremely good. Nothing wrong with somebody massaging your neck, after all. Quite innocent. Even though it was making her feel slightly moist below.

Meeting no resistance so far, Jean-Luc pressed on. He lifted the hair from the back of Ros's neck and put his lips against her skin. Ros gave a little shiver as he did so and noticed that her nipples appeared to be hardening. Must be the breeze from the open window.

Jean-Luc put his hand around Ros's shoulder and gently turned her towards him. He looked into her eyes and moved in to kiss her lips. Ros closed her eyes. OK. Well just a kiss, that's not too bad is it. The trouble was that it was rather a long and deep kiss, nothing wrong with that in itself, except that, in the process, her breasts pressed up against Jean-Luc. She could feel his hairy chest against her hard nipples.

She surfaced for air, moving away from him and looking into his eyes again. All right, she thought, just one more kiss. And moved in again. This time she felt Jean-Luc's right hand, previously stationed round her back, move under her arm and towards her left breast. Now that was going a bit far, thought Ros. And made not the slightest attempt to prevent Jean-Luc cupping her nipple in his hand and then squeezing it gently. She did however allow herself to moan slightly, during a gap in their kissing.

Still holding her left breast in his hand, Jean-Luc's lips slid off Ros's and round to the right hand side of her neck. She involuntarily moved her head back and sideways, eyes closed. He then moved his lips downwards until they were gently kissing her right breast, and heading towards her nipple. She must stop him right there, she thought, wrapping both arms around his head and kissing his hair.

Jean-Luc took her nipple gently between his lips and licked it with his tongue. Well this is going a bit far, thought Ros, but it still is only a bit of innocent petting. Just like you used to do as a teenager. It's not really sex after all.

Jean-Luc was sitting up on the bed whilst engaged in this activity while Ros was still sitting turned towards him on the side of the bed. She hadn't moved much since she sat down. Apart, that is, from returning his embraces.

Jean-Luc now moved his hand away from her breast and put both arms behind Ros's back, pulling her towards his head which now nestled between both breasts, well-placed to lick, kiss and nuzzle each of them in turn. Which, unsurprisingly, he proceeded to do. This is still OK, thought Ros. Look, I've got my feet on the floor, as the censor used to insist on in old Hollywood films. Nothing wrong in that.

At this point Jean-Luc raised his face from her bosoms and kissed her again. This time he turned his body more towards her and suddenly she found herself flat on her back, but again with only the top half of Jean-Luc pressed against her. It was a bit uncomfortable to have her feet still on the floor so she moved them onto the bed. That was a bit more comfortable, she thought, as she put her arms around Jean-Luc's hard back, feeling the taut muscles. And returning his kisses. Well, he was making an effort to kiss her. It was only polite to respond. Anyway, she reasoned, even though I'm now lying on the bed on my back, all the action is still only above the waist.

No sooner than she'd had this thought, than Jean-Luc broke off his kissing and once again headed south towards her breasts. Stopping briefly to give them a quick nuzzle, he continued his journey, licking and kissing her abdomen. She must stop him there. This was really getting beyond a joke, thought Ros, arching her body slightly towards his lips and parting her legs just a little.

Jean-Luc's head had reached his final destination. Ros wondered from a comparison point of view how a Frenchman might carry out this operation. It would be interesting to find out. She did. Using only his lips and tongue, he licked and kissed her. At this point, Ros's only thought was 'Yes! Yes! Yes!' Well, she was only human after all, wasn't she?

Jean-Luc raised his head from his work and shifted back up the bed to kiss Ros again. This time, he was on top and she could feel a very hard muscle against her, which she thought she'd investigate with her hand. Living up to her expectations when she'd first seen Jean-Luc nude and flaccid, the member she had in her hand could only be described as substantial.

Taking this as a signal, Jean-Luc moved his own hand down to take his organ. My God! He was going to put it inside her!

'Wait! Stop!' Ros cried, pushing Jean-Luc off and raising herself on one hand.

Jean-Luc looked shocked and dismayed. Surely she wasn't going to stop him now, after all the hard work he'd put in.

'What's the matter,' asked Jean-Luc gently, whilst aware of his throbbing erection, seemingly with a life of its own.

'Durex!' said Ros.

'Durex? What is that?'

'You know. Durex.' Ros searched around for another word he might understand. 'Condom!'

'Condom?' This was even more mysterious. Why was she talking to him about a town in France?

'No, oh, what's the word. That's it. Preservatif!' said Ros, although it sounded like something you put into canned food.

The centime dropped. 'Ah preservatif. Certainement.' Jean-

Luc lapsed into French, relieved that she wasn't going to pull out, so to speak, at this late stage in the proceedings.

He swung his legs over the side of the bed and opened the bedside cabinet drawer. Ros, propped up on one hand, looked over his shoulder to admire his organ. Whilst doing so, her eyes were drawn to the fair number of preservatifs in the drawer. Many of the packets, she also noted, were empty which was why Jean-Luc was rummaging around for a full one.

Jean-Luc suddenly stopped, mid-rummage. Dead still. He turned his head towards the door as if listening.

'What's the . . .' Ros began, but stopped when Jean-Luc raised his finger to his mouth in a "shhh" gesture.

Ros listened. Yes, now she could hear it. There was someone walking around downstairs. Shit!!!!! It could only be Nick!

He must have figured out that she might be coming over to see Jean-Luc and had decided to check for himself. What the fuck was she going to do? Don't panic. After all, perhaps he would find nobody there and go away. He wouldn't possibly come up here to a stranger's room. They heard a creak on the stairs as someone slowly and carefully started to climb towards the bedroom.

Jean-Luc looked like a startled Bambi who'd just seen his mother shot by hunters. He seemed incapable of doing anything but sit there, with a somewhat reduced in size, but still substantial, hard-on for Nick to admire when he arrived.

Sheer panic made Ros act. She leapt to her feet and went round the side of the bed to Jean-Luc. 'Quick!' she hissed quietly. 'Lie on the bed. Face down.'

Still in a daze, Jean-Luc swung himself back onto the bed and onto his front. Erection now safe from prying eyes, Ros quickly ran her hand through her hair, to give it the semblance of tidiness, and ripped the fresh dressing from Jean-Luc's thigh. So violent was her action that Jean-Luc cried out in pain. 'Ouch! Merde!'

'Jean-Luc is that you?' called a voice from the stairs.

Ros nearly fainted. With relief. The voice was not Nick's but that of a woman. She picked up the first aid box, opened it and had just taken out a fresh piece of cotton wool when the door opened and in walked Shareen.

Shareen was slightly taken aback to find a naked Ros sitting on Jean-Luc's bed and Jean-Luc lying there with his arse in the air. The way she actually expressed it was 'What the fuck's going on here?'

In any other place, anywhere in the world, someone catching a man and a woman nude in a bedroom together would mean that particular couple were preparing for, having or recovering from having, sex. This was not necessarily the case in a naturist resort. In Le Paradis, Ros was fast discovering, nudity only occasionally equated with sex. Not often enough, she was beginning to think.

'Hi Shareen!' said Jean-Luc, regaining the power of speech and thinking that, if he played his cards right, he could still escape from this situation with his balls intact. 'Ros dropped by to change my dressing. How does it look?' The last question aimed at Ros, not Shareen.

'Not too bad. Healing nicely,' said Ros, remarkably calmly she thought, although inside, her heart was pounding. It had been a close call.

As she turned to get some antiseptic, her heart rate increased still further. In the rush to get Jean-Luc back on his front, she'd forgotten about the bedside cabinet drawer. She noticed it was still half open, with preservatif packets on full display if Shareen happened to look that way.

Ros shifted her position slightly on the bed to shield the drawer from Shareen's eyes. Fortunately, Shareen was more interested in looking at Jean-Luc. She stood, leaning against the door jamb, arms folded under what, even Ros had to admit, were very shapely breasts.

She looked mightily suspicious and seemed to be weighing up what to think and do. Was this as innocent as it appeared? Or were these two up to no good? The answer to these questions was right there in the room in the open drawer.

Ros thought quickly. 'Er, Shareen?' Shareen turned to face her. 'Do you think you could get me some water? I just want to wash the area round the wound.' Ros gambled on there being no water upstairs. And she was right.

'Sure,' said Shareen, a touch reluctantly, straightening up and unfolding her arms. 'How much do you need?'

'Just a cup will do fine. It's only a small area.'

'There's only cold water.'

'That'll be all right,' said Ros. Perfect bedside manner.

Shareen turned and left the room. Ros realized she'd been holding her breath and let it out with a long whoosh. Reaching behind her, she gently pushed the drawer closed. She didn't think they'd be needing the contents now, anyway.

Jean-Luc was looking at her but not speaking, thinking that on the one hand he'd probably blown his chance with Ros, but on the other that he should be grateful for Ros's presence of mind, which seemed to have allayed Shareen's suspicions – if only for the moment.

Now that it was no longer necessary to sit on the bed, Ros got up and walked over to the balcony, indicating to Jean-Luc that he should stay put.

Stepping outside, she realized how much she needed the breeze. Looking over at the table, she saw again the two glasses and joint stubs she had seen yesterday. Now she knew who Jean-Luc had been sharing them with. Shareen. She wondered how long they'd been an item. For as long as this summer season, she suspected. Shareen clearly knew her way around the boathouse. And around Jean-Luc.

Having washed and dressed Jean-Luc's wound – again – Ros bade them both farewell and left the boathouse. She was relieved to be outside in the now slightly cooler air.

It was only then that the full realisation of what had happened really hit her. What had she been thinking about? Hang on a minute, though. OK. She'd had a bit of slap and tickle with a French guy. What's wrong with that? A French guy who'd gone down on her, admittedly, but no real sex. She could say, as truthfully as Bill Clinton had been able to, that she'd had "no sex with that person". Although she'd come within an inch – well several substantial inches – of the deed, she'd emerged white as snow. Well, snow that had lain around in the gutter for a week or two.

It was a chastening walk back. She wasn't proud of what she'd done. She'd been tempted but that was it. End of story. Her next concern was Nick. Her main fear was that Shareen would mention to Nick that she'd found them both in Jean-Luc's bedroom. If Shareen *was* going to tell him, then Ros had better mention it first. But if Ros did tell him, he'd become even more suspicious – with some reason now, thought Ros guiltily.

She also wondered if Nick knew about Shareen and Jean-Luc? If he didn't – and she was sure he didn't – should Ros give him the information? That might put a stop to . . . to what? Surely nothing was going on between them. Not with Shareen going out with Jean-Luc. But who could tell? She actually lived with Nick, for Christ's sake, and nearly had sex with Jean-Luc. No, if Nick was going to find out that Shareen and Jean-Luc were sleeping with one another then Ros certainly wasn't going to give him the information. Let him find out, if he must.

Yes, Ros had a great deal to occupy her mind, on the long walk back from the boathouse.

19

That didn't go too well, thought Nick, just after Ros had rattled the insubstantial frame of the cabin as she stomped out. What on earth had got into her? As a doctor, she should know better than most that men can't always perform at the drop of a pair of knickers. There's no shame in that. When he got out of Le Paradis his libido would kick in again — always assuming they ever did get out.

Unusually for him, Nick decided, exactly as Ros had done earlier, that the only solution was a cup of tea. He put on the kettle and opened the cabin door to let some air in, idly looking out whilst waiting for the kettle to boil.

Nick had to admit to being a little shocked by Ros's outburst. Whilst they often had small disagreements, they never ever came to this. Maybe Ros was feeling the tension of being trapped here as much as he was.

But what was "here" he mused. Did it mean the physical boundaries of Le Paradis? Or the less obvious ones of their relationship? Come to think of it there were similarities.

At this moment most of the inmates of Le Paradis were under the impression that they could leave the resort any time they pleased. However, if they tried to get out they would soon discover they were actually prisoners. Until Lagardère saw fit to let them go, they were trapped, unable to escape.

In his relationship with Ros he felt free to go at any time. But was that freedom just as much an illusion for him as it currently was for the Le Paradis inmates? Sure, unlike them he could get beyond the "gates" of his relationship but then what? He'd be faced with the fear of the outside, the unknown.

Nick poured the water over his Lipton's teabag-on-a-string and gently swirled the spoon from side to side until the water started looking orange-ish.

Once outside, he'd be starting again. In the world of singles, dating and casual sex. Yes, he was free to leave but – like someone who'd been incarcerated a long while – he found the thought a bit frightening. Just like an old lag leaving prison, it could be a terrifying world out there in single freedom land.

And like the ex-con who immediately re-offends in order to get banged up again, what do new singles do? Immediately look for another relationship. A pattern of serial re-offending. Maybe it was far cosier and safer to be in a relationship, even if it wasn't always perfect. Then again, was anything ever perfect?

Nick sighed, hooked out the teabag, put it on the drainer and stirred some milk into his tea. It still looked a bit weak. He contemplated carrying the mug out onto the verandah, but that had inherent dangers. He might have to talk to Pike or Lagardère. So before venturing outside, he peeked round the door. No sign of either.

It was actually quite nice sitting on the verandah. Shaded from the sun and with a pleasant breeze, he almost began to feel his old self again. He wondered where Ros had gone. Probably to the pool, he suspected. Should he follow her and try to make up? No, that hadn't worked just now. He was sure she'd have got over it by the time she returned. Or hoped she would.

He supposed he could go down to the bar for a consoling glass of beer with Shareen. No. His heart wasn't in it. And to be truthful, he'd already drunk more than enough at lunchtime. With the promise of more drink ahead tonight he wanted to keep something of a clear head.

He looked at his watch. Still hours to go before he could get dressed for the barbecue. He presumed Ros would be back by then. Maybe now *was* the time to go and see Lagardère and tell him that Charles and Camilla were probably the last to see Giles Curtis alive.

Nick wondered if the inspector was in. He glanced over at the cabin. The door was closed, the windows shut. The last time he'd spoken to the inspector, Nick had the disadvantage of being nude. How to get round that and still look cool was the problem. But strangely, one that he seemed less worried about today than he had yesterday. Perhaps, just as he seemed to have developed an immunity to naked women, he was developing an immunity to public nudity.

He looked down at his lately under-employed tackle and didn't feel the urge to cover up – or the same panic at being naked he'd experienced yesterday. He began to think Lagardère had a point. You *could* get used to anything eventually.

Nick took another sip of comforting tea. It reminded him of home and, by association, Phillip and Kathy. He should try phoning them once more. They must be worried sick. He sighed. He seemed to be doing a lot of that recently.

Taking his mug indoors, he emerged with coins and phone number – although by now he almost knew it by heart – and set off in the direction of Reception.

*   *   *

The phone box was oppressively hot. He dialled the number. It rang and rang and . . . 'Allo?' Phillip's voice came on the line.

Nick was so surprised he nearly dropped the receiver. 'Phillip, it's Nick!'

'Nick! Where the hell are you?'

He heard Phillip's voice calling out, presumably to Kathy, 'It's Nick', although he couldn't catch her reply. 'We've been wondering what happened to you both. Thought you'd changed your mind. Got a better offer.'

'No, nothing like that. Well, I suppose you could say we've been unavoidably detained.'

'Detained? Where are you then?

'Not too far away from you, I think. We *are* in France.'

'Did you leave late? Have a last minute job? I know you freelancers. Any chance of earning some extra cash and you jump at it. Can't say I blame you, though,' Phillip continued jovially.

'No. We left on time but, as I said, we've been detained.'

'I don't understand. Detained by what? Car break down?'

'Well, er, initially, yes, but now we've been detained by the police, actually.' Nick said.

'Why, did you have an accident? Are you in jail?' Phillip sounded concerned.

'No accident but, yes, we are in a sort of jail.' He had to tell the full story at some time, so here goes. 'We're actually under, what you might call, house arrest. In a naturist resort.'

'Have you been on the piss? Arrest? Naturist resort? Come on!'

'No, unfortunately, Phillip, it's true,' although telling the facts to someone else made it sound even more far-fetched.

'Why are you under arrest? It couldn't have been for exposing yourself,' asked an increasingly sceptical Phillip.

'Much more serious than that. I'm suspected of having committed a murder?'

There was silence at the other end of the phone. He could hear, in the background, Phillip giving the story so far to Kathy.

'I don't believe all this. You'd better start from the beginning. If this is your idea of a joke . . .'

'If only it were,' sighed Nick. He gave Phillip a précis of the events of the past two days. Which took up most of his supply of coins. And resulted in him probably losing a couple of pounds' weight in sweat, even with the phone booth doors ajar.

Phillip listened attentively and when Nick had finished asked, 'Are they allowed to keep you there? You know, without charge or anything?'

It was a question that had occurred to Nick. He remembered Lagardère being vague about it when he'd asked him. 'I don't know. I'm no expert on French law.'

'I'll find out for you. We have a neighbour who's a retired advocate. We'll ask her.'

'Thanks.'

'Has the police inspector, what's 'is name, informed the British consulate or authorities that he's holding perhaps tens of British subjects against their will?'

'That's not strictly the case. I'm not even sure they know they're being held captive.'

'Well, you and Ros are and that's good enough for me. Where did you say this place is you're staying?'

Again, this was an excellent question. And one to which Nick had no answer. 'I'm not sure. The owner tells me it's about half hour from Perpignan.'

'Tell me what it's called again?'

'Le Paradis.'

'OK. We'll look up the telephone number and address on the minitel. And inform the local British consulate.'

Nick suddenly thought of all the others in Le Paradis. Not to mention himself and Ros. 'I appreciate the thought, Phillip, but I think it's best if you leave the consulate out of this.'

'Why?'

'Well, it's bound to generate a great deal of publicity. Get back to the British press. If the story gets out, well, it could be very embarrassing for us all. Just think of Ros, for instance, trapped in a nudist colony. She'd never hear the last of it from her patients.' Nor me from my clients. Let alone mates down the pub, thought Nick.

'I see what you mean. OK. We'll save that as a last resort. Do they allow visitors in this place?'

Nick's heart leapt. It was one thing having Phillip and Kathy see them with their swim-suits on. Quite another seeing them naked. And vice versa. 'I don't think so. I'm not sure the inspector wants anyone going out or coming in.'

'We'll find out. Leave it to us,' said Phillip. 'How can we reach you?'

'I expect you can leave a message at Reception – if you can find the number. Ask for Jack. He'll pass on any messages.'

'Apart from all this, how are you enjoying your holidays?' chuckled Phillip.

Nick walked back from Reception, buoyed up by his conversation with Phillip. At last, someone outside was trying to do something to sort out the situation. The *least* Nick could do was to try to do as much as possible himself to help the process along *inside* the resort. He resolved to go and find Lagardère.

It wasn't much of a search. Rounding the corner to Avenue A he saw that a clothed Lagardère was sitting on his verandah. Oh, no! He was talking to Martin Pike.

Nick had to walk past the cabin to get to his, so there was nothing for it but to acknowledge their presence. He decided to wait for Pike to go before talking to Lagardère. That plan didn't work either.

Lagardère spotted Nick and beckoned to him. 'Nick! Hi! Come on over. I've got some news which may interest you.' Lagardère seemed to think it all right to address Nick by his Christian name now. Was that a good sign?

Nick went over to them, pausing only to grab one of the chairs from his own verandah. Lagardère and Pike made room for Nick. They were now all snugly squeezed around a tiny table, on which were wine glasses and a half-empty carafe. The inspector offered him a glass of red wine. Churlish to refuse, thought Nick.

'Santé!' Lagardère raised his glass to Nick, at the same time seeming to give him a head-to-toe once-over. Strangely Nick didn't feel too bad being nude in front of Lagardère today. Maybe with Pike also present there was safety in numbers. Naturists 2, Textiles 1.

'As I was saying,' Pike continued, leaning forwards in that earnest way of his, eyes glinting behind thick lenses. 'Many people confuse nudity with sex. The two are very different you know. Just because most people take all their clothes off to have sex . . .'

'Sometimes just taking some of them off is sufficient. And more enjoyable,' said Lagardère, with a smile.

'Yes.' Pike gave a small forced smile himself, not pleased at being interrupted in full flow. 'As I was saying, just because most people get naked to have sex, it doesn't necessarily follow that nudity *equals* sex. It's come about totally by association. So when people think about naturism, the first thing that comes to their mind is that we're all sex maniacs.'

If anybody looked less like a sex maniac it was Pike, thought Nick, though who knows what he got up to in the privacy of his own home? Or, here's a scary thought. His own cabin?

Pike continued. 'I have a whole section on the subject in the Naked Guide, you know.'

'You don't say?' Nick couldn't resist adding.

The Naked Guide has this to say about sex and nudity:

For many 'textiles', there is a direct relationship between nudity and sex. Nudity in their eyes equates with sex. Therefore naturists, being nude, are considered in some ways to be undressing merely to facilitate, or encourage, sexual behaviour.

The misunderstanding occurs probably because most people undress to have sex. Lack of clothing equates with the readiness to indulge in sexual activity. Add to this the prudishness of most modern-day religions about the naked human form and it becomes axiomatic that, if you're nude, it's only a short time – or distance – from having sex.

Naturists believe that social nudity is not by itself sexual in nature and is certainly less titillating than the partial clothing and skimpy costumes encountered on textile beaches. Most naturist groups go out of their way to discourage sexual activity in public in order to counter the perception that nudity equals sex.

Of course, naturists do have sex. They are human after all. They just don't have sex as part of their naturist activities. Just as textiles wouldn't have sex as part of their visit to the gym for a workout or sunbathing on a beach in the Mediterranean.

Once Pike had descended from his metaphorical soap-box, Lagardère turned to Nick. 'Mr Pike was telling me about his relationship with the murdered man.'

'Dreadful waste,' said Pike, staring into the bottom of his wine glass, seemingly affected by the murder. 'Didn't know him long but did count him truly as a friend. A kindred spirit indeed.'

If Pike *had* murdered Giles Curtis, he was giving a RADA-rated acting performance.

'Have you found out anything more about him?' enquired Nick of Lagardère.

'Some. We now know that he had no criminal record. We got indirect confirmation from New Scotland Yard. They have no finger prints on Mr Curtis for any crime or arrest. I didn't expect them to,' said Lagardère, gazing calmly out at the Avenue.

'Have you found his next-of-kin? That sort of thing,' asked an increasingly frustrated Nick.

Lagardère said, in a more soothing tone, 'We are as anxious to clear this crime up as you are. But we are very much in the hands of your countrymen in this respect. They don't seem to be giving the case too much priority. Besides we only have the evidence of the check-in card that he actually lived at the address in Tottenham.'

'That's where he told me he lived. In Tottenham,' added Martin Pike.

Nick had forgotten he was still there, so quiet had he been. 'He also mentioned it to Garry,' added Nick impulsively. He looked at Lagardère to see if he would ask any further questions about Garry.

'Ah yes. You mean Mr Hollins,' said Lagardère, turning to Nick. 'The family with the two boys.'

Nick was not sure whether Lagardère had added that fact to differentiate the witnesses in his own mind or to indicate to Nick that he knew more than he was letting on.

Lagardère continued looking at Nick. 'I hear that Mr Hollins – Garry – was seen having a violent row with the victim earlier that day. Would you know what that was all about?'

Nick couldn't bring himself to betray his confidence with Garry. 'How could I? I wasn't even here at the time. And that's something I *can* prove,' Nick added, a touch unnecessarily.

Lagardère looked away from Nick towards the Avenue. 'I

called the Yard again this afternoon. They seem to think they'll
be able to let us have some more information tomorrow.'

'Isn't that what they said yesterday?' said an exasperated
Nick.

Lagardère poured himself another glass of wine. He offered
the carafe to the others. Both declined. Lagardère shrugged —
either to demonstrate that it didn't matter whether they took a
glass of wine, or as if another day or two's delay in the
investigation wouldn't make the slightest difference to him.
And it probably wouldn't, thought Nick.

It must be quite pleasant for Lagardère to stay here in the sun
at the French taxpayer's expense. Almost like being on holiday.
And unlike everyone else, Lagardère had the added advantage
of being able to keep his clothes on.

'Well I must be off.' Martin Pike raised himself off his chair,
turning to retrieve his towel. 'Thank you very much for the
wine, Inspector, it was most appreciated. And nice talking with
you.'

He held out his hand and shook the inspector's. 'If there's
anything I can do to help catch the fiend who perpetrated this
foul act, then don't hesitate to ask.'

'Thank you, Mr Pike. I will,' the inspector replied, as Pike
toddled off, a little unsteady on his feet, to his own cabin.

Nick didn't quite know how to broach the subject of Charles
and Camilla with Lagardère, so he chose a roundabout method.
'Er, have you been getting very far in tracking Giles's last
movements?'

Lagardère was non-committal. 'We've got a fair idea, yes.
But there are some gaps.'

'Did you know, for instance, that he had dinner that evening
with a couple in their caravan?'

'Ah. You must mean the quaintly named Charles and
Camilla.'

Nick was taken aback. 'How did you know that?'

Lagardère turned to Nick. 'The same way you did probably. By talking to the English people in the resort. In fact, we got that information from someone called, er . . .' Lagardère for once was lost for a name. 'You wouldn't forget her. She had rather large breasts,' He demonstrated with a two-handed gesture any man in the world would recognize, 'with rings through her nipples.'

The nipple rings weren't a give-away. Lagardère's description was. 'You must mean Janet,' said Nick.

'Yes, that's the lady. Most extraordinary. You know she even has piercings in her . . .'

'Yes, I do know that.' Nick interrupted quickly, not wishing to discuss the finer points of Janet's body jewellery with Lagardère.

'She told us she'd heard that Charles and Camilla were the last to see Giles Curtis alive. So we went to question them this afternoon.'

'And what did they say?'

Lagardère took a small sip from his glass and placed it down on the table in front of him. 'They admitted he'd been round for dinner and left about eleven o'clock that night.'

'And did you believe them?'

'Not until we'd corroborated their story with a Belgium family in a nearby trailer. They'd heard a noisy, but amicable, farewell at about that time. Looking out to see what the fuss was, they saw Giles Curtis leaving the caravan and walking down the Avenue. They identified him from the photo we have.'

'That seems to put Charles and Camilla in the clear, then,' said Nick, sounding slightly disappointed.

Lagardère stared into his wine. 'Not necessarily. They could have followed him and murdered him later. When it was quiet.

And I've been making enquiries about our friend Charles via the computer in London. It seems he has a criminal record.'

'Really?' Nick perked up.

'It was a long time ago, of course, and he served time in prison for it.'

'What did he do?'

'It was for receiving stolen goods. Fencing, I think the slang is in English.'

Nick thought that as Charles was in antiques, it wasn't that surprising that he not only sold but also got up to the odd fiddle.

For a change, Lagardère was forthcoming with the details, as if trying to sort out the recently acquired knowledge in his own mind. 'It was for handling some of the proceeds of a gold bullion robbery. From a bonded warehouse at Heathrow in the 1980s. The gang got away with ingots worth some ten million pounds. That's a lot of money even today. Then, well . . . it was a small fortune.'

'And Charles handled all that bullion?'

'No, no. Apparently Charles was only relatively small beer. He was convicted of handling just a few gold bars – but even so, worth around a quarter of a million pounds. It was enough to get him five years inside.'

'What happened to the rest of the criminals?' Nick enquired.

'The English police caught one or two. But never apprehended the ringleaders. Probably disappeared into the Spanish Costas. There was no extradition in those days, remember.'

Nick suddenly remembered that Hamish lived in Southern Spain. And he was about the right age to have been a bit of a rascal in the 'eighties. But Hamish? No!!! Impossible!

'And what happened to the gold?'

'Some was recovered but the majority was never accounted for. As if disappeared into thin air,' said Lagardère, putting down his glass. He thought about filling it up again and decided against it. 'Probably in a Swiss bank now. Or spent on trifles and baubles.'

Nick immediately thought of Camilla's gold bracelets, necklaces, ear rings and such.

Lagardère continued. 'I'm not sure where that gets us really. If Giles Curtis recognized that Charles was an ex-con, he might have tried to expose him unless Charles paid him some money. But then again, it was all so long ago. The world's moved on. Who cares that Charles has served time in jail. Some of the most prominent politicians from both our countries have been inside for worse.' Lagardère sounded a bit tired. Maybe the investigation was getting to him as well. 'And scarcely reason to kill a man.'

Nick and Lagardère sat in silence. Nick was mentally turning these new pieces of information over. He didn't get very far, except to use up valuable brain space.

Lagardère looked up and smiled at Nick. 'But let's look on the bright side. The only real suspect we've still got is you.'

'I had no reason to kill Giles Curtis either,' said Nick for the umpteenth time. Perhaps he ought to buy and train a parrot to repeat this mantra as and when required.

Nick suddenly remembered his conversation with Phillip. 'Incidentally, are you allowed to keep us here? I mean, officially? Don't you have to have a warrant or something?'

Lagardère shrugged. Like all Frenchmen, he was good at shrugging. In France, they probably had a GCSE in it.

Getting no other reply, Nick continued. 'I've got a French legal representative looking into this.' Lagardère raised his eyebrows slightly at this news. 'And I can promise you that if you're holding us here illegally, well I, I . . .' he couldn't actually tell Lagardère what he'd do because he hadn't the faintest idea of French legal procedures. But by God he would, once he found out what they were!

'Are you threatening me, Nick,' said Lagardère, in a none-too-friendly manner.

Nick backtracked. 'No, not threatening. It's just that, well, we don't think we should be held without a charge.'

'So you'd rather I charged you with murder? You could then spend the whole of your holiday – or longer – in a stifling and unhygienic holding cell in Perpignan. Would you prefer that to walking around like this . . .' once again indicating Nick's nude state '. . . in a nice place like Le Paradis. Because if you would prefer it, I think I can arrange it very easily.'

Nick shifted uneasily in his chair. 'Well, obviously I don't want to be charged. I just want to be released.'

Lagardère leaned over and put his hand on top of Nick's, in a comradely rather than gay way, at least that was the interpretation Nick preferred. 'Be patient, Nick. I'm sure the murderer is still on site. And I'm sure we'll get him – or her.'

But Lagardère didn't sound too sure of himself.

20

Nick let himself back into the cabin. Still no Ros. Again he wondered if he should have gone out to find her. Would she be alright on her own in the resort? Of course. Yet she didn't seem to be as blasé about walking round nude as she had yesterday. Must have been a delayed reaction to the shock of their naked dinner last night.

Nick walked into the bedroom with the intention of getting ready for a shower, suddenly realising he was already un-dressed. Nudity could be convenient at times, he thought, stepping next door and directly into the shower tray.

Whilst soaping, Nick pondered. His conversation with Lagardère had given him a whole three-course meal for thought. So Charles was an ex-con jailed for handling stolen gold? Could there be a connection with Giles Curtis? Perhaps Giles Curtis was threatening Charles. Then why invite him round to dinner? And could Hamish be a Mr Big of the underworld – albeit a very small and hairy one?

Then again, perhaps the whole thing was much simpler and Giles Curtis had been bludgeoned to death by Garry for molesting his kids. Or by the phantom serial killer, beginning his murder spree. Nick shook his head as if to clear it. He wasn't sure that what he'd learned had helped or hindered him in his quest for freedom.

He got out of the shower and towelled himself down. What about Shareen, his erstwhile 'Dr Watson'? Perhaps she could throw some light on it. After all, she was a highly intelligent woman. And incredibly fanciable with it. Nick wondered whether she'd be at the barbie-wake tonight. Perhaps they could find somewhere to have a quiet chat.

Nick turned to the bathroom mirror and shook a tin of shaving foam to get the stuff inside to thicken up. There was nothing worse than pressing the button and getting a thin trickle of soapy gunge. He lathered his face and started to shave.

Come to think of it, he also hadn't liked the way the inspector seemed so prepared to throw him into jail and chuck away the key. Maybe that was just a bluff? Maybe. Best not find out. He resolved to go quietly on the French legal system approach in any future discussions with Lagardère.

Finishing his ablutions, Nick walked back into the bedroom and did something he hadn't done since he'd arrived. He took out his case from under the bed and contemplated its contents.

He hadn't packed many clothes, reasoning that he wouldn't need many in this sort of climate. Little did he know at the time how few he'd actually require.

He lifted out his bathing shorts. They did look very strange. Pieces of cloth you wrapped round your privates. Cloth that got wet and soggy, when waterproof skin was a much more practical alternative. Looking at them, much as a Borneo headhunter would a Paul Smith suit, Nick dropped them back in the case. He contemplated his limited wardrobe of slacks, jeans and t-shirts. What did one wear at an event of this type?

Before Nick could reach a decision, he heard the cabin front door open. 'Ros? That you?'

'So who else are you expecting?' she said coming into the bedroom. She looked calmer than when she'd left. Hard not to be. She came over to him, put her arms round his neck and gave him a kiss. 'Let's not argue again, love.'

'Er, no,' said Nick, slightly taken aback. 'I didn't really want to. It's just the tension, you know.'

Ros unwound herself from him and went to the dresser to brush her hair. 'I know. I'm feeling it too. If only we could just get out of here.'

Nick sat on the bed. 'I've got some news on that. Would you believe that I finally got through to Phillip and Kathy this afternoon? Had a long chat to Phillip.'

Ros turned to face him, mid-brush. 'Did you explain what's happened?'

'I did. And eventually he believed me. They actually think that Lagardère might be holding us here illegally. They're going to check with a retired lawyer to see what French law has to say about it.'

Ros became animated. 'That's great! So if they find we're being held illegally, does that mean we'll be free to go?'

Nick thought he'd better not mention Lagardère's threat to arrest him. He didn't want to spoil Ros's improved mood. 'Well, I shouldn't hold your breath. But at least something's being done.'

Ros turned back to the mirror, examining her reflection in a rather disapproving fashion, as if looking at some feature she didn't quite care for. She caught Nick looking at her in the mirror. 'I must wash my hair if we're going to this "do" tonight.'

'The bathroom's all yours.'

She needed it, she thought. If she couldn't dry clean her conscience, she could at least thoroughly wash away the dirt of the afternoon.

Having given herself what her mother would have described as "a good scrub down", Ros returned to the now empty bedroom. One towel was wrapped around her body, the other she was using to dry her hair.

'How about a drink before we set off?' Nick's voice called from the kitchen.

'Just a small one,' Ros replied. She sat on the bed, head to one side and carried on drying her hair.

Nick pushed his way backwards through the beaded curtain and turned to reveal the two tumblers of cold dry white wine he was carrying. Ros noticed that he was still nude. 'Put mine on the bedside cabinet, would you please, love,' she said.

Nick obliged and sat down on the dressing table stool, facing her. He had picked up more of a colour today and was looking fairly brown. Even the white bits were beginning to merge with the general colour scheme. Was it her imagination or was he looking slightly thinner? Must be the tan.

'Shouldn't you be getting ready? You know, getting dressed?' Ros said.

'Plenty of time yet.' Nick replied. In fact, he'd actually been putting off putting on clothes. 'It's so hot in here, I don't want to get sweat marks on my t-shirt. How can you wear that towel? It must be stifling.'

'I suppose it's comforting in a peculiar sort of way.' Ros replied.

'So what have you been doing with yourself?'

It didn't sound a threatening question. Just as if Nick was genuinely interested in where she'd been. She knew him well enough to know that the last thing he would want would be to resurrect their row. She answered in a similar tone. 'Oh, you know. Walked around a bit. In fact quite a long way, actually. Right round the lake.' No reaction from Nick at the mention of the word "lake". She continued to explain. 'I was thinking. Trying to calm down.'

'I'm sorry,' said Nick, automatically.

She continued drying her hair. 'That's all right. It takes two. I also went to the pool for a bit of a swim.' She had done this after her walk back from the boathouse, almost as a symbolic total immersion to rid herself of every trace, smell and taste of Jean-Luc.

'See anyone we know?' Nick asked, innocently.

The moment Ros dreaded had arrived. She lifted her glass from the bedside cabinet and took a sip. She didn't look at him. 'Like who?'

'You know. Geoff and Lynne? They seem to pop up everywhere.'

'No, I think they must have been sleeping-off lunch. Something perhaps we should have done,' said Ros, and then, realising it sounded like a slur on Nick's sex drive, added 'to get some rest for tonight.'

'Anybody else?' Nick was thinking of Shareen. Ros thought he was talking about Jean-Luc.

Here goes. Decision time. She took a deep breath. Fortunately, Nick was staring into his glass at the time. 'Well, I did bump into Shareen.'

'In the bar?' asked Nick, in a seemingly disinterested fashion.

'No, near the boathouse, actually.' There she'd said it. How would Nick react? She looked at him over the top of her glass.

'Wonder what she was doing down there? Long way from the bar,' Nick mused, almost to himself.

'Yes, well, there you are,' said Ros, and quickly got to her feet before he could conjure up any other questions. 'Can I get to the dressing table. I need to do my make-up.' She hadn't denied seeing Jean-Luc. She just hadn't mentioned it. So she had a fall-back position, Ros reasoned, should the subject ever come up again.

'What? Oh sure,' said Nick, moving out of the way and to his side of the bed. He peered into his travelling wardrobe of clothes as if inspecting an alien space craft.

Ros watched him in the mirror as he took out one t-shirt, held it up, put it back and took out another. 'I can't wait to put on clothes again,' she said. 'Isn't it a real relief to be able to get dressed tonight?'

'Strangely enough, I can't say it is really.'

Ros carried on applying foundation. 'What do you mean?'

'Well, I'm getting used to it. You know, nudity. It doesn't seem such a bad idea after all.'

Ros stopped what she was doing and turned towards him, incredulous look on face. 'What?!! Is this the same person who was worried about exposing his genitals to public gaze less than 48 hours ago? The man afraid of people seeing his arse? The man who tried to turn a towel into a dressing gown? What's brought this on?'

Nick looked at her with a slightly abashed expression. 'I don't know. It's not anything to do with all that "freedom" and "classlessness" bollocks. It just seems to make sense in this climate. Dress for cold. Undress for heat. After all, it's what all our primeval ancestors used to do in the dim and distant past.'

My God! He's beginning to sound like Martin Pike, thought Ros. It must be what living in close proximity to him does to you.

She turned back to her face in the mirror. 'Well I for one will be absolutely delighted to get some clothes on. Believe me, the memory of last night will remain for a long time.' Not to mention the memory of this afternoon. Maybe there was just too much temptation, for her at least, in being naked.

Having finished tarting herself up, Ros removed her towel. She'd decided to wear a very light black cotton dress. She also pulled out of the case matching black bra and pants – bought specially for the holidays and nights of passion with Nick. Might as well have saved her money, she thought, a trifle bitterly.

She slipped on the pants and hooked the bra into place, arranging it in the mirror. She noticed Nick looking at her. 'Yes?'

'Just admiring the goods.'

'Yes, well when you've finished window-shopping, perhaps you'd care to come inside and buy.' Damn. Ros hadn't meant to say that. Would it re-kindle the argument?

Nick seemed to take it in a good-humoured fashion. He laughed. 'Perhaps I'll do just that.' He kissed her briefly on the back of her neck, something he almost certainly would not have done if he'd known whose lips had been there a few hours' earlier.

Guiltily, Ros pulled on her dress, Nick obliging with the zip. 'Nick will you please get ready. We're almost late as it is.'

Reluctantly Nick addressed his case again. 'I suppose black is the right colour to wear in these circumstances.' He pulled out a pair of black Dockers chinos and a plain, but expensive, black t-shirt. There was nothing he could do about shoes, so wore his brown Sebago deck shoes – without socks, of course.

Ros checked her appearance one more time in the mirror, stepped into the same heels she'd been wearing yesterday and, feeling more confident than she had since she arrived, set out with Nick to "celebrate a life" – the life of Giles Curtis. The man Nick was supposed to have murdered.

21

They set off to find Avenue E, home of Camilla, Charles and "the Daimler".

Nick felt most peculiar wearing clothes again. The boxers tight against his genitals. The lack of breeze around his chest and legs. The restriction of shoes. It was all very weird. And much stranger than he thought it would have been after a mere couple of days in the nude.

By comparison, Ros was transformed. She seemed happier and more confident than he'd seen her for some time. If it didn't sound too corny and Womans Weekly, she actually looked radiant. He felt a sudden glow of warmth and affection for her. He took her hand which she gave willingly and they wandered down the tree-lined Champs-Elysses like two Start-Rite kids.

It was getting near dusk. But still passably light. And still impossibly hot for the time of day. Nick could feel and see a patch of sweat forming in the middle of his t-shirt.

As they walked, he couldn't help but notice the inhabitants of Le Paradis who seemed too pre-occupied with preparing their evening meals to take much notice of them.

The barbecue option seemed to be favourite, if the smell of burning charcoal and singeing flesh was anything to go by.

Nick became fascinated by the fashion adopted by many of the men. Put at its simplest, it could be described as the bottomless look. A t-shirt, preferably with infantile cartoon or inexplicable French saying imprinted on it.

This season's look was to wear said garment "au naturel", which in practice translated as having the t-shirt end just above or below the waist. And below that? Nothing. What else did you need, they probably reasoned?

It was probably OK from a practical point of view but left a lot to be desired aesthetically. Seeing male genitalia dangling into view below the t-shirt didn't quite do a lot for the overall ensemble.

Avenue E was quiet and tree-shaded. He knew it was fanciful, but Nick thought it a little like Hampstead Garden Suburbs in relationship to the rest of Le Paradis.

There seemed to be more hedges and greenery. The caravans were larger and had more of a permanence to them. Some looked as if they hadn't moved for years and had mature flower beds and garden gnomish ornaments. He guessed, correctly as it happens, that these caravans once in position would never move back onto a main highway to irritate the shit out of other drivers. They'd found their final resting place.

Towards the middle of the avenue sat a Daimler-badged late model Jaguar saloon with Portuguese plates. Looking sleek, powerful and alert, it sat as if guarding a small, white wooden gate.

Nick and Ros pushed the gate open. Charles and Camilla's

caravan was end-on to the road. They followed a path round to the left and there was a small but well-kempt lawn. The front of the caravan had a white awning which spread out over part of the garden. Beneath this, a white plastic table was, if not groaning then at least complaining mildly about the huge number of bottles and glasses it had been called upon to support. Below it, in plastic buckets, were yet more bottles – beer, white wine and mineral water. Giles Curtis was to be sent off in some style.

At the far end of the lawn, there was a heavy smoke haze. Through it, they could just detect a figure waving his hand over what must be the barbecue. He looked up and directed his wave briefly in their direction before re-addressing the coals. Wearing a long chef's apron and, Nick noted, nothing else, it was their host and ex-jail bird Charles. Nick remembered that he hadn't told Ros about their host's "previous" yet.

By now they'd reached the caravan. Nick called through the door. 'Hello? Anyone at home?'. It sounded naff even to him. But what else did you say? You couldn't just walk in.

A plummy voice answered from inside. 'I'm in the kitchen. Do please come in.'

Ros entered the caravan, followed closely by Nick. Nick had never seen the attraction in camping or caravanning. Why go on holiday and replicate exactly what you have at home but in more uncomfortable and cramped surroundings? Charles and Camilla's caravan went a long way to change his view – faster than you could say "chemical toilet".

It was enormous. The interior stretched about 30 feet and there were further doors to the rear. He noticed an air conditioning unit which was quietly doing its job, lowering the temperature to something that resembled comfort.

The kitchen itself was better appointed than the one in their house in Stoke Newington. And at the work surface – to be

more accurate, one of the work surfaces – stood a very brown
and bejewelled Camilla. She was wearing a pair of Marigold
gloves and, like Charles, a full length chef's apron. And nothing
else.

She turned from what she was doing, which looked like
something illegal involving an olive and an anchovy.

'Hello, there!' Camilla said in a jolly hockeysticks way.
'Forgive me if I can't shake hands.' She referred to the gloves
and the sharp knife in her hand. Instead, she leant towards
them, proffering each cheek to be pecked by both Nick and Ros
in turn.

'Lovely to see you both. Someone always has to be the first
to arrive. You will excuse me, won't you. We're a bit behind
with preparing the food,' said Camilla. It was strange. From
this side the apron covered most of her and she looked clothed.
When she turned round she was stark naked, apart from the
apron straps, of course.

'Er, is there anything we can do to help?' Ros offered.

Camilla turned to face them again. 'Too kind. Ros isn't it?'
Not waiting for a reply, Camilla ploughed on.

'Very nice frock. Although it's not formal you know. Still
very appropriate for this evening. Would you mind awfully
taking these out front please Ros?' Camilla indicated a number
of plates of hors d'oeuvres including smoked salmon, stuffed
olives – and other things Nick couldn't recognize. 'Just a few
nibbles until Charles gets the fire tamed. I did tell him he'd left
it to late, but will he ever listen? That's men for you, isn't it
Ros. Just won't be told. Even when it's for their own good.'

Ros could do little more than smile in agreement, giving
Nick an eyes-raised look as Camilla turned back to olive-
stuffing, or whatever she was doing. Ros picked up the plates
and took them outside.

Camilla became aware that Nick was still standing there. He

was actually looking round the place and trying hard not to look at Camilla. The Sloane accent, haircut, jewellery were all so typical of that type of woman, it was incongruous seeing her standing there with no clothes on. Particularly indoors. It was made even more incongruous as Nick himself was now fully clothed.

'Well, don't just stand there Nick. Make yourself useful. Give Ros a hand. And get yourself a drink. Don't stand on ceremony.'

Nick took some plates and went outside. It was distinctly hotter away from the cool interior of the kitchen. He found Ros looking a bit puzzled, arranging plates. He helped himself to a beer from one of the ice buckets.

'Nick, have you noticed that Charles and Camilla aren't wearing anything?'

Nick tipped the bottle neck upwards and took a swig. 'Yes, so what? This is a naturist resort, you know', giving a fair imitation of Martin Pike. 'They'll probably get dressed once they've finished preparing the food. Don't want to mess up their clothes. What can I get you, gorgeous? Glass of white wine OK?'

Ros smiled at him as he handed her the glass. She took it in her hand and the smile froze, just as if someone had freeze-framed her on a video recorder. She was staring at a spot behind Nick's head, which approximated with the entrance to the garden.

Nick turned and followed her gaze. There, just a few yards away, were Geoff and Lynne, making their way towards them.

Geoff was, well, just Geoff. But Lynne looked particularly attractive. She was wearing make-up, which Nick up to then had thought an action punishable by expulsion from the community by the Stoke Newington Health Police. On her feet were some strappy, high heeled sandals which could probably best be described as "fuck me shoes".

And that's all she *was* wearing. Because, like Geoff beside her and Charles and Camilla, she also was stark naked. Which explained Ros's open-mouthed impression of a gaffed flounder.

Lynne led the way over to where Ros was standing and kissed her on both cheeks. She turned to do the same to Nick, smiling mischievously. 'Hi Nick. Didn't recognize you with your clothes on.'

'Oh, hi Lynne. Geoff. Er, can I get you both a drink? I seem to have become honorary barman.'

Without waiting to be asked, Geoff had already got himself a beer and twisted the cap off. 'Cheers!', he said, as he uptilted the bottle and took a good slug. Geoff clearly meant to start as he was going to finish. He lowered the bottle, perhaps to take in some air, and was about to raise it again when he looked at Ros. 'You're dressed.'

'Good marks for observation, Geoff,' said Lynne, taking a glass of wine from Nick. She somehow didn't seem able to remove that smile from her face. Which set the rest of her ensemble off very nicely thought Nick.

Ros looked distinctly put out. Nick could sense that she was not happy. She addressed her remarks to both Geoff and Lynne. 'Look, don't mind me asking but . . . but why aren't you two wearing any clothes? And please don't tell me it's because we're in a naturist resort. I have worked that out for myself you know.'

Geoff shrugged, cradling his beer in one enormous paw. 'Well, it's a barbecue.'

Ros continued in increasingly bad mood. 'Yes, I think I've even noticed that as well. What I mean is, how come yesterday evening it was "de rigeur" to wear clothes and tonight it isn't?'

Just as last night in the restaurant, it was clear that Lynne did not want any part of this conversation. She stood quietly sipping her wine, leaving Geoff to continue with the explanations.

'Ah, now yesterday was dinner in the restaurant. A formal occasion, so people like to get dressed. You know, like black tie in the world of the textiles. Same goes for the night club. But here, well it's just a barbecue in someone's backyard. Informal. Q.E.D. No reason to get dressed.'

'Does that mean we'll be the only two people wearing clothes?' asked Ros.

Geoff seemed to weigh up his answer carefully. 'Erm, yes, I suppose you will be. Except of course Janet and John. They're always what I call "semi-dressed".'

Ros didn't seem appeased by Geoff's description. 'Well I wish someone had mentioned it to us, that's all.'

This was turning into a repeat of last night in the restaurant. Then Ros had wondered why nobody had told them to get dressed; here no-one had told them they needn't get dressed.

Before anybody had time to continue the discussion, Charles materialized next to them. As a possible suspect, Nick looked at him with renewed interest. He was quite brown, like Camilla, and slightly stocky and overweight. In his fifties, he still had brownish greying hair, with an old-fashioned parting and quite short round the back and sides. He looked as if he had once been fairly powerful, with broad neck and shoulders but now run a bit to seed.

'Good. I see you've got drinks,' he said, not bothering to shake hands. 'Barbecue bit bothersome. Have to get back to it.' A man of few words, he took a glass of red wine and returned to the smoke at the bottom of the garden.

Camilla bustled out with a final tray of canapés and placed them on the table. 'Thank goodness for that. Now one can relax.' So saying she took off her apron, tucked it under the table, poured a generous glass of red wine and came over to welcome Geoff and Lynne.

Nick felt his arm tugged by Ros. The signal for ''let's talk''. They moved a few yards away down the garden, out of earshot.

'I simply can't believe this,' said Ros. 'I look forward to a whole evening in civilized company, with everyone fully dressed, and find that yet again we're the odd ones out. This time surrounded by naked bodies instead of clothed ones.'

'There is a major difference between now and last night however.'

'Which is?'

'Last night we were several hundred yards away from our clothes.'

'Yes, I know that,' Ros said testily.

'And we couldn't reasonably go back and get dressed without a great deal of disruption, loss of face, etcetera.'

'The point being?'

'Well, there's a very simple solution to tonight's little predicament.'

'Which is?' Ros was getting irritated with Nick's game.

'Here, hold this.' Nick gave Ros his glass. He reached down with both hands, pulling his t-shirt out of his trousers. 'We simply undress.'

If Ros had a spare hand she would have grabbed his. Instead she hissed. 'Nick!!! Don't you dare!!

He stopped what he was doing. 'What? What's the problem? We can put our clothes to one side. Pick them up when we leave.'

Ros now looked very angry indeed. 'If you take a stitch of clothing off, I'm leaving. I mean it.'

'But won't it be embarrassing being the only person dressed?'

Ros thrust Nick's glass back into his hand. 'Not for me it won't. Anyway, I will not be the only one dressed. You will be as well. And if you think I'm going to let you strip off, making me the only one clothed, like, like . . .' she searched for an analogy '. . . like the opposite of that painting "Dejeuner sur l'herbe" then you've got another think coming.'

The last thing Nick wanted was another quarrel with Ros. He raised his hand in a conciliatory gesture. 'OK, OK. We'll stay just as we are. All right?'

Ros seemed to calm down slightly and said to nobody in particular. 'This place is really beginning to drive me totally fucking crazy.'

22

It was almost dusk before the first batch of semi-burned food arrived. With Geoff by his side, doing serious damage to some chicken pieces, Nick nibbled gingerly on a hot sausage held over a paper plate and looked around. Things seemed to be going well, guests mingling supervised by Camilla, who, whatever her faults, was no slouch in the hostess stakes.

Over near the table, Hamish and Martin Pike were talking amiably to Garry, as they helped themselves to some salad. Garry's kids, having already finished their burgers, were kicking a ball about at the end of the garden, watched anxiously by Sam, who in turn was talking to Lynne. As he looked over, Nick thought he caught Lynne smiling at him over the top of her glass.

He instinctively checked to see where Ros was. She was talking to Charles and Jack – the proprietor of Le Paradis – who'd somehow made an effort to turn up, finding a relief receptionist. Which could explain why there was no sign of Shareen.

Camilla, who was circulating with bottles of red and white wine, reached Geoff and Nick. 'Do have some more wine. Can I give you a refill.'

Geoff, mouth full of food, uttered a sound which Camilla correctly interpreted as "yes". Particularly as Geoff, having switched to red wine, was proffering an empty glass.

'Nick? White or red?' Camilla politely enquired.

'Red, please Camilla.' As she poured Nick said 'Nice party.'

She smiled at him. 'Thank you so much. Yes it is rather jolly isn't it. Makes one almost forget why we're here tonight.'

'Yes, quite.' Now Nick was beginning to sound like Camilla.

'We're going to say a few words for Giles a little later on. I do hope you'll be able to stay for them.' Without waiting for a reply, she continued, 'Now if you'll excuse me.' And wandered off.

He didn't think he would, but in fact Nick was coping quite well with being clothed while everyone was nude. He would, of course, rather be naked if it wasn't for Ros's objections.

Surveying the gathering, he thought that this was what it must have been like for early British explorers discovering naked tribesmen on some distant foreign soil. And mingling with them fully dressed. He pictured Ros and himself as ambassadors, imagining conversations that began 'and what do you do?' and 'have you travelled very far' and 'that's a very attractive shrunken head you're wearing'.'

He contentedly took another bite of his sausage. Come to think of it, Le Paradis could be said to be a foreign land with its own rites and customs, as alien to outsiders as a south sea island would have been to Captain Cook. But perhaps not as dangerous – although it had been for poor Giles Curtis.

His thoughts were interrupted by Geoff nudging Nick's elbow, which nearly made him stick the sausage up his nose. 'Well, look who's here?'

Nick turned to follow Geoff's gaze, and nearly dropped his plate as well. Just turning the corner were Janet and John. When Geoff had told Ros earlier that they were usually "semi-dressed", he hadn't been exaggerating.

Unlike yesterday, Janet was dressed less formally. That, noted Nick, trying not to make his eyes goggle so much, meant first discarding her bra. Exposing breasts which defied gravity and probably nature as well. Adorned with silver nipple rings, her breasts were enormous. And silicone-firm. He was sure that when she lay on her back they stayed exactly facing straight up, pointing at the ceiling. He immediately stopped himself thinking any further along those lines.

Janet seemed to have made some concession to the solemnity of the occasion by wearing a black leather skirt that made the one she was wearing yesterday look positively modest. It ended half-way up her hips, below which he could see she was wearing a black leather thong. The outfit was completed with thigh length black boots.

Nick had never been into leather and bondage, but just looking at Janet instilled a "that looks interesting, perhaps I will give it a go after all" mentality.

John was also dressed, if that was the appropriate word, in black. He was wearing a black open leather waistcoat and a black leather thong. Nick imagined that they got their matching thongs in a "his and hers" bondage shop.

Nick was relieved that John was wearing a thong. He couldn't stomach both the half-cooked sausage and the thought of seeing John's rumoured assortment of genital hardware.

What was most remarkable was that nobody else batted an eyelid. As Geoff and Nick were the nearest guests, Janet followed by John came over. Nick managed, with great difficulty, to raise his gaze to Janet's eye level as her breasts inexorably made their way towards him, followed – seemingly a few minutes later – by the rest of her body.

'Hello Geoff,' Janet leaned forward to give Geoff a kiss on both cheeks, a manoeuvre which just couldn't avoid involving her chest connecting with Geoff's. Nick thought he saw Geoff blush, even in the twilight of the garden.

'Hi Nick.' Nick waited for her kiss him as well, but apparently they didn't know each other well enough. Shame.

'Sorry we're late. We were . . .'

'A bit tied up?' said Geoff, the old wag, reprising Janet's line from last night, to her obvious disappointment.

'Yes, how did you guess?' said Janet.

John joined her, pushing back his long black hair with both hands. He looked uncannily like Geronimo, about to do battle with the paleface horse soldiers. If, that is, you could imagine Geronimo wearing a thong and Timberland boots.

Camilla bustled up. 'Hello you two. So glad you could make it. There's still some food left.'

'That's OK,' said Janet, 'we had something before we came out.' She smiled at John, who remained impassive.

'A drink then? Beer? Wine?'

Having taken their orders and having brought them both beers, Camilla left to see how the others were doing.

Janet looked Nick up and down. 'Aren't you a bit warm in all those clothes?'

He was, actually. And a great deal warmer since Janet had come and stood near him. Maybe the large surface area of her breasts radiated heat – a bit like solar panels. This could be the solution to the world energy crisis. 'Er, yes,' was all he could reply.

Geoff stepped in to elaborate. 'Nick thought it was like having dinner in the restaurant, so he got dressed for it.'

'But he was naked in the restaurant last night.' Janet was having difficulty coming to grips with the logic.

'Yes, that was because he didn't know at the time he needed to get dressed for dinner,' Geoff explained, patiently.

'So he thought tonight was a formal occasion, like dinner, and wore clothes even though he didn't need to.'

'That's it!' said Geoff. 'That's why he's dressed. Simple really.' Nick had the distinct feeling he'd become invisible and had a sudden flash forward to a time when he might be imprisoned in an old folks' home, in a wheelchair, with care workers talking over his head.

'Yes, but now you know you don't have to wear clothes, and you're hot wearing them, why don't you strip off?' Janet asked Nick, acknowledging his presence at last.

Nick could feel himself losing the will to live. 'It's a long story.'

Before he had time to say any more, Geoff said 'Right, if you'll excuse me, I'll just see if there's any more chicken left.' He headed towards the barbecue, leaving Nick alone with the Leather Village People.

For the sake of something to say, and to deflect any more questions about his own outfit, Nick commented on Janet's. 'I like the skirt and boot combination. It looks good on you.' He glanced at Geronimo to make sure he hadn't caused any offence. He couldn't tell. He was still staring into the middle distance.

'Thank you. Are you and Ros into leather at all?'

'Only for shoes, wallets, handbags, that sort of thing,' said Nick.

'Silly,' said Janet, giggling and giving him a nudge, which brought her chest even closer to his, raising his temperature a few more degrees. 'You know what I mean. Plastic's good, too, of course. But we prefer leather don't we John?'

John nodded, showing that he was at least listening and had a fair grasp of the white man's tongue.

Janet continued. 'You ought to give it a go. You don't know whether you're interested in submission and domination until you've tried it.'

There were quite a few things Nick might have liked but certainly had no intention of trying. Like free-falling out of an aeroplane, potholing, white water rafting. All had one thing in common. The risk of doing yourself a serious, if not fatal, injury. He preferred to remain in one piece. 'Doesn't it involve, you know, I mean, pain? We're not much into pain.'

'Ah,' said Janet, 'there's pain and then there's pain.'

There wasn't a lot that Nick could grapple with in that utterance, so he just sipped his wine.

Janet continued. 'Lots of people are into it. Not just young but old as well. It's great fun.'

If you had just joined the conversation you would have thought Janet was talking about a game of Happy Families, not having your penis stamped on with a high heeled boot, or whatever else they got up to.

'I'm not sure it's really for us,' said Nick, now regretting having brought up the subject in the first place. Although, come to think of it, he didn't remember doing so.

John spoke, making Nick start. 'You ought to come down to the Dungeon one night, just to see for yourself. Can't do any harm.'

Nick's understanding was that "doing harm" was the point of the exercise. 'The Dungeon? Well, when we get back, perhaps we will,' said Nick, thinking that would be the end of the matter.

'You don't have to get back, silly. The Dungeon is here.' Janet giggled again. Nick wished she wouldn't do that.

'What, here?' Nick said, looking around the garden.

'No. Here in Le Paradis. In the basement of the night club,' Janet explained, patiently.

Nick shook his head as if to clear it. 'Let me get this right. Are you saying that there's an S and M, or whatever you call it, club in the basement of Le Paradis night club?'

'Yes. It's very well-appointed. It's got stocks. Iron rings. Handcuffs. Rope. Whips. Everything you need actually.' John now seemed to be slightly more animated. Must be a subject dear to his heart.

'And do many people go there?'

'You'd be surprised. It's not just couples either. It's open to single men as well. So even if Ros isn't interested . . .' said Janet, eyeing Nick up.

Now normally, Nick would be flattered if a half-naked woman, especially one with stupendous breasts, gave him the slightest piece of encouragement. Not this time. All he could think about was the pain that Janet and John could inflict on various parts of his anatomy.

John now proved his point by elaborating, in what for him was a long speech. 'It's the danger that excites them. The tightening of rope around the neck. Semi-strangulation heightens the pleasure of orgasm, you know.'

Nick gulped. He'd never quite worked out what S and M was all about. M and S yes. That's where one bought one's knickers and tartare sauce. But sado-masochism. He only knew what he'd read in seedy papers like the News of the World. He vaguely remembered that Tory MPs had a penchant for such things. Hadn't he read about one that had hanged himself with an orange in his mouth? Or had he just imagined the last part . . .

Janet interrupted his thoughts. 'Yes, even the most unlikely people are regular visitors to the Dungeon.'

Nick couldn't resist asking. 'Er, apart from you two, obviously, is there anyone here tonight who's a regular?'

Please don't let it be Geoff. He would never be able to look him in the face again.

Janet looked round the assembled gathering. 'No-one we recognize. Although Giles Curtis did pay a few visits.'

Nick thought that he saw John's eyes flicker towards Janet at that point, as if to warn her away from the subject. But she didn't notice.

'Giles Curtis?' asked Nick.

'I told you even the most unlikely people indulged. Like you, he was interested and wanted to try it out.' Nick wasn't sure how he'd given her that impression but decided to let her continue. 'So we took him along with us one night.' John was now impassive again, but appeared to be listening more attentively to what Janet was saying.

'And did he try it out?' Nick had to ask.

'Oh yes! He enjoyed being tied up, did our Giles.' Janet now seemed to catch a look from John and promptly shut up.

'Did you know Giles before this holiday?' asked Nick.

John answered. 'No. Just met him here. Terrible shame what happened to him. Nice guy as well'

Nick found this conversation with Janet and John revealing, in more than one way. He remembered the marks around Giles Curtis's ankles and wrists, which at the time were felt to have been caused by his body being tied up and dragged to the spot where he'd been found. It hadn't occurred to anyone to think that Giles had acquiesced in his own bondage. And for fun. Some fun! And he remembered Lagardère commenting that the marks looked terribly recent.

He wondered if Janet and John had seen Giles on the night of his murder? Should he ask?

'Did you see Giles on the night he was murdered?'

Janet's eyes flickered briefly to John's. 'No, I don't think we did, did we John?'

John shook his head.

They were lying, thought Nick. They had seen Giles that last night. But S and M, no matter how painful, surely precluded bashing someone's head in? And surely not something that a tax inspector and primary school teacher from Orpington would get involved in?

23

Standing with Jack and Charles and sipping her white wine, a fully clothed Ros felt, if not at ease with the world then slightly more comfortable. The dress was one which she caught both Jack and Charles glancing down on odd occasions to see how much they could see of her breasts. Old habits must die hard amongst men, even naturists.

She turned to Charles. 'It's a very nice caravan you've got.'

Charles was doing his usual staring into mid-distance trick, strangely enough in the direction of Janet's naked breasts, which, Ros noticed, Nick was standing just inches from and holding an animated conversation with their owner.

Without noticeably looking at Ros for more than a couple of seconds at a time, Charles replied. 'We don't call it a caravan. It's a mobile home. Although admittedly not very mobile. We've had it since Jack bought the place. What must that be, Jack, twenty years' ago?'

Jack, cigarette in one hand and beer in the other, had a think before replying. 'Yeah. That must be 1983. Where do the years go, eh?' He looked pensive as he took another drag.

'So you two have known each other all that time?' Ros was both surprised at their long connection and struggling to keep the conversation alive.

It was Charles who replied. 'Yes. We knew each other when we lived in London. We go back a long way, Jack and I.' He looked over at Jack, who seemed not to notice.

Ros remembered that Nick had told her about Charles's criminal record and wondered if Jack was also a part of that past. It didn't seem polite to pry.

Remarkably, unprompted, Charles continued speaking. 'Camilla and I came down, liked the look of this place . . .' nodding at his mobile home, '. . . and decided to buy it on the spot. Been improving it over the years. It was pretty decrepit then. As was the rest of Le Paradis, I seem to remember.'

He looked at Jack, Ros could have sworn, with a twinkle in his eye. The first indication she'd seen that either Charles or Camilla had the slightest sense of humour or irony.

Again, Jack seemed to be elsewhere, but picked up on the point made by Charles. 'Le Paradis was very run-down when we took over, but we're getting there. Slowly. Almost full this month and a fair few bookings for September and October. Mostly naturists from Germany, Holland and the UK. They prefer it a bit cooler, bit quieter than July and August.'

Ros asked Jack. 'All this can't be good for business though, can it? I mean, if word got out about the murder, would people still come to the place? Let's not forget there might be a homicidal maniac on the loose.'

As Ros said this, she looked around the garden and into the darkening trees and hedges, which suddenly, in the increasing twilight, seemed much more threatening.

For no reason that Ros could fathom, Jack smiled. 'You're right. It's not exactly good for our reputation. We've never had a murder here before. Well you don't, do you. Despite what they show on television, it's a rare event. Of course, we've had one or two deaths over the years. Natural causes. Too much "fruits de mer" putting a lethal strain on French tickers, that sort of thing. Never something like this though.'

Not wearing any shoes, or anything else, Jack had to bend down and stub out his dog-end on the grass. He got up again and continued. 'What worries me is what happens at the end of the week, when everyone wants to leave. I can't see our French clientele taking their imprisonment lightly. If they burn sheep at the drop of an EU edict, I dread to think . . .' Leaving the sentence unfinished.

The prospect of still being there in five days' time also filled Ros with dread, although for very different reasons. With all three of them thinking their individual thoughts, the conversation died.

Ros thought she'd try artificial respiration. Turning to Charles, she asked brightly, 'Camilla tells me you're in the antiques business?'

Charles looked at her, briefly, before fixing his eyes again on Nick and Janet. 'Yes. Import and export mainly. We don't have a shop in Portugal, although we do have some good customers. There are a lot of wealthy retired people on the Algarve. With time and money on their hands.' Ros thought Camilla herself perfectly fitted this category.

So the conversation continued. To call it "desultory", would be an insult to the word. Ros's mind went for a stroll. It was interesting that Charles and Jack knew each other from the past. She wondered if the inspector had that piece of information on file. And if she should tell him. But what relevance could it have? It seemed to her that most of the people at the barbecue were connected with one another – and with Giles Curtis.

Having learned enough about S and M to last him several lifetimes, Nick reluctantly heaved himself away from the magnetic attraction of Janet's bosom to hunt down a drink.

Spotting Geoff chatting to Hamish at the food table, Nick wandered across. Taking a bottle of red, he filled his glass and insinuated himself into the conversation. He immediately wished he hadn't because he found that both of them were talking about accountancy. How unlikely was that?

'So you see,' explained Hamish, to a clearly fascinated Geoff, who was grasping a beer glass full of wine, 'double entry book-keeping derives its origins from those very early days.'

Hamish looked at Nick, acknowledging his presence, as Geoff enquired, 'But what I don't understand is that if you're completing your tax return and you have to get the calculation correct, what is there to stop the Inland Revenue re-investigating that particular area?'

Nick's mind glazed over. It was something of a cliché to find accountants and accountancy boring but nevertheless held true. Nick always gave his accounts to a book-keeper who lived in Hampstead and let her do all the hard work, before sending them off to his accountant in Gant's Hill. Much simpler that way. All that "double entry" meant to Nick was something that they had a habit of doing in porn movies.

After some minutes of similar fascinating banter between the two of them, Geoff seemed satisfied and concentrated on re-filling his wine/beer glass.

Nick took the opportunity to say to Hamish 'I didn't know you were an accountant?'

'Used to be, laddie, used to be.' Hamish seemed to have got

even more Scottish. 'Now retired. But there's still a fascination in numbers. You just have to know what you're looking for.'

Before Hamish could elaborate, Geoff returned. 'Hamish and I are going to play boules in the morning. Trying to get a group together. Why don't you come and join us?'

Having only played once or twice, Nick admitted, 'I'm not very good.'

'That's all right, isn't it Hamish?' said Geoff.

Hamish replied with a grunt, which could have meant anything.

Nick wondered what he would be doing tomorrow morning. There was the off-chance that he and Ros would be in their car en route to Phillip and Kathy's.

'Be a sort of "men only" game. Get away from the girls for the morning,' said Geoff in a sexist manner which, if Lynne had been around, would have resulted in her grabbing his ear and dragging him off to his room where he would have had to stay alone for the evening – facing the corner.

Given the current state of play with Ros, the idea held some attraction for Nick. 'All right. As long as you've got your toes insured for accidental damage caused by stray boules.'

At this point Martin Pike joined them.

Geoff said to Pike, 'Interested in a game of boules tomorrow morning? Bit of exercise?'

Pike appeared to think about it for a moment. 'Why not. That would be most agreeable. Naturism isn't just about sunbathing, you know. It's fitness and health that are important. That's why the magazine "Health and Efficiency" was so titled when it was first printed all those years ago.'

At that point, Geoff made a fatal mistake. He expressed interest. Which led to a history of the original, and at the time only, British magazine where you could see totally nude

women, albeit with pubic hair and genitalia discreetly air-
brushed out.

The Naked Guide has this to say about "Health and
Efficiency":

> For schoolboys in the fifties and sixties, Health and Efficiency was
> the only magazine to turn to for pictures of the naked female form.
> Today, the magazine still sells over 20,000 copies a month.
>
> Despite this, Health and Efficiency (H&E) was a true pioneering
> publication in the history of British naturism. But, interestingly, it
> began life in 1900 as a magazine covering health topics such as
> diet, exercise, herbalism and general advice on living a healthy and
> efficient life.
>
> In the 1920's, when naturism was even more of a minority
> interest than it is today, it was aimed at middle class occupations
> such as doctors and solicitors, becoming an early champion of their
> cause.
>
> H&E advocated the benefits not simply of sun, but also of a
> healthier way of living. Out went smoking and drinking; in their
> place came vegetarianism and callisthenics. It could be said that it
> was the birth of the cult of body fascism which is so prevalent in
> today's society, with an emphasis on exercise, healthy eating and
> looking good, rather than just an enjoyment of the sun and naked
> outdoor living.
>
> Today, Health and Efficiency is under the unlikely stewardship of
> the Goole Times group of publications. It is no longer fascist-inspired;
> it no longer shows pictures of naked children (outlawed in the 1980s)
> but does show fully nude, if imperfectly formed, people enjoying the
> benefits of naked living. And it does espouse a much more majority
> way of life than ever its founders could have imagined.

It was now totally dark. Lights under the caravan awning had
been illuminated. The noise level had risen as more drinks had

been consumed. Nick couldn't see Ros around. Oh, there she was! Talking to Geoff and Lynne in the far corner of the garden. Her black dress blended her into the background, so at first glance you could only see the other two.

Aware of the fact that he hadn't spoken much to Ros all evening, he was about to walk across to join them when Camilla appeared at his elbow. 'Oh Nick, would you mind awfully giving me a hand with these glasses?'

'Not at all,' said Nick, putting his own half-full glass onto the tray of empties to take into the caravan. He followed her ample brown backside up the steps and into the kitchen. 'They need to go into the dishwasher, if you'd be so kind? I'm just putting the finishing touches to my eulogy to Giles.'

With that, she disappeared down the far end of the caravan, presumably to a study or bedroom, and closed the door behind her.

Nick crouched down to work out how to open this particular dishwasher door and turned to begin to load the glasses. He found he was at eye-level with a v-shape of dark female pubic hair – definitely not air-brushed – barely a foot away from his face.

He looked up and found it belonged to Lynne, who was looking down at him. He felt himself blush slightly as he got to his feet.

'Hello Nick.' Lynne sounded just a tiny bit as if she'd had too much to drink. Which in itself was unusual. Members of the Stoke Newington Health Police *always* counted alcohol units and made sure they didn't exceed Government-recommended levels – whatever they happened to be that week.

'Hi!' said Nick. Lynne was, as usual, standing just a little bit too close. Normally, at parties at home, this wouldn't matter too much, but when all she was wearing were those high heels and a very attractive perfume – which Nick couldn't identify (probably made from some ecologically sustainable rain-forest plant) – her closeness was unsettling.

She could have been reading his mind. 'It's strange you standing there fully clothed and me naked, isn't it?'

''Strange'' wasn't the word that Nick would have used. 'Er, yes.'

'I don't know why you don't strip off. It's awfully hot and stuffy to be wearing clothes,' Lynne continued, making Nick's heart beat even quicker. She accompanied this with a gesture she must have got from some movie or other, which was a light touch along the neck of Nick's t-shirt with her forefinger, temptress-style.

'Er, it's Ros really. She didn't want to undress, so, well, I thought I'd better, er, keep her company.

'Ros can be so uptight at times,' said Lynne. Before Nick could consider this statement, she continued. 'Anyway, if you were mine, I'd positively encourage you to go around naked.' Nick gulped. Lynne continued with her theme. 'You look good nude, you know. I remember thinking so the other day when we first met in the restaurant.'

If it were possible, Lynne was now even closer to him than before. Almost close enough for Nick to have to concentrate on getting her face into focus. He took a step back and found himself trapped by the kitchen work surface. 'Well, I have put on a bit round the middle here.' He indicated his slight paunch.

'Nonsense. Let me see.' Lynne laid her hand on his stomach – and kept it there. 'Nothing to be ashamed of. That's what I like about naturism.'

'What's that?'

Lynne took her hand from Nicks's stomach and stared into the distance as if collecting her thoughts. Which, Nick thought, must have been difficult if she'd drunk as much as she appeared to have.

'It was Geoff who wanted us to try it first. Originally I wasn't very keen. Bit like you, really.' Nick was about to protest but Lynne continued. 'Then I began to enjoy it. It stops me eating too much.'

Nick couldn't quite follow that train of thought. 'How does that work then?'

'Well, during the year, if I know we're coming to a naturist resort I think what I'm going to look like in the nude to others.' She moved slightly away from Nick. 'So, you see, I do a little twirl in the mirror in the bedroom to see what I look like from all angles.'

So saying, she demonstrated said twirl, holding both arms away from her body and doing a very slow 360 degree turn in front of Nick, which might have induced a fatal cardio-vascular infarction in an older man. She came to something of an unsteady halt and staggered slightly against Nick, holding his shoulder for support.

'If I look a bit podgy, then I diet more and watch what I eat and drink.'

Lynne showed no sign of taking her arm off Nick's shoulder and he couldn't think of a way of escaping without physically manhandling her nude body out of the way.

'It doesn't seem to bother Geoff,' Nick said. Lynne looked confused at this mention of her husband. 'I mean, he doesn't seem to care what he looks like, nude or clothed.'

Lynne looked drunk-serious. 'No he doesn't. He says all of us are different and we should have no shame in our body shapes and sizes.' She staggered, putting her arm a bit further round Nick's shoulder, tightly, to prevent herself slipping. She leaned her head against his shoulder. 'I think that's bollocks, myself.'

She suddenly went very quiet. If she had gone to sleep or passed out, he'd have a real problem getting her off his shoulder and to a place she could lie down. No difficulty in lifting her, as she didn't weigh a great deal. But in having to hold her naked waist and legs as he did so, he'd feel like a pervert. And what if Ros appeared as he was carrying her across to a sofa? Talk yourself out of that.

He decided to look down to see if she was asleep. It was a mistake. She was looking up at him, her mouth only inches from his own. She moved her mouth towards him. There wasn't a lot he could do about this he thought, I'm just going to have to kiss her back. Which he did.

This time, he really did feel something rise. He knew that Lynne could as well, as by now she had both arms around his neck and was pressing herself against him. In all truth, with his arse against the kitchen work-top, he couldn't really move. Part of him told him he didn't really want to.

She broke off, probably for air but still had her arms round his neck. 'Naughty Nicky. Taking advantage of a girl just because she's not wearing anything,' she giggled.

Nick now became acutely aware of the danger of their surroundings. Anyone could walk in at any time. What the fuck would he do if that person was Geoff? Or Ros? He was in serious jeopardy.

He took both her arms, managed to prise them away from his neck and he moved her slightly back, taking sure not to touch any other part of her body but her shoulders — and very nice they were, too. To the casual bystander, they now appeared to be two people having an innocent conversation in the kitchen, at a party. Albeit one of them completely nude.

Nick suddenly wondered if he had any lipstick on his face, until he remembered that lipstick was especially 'verboten' by the Health Police.

Lynne seemed to have sobered up slightly, although she didn't seem the tiniest bit embarrassed about their clinch. 'That was nice, Nick. I enjoyed that.' As she said this, she looked down at the bulge in his trousers, which was still prominent. 'Where's my drink? Ah, there it is.'

She reached over for her glass of red wine which she'd put on the counter. She showed no signs of leaving, so Nick decided he'd better get on with the dishwasher task, trying not to look behind him where she was resting against the other work surface, ankles crossed, fuck-me shoes in evidence.

'Have you been to the night club yet, Nick?' asked Lynne, and then answered her own question. 'Silly me. I forgot. This is only your second day.' Yes, thought Nick, two days that have seemed like a life sentence. In Broadmoor. 'You, me, Ros and Geoff ought to go down there one night. It'll be fun.'

'I've just been talking to Janet and John about it. You know, the Dungeon? Doesn't sound my idea of fun.' Nick finished loading the glasses and, leaning against the dishwasher, turned to face Lynne. He picked up his own glass of wine.

Lynne giggled. Women around him seemed to be doing a lot of that, thought Nick. Nice to know he was the cause of such amusement. She said 'No, not that horrible Dungeon place. That's for the S and M wierdies. No, there's more downstairs than that.'

'Such as?'

'Well, there are quite a few private and communal rooms for couples. And more, if the fancy takes.'

'What, you mean these rooms are there for, for, er, for . . .'

Again Lynne laughed. 'Yes Nick, for having sex. The French are heavily into, what I suppose they'd have called in the 'sixties, "swinging". Swapping partners. Being involved in three-somes, orgies, that sort of thing. They have large circulation contact magazines devoted to it. It's almost a national sport.'

'After rugby and football, I presume,' said Nick, for want of

something to say. And to lighten this new direction of attack
from Lynne. What on earth was she suggesting? He didn't have
to wait long to find out.

'You know, we could go to the night club. Upstairs is quite
respectable. Be nice to have a bit of a bop as well. At least Ros
could keep her clothes on. And perhaps we could slip away
down into the basement. Just you and me. Nobody need ever
know.' Lynne said, twiddling the stem of her glass. She looked
candidly at him, as if to brook no misunderstanding of what she
was saying.

To be honest, Nick was feeling a bit dumbstruck – an
increasingly common by-product of being trapped in Le Paradis. On top of everything, were boring old Geoff and,
admittedly attractive, psychotherapist Lynne, into wife swapping? He had to find out.

'Do you and Geoff, you know, go and join in. You know,
swap partners? Get involved in three-somes?' Nick was somewhat embarrassed asking Lynne these questions, but she didn't
seem at all fazed.

'Of course we don't. It just occurred to me that it might be a
good opportunity for you and me, that's all.'

Oh no! Thought Nick. She's on her way over again. Lynne
put her glass back down on the surface, uncrossed her legs and
tottered a few steps towards him, in her high heels.

She reached Nick as he backed away as far as the dishwasher
would allow. He kept his hands down at his side as she once
again leant her body against his. She put one hand around his
neck to pull his mouth down to hers. The other hand, my God,
she put on his crotch, almost immediately restoring his erection
to full rude health.

Just at this moment, three things occurred in quick succes-
sion.

First, Camilla appeared in the kitchen, papers in hand.

'Nick, have you . . .' Camilla began. 'Oh terribly sorry! I . . .' She stood there lost for words, which must have been a new sensation for her.

Lynne removed her hand from Nick's crotch, which was just as well as the second thing to happen was Ros appearing just behind Camilla, taking in the very unwelcome sight of Lynne with arm around Nick's neck, pressed against him as if playing sardines.

And the third thing? The pressure of Nick's backside started the knob on the dishwasher which groaned into life. All Nick managed to say with a rictus smile, that would not have disgraced a corpse, was 'Er, just doing the washing up.'

24

'We are gathered here this evening to celebrate a life. The life of our erstwhile colleague, and fellow naturist, Giles Curtis.'

Camilla was standing under the awning of the caravan, where it was light enough for her to peer occasionally at her notes through half-moon Dior reading spectacles. Listening to her eulogy, with wine or beer in hand, were the everyday motley crew of Le Paradis English folk.

Lynne was swaying ever so slightly against Geoff, whose arm was wrapped around her shoulder to prevent her toppling over.

Hamish and Martin Pike were looking serious, standing shoulder to shoulder and paying strict attention to everything Camilla had to say. As were Janet and John, next to them.

Charles was gazing into the distance, whilst Jack was placidly smoking another cigarette.

Sam and Garry were trying, mostly successfully, to shush the kids.

And to one side were two people, distinguishable from the

rest in that they were clothed, who looked as if they'd rather be anywhere else but in each other's company.

Camilla continued. 'Charles and I only knew Giles in the last week or so, but during that time we came to know him almost as one of the family.'

'Here, here!' was the response from Pike.

'Quite, thank you Martin. It truly is tragic that he's been cut down in his prime by the evil hand of an unknown assassin. An assassin that may even now be in our midst.'

This caused a certain amount of looking about by the assembly until Camilla added, 'I'm sure none of us here would have partaken in this heinous deed. We all live here in Le Paradis in a spirit of sisterhood and brotherhood, helping one another, yes, even loving one another.'

That may be the problem, thought both Nick and Ros separately. There was a certain temptation in Le Paradis to take the "love one another" message far too literally.

Camilla continued. 'Let us hope that the culprit is quickly found and punished.' Sounding like the headmistress of a public girls' school in Weybridge, talking about someone who's stolen another girl's ruler. 'Then we can all rest easy in our beds in the knowledge that Giles' death will have been well and truly avenged.'

There was another 'Here, here' from Pike's direction.

'There is no good time to die,' Camilla carried on, 'but it was a particularly unfortunate time for Giles. Thrown on the employment scrapheap at an early age, things were about to take a turn for the better for him.'

At this point, Nick started to pay attention. Ignoring the intense bad vibes he felt emanating from Ros, he metaphorically pricked up his ears.

'He was only telling us on the day he died that he had a business deal that was about to pay off. A transaction of some sort which would help make his retirement more comfortable and allow him to do the travelling he still felt he had to do.' Camilla paused, to see where she had reached in her script.

This was news to Nick. Nobody had mentioned before that Giles Curtis was about to better himself financially. This, perhaps, tied in with the blackmail idea Nick had shared with the inspector – of Giles blackmailing Charles about his past criminal record. Maybe there was something in it after all. But why would Charles's wife be the one to impart this knowledge? If she knew, then surely she would have shut up about it.

'There's a lesson for all of us in his untimely demise. And that is 'seize the day'. Do the things you want to do. Don't delay or put them off.' Both Ros and Nick thought independently about Jean-Luc and Shareen/Lynne. 'Because we are here only for a little while. Who knows when we may be recalled, just like Giles, before we have had an opportunity to fulfil our individual destinies.'

Camilla seemed to have come to a halt. Unfortunately, it was only for dramatic effect. 'So then let's remember Giles Curtis and let's raise a glass to him and his life. Let's remember the good times we've had with him, and not the sadness of his death. I propose a toast for us all.' She raised her glass. 'To Giles. May he truly rest in peace.' The sentiment was echoed by the assembled gathering. 'And may God grant that his killer be found and punished.'

Nick didn't know whether applause was appropriate at this point so didn't do anything except look sideways at a glowering Ros as he raised his glass. Pike thought otherwise and clapped his hands. At first he was alone but, as he looked around at the others with his best Mussolini glare, they all joined in – with varying degrees of enthusiasm.

Pike then strode over to where Camilla was standing. 'If I

may Camilla,' he said and, before she could answer, said 'Thank you.'

Martin Pike looked out at the Brits almost as if, thought Nick, they were a gathering of blackshirts in Rome. His eyes glittered behind his glasses. 'I'd like to just add my own few words to those excellent ones of Camilla.' He acknowledged Camilla by turning towards her and nodding. She almost simpered. 'I also only knew Giles for a short period, but in that time we became very close. Very close indeed.'

Nick wondered how close that was. Could Giles and Pike have been, well, lovers? No. It was impossible. But was it? Who could bloody tell in Le Paradis. It seemed everything here was possible. And nothing was possible.

Pike continued. 'I feel the loss keenly. He was a great bloke. He loved life. He loved naturism. And he was looking forward to a brighter future.' Again that reference to a change in circumstances.

'We had plans when he returned to Britain. He was going to join my club.' Nick felt sure Pike wasn't referring to Soho House or the Groucho. 'And we were going to collaborate on completing the research for the Naked Guide. Now, alas, none of this will happen.' Pike did seem very upset. 'So I'd just like to add my toast and farewell to Giles Curtis.'

He raised his glass and, surprisingly, everyone else raised theirs and uttered a round of 'Giles Curtis'. Who knows, perhaps Martin Pike had missed his vocation as Italian dictator by a mere seventy years. He stepped away from Camilla and back to Hamish, who shook his hand.

'Thank you for those touching words,' said Camilla. 'Now please carry on enjoying yourselves.'

That would have been a tough call for most of those present. Lynne could hardly stand. Pike and Hamish looked sad. Charles and Jack, enigmatic. Camilla pensive.

Janet and John looked as if they had other places to go, men to flay off, people to torture, and were clearly getting itchy feet to leave and join the night shift at the Dungeon.

As Nick stood there, wondering what Ros would be saying to him once they were truly alone, Garry and Sam came up. They still had the kids with them.

'Gotta go.' Sam said to Ros. 'Get these little bleeders into bed.' She gave Ros a kiss on each cheek in farewell. Ros smiled, briefly. After all it wasn't Sam's fault that Ros's partner was such a bastard. Studiously ignoring Nick, Ros showed him she still had the power of speech by chatting to Sam.

While she was doing this, Garry engaged Nick in conversation. 'Nice do, eh?'

Nick could not but agree, with a vivid image of a naked Lynne with her hand on his crotch springing instantly and unbidden to mind.

Garry continued, taking a cigarette from a pack he kept in a small shoulder bag and firing it up. 'I meant to tell you. You know we were having a chat about Charlie boy today?'

'Yes?'

'Well I was looking at him standing with that other geezer, Jack, and I'm sure Charles looks familiar.' Garry took a long drag of his cigarette.

'Where from?' asked Nick.

'Long, long time ago. Never forget a face. Names, yes. Faces, never.' Garry looked puzzled and, to be truthful, a bit pissed. 'When I remember, you'll be the first to know my son.'

So saying he gave Nick a handshake and a bit of a bear hug, which reminded Nick a bit of the nude wrestling scene in "Women in Love", only with one man clothed, and he was gone with a final 'See ya later!' following Sam and the kids.

Peace descended on the garden. Only for a short time

because he was there with Ros, who was now looking as if she had a few words to say to him, and none of them the slightest bit complimentary. Was it sixth sense or did he feel that there could be yet another row scheduled to take off soon?

The party broke up shortly afterwards. Geoff, seemingly blissfully unaware of Lynne's impersonation of a "femme fatale", reminded Nick of tomorrow's boules date. He then left with Lynne, who seemed very slightly the worse for wear — well, make that very much the worse for wear.

Jack had gone back to Reception, presumably to take over the night shift from Shareen. Janet and John had already gone off in search of whatever it was they were looking for in the way of family entertainment. And Hamish toddled off to his caravan, looking forward to a bedtime dram or three.

This left Nick and Ros alone outside the gate guarded by "the Daimler". Nick had a feeling the walk back would not be a pleasant one. He knew that Ros would want to talk about the fetching little tableau she'd stumbled across in the kitchen and he just didn't feel up to another quarrel. Particularly this late at night when he was also feeling the effects of perhaps too many red wines.

Just as Ros opened her mouth to start the attack, right on cue, the cavalry arrived.

'Hey! You two! Wait for me!' a voice called from behind. They both turned. Martin Pike was hustling towards them.

Nick had forgotten that Pike was still there. He must have been in the caravan, using the lavatory or saying his goodbyes to Charles and Camilla. For the first time in the past two days — make that "ever" — Nick was genuinely pleased to see him.

'Mind if I join you for the walk back?'

It was a rhetorical question because he immediately fell in alongside them. There was nothing that they could say or do to prevent it, although Ros did try.

'Actually Martin, we were having a private . . .'

Nick cut in. 'Please do. Seems silly to go separately as we live next door to one another.'

Nick and Ros didn't have much to say on the way back to the cabin. Even if they had wanted to talk, Martin Pike, in his normal fashion, monopolized the conversation.

'It's strange, isn't it, all this.' Pike waved his hand in a general direction to take in the resort and its grounds. Nick suspected that Pike may also have imbibed a bit more than usual.

'Is it?' Nick asked, clearly going to be on the receiving end of what was on Pike's mind anyway, whether he answered or not.

'All in just a hundred years.'

What was he going on about? 'A hundred years?' Nick was beginning to feel like a parrot. But it was preferable to being berated by Ros.

'Yes, you can date back the recent history of naturism a hundred years. We've come a long way in that time. This would not have existed before then – no naturist resort would.'

'I expect you've got a passage on this in The Naked Guide,' said Nick, a touch sarcastically.

Pike ignored, or probably simply didn't notice, Nick's tone of voice. 'Indeed I have!'

The Naked Guide has this to say about the modern day origins of naturism:

After the dark ages of Victorian repression, where even table legs had to be clothed to prevent impure thoughts, the new century dawned bright and clear. But it was to Germany that naturism in the 20th century had to look for its current incarnation.

Called 'Freikorperkultur', now abbreviated to FKK, meaning free body culture, the movement was influenced by two seminal works.

Heinrich Pudor's book published at the turn of the century called

'The Cult of the Nude' acted, as one website history puts it most aptly, 'as a timely beacon' to the movement. The movement gained momentum with the publication of Heinrich Ungewitter's 'Nakedness', a utopia of nude living which was reprinted several times.

In 1903 the first nudist club was opened in Hamburg, called the Free-Light Park (Freilichtspark). By 1930, in fact, Germany had an estimated 3 million naturists. And although the German naturist organisation, like every other non-National Socialist organisation, was banned by Hitler, the practice still remained — even though it had to go underground, so to speak.

By the twenties and thirties, Britain too was beginning to shed its old inhibitions about nudity. As was America. On one particularly hot summer in the 1930s, thousands of men on Long Island, New York disobeyed the law and went topless, the law changing in 1936 to decriminalise topless male bathing. By . . .

The trawl through the history of naturism occupied, somewhat unsurprisingly, the total travel time to their respective cabins. It gave Nick pause to ponder on what might occur when they did get back.

OK, so Ros had caught Lynne draped all over him like an ill-fitting suit. But it truly hadn't been his fault. She'd just jumped him. And without any warning. What was the problem there?

Surely even Ros could tell Lynne was just a touch out of it? She could see it was all probably harmless. So what was he worrying about? What on earth could she complain about? She'd find something, he thought gloomily.

By contrast, if Nick had but known it, Ros's mind was in something of a turmoil. Yes, she had found him with Lynne, but to be fair to Nick he had been fully clothed. Unlike Jean-Luc and herself this afternoon. And, but for luck and the vagaries of fate, it could just as easily have been Nick that walked in on her, rather than the other way round.

But then her more unreasonable self kicked in. What the fuck was he doing with that skinny bitch anyway? Please! Normally you'd have to have a clean bill of health signed by three doctors before someone like Lynne would even let you breathe on her, let alone consent to sex. Oh yes, and a sterile room was also a pre-condition. Rubber gloves and surgical masks optional.

She calmed herself down. What really was at the root of her problem, she decided, was that once again they had both been out of step with the customs of Le Paradis. That was pissing her off for a start. And if she was being totally honest with herself, well, she was simply sexually frustrated. After all, it's not everyday you have the undivided – or should that be divided – attention of a nude young Frenchman.

They reached their cabins. But it was a further five minutes before Nick and Ros could extricate themselves from listening to the final chapter in the 20th century naturist saga. It took a further minute for Ros to fish the key from the deeper recesses of her bag. And they were "home".

The cabin seemed to Nick synonymous with "arguments" and "bad temper". It was like one of those places, in a horror movie, that was imbued with evil.

The cabin was stifling. Nick got some water from the fridge and poured it into a glass. He took a few swallows whilst looking out of the open door into the darkness, listening to the sounds of the cicadas.

He was stalling for time, dreading the impending quarrel with Ros, which loomed over the cabin like a gathering storm. He sighed, rinsed the glass and put it on the draining board. Better get it over with. Let her have her shout. Then maybe things would blow over.

He turned away from the sink and found that Ros had been

watching him from the beaded curtain leading into the bedroom. Leaning casually against the door frame, she had discarded her dress but retained the new black bra and pants.

She didn't seem as if she was about to brandish a metaphorical rolling pin. In fact, she looked as if she was offering her services to passing punters from a red-lit doorway in Amsterdam – an impression heightened by the fact that she was also wearing high heels.

'Are you going to stand there all night?' Ros said. 'I think you and me have some unfinished business.'

He closed the door and walked across to her. 'Look, if it's about Lynne, then I'm . . .'

Before he could apologize, Ros put her fingers on his lips to shush him. She then put her arms around his neck and kissed him, long and deeply. Christ! Nick thought. She hadn't kissed him like that for years. He responded and, unlike yesterday night, felt a reciprocal stirring below.

Ros could feel it as well and smiled up at him. 'I think it's time we got you out of those restricting clothes.'

'If you insist, doctor.'

Ros pulled him into the bedroom and sat on the side of the bed facing him. Nick removed his t-shirt and flung it aside. He was just going to do the same with his trousers, when he felt Ros's fingers unzipping his flies. 'Something seems to have come up,' Ros said, almost playfully, as she leaned forward to take him in her mouth. It had been so long since they'd last had sex, she'd forgotten that Nick himself didn't have a lot to worry about in the size department.

From that point, it all became a bit of a blur. Reluctantly moving Ros's head from its current resting place, Nick removed his trousers and boxers. He then had fun taking off her bra before attending to her black pants. Typical, thought Ros. Just like buses. Wait for months for one man to go down on you and two come along on the same day. Not that she was complaining, you understand.

Things progressed, as they are apt to do, until she could wait no longer for him to put it inside her. 'Now, Nick, now. Come on! Fuck me!' Ros liked to talk a little dirty in bed. Just a little.

In a strange reprise of a scene earlier that day, a scene of which Nick was totally unaware, Nick turned to the bedside cabinet drawer to take out the packet of Durex he'd put there when he'd unpacked his toiletry bag.

Ros saw what he was doing and, unlike this afternoon, said 'No, Nick. No preservatifs tonight.' Fuck! What had she just said!

Nick stopped what he was doing, which was tearing open a pack of condoms, to look at her. 'Pardon?'

'Preservatifs. French for condoms,' Ros said, in what she hoped was a casual fashion.

'Oh,' said Nick, returning to the task in hand. He then stopped again. 'What was the rest of that sentence?'

'I said no, er, condoms tonight. Please. Thank you.' As if she was asking a waiter for a salad without the dressing.

By now Nick had the said article half-rolled down, or up, his penis, depending on your point of view, and wasn't amused. 'But you could get pregnant?'

'Could, yes, but probably not.'

' "Probably" is not good enough.' Nick had now completed the task and was about to roll over on top of her.

Ros looked up into his eyes. 'Would that be so bad?'

'Would what be so bad?' Nick was still nursing his erection through this conversation.

'Getting pregnant.'

'Well, yes it would. Now hold still. This won't hurt a bit,' said Nick.

Desperate though she was for sex, Ros stopped his hand and

closed her legs. 'Just take it off Nick. And let's see what happens, shall we.'

'No Ros. We agreed that we need to talk this baby business through. You just can't spring it on me when we're about to fuck. It's not fair.'

Ros bridled at this remark. 'What's fairness got to do with it? Is it fair to deny me the chance to become a mother? Is that fair in your book?'

Nick became exasperated. 'No, I agree that's not fair either. Now can we talk about this some other time.' He was rapidly beginning to go off the boil. If he waited much longer, the condom would drop off of its own accord. Not that the member beneath would be much use to Ros by then.

Ros still looked up at him. She was not amused. 'No, Nick. We can't talk about this some other time. You're always putting it off. You can have me now but you are not using a *preservatif* . . .' Fuck!!! Why did she keep saying that. She was too angry to care now. '. . . and you're not pulling out either. I'll make sure of that.'

Nick turned away from her. 'I can't do that.'

'Why not?'

'I've already said. We need to talk about this.'

'And I've already said that the time for talk is over. Don't you want children?'

Nick sat up and put his legs over the side of the bed. The *preservatif*, or whatever the hell Ros insisted on calling it, had now removed itself together with his erection. He turned to look at her. 'Well, yes. In the fullness of time.'

'Nick, we don't have time. *I* haven't got much time. This is something I need to do. And I really do want you to be the father of my child, our child, our children even.' She reached out to take his hand.

Nick was quiet. 'I couldn't do it now anyway, with or without a "preservatif".'

Ros noticed the disappearance of his erection. She tried to make some amends. 'It is important to me, you know.'

'Yes, I know that. It's just that, well, I'm not too sure I'm ready for such a move. Such a life-changing commitment.' Nick looked down at her.

Ros thought she'd never seen him quite that serious. What had she started? It was too late to go back. She had to go on, whatever the consequences.

'Just think about it, OK? There's no hurry but don't take a long while to make your decision.' She pulled his hand and he moved down next to her on the bed. She put her hand gently on his face. 'You don't have to say anything now. But I do want children. And if you don't, then I'm going to have to find someone who does. Much as I love you. Much as that would hurt.'

It hadn't been the easiest of days for Ros and, with this last statement, she burst out crying. Fuck! That wasn't supposed to happen.

Nick held her close to him, feeling her tears wetting his chest. At that moment he knew he didn't want to lose her. And he knew he didn't want kids just yet. Heads you lose. Tails you lose.

Ros's sobs subsided and were replaced by gentle deep breathing as she fell asleep. The end, thought Nick, of yet another perfect day of their holiday in Paradise.

DAY THREE

'Civilisation held nothing like this in its narrow and circumscribed sphere, hemmed in by restrictions and conventionalities. Even clothes were a hindrance and a nuisance. At last he was free. He had not realized what a prisoner he had been.'

Edgar Rice Burroughs, Tarzan of the Apes

25

Ros woke up. Her first thoughts were of their argument last night. This was serious. After all she had given Nick, in effect, an ultimatum. It had made sense at the time but what did it look like in the morning sunlight currently streaming through the flimsy cabin curtains. Not too good, were her first reactions. More importantly, how was Nick feeling about it?

In fact, where was Nick?

She was alone in the bed. Surely he hadn't gone off to sleep elsewhere? She got wearily out of bed, ran her hands through her hair and walked into the kitchen.

No sign of him. The brown shag pile sofa bed remained unopened. Only one more place to look.

When Ros entered the bathroom, all thoughts of their argument were involuntarily thrust from her mind by the bizarre sight that greeted her.

Nick, nude of course, was standing with one foot resting on

the bidet, safety razor in hand. Much shaving foam was in evidence, but not where it should normally be, that is, round his face.

He looked at her a touch sheepishly, she thought, as if to gauge how she was feeling after last night. 'Hi. How are you this morning?'

Ros couldn't get round to answering that question. She had one of her own. 'What on earth are you doing?' she said, trying to inject a calmer, ''more tea vicar'', tone into her voice than she clearly felt.

'Shaving my balls,' came the prompt reply.

Ros could feel a mixture of irritation and slight distaste rising inside. Almost as if she'd discovered him doing something slightly obscene – such as accessing ''red hot teenage babes'' on the internet.

'Yes I can see that.'

Which was a lie, really, because large areas of his genitalia were covered in creamy white shaving foam, making them impenetrable to casual gaze. All she could clearly see was his penis, which he was lifting with his left hand to allow easier access to the foamy areas beneath.

'What I really meant was why?'

Without diverting gaze from his scrotum, Nick replied quite evenly, all the time scraping away, albeit tentatively, at his testicles: 'Well it seems to be what the well-undressed man is wearing this season. Haven't you noticed? Many of the blokes round these parts, if you'll forgive the expression, have shaved genitals.'

'You may find this hard to believe,' said Ros, 'but I don't go around all day looking at men's balls.'

If truth was told, she tried to avoid looking at them, which wasn't that easy given their current situation. She felt a particular pity for the poor middle-aged check-out woman in the supermarket whose eye line was on precisely the same level as the genitalia of her customers.

'Except Hamish of course,' continued Nick, now giving the razor a quick rinse before resuming the task in hand.

'Sorry?' Ros's attention had wandered.

'Except Hamish. Hamish looks as if he's wearing a fur coat, and a sporran, all the time.'

'But why?' said Ros, clearly feeling that she was rapidly losing any plot she may have understood so far.

'Because he's so hairy of course.'

'No, not Hamish. Why shave your balls?' she tried to keep the rising hysteria out of her voice.

Nick looked up from his labours and spoke to her slowly and evenly as if to an imbecile. 'I suppose you could say it's a fashion statement. If you can't wear clothes, then you want your body to look at it's best. And that includes your privates. They say it's more hygienic as well.'

'They also say that about circumcision, so the next time I come in here am I going to find you with a scalpel in your hand?'

Ignoring the comment, Nick was now drying himself off and turned proudly to Ros. 'There, how does that look?'

Despite herself, she looked down as he proudly displayed his shaven testicles. She thought they looked better hidden by a layer of hair. Bereft of any covering, the image of turkey necks hanging upside down in butchers' shops came unbidden to mind. Pink, wrinkly and shiny. And very unappealing. Not a pleasant image in theory or, from where she was standing, in practice.

How come Nick seemed to be concerned with such a trivial matter as shaving his balls when they'd had such an important set-to last night? Was it some sort of displacement activity to stop him from thinking too deeply about it? Had he taken their argument last night as seriously as she had? She wondered if she should raise the subject again. Just to check which way the wind was blowing.

If only she knew. Last night's argument had badly shaken Nick up. He hadn't realized the strength of Ros's feelings about the baby issue until that point. Well, perhaps he had but thought that not mentioning it would somehow make it go away. The good old ostrich "head in sand" routine. Hey, it had worked before, maybe it would work again. Then perhaps not.

Naked, and newly-shaven, Nick went back through the bedroom to the kitchen. Ros followed him as far as the bedroom and looked around for a wrap or robe. For some reason she felt even less like being nude today.

'Like some coffee?' Nick called into the bedroom from the kitchen, putting on the kettle.

'Please,' came Ros's reply.

As he was making the coffee, Ros came into the kitchen dressed in a cotton wrap, tied over her breasts but at the same time leaving tantalising glimpses of her pubic hair. Nick noticed the cover-up but didn't comment.

Instead, he decided to raise the subject of last night – before she did. He put a cup of coffee on the table and joined her with his own. The cabin door was open. It looked as if it was going to be another peerless azure sky day.

'How you feeling?' he asked.

She smiled weakly at him. 'Oh a bit raw, you know.'

Nick put his hand on hers. 'Yeah, well what was said was said. And I haven't forgotten any of it. A decision has to be made about our future and I appreciate that as much as you. But from a practical point of view it just isn't something we can do right now. We're still stuck here and I'm still a murder suspect.'

Nick continued. 'So I think we should be sensible about this. First things first. Let's sort out this little mess before anything else. I promise when we get out of here, the baby issue will be number one priority. I really, really do mean that.'

It was quite a long speech for Nick and he had meant every word. He watched Ros to see how it had gone down. She leaned over and gently kissed him on the cheek. Not that badly, then.

'OK. But don't leave it too long once we leave this hell hole, all right?'

Nick got up and searched around for something to go with the coffee. It didn't take long. They were totally out of bread and croissants. Not to worry, he thought. Time to give his newly shaved balls their first moment of glory on the Le Paradis catwalk.

'There's nothing to eat. I'll go down the supermarket,' said Nick, getting to his feet.

'No you finish your coffee. I'll go. I think I'll take a bit of a walk first,' said Ros. She picked up her bag and, noted Nick, went out wearing her cotton wrap. Not totally within the rules of Le Paradis, but probably just acceptable, he thought. Good God! Not only was he beginning to talk like Martin Pike, he was starting to *think* like him as well.

Nick poured some more coffee and debated taking it outside. Whenever he did this, he became embroiled either in a conversation about naturism, which he just wasn't in the mood for this morning – or any morning, come to think of it – or a third degree grilling by the Sureté.

Instead, he thought he'd take his coffee back to bed with him and read. He pushed through the beads, put the coffee on his bedside table and half-lay, half-sat up on the bed, leaning against the headboard.

He couldn't resist admiring his newly exposed testicles. He

didn't care what Ros thought, he thought them a great improvement. Sort of neater and tidier. He wondered whether he should trim his pubic hair to go with them.

As he was pondering this important issue, he heard a creaking from the front porch steps. He hadn't closed the door. Who the hell was that? Ros back so quickly? His question was quickly answered as he heard the unmistakable Australian tones of Shareen. 'Hello? Anyone home?' followed by a tentative knock on the door.

'Yes, hi. Through here,' Nick called back. Hang on. Why had he done that? Why hadn't he got up to go to the kitchen to meet her. Too late. Shareen pushed through the beaded curtain and was standing just inside the room, leaning against the door frame just as Ros had last night, but facing into the room rather than out.

Shareen was wearing what she always wore. Nothing. And it looked amazingly good on her. She smiled down at him. 'You still in bed? Alone as well, I see?'

'Er, yes. I mean, no. I just came back here to avoid a chance meeting with Pike or the Inspector,' Nick explained, and made as if to get to his feet.

'No, you stay there. Any more coffee?'

'In the kitchen.'

Shareen bustled out and returned quickly with a cup. She sat down on Ros's side of the bed, feet on floor, putting her cup on Ros's bedside cabinet and turning slightly to face Nick.

This wasn't doing him much good. On every count. He'd imagined, of course, being in bed with Shareen, but he hadn't quite envisaged it like this. And with Ros due to re-appear any moment. What with the anti-climax of last night, or should that be non-climax, he was also having great difficulty keeping his member under control. He guessed it was only fear of what might happen if Ros walked in that helped him manage the feat.

Being caught clothed in a kitchen with a naked Lynne paled into insignificance on the infidelity scale in comparison with being found lying naked on a bed with a nude Australian woman both drinking, what could possibly pass for, post-coital cups of coffee.

Worryingly, Shareen looked as if she was there for a prolonged visit. 'You needn't worry about bumping into the inspector. Jack said he went off early today to do something. Didn't say what.'

'There's still Martin Pike though,' said Nick with a smile. 'The words "plague" and "avoid like" come to mind.'

Shareen seemed pre-occupied and didn't even smile at this. Well it wasn't that amusing, thought Nick, but pretty good in the circumstances.

'How'd the party go? Jack said it went well. I would have loved to have been there,' said Shareen.

Nick thought back to the scene in the kitchen. 'Yes, it was quite an evening. It's a pity you weren't there.' An image of a naked Shareen instead of a naked Lynne in the kitchen popped in to his mind and didn't do a great deal for his already perilously high blood pressure.

Shareen looked down at her cup of coffee. Nick felt she had something to say. Maybe she was also feeling uneasy sitting here in the bedroom. Although she'd had a chance to go into the kitchen and turned it down. What was on her mind? Surely she didn't expect him to, well, try anything on?

'Penny for them?' Nick asked.

Shareen looked up and gave him a shy smile. As she did so, just for an instant, she looked incredibly young and somewhat vulnerable – unsure of herself. 'It's nothing.' She changed the subject, enquiring brightly, 'How's the sleuthing going?'

'Not brilliantly. I keep learning little bits of information that don't really add up to much.' Nick was thinking about what he'd found out last night. That Charles and Jack went back many years. And that Garry thought he recognized Charles from the past. He wondered if Shareen could add anything. 'Do you know what Jack did before he bought Le Paradis?'

Shareen looked at him. 'Jack? No idea. Why are you interested?'

'Not sure, really. Just reviewing the facts in the case.'

Reviewing the facts also kept Nick's mind off the attractive woman sitting just a couple of feet away on the bed.

He wondered how interested Shareen really was in him. When they were sitting on the jetty near the boathouse the other day, he'd had the distinct impression she was. When was that? Well, only yesterday. Christ! It seemed as if they'd been in this place for weeks. The opposite of time flying when you're having fun.

Nick continued. 'I found out last night that Giles Curtis said that his fortunes were about to take a turn for the better. Any idea what he meant by that?'

Shareen gave a tiny very fetching shrug of her shoulders. Nick had to admit he would have given her an A grade in the French GCSE Shrugging paper – on the spot. 'No. He never mentioned it to me. You tried the others? Hamish, Garry, you know? See if they know anything?'

He hadn't. Maybe he'd mention the subject at the boules later. 'No. That's a thought.' Nick gazed forward at the wall. Less risky than staring at Shareen's naked form. 'Not exactly Poirot and Hastings are we.'

Shareen laughed. She seemed to be less pre-occupied, less serious than when she arrived. Loosening up. But Nick still had the feeling that she was holding back some piece of information. Something she wanted to tell him but couldn't – or wouldn't.

Nick suddenly wondered exactly why Shareen had come over here in the first place. He was just about to ask, when the front steps once again creaked. Shareen heard them as well and guiltily jumped to her feet, still holding the cup. Within what seemed like a nano-second, Ros was standing in the beaded curtain doorway, stopped dead and staring at the touching little tableau in front of her.

For a second nobody moved or spoke. It was like a scene from an erotic Madame Tussaud's exhibit. It was Nick who broke the silence. 'Hi, Ros. Get the croissants?'

Ros raised a paper bag that she was holding in her hand. She did not look that happy, thought Nick. And seemed to have lost the power of speech.

Shareen filled the gap in the silence. 'I just popped in to give you a message? From the office?' So that's why she was here.

'A message that you have to deliver in the bedroom?' Ros had learned to speak again – but in question marks, just like Shareen.

Nick thought he'd better help out. 'I asked her in here.' Shit! That didn't sound right. 'What I mean was, I was in here lying down and Shareen came through to deliver the message.'

'And is that all *she* came through to deliver?' said Ros, stonily pointing at Shareen whilst looking at Nick.

'Now wait a minute!' Shareen decided to join in. 'Who's this "she" you're talking about? Just what are you insinuating?'

Oh no, thought Nick. There's going to be a fight any minute. His second, more unworthy thought, was "this might be interesting".

Ros turned to Shareen. 'That you've had your eyes on Nick from the moment we arrived. That's what I'm insinuating.'

'You what?' said Shareen, screwing up her face in a none too attractive fashion. 'After your man? When I've got a perfectly good one of my own? As you well know!'

Hang on. He didn't know Shareen was going out with anyone. And if he didn't, how come Ros knew?

What was even more peculiar was that this speech appeared briefly to give Ros pause. It didn't last long. 'What else am I expected to think when I catch you here − in our bedroom?'

Instead of getting angry, Shareen now smiled, and continued in a very sarcastic tone. 'Oh yes. In your bedroom. It does look bad doesn't it when someone catches you in someone else's bedroom. And you both happen to be nude. That does look very suspicious indeed.'

Ros backed off. 'Well, I suppose there's an innocent explanation for it.'

Shareen continued. 'Yes there is. In this instance.'

To Nick's amazement, Ros now looked down and seemed to have not a lot to add. The argument had fizzled out and he couldn't quite work out why.

Shareen sensed victory. She turned to Nick. 'What I came over to tell you was that there was a phone call. From someone called Phillip? He's going to ring back in an hour's time − at . . .' Shareen looked at her watch to make the calculation '. . . ten. I said I'd try to get you there to take the call.'

'Oh, right. Thanks, Shareen.'

'Don't mention it. See you around,' Shareen said, giving Nick a radiant smile and making a move towards the beaded doorway. Ros stepped aside to make room for her. Shareen had to have the last word. 'Bye Ros. And I hope I *don't* see *you* around.'

Both of them remained motionless as they heard Shareen leave the cabin. Nick found that he'd been holding his breath and now let it out. He also realized he'd been lying on the bed for what seemed ages. He got to his feet with slight cramp in his calves. Without a word, Ros turned and walked into the kitchen.

When Nick joined her, the kettle was on and she was looking out the door, arms folded. She seemed to have calmed down. Hearing him, without turning around, Ros said wearily, 'Is there any risk of me leaving you alone for a moment and not catching you with a naked woman about your person?'

Nick didn't quite know what to say in reply. Anything he did say he was sure would be incriminating. So he said nothing, taking a croissant from the paper bag on the kitchen table and chewing it whilst looking out at the view. It seemed as if it was going to be just as hot today as it had been yesterday.

Nick left the cabin in good time to get to Reception by ten. In fact, he exited early to escape from the not-too-great atmosphere that had settled on the place in the wake of Shareen's departure.

He was rapidly coming to the conclusion that, if he were being blamed by Ros for womanising, he might as well have a go at it. Here he was taking all the flak for events in which he was a fairly innocent bystander. Why not actually do something to warrant being attacked!

By this time he had reached the supermarket across the way from Reception. It *was* really hot again. Nick could feel the sun burning into his factor 8-protected shoulders. The only other thing Nick was wearing was a small towel, draped around his neck. To sit on when he got to the office. Oh yes, and a pair of flip-flops to stop his feet from burning on contact with the hot surface of the ground.

Just as he was about to cross the road, Camilla came out of the supermarket, plastic shopping bag in hand. She spotted Nick and approached him.

'Good morning Nick. How are you today?'

Nick felt she was enquiring as much about his mental as his physical health. With a woman's intuition, Camilla probably guessed that Ros wouldn't have taken catching him with Lynne lying down, so to speak. Acknowledging the possible double meaning of the question, Nick smiled, 'Not too bad in the circumstances. Great party, by the way.'

'Yes, you seemed to enjoy it, I noticed,' Camilla said, looking briefly down at Nick's crotch, as if reliving Lynne's hand round it.

'It's difficult when some people can't hold their drink,' said Nick, feeling very slightly embarrassed, both by her sudden interest in his genitals and at the situation she'd witnessed last night.

'Incidentally, you don't take the Daily Telegraph by any chance?'

Nick couldn't see any connection with what they'd just been talking about. Probably because there wasn't any. 'No, we're more Guardian and Independent types ourselves.'

'Yes, I thought so,' said Camilla in a tone she might use to describe people that she'd discovered were into necrophilia. 'But I wondered if you've been buying any papers here in the resort?'

'No. We've had a lot of other things on our minds.'

'I noticed,' said Camilla, once again breaching naturist etiquette by glancing down at his genitals. 'No, what I mean is that there appears not to be a single English newspaper today. In the supermarket. There's usually the odd Mail, Times or Telegraph, but today nothing.'

'Maybe they haven't arrived yet,' Nick suggested. 'I'm going over to Reception. I'll ask Jack for you.'

'Would you? That would be so enormously kind of you,' said Camilla. She laid her be-ringed podgy brown hand on Nick's forearm and continued, as if letting him into a state secret, 'and could you ask him to put aside a Telegraph for me if and when it arrives. I'd be so grateful.'

'OK' said Nick. He looked at his watch. Three minutes to ten. 'Look must rush. Got to take a phone call.'

'Goodbye. And don't forget.'

*　　*　　*

Nick entered the Reception building, wondering if Shareen would be there. She wasn't. Probably out preparing to open the bar. He could see into the office where Jack looked out at him.

'Nick. Hi. Come on through.'

Nick accepted Jack's invitation and sat down on his towel on a chair. It was strange but he didn't feel at all self-conscious about being nude. Yesterday he would have thought twice about coming into the office so obviously naked. Today, well it didn't seem that much of a big deal.

He was not only coping with 24/7 nudity but, he had to admit to himself, even beginning to like the sensation. And, here was another worrying thought. He might even be having a good time by now. If, that is, he could forget the murder, Ros and the relationship, the baby issue, Lynne's proposition, Janet's invitation to the Dungeon, Shareen and Shareen's prize-winning argument with Ros. On reflection, enjoyment was probably several light years' away.

'Like some coffee while you wait?' Jack asked sociably, lighting a Gauloises.

'Great. Thanks Jack. It's good of you to let us use your phone this way.'

'No problem. It was your mate Phillip who suggested phoning back to save us the cost of the call. I told him there was no need but he insisted.'

Jack poured a mug of coffee and placed it in front of Nick, who added milk. 'Thanks. Incidentally, I bumped into Camilla outside and she wanted to know what's happened to the papers.'

Jack looked puzzled. 'Papers? What papers?'

'You know, newspapers. The English newspapers. Seems like there haven't been any today.'

'Oh, those. Yeah, well they can sometimes get held up.

Industrial dispute probably. Can never tell when the bloody Frogs are going on strike next. Or over what.'

'If they do turn up, she asked me to ask you if you could reserve her a Telegraph.'

'Sure. Not a problem.'

The phone rang. Jack picked it up. 'Allo. Le Paradis.' He listened. 'Yeah, he's here. Put you right on.' He handed the phone to Nick. 'It's your mate Phillip.'

'Phillip. How are you?' asked Nick, taking the phone.

'We're both well. More to the point, how are you two making out? You know, "naked as nature intended"?' Nick could swear that Phillip chuckled as he said this.

'Actually it's not too bad, quite enjoyable really, once you get used to it.'

'Well don't get used to it too much. Don't want you swanning around our pool without your kit on. Scaring the natives. I'd have to lock Kathy up as well. Don't know I could control her if she saw you in the all-together.'

Nick laughed. 'Believe me, I'd swap being nude here with wearing a suit of armour if we could only get out of this place.'

Thinking he'd unwittingly insulted Jack's pride and joy, Nick guiltily looked over at him. He seemed to be engrossed in a French newspaper and gave no appearance of listening to the conversation.

'That's the specific reason we phoned.' Phillip continued, 'We've been talking to Françoise, you know, the retired advocate I told you about? And she feels that you are being held without charge. And that's against the law. You do really have a case to pursue against this inspector chappie. I can kick it off for you. Get the right papers. At least do something, although I'm not sure how swiftly French justice works – especially in August.'

'I don't think that would be a good idea, Phillip, although

thanks for trying.' Nick outlined his conversation with Lagardère and the threat of his being hauled off to gaol.

'That's a pity. Oh, incidentally,' Phillip continued. 'Your crime has reached the English newspapers.'

'Has it?'

'It's hardly front page stuff. I found a couple of paragraphs tucked away in today's Telegraph. Well, not today's Telegraph, of course, the day before's. We always get the papers a day late down here.'

'What does it say?'

'Wait a minute, I'll go and get it.'

Nick could hear silence and then rustling, as of pages being turned. Phillip came back on the line. 'Here it is. I'll read it to you. Won't take long. The headline reads: "Ex VAT-man killed in French camp-site" '

So Giles Curtis was a VAT man? Or had been. How innocuous is that? Checking that tobacconists have the proper receipts for their ciggies, and such like.

Phillip continued reading: ' "The badly battered body of Briton Giles Curtis, aged 55, was discovered yesterday on a campsite in South West France." Funny, they don't mention it was a nudist camp. "French police suspect foul play. Curtis was unmarried with no children." Are you getting all this, Nick?'

'Yes, carry on.'

' "Recently retired, Curtis was a senior Customs and Excise Officer. His biggest case was the notorious Heathrow Heist in 1983." I remember that.' Phillip continued reading: ' "A £10 million bullion robbery from a bonded customs warehouse, most of the gold was never recovered and few of the perpetrators arrested. French investigation of Curtis's murder continues".'

'That's it?'

'All there is, Nick. Probably doesn't help much or tell you

anything you don't already know. I'll keep the cutting as a memento when you finally get here. Any idea when that'll be?'

'If only we knew. It seems the inspector's off somewhere today. Let's hope that he's half-decent at his job.'

'Well, we'll keep towels on loungers for you and Ros.'

'Towels? How do you know about that?' Nick was surprised.

'You know, towels? As in Germans and reserving sun-beds? It's a joke, Nick. Well, obviously not.' Phillip laughed.

'No I thought it was . . . well, never mind. Thanks again Phillip and I'll be in touch the minute we have any news.'

Once they'd said their farewells, Nick sat in front of the phone digesting this fresh piece of news. So Giles Curtis had been a VAT inspector, not one that came round and checked your books but a senior investigator. If the bloody Daily Telegraph could find that out, why couldn't Lagardère? Or perhaps he had and was keeping quiet about it.

'Everything OK?' Jack looked up from his paper.

'Fine, thanks,' said Nick. 'You don't happen to know where Lagardère is, do you?'

'Not a clue. Doesn't tell me a thing. But if I see him I'll tell him you're looking for him.'

'Thanks. And thanks again for the use of the phone.' Nick got up and Jack waved one hand in a "think nothing of it" gesture, whilst utilising the other to light a cigarette.

Nick slung his towel round his shoulder and left Reception, heading back for the home comforts of the cabin of doom.

26

Back at said cabin, Ros had showered and now had a towel round her as she dried her hair in front of the dressing table mirror. She had a lot on her mind. Mainly the argument with Shareen. Ros knew that she'd had a close shave, not as close as Nick with his balls earlier that morning but still pretty unpleasant.

When they started their slanging match Ros believed that Shareen didn't know what had happened between Ros and Jean-Luc yesterday afternoon. She was fairly sure Jean-Luc wouldn't have told her – he was probably still thinking he'd get another crack at Ros. Yes, Shareen may have had her suspicions, but she couldn't prove anything untoward had taken place. That was before the argument.

After the argument, Ros thought Shareen must know something *had* taken place. Ros capitulated just too easily for her to be Miss Innocent Goody Two Shoes. The next concern for Ros was whether Shareen would impart the unwelcome news of catching Ros and Jean-Luc together, virtually *in flagrante,* to Nick – purely out of spite. It had been known.

And what had Nick made of the argument? This was even trickier. Did he pick up on the fact that Shareen had a man? Nobody actually named names during the argument. Nick would probably want to know who it was. And if he found out that it was Jean-Luc, would that result in a further line of questioning that led to, well, who knows what?

The cabin door opened at that point, making Ros start. 'Ros? You in?' It was Nick.

'In the bedroom.'

Nick pushed through the beads and threw first his towel on the bed and then himself. She could see him looking at her in the dressing table mirror. She couldn't quite read his expression although, as far as she could tell, he seemed fairly calm.

'Just spoke to Phillip. Our crime has reached the English newspapers. Well, one of them at least. Well, the Daily Telegraph. It seems Giles Curtis was a retired Customs and Excise senior investigator.'

Ros didn't know what to say about that so didn't say anything.

'Not sure if it has any relevance at all. Maybe it'll give Lagardère a lead to follow. Oh, yes, and I bumped into Camilla, thanked her for the party.' Nick wished he hadn't mentioned the party but, wait a minute. The thought of Lynne was swiftly followed in his mind by that of another attractive nude woman. Shareen. Just who was Shareen's man?

'Er, this morning?' said Nick, even at the risk of Ros going "off on one" he had to know.

Oh, no! Ros thought. Here it comes. 'Yessss?'

'When you were having that, er, slight disagreement with Shareen?'

'Yesssssss?'

'And she said that you knew she had a man?'

'Yesssss?' Ros didn't have a lot more to say at this point.

'Well *did* you know she had a man?'

'Yes.'

'And just by chance, can you put a name to that man? Just out of idle curiosity, you understand.'

'Yes.' She couldn't actually go on saying "yes" for ever. She was finding that it was limiting her conversational style.

'So, er, is it anyone we know?'

'Yes.'

'Any fear of, you know, actually giving me a name?'

Here goes. 'Jean-Luc,' she said, as casually as she could manage.

She watched his face for a reaction. He looked puzzled. 'Jean-Luc is going out with Shareen?' he said, almost to himself.

'Yes.'

'How did you find out?'

'I saw them together down by the boathouse.' At least she'd stopped saying "yes" that was some improvement. And it was a true statement. Almost. 'I believe that's where Jean-Luc lives.'

Nick still seemed to be taking in this information. He spotted Ros looking at him in the mirror and got to his feet.

'That's interesting,' he said, as if it was the most boring piece of information he'd ever heard.

She waited for him to ask when she saw them together down there. He didn't.

'Well, better get ready,' although he couldn't think what he needed to do before going out except comb his hair. One thing about naturism was that you were always ready to go out. Whether swimming, partying or shopping, you were always suitably dressed for every occasion – once you knew the rules, of course.

'Where are you going?' asked Ros, glad for the change of subject.

'Out to play boules.'

'Who with?' Ros sounded like a suspicious housewife, thinking Lynne might fit somewhere into the equation.

As Ros was still monopolising the dressing table mirror, Nick walked into the bathroom to comb his hair 'Just the lads,' he called into her.

'What lads?'

'You know,' said Nick, re-appearing and giving his hair a final slick-down, 'Geoff, Hamish, Pike and Garry.'

Ros didn't know why this irritated her so much. Perhaps the thought of Nick having made all these contacts in just a couple of days when the best she'd managed was a brief fling with Jean-Luc. Well, that was quite an achievement, she supposed, but something she couldn't tell anybody about. Instead she said to Nick, 'The Famous Five, eh?'

Nick glanced at her in the dressing table mirror, adding 'Yes, and it's "boys only", so there'll be no distractions from the opposite sex.'

Was that a disguised apology for last night's incident with Lynne and today's to-do with Shareen, thought Ros? Or was it a coded message that he knew something had gone on with Jean-Luc?

Nick continued. 'Although, if you like, you could come over and watch. Give me moral support.'

Ros didn't feel she was in a position to give any support at the moment, moral or otherwise. 'It's OK. Just leave me here. I'll find something to do. Probably stay and read out front, if that's all the same to you.' Even to herself she sounded simultaneously both sulky and petulant.

This time Nick was annoyed. 'Look, Ros. I've got to do something to keep my sanity here. Listen, it's a nice day. It's sunny. It's too hot to be stuck inside. We've just got to make the most of this until we can get the fuck out of here.'

Nick countered these words by coming over to her, kissing

her on the cheek and stroking her neck. 'How about lunch, later? It seems to have become a custom.'

That custom, thought Ros, unfortunately seemed to involve Geoff and Lynne. She wasn't sure she could face Lynne today after last night. 'Maybe.'

'About one o'clock? Meet you in the bar? I'm sure the lads will want a refresher after the match.'

Served by that Australian slut! This place had turned into a bit of a nightmare, thought Ros. Wherever she turned she bumped into women who she'd caught naked with Nick. Or women who'd caught her naked with Jean-Luc. And mostly they were one and the same. 'I'll think about it.'

'Suit yourself.' So saying, Nick picked up his towel and was off.

Ros stared at her reflection in the mirror, straightening her own hair as she did so. Apart from any of the other issues, she was concerned about Nick's new blasé attitude to being nude.

In a couple of days he'd gone from walking around with his voluminous beach towel covering as much as he could of his privates, to slinging a small hand towel round his neck and setting off much as he would if he were leaving for work. She vaguely recalled that sociologists might call this "going native".

By contrast, she'd become increasingly uneasy about her own nudity. Perhaps it was the shock of nearly being caught by Shareen yesterday. Or perhaps nudity for her was just too uninhibiting, making her willing to do things she wouldn't dream of in her everyday life. Jean-Luc being a classic example. Sure, she enjoyed the admiring glances of the males of Le Paradis – who wouldn't? – but she just felt less and less easy in her skin than she had been.

If she had discussed this with Martin Pike, he would have probably pointed her in the direction of a resort where she could choose precisely how much or how little to wear. And where she could have chosen her own combination of clothing or nudity. Namely a place denoted as "clothing optional". The Naked Guide has this to say about "clothing optional"

As attitudes to naturism have become more relaxed world-wide, the past decade has seen an increase in the number of hotels and resorts styling themselves 'clothing optional'.

As opposed to a naturist resort, where nudity is obligatory, 'clothing optional' gives one the choice — of wearing clothes, going topless, even bottomless should the fancy take, or of being totally nude.

There are now many resorts that offer a whole range of 'clothing optional' vacations.

At one end of the scale, some ordinary textile hotels have private pool and beach areas for naturists.

There are also hotels that are clothing optional in all areas, except in public spaces such as restaurants, bars and night clubs.

And ones which are totally clothing optional. Here one can conduct most of life's functions dressed, under-dressed or totally undressed as one pleases. Activities that include golf, working out in the gym, playing pool in the bar, eating and drinking or even dancing in the night club, all can be conducted wearing as much or as little as one chooses.

Whilst on the one hand 'clothing optional' could be said to encourage the faint-hearted to sample the delights of going naked, on the other hand it also creates a strange nether-world where the clothed and unclothed rub metaphorical and, occasionally, actual shoulders together, with neither party feeling quite at ease with the situation — or one another.

'Clothing optional' can, therefore, be seen as a mixed blessing for naturism. On the plus side, it does offer an easy route into the lifestyle for those who may fear to go naked immediately. On the negative side, purists would argue that it leads to confusion and dilution of the original principles and precepts. The jury remains out!

27

On his walk over to the boules court, Nick pondered the latest piece of news from Ros. So Shareen was going out with Jean-Luc. That must mean she really didn't fancy Nick, after all. At least Jean-Luc was the right side of thirty — as was Shareen, thought Nick gloomily. And he was way the wrong side.

Yet on the jetty the other morning, she had seemed so keen. Wait a minute though. If Jean-Luc lived in the boathouse, it might account for her enthusiasm. Maybe she knew he was watching. That also explained the flashes from the upstairs windows. Must be Jean-Luc's room. She was just trying to make Jean-Luc jealous. But why? He sighed. He'd never really understand why women operated the way they did.

As he got to the boules court, he saw a large figure practising at the far end. It was Geoff. It suddenly occurred to Nick that Geoff may have found out about Lynne doing her impression of a rash all over Nick last night. Well, it really wasn't his fault that he was forced into a clinch with Geoff's naked wife, was it? Still better to be safe than sorry.

Nick approached tentatively. Geoff spotted him. 'Nick. Hi. I've brought the spare set of boules for you.'

As it seemed relatively safe, Nick proceeded over to Geoff. 'First here, I see?' Nick said for an ice-breaker.

'Yes. I think everyone must be suffering from the after-effects of last night's bash,' said Geoff amiably, whilst liberating a set of boules from their case for Nick.

'How you feeling?' Nick asked a deliberately open-ended question.

'Great! Took a couple of heavy duty ibuprofen tabs and out like a light. Very slight hangover this morning and then nothing. Right as rain.'

It seemed Geoff was unaware of the kitchen incident. He continued, as he was wont to. 'You mustn't mix your drinks, that's the secret.'

'Hang on! I saw you drink beer and red wine last night. I would have thought that was a pretty lethal combination?'

'Ah,' said Geoff, touching forefinger against side of nose, 'It depends on what order you drink them.'

'Sorry?'

'There's an old saying "Beer before wine, fine. Wine then beer, oh dear!" So, the message is, don't drink wine then switch to beer.'

'I've never heard that before,' said Nick, and wasn't sure he'd missed a great deal.

Geoff lined up a boule for a shot at the jack. They were both having a practice now. 'Lynne must have drunk quite a bit last night,' said Geoff. 'Very unusual for her. She normally sticks to set limits.'

'Really?' Nick was non-committal.

'She was sick as a dog on the way back. Threw up all over me. Lucky I wasn't wearing any clothes, eh?' Geoff laughed.

Just the thought of someone vomiting over his bare skin made Nick feel very queasy indeed.

Unfortunately, Geoff continued with the story. 'Yes, made quite a mess. Stuck both of us in the shower when we got back. Took a while to clean up the stuff. You know it looked just like . . .'

Nick interrupted at this point. 'Er Geoff, please spare me the details. I'm not feeling a hundred percent myself today.'

'Oh sorry! Forgot you were squeamish about bodily functions. Lucky you live with a doctor, eh? She can do all that sort of thing for you.'

Nick picked up a boule in each hand and was holding them down by his side, waiting his turn, when they heard a loud 'Oi!!!'

It was Garry coming towards them loaded down with boules in a case in one hand and a huge plastic ice box dangling from the other. He stopped and put them on the bench to the side of the court, under the shade of a tree. He sat down, took a pack of cigarettes and his lighter out from a pouch strung round his neck and lit up, with much coughing.

Geoff and Nick walked across to him. Garry looked at Nick. 'Like your balls, Nick.'

Nick misheard. He looked down and said. 'They're not mine. They're Geoff's spare set.'

Garry dissolved into a fit of laughter and spluttering. When he could speak again he said. 'No. I said I like your balls, not your boules,' pointing at Nick's newly-shaved testicles.

Nick coloured slightly.

'Given 'em a number one crop I see. Suits you. Well done my son.' Garry said.

Nick wasn't sure that he welcomed a discussion about his

privates. And with a man. But Garry didn't seem too concerned. Geoff had a glance down at them but merely shrugged as if this meant totally nothing to him. Which, in all probability, was the case.

Garry reached over for the cool box and cracked off the lid. Inside were cold bottles of beer swimming in a fair amount of ice. He took one out and offered one to each of them. 'Ere you are boys. Hair of the pooch. Can't do any harm. Get that down you.'

All three of them stood or sat, drinking from the bottles, enjoying the peaceful surroundings. Light filtered through the trees shading the side of the boules court. The sun beat down on the exposed hard earth of the court itself. Beer was contentedly supped.

Hamish and Martin Pike arrived together. Pike was having an animated conversation with, or should that be at, Hamish.

Garry, seeming to have taken control of this little gathering, offered them a drink: 'Beer lads? Help yourself.' It was an offer briskly taken up by Hamish, but turned down by Pike. 'Far too early for me.' He looked disapprovingly at the other four, all swigging from bottles, as if he'd caught them smoking behind the bike sheds.

'Right!' said Garry, having finished his beer. 'Suppose we'd better get on with the game.'

Boules progressed at a leisurely pace, punctuated by the odd beer and, in Garry's case, the frequent cigarette. Nick felt quite at ease in the gathering. At times, he found himself forgetting totally that he was nude and with four other naked men. Something that, when he'd first arrived at Le Paradis, would have had him quite literally running for cover-up.

He was musing on this, when he found himself on the bench next to Garry, cool box conveniently situated between them. They were sitting out the current game, taking a breather.

Nick recalled that he hadn't told anyone the news about Giles Curtis. Here was a good place to start. He helped himself to a beer and twisted off the cap. Garry lit a cigarette. 'Good shot!' Garry shouted as Geoff sent Pike's ball flying.

'Er, Garry?' said Nick.

'Yes, my son?'

'I found out today that the murder has made the English papers.'

Garry looked at Nick. He had his full attention now. 'Oh yeah? What do they say?'

'Well, as far as I can tell, it's only a couple of lines in one of them.' Although, thought Nick, for all he knew, it could be splashed all over the front page of the Sun. He told Garry what Phillip had told him this morning.

Garry looked pensive, puffing on his cigarette, and turned back to watch the game. 'A VAT-man, eh. No wonder Giles kept it quiet. Must rate with tax inspectors in the job popularity stakes.' He laughed to himself.

Nick was thinking aloud. 'Why do you think Giles suggested to Camilla that he was about to have a change in fortune?' asked Nick. 'You know. In her eulogy last night?'

'Beats me. Perhaps she didn't hear him right. We all know she's not the world's greatest listener.' He stubbed out his cigarette and turned to Nick. 'Speaking of last night, do you remember me mentioning that Charles looked sort of familiar?'

'I do.'

'Well it came to me this morning in the shower. His face looked like I'd seen it before because I have. It was donkeys' ago. I was only, what, a teenager at the time. He's a local lad from my manor.'

'What? Islington?'

'Yeah. Charlie, as he was known in them days, was a member of one of those crooked families we're famous for.'

Garry smiled. 'Right load of villains. Mind you, you can't tar the man with the same brush. He's probably a reformed character today.'

'Lagardère did tell me that Charles has a criminal record,' added Nick.

'Oh yeah?' Garry looked interested. 'What for?'

'It was for receiving. Long time ago.'

'Doesn't surprise me. They were into all sorts. Still, you have to admit the boy's done good since. The Daimler, the antiques business, the house in Portugal. Yeah, apart from Camilla, that is.' Garry coughed. 'No, only joking. Who'd imagine that a lad from the estates would have done so well.'

'You are sure it's the same Charles? I mean, it was a long time ago?'

Garry looked at him. 'Just as certain as I am that your name is Peter and that Arsenal play in blue and white.' Garry laughed. He clapped Nick on the shoulder. 'Course I'm sure. I told you. I never forget a name and face.'

They both gazed out at the peaceful bucolic scene — of three nude men tossing pieces of metal about. Garry seemed to be musing on something. Nick was content to sit and think.

Nick's mind wandered back to review what he knew about the murder. Part of the newspaper story that Phillip had read to him had faintly rung a very rusty bell in his belfry of a brain.

Hadn't Lagardère mentioned that Charles had been sent down for receiving gold from a bullion robbery? What was it? Five years inside? And hadn't Lagardère also said that the robbery was at Heathrow? That was about the same time as the newspaper had reported Giles Curtis's involvement with the investigation. Lagardère said mid-80s; the newspaper 1983.

Nick thought it was a bit too much of a coincidence. Giles Curtis had been the investigating Customs official on the infamous "Heathrow Heist". Giles was staying here in Le

Paradis at the same time as Charles, who had been involved in the robbery, albeit peripherally. And he was with Charles and Camilla the night he was killed. In fact, they were the last ones to see him alive.

When Lagardère had talked about Charles as a suspect, he didn't think it added up. If Giles was blackmailing Charles and threatening to expose him as an ex-jailbird, it didn't. However if Charles had played a larger part in the "Heist" than the police ever suspected, or could prove, and Charles still knew where the un-recovered bullion was, then blackmail was definitely on the cards. And what had Camilla said about Giles looking forward to a brighter future. Some brighter future!

Nick wondered how much Lagardère knew about all this. Did he have his suspicions about Charles? When they'd last spoken, he appeared not to. But seemingly, at that time, Lagardère hadn't known what Giles Curtis had done for a living. When they next met, Nick would talk about his theories to him. Swap clues and explore the evidence, just like the old crime-solving professionals they both were!

Garry nudged him. 'We're on. Stir your balls!' So saying he lumbered to his feet and set off boules in hand, cigarette in mouth. He was followed by Nick, who thought he could see an end in sight to his captivity. Strangely enough, it didn't seem such a welcome prospect as it had a couple of days' ago.

While the "lads" were playing boules and drinking beer, Ros spent the morning with her bonkbuster and cups of tea on the porch of the cabin. Although, to be honest, the exploits of Lady Louise and Sir Jonathan's head groom seemed a bit tame compared with those she'd been party to in Le Paradis over the past couple of days.

Making sure she had her cotton wrap covering her breasts and as much of her thighs as possible, Ros couldn't really bring

298 • A W Palmer

herself to concentrate on the text. Like Jehovah Witnesses on the doorstep, other unwelcome thoughts kept intruding,

There was Lynne, of course. How to deal with her when they next met. What on earth did she think she was doing last night? Hadn't she heard of making a foul mess on your own doorstep? Perhaps like Ros, Lynne felt less inhibited swanning around naked and more tempted to indulge. No wonder Adam and Eve had adopted the fig leaf. If they hadn't, the world would be even deeper in people than it already was.

Then there was Shareen. If she *was* going to tell Nick about Ros and Jean-Luc, she'd had a great opportunity to do so this morning. Instead, she'd just hinted at it. Ros found this slightly reassuring.

But would she take some other revenge for Ros's fling-ette with Jean-Luc? By seducing Nick, for instance. That would serve two purposes at once. It would punish Ros for encouraging Jean-Luc, although Ros didn't notice him needing much encouragement. And it would also punish Jean-Luc for going with Ros.

If Shareen was going to take this course of action, thought Ros, would Nick rise to the bait, so to speak? Ros had no reason to think that Nick had ever been unfaithful to her, so that's a mark in his favour. He was, she thought, a serial monogamist.

On the negative side, Ros had given him an ultimatum on the baby issue and she didn't know which way he'd jump. She hoped he'd stay with her, but she couldn't know for sure. He also hadn't had sex for a very long while and was randy as hell last night. Any encouragement could push him over the bed edge.

He was also always nude and she knew from experience how easy it was for kissing to turn into full blown sex in a very short time — well, almost full blown sex. And the other factor which clinched it for the prosecution was that Shareen was also nude, in her early twenties, and extremely attractive with a great body. She tried to think of a heterosexual male who, if presented with this package, would be able to resist – and failed.

Ros comforted herself with the thought that it was no use worrying about it until, and if, it happened. Then she'd go and tear the little bitch to shreds!

Ros's mind then wandered to their present situation. When the fuck were they going to be let out? Surely they'd find the murderer soon. Although she'd seen no movement on that front. The gendarmes still guarded the gates. Lagardère seemed to have gone walk-about. And as far as she could see, nobody seemed in the slightest hurry to progress the investigation.

She sighed. She supposed she couldn't really stay here all day. The sun had moved round and was now beating on the wooden verandah roof, making it even hotter. There wasn't a breath of wind and Ros felt sweat puddling under her breasts and the tops of her legs.

Ros went inside the hut, removed her wrap and gave herself a dry down. She looked at herself in the mirror. She had managed to go quite a nice all-over brown in the past couple of days. She liked how it looked. No white marks. She turned to look at her bum. It seemed smaller brown than white. Perhaps that was one good thing to be said for naturism – probably the only good thing.

She tried various ways of tying her cotton wrap for maximum coverage. It was just that bit too small. It had been designed to tie round your waist to modestly cover your bikini bottom. It wasn't supposed to double as a frock.

If she tied it over her breasts, when she walked it exposed the v-shaped pubic hair area which, she felt looked much more revealing – and more erotic – than full nudity. If she tied it under her breasts, it covered her lower area fairly efficiently –

up to mid-thigh anyway. She settled for this, christening it the Tahitian topless look and reasoning that her breasts could benefit from extra tan.

Once "dressed" she thought she would walk her bonkbuster down to the pool. She wasn't so concerned about being nude round the pool. That seemed totally natural to her. It was just the rest of the experience — sitting in the restaurant, selecting items from the chilled cabinet, playing boules, being in a Frenchman's bedroom — that really bothered her.

Packing her beach bag, Ros set off. She could decide later whether she wanted to meet the "lads" for a drink. In the circumstances, she thought perhaps not. The prospect of being surrounded by five naked men in a bar, each with half an eye on her breasts, was not one she felt she could deal with today.

28

Having finished their game, the five naked men in question had indeed adjourned to the bar for liquid refreshment. For a change, they took an outside table under a large parasol.

There was a good view of the pool area and the grass and footpaths down to the lake and beyond. In the far distance, beyond the lake, was a building Nick presumed was the night club, home of the Dungeon, where Janet and John held court nightly to S and M supplicants.

'Right, Geoff. I think that as you won, you can get the first round in,' said Garry.

If Geoff had any faults, and Nick could name quite a few, meanness wasn't one of them. 'Be delighted to have you toast my victory. The best man won, obviously. What about some nice cold Chablis?'

'Sounds good to me,' said Garry.

The others concurred, except Pike 'Just a sparkling water for me please, Geoff.'

A brown overweight child appeared at Garry's elbow. 'Dad?'

'Yes, Mason,' Garry replied, ruffling his son's hair – much to his irritation.

'Mum said to ask you if I could have some money for an ice lolly.'

'Sure,' said Garry, fishing a couple of euros out of the bag round his neck, together with his cigarettes and lighter. He gave the boy the euros. 'Get one for Gareth as well while you're at it.'

'How have they taken Giles not being around any more?' asked Nick, watching the boy run off.

'Not too bad. They soon forget. You know what it's like with kids.'

Nick didn't. And wasn't too sure that he wanted to find out. He didn't know how anyone ever did it. The mess. The late nights. The early mornings. The weeping and crying. And that was just the parents. Was he really ready for all that? At this point in his life, if he wasn't, would he ever be?

His mind was totally taken off this line of thought by the arrival of Shareen. 'G'day you bunch of reprobate poms! Too bloody idle to come into the bar now are you?' She smiled a dazzling smile which encompassed all of them. Nick thought it lingered on him slightly longer – well you would, wouldn't you?

'Shareen, your very best bottle of Chablis please,' ordered Geoff, in pompous fashion.

'And shove it in an ice bucket, darling would you,' added Garry, rather spoiling the effect of Geoff's order.

'And a bottle of sparkling water please,' said Geoff.

'Coming right up,' said Shareen, executing a smart turn and giving them all a most excellent view of her swaying rear as she walked back inside the bar.

It was a sight guaranteed to silence even Pike — not that anyone was complaining.

'If I was a few years younger — and didn't have that little lot,' said Garry gesturing down towards the pool area, 'I wouldn't crawl across her to get to you. Even with your new balls.' This last remark aimed at Nick, as Garry lit a Marlboro Light.

It might have been Garry's laddish behaviour that encouraged Nick to say. 'Actually, Shareen was on my bed earlier this morning.'

This got their attention, especially Geoff, who raised his eyebrows in disbelieving fashion.

'Now you really are pulling our plonkers,' said Garry.

Nick laughed. 'No it was nothing like that.' And explained that she'd come to tell him about a phone call in the office and stayed for a cup of coffee and a chat. He somehow forgot to mention the slight disagreement that had occurred between her and Ros.

Shareen returned with the wine, ice bucket and glasses.

' 'ere, Shareen,' said Garry, taking a pull on his cigarette, 'Nick here tells us you was in his bedroom this morning? Is that true?'

She looked at Nick as she was removing the cork from the bottle, 'Yeah I was, as it happens.'

'Well, if you're in the habit, can you pencil me in for a visit as well some time,' Garry laughed.

Shareen punched him playfully on the shoulder. 'Wait 'til I tell that wife of yours. Only good-looking *single* guys get house calls.' This last remark clearly aimed at Nick.

Garry added, 'I told you you were in there Nick, didn't I?'

Shareen raised eyes to heaven, good-naturedly, put the glasses down and treated them all to a welcome reprise of that behind and that walk.

Geoff did the pouring honours and Nick raised his glass to Geoff 'To the victor.' The others did likewise. The Chablis was surprisingly good. Conversation started between Geoff and Pike on bird-watching, while Hamish and Garry appeared to be debating the relative merits of English and Scottish football.

As both subjects held little appeal for him, Nick savoured the wine and thought about Shareen. She didn't seem to have taken this morning's spat to heart. If anything, as far as he could tell, she seemed warmer towards him than previously.

He looked around to see if this was for the benefit of Jean-Luc, lurking in the shrubbery. He didn't seem to be about. Maybe she'd split with Jean-Luc, or just fancied a change. He sighed inwardly. Even if it was on, he just couldn't afford the risk of Ros finding out.

Actually, where was Ros? He presumed she was still at the cabin. He looked at his watch. Gone one o'clock and no sign of her. Perhaps she hadn't wanted to meet the gang. Or more likely Shareen.

Unknown to Nick, Ros was but a few hundred yards away at the far end of the pool. Concealed from the bar by a forest of parasols, tanned bathers and sunbathers, she'd been there long before the "lads" got back from their game.

She'd taken a lounger close to Sam. 'So you're a boules widow as well?' she said to Ros, rubbing sun cream onto her smooth brown skin. 'Bloody men. They're just like kids themselves.'

Ros smiled. She didn't really want a conversation with Sam but felt comforted by the presence of a fellow nude woman companion.

'Good "do" last night,' said Sam. 'Nice speech by Camilla, I thought, as well. Brought a tear to the eye.'

'Yes it was – and did.'

'Garry was a bit the worse for wear, but then again he usually is.'

'Yes.' Ros smiled as she applied her own sun cream to breasts and thighs.

'I'm afraid you've missed Jean-Luc.'

Ros stopped what she was doing and looked at Sam. 'Sorry?'

'Jean-Luc, you know, the aquarobics? You've missed the session,' explained Sam.

'Oh, right.' Ros continued applying the cream.

'Only I know you have a bit of a soft spot for him,' smiled Sam. If only she knew, thought Ros. Actually, she really had forgotten that Jean-Luc did a session in the morning.

Sam interrupted her thoughts. 'It's too hot for me today. I'm off for a dip. Coming?'

'Maybe later,' said Ros.

Sam got up and slipped, seal-like, into the pool.

Ros relaxed. She lay down nude on her lounger, legs slightly apart. The sun felt good on her skin. She picked up her book. There was one other thing she'd forgotten as well.

'That's normally five euros, but today there is no charge. Compliments of the management.'

Ros's head came up with a start. Crouching down beside her lounger, his head not a foot away from hers, was part-time sunbed and parasol attendant Jean-Luc.

Ros couldn't help her heart beating faster and, at that precise moment, couldn't think of any words.

Jean-Luc took hold of one of her hands and looked into her eyes. 'How are you today, Ros?'

'Er, fine thanks.' Well she could manage a few.

He looked at her body. It was the way he looked at it that made Ros get hot. And it had absolutely nothing to do with the sun. 'You are getting a nice tan. It looks good on you.'

Despite herself Ros thought that Jean-Luc would also still look good on her. Instead she said 'Er thanks.'

'No. Thank *you*. For what you did yesterday.'

She didn't remember doing much. Jean-Luc seemed to have been doing most of the work. 'Sorry?'

'You know. Saving me from Shareen.'

'Oh, that. Sheer adrenalin, I think.' And fear of being caught by Nick.

'Shareen, she can be very jealous,' said Jean-Luc.

But not vindictive, thought Ros. Well, at least not yet. 'Yes, I saw her this morning. She seemed very suspicious.'

Jean-Luc looked worried and glanced towards the bar, dropping Ros's hand at the same time. 'You didn't tell her about us, did you?'

'No, Jean-Luc. And I'm not going to. It's all forgotten as far as I'm concerned.' Although she would remember that afternoon for many years to come.

'Forgotten? But maybe we can . . .'

'No. Jean-Luc,' Ros said, more firmly than she actually felt. 'We were nearly caught last time. It's too dangerous.'

He wasn't going to give up without a struggle. 'Maybe if we found a quieter place. I have a key to one of the rooms in the night club. Perhaps . . .'

'Jean-Luc,' it was Ros's turn to take his hand, breaking the news to him gently. 'No. It's over. The moment's gone.'

He looked like a little boy that had been told he couldn't have another biscuit.

Ros suddenly became aware of a figure standing over them. It was Sam, newly returned from her seal pool. She was watching, with a puzzled frown, this touching scene being played out in front of her.

Jean-Luc noticed Ros looking up, saw Sam, removed his hand and stood up. 'Au revoir, then madame,' he said to her, in what she thought was an unnecessary bitter fashion. "Madame"? What happened to "Ma'm'selle".

Jean-Luc shook his hair out of his eyes and walked off, with both Ros and Sam admiring those lean brown buttocks of his.

'I see you found Jean-Luc then?' said Sam, with a very suspicious look on her face.

'Er yes.' And lost him again. For good.

29

Back at the reprobates' table outside the bar, debate turned to whether it would be a sound idea to order another bottle of the very fine Chablis they'd just demolished.

Strangely enough, it was Geoff who put the kibosh on it. He looked at his watch. 'Much as I'd love to, especially as I'm not paying for the next one, I've got to get back. Promised to prepare lunch for Lynne.'

'How is she?' asked Garry, tactless to a fault. 'Looked pissed as a fart last night, if you ask me.'

Geoff smiled wrily. 'Can't argue with that. She's been sleeping it off this morning. I left her in the dark with a bag of frozen broccoli spears on her forehead – organic, of course. The broccoli spears not the forehead. Promised to make her something nourishing. Preferably something she'll find easy to keep down.'

Geoff turned to Nick. 'Talking of which, I don't want to be a pain, but I'm a bit worried about Lynne.'

You'd be even more worried if you'd seen her with her hand round my crotch, thought Nick. 'Why's that?'

'Well she took her temperature this morning and it's very high. Might be food poisoning or something. Do you think you could ask Ros to pop over and take a look at her? You know, give us her professional opinion? It's probably nothing, but . . .'

'I'll ask her,' said Nick, not sure how Ros would react to seeing Lynne again, so quickly after yesterday evening.

'Why don't you come over as well? You've never seen our place, have you? It's small but homely.'

Nick could believe this as they were living in the large but aged camper van that was normally such an eyesore in their street back home. Nick wondered how it had made it this far south. And more to the point, how long it had taken to coax it down here. He wouldn't want to risk driving it further south than Peckham. And then with an RAC van in tow just in case.

'Thanks Geoff. Might do that,' said Nick, thinking that it may not be too good an idea for both him and Ros to be there with Lynne. 'Where you based?'

'Avenue D. One up, same side of the Champs as Charles and Camilla.' So saying, Geoff lumbered to his feet and collected his towel and sets of boules. 'I'll pay inside. See you all later.'

With that he was off. 'So,' said Nick. 'Shall we get another bottle? My round I think.'

Hamish looked at Pike; Pike at Hamish. Pike spoke first. 'Actually, Hamish and I are going back to my cabin for lunch. A nice chicken caesar salad. Accompanied by a dry riesling. I think we'd better be on our way.'

They followed in the footsteps of Geoff, and were gone.

Nick watched them go. 'Do you think they're an item? They seem pretty inseparable.'

Garry smiled. 'Hadn't really thought about it. Wouldn't like to, either. Can you imagine going to bed with Hamish? It'd be like wrestling a polar bear.'

For an ex-Islington scaffolder, Garry was very liberal about expressing his views on male sexuality, thought Nick. 'What do you know about Hamish?'

'Not a lot really,' said Garry, screwing up his eyes against smoke that was blowing back into his face from his cigarette. 'I know he lives in some Spanish Costa or other. That he's here every summer, and has been for years. And that he knows Charles and Jack very well. You would, really, if you've been coming here donkeys, wouldn't you.'

Nick agreed. 'Well, I'm sure I can get *you* a drink?'

'Yeah, that'd be good. I think I'll stick with the white,' Garry said. 'On second thoughts, hold up a minute.'

Nick followed Garry's gaze and coming towards them were Sam and the two kids, loaded with beach bags, swim rings and other assorted paraphernalia. Oh the joy of children. They were soon by their table.

'Allo love,' said Garry, not bothering to get up. 'Join us for a quick one?'

'No, these two need feeding. I'm surprised you don't want to stick your face in a nosebag by now.' Sam turned to Nick and looked at him with a strange expression which, if Nick didn't know better, looked almost like pity. 'Hello Nick.'

'Hi Sam.'

Garry began the task of getting to his feet and assembling cool box, boules, ciggies and so forth. 'Well, I must say that I could be tempted to the odd bit of foie gras and smoked salmon.'

'We're having fish fingers, chips and beans,' said Sam. 'The kids' favourites.'

'Yum, yum,' said Garry, now ready to leave. 'Right. Well see ya round Nick. Good game.'

Sam looked at Nick again in that strange way and said 'If you're looking for Ros, she's down by the pool. Far end. See ya later.'

With that Nick was alone at the table. He got up and extricated himself from the shading parasol, looking to see if Shareen was anywhere about. She didn't appear to be.

Towel around neck, he made his way through the thinning numbers of sunbathers – French lunchtime called – to the far end of the pool. Ros was lying naked on her front, giving a very good impression of the pose she'd adopted a few nights back in the cabin. Then he wasn't too interested. Now he felt a slight stirring in his loins. He bent down towards her. She was asleep and lightly snoring.

He gently shook her shoulders. Her eyes opened and she looked up at him. 'Hello,' she smiled.

'Just wondered if madame would care to join me for lunch,' said Nick.

Ros struggled over onto her front and sat up. 'What time is it?'

'Half one. Better hurry if we're going to make it before they stop serving.'

'Right.' Ros got up and wrapped herself Tahitian style, exposed breasts to the fore. Quite brown breasts, Nick noted with interest.

She left her book and sun cream on the plastic table to the side of the lounger and picked up her beach bag. Ros looked at Nick, sudden thought crossing her mind. 'We're not having lunch with bloody Geoff and Lynne again are we?'

'No. You'll be pleased to hear that Lynne has taken to her bed, the worse for wear. Which reminds me. Geoff asked whether you would mind popping over to see her later. You know, in a professional capacity. She's got a high temperature and he's worried she's got some sort of food poisoning or something.'

'Alcohol poisoning more like,' Ros scoffed.

'It wouldn't do any harm,' said Nick.

No, and perhaps it'd give Ros a chance to ask Lynne what the fuck she was playing at last night, using Nick as a coat hanger. 'I suppose if I must.'

'That's later. Now, for a change, you and me are going to have lunch alone. And without the slightest risk of naked women anywhere about my person. Except you, of course.' Nick gave Ros a hug, and they walked hand-in-hand to the restaurant.

30

A bottle of rosé was cooling nicely in an ice bucket as Nick and Ros studied the menu. Although to be truthful it didn't take a lot of effort as the menu hardly changed from day to day.

Ros felt slightly more at ease now she was sitting down, and untied her wrap to let air and sun through to refresh the parts air and sun normally didn't reach.

She put her hand on Nick's arm. 'This is nice. Do you realize that since we've been here, we've hardly spent any time at all with one other. And whenever we have been together, others have always been around.'

Nick thought about it. 'You're right. The only time we have been alone is in the cabin of evil. And that hasn't been too great.' Remembering the last couple of nights.

He poured the rosé into their glasses and raised his glass to hers. 'Here's to more time together. You and me. Alone.'

'You and me. Alone,' Ros replied, and clinked her glass against his.

314 • A W Palmer

'May I join you?' a voice behind them inquired.

Glasses poised in mid-air, Nick and Ros turned to find Lagardère standing there, about to pull up a chair to their table. Looking slightly hot and dishevelled, he was wearing his usual chinos and short-sleeved shirt combo and carrying his leather briefcase.

Lagardère must have noticed the looks on their faces because he added, 'I thought you'd be interested in how the investigation is going.'

Nick looked at Ros, who was already pulling her wrap over her thighs. She wasn't amused at this interruption. But then again, if it would help them get out of here, she'd put up with it. Come to think of it, if it hastened their departure, she'd put up with listening to a three-hour lecture on naturism in the Solomon Islands, delivered by Martin Pike.

'Have you eaten?' asked Lagardère, joining them at their table. Not much of a detective thought Nick if he couldn't work that out.

'We were just about to order. Have you?' enquired Nick.

'No, I've been a bit busy this morning.'

'Yes, we heard you were off somewhere. Learn anything interesting?

'All in good time, Nick, all in good time. Now let me get a menu. Don't worry, I'll pay for my share.'

So saying, he took a menu from the table behind and studied it. As he was doing so he commented on the heat in best British conversational style. 'It's terribly warm again, today, don't you think? You are so lucky to be able to walk around naked,' he said looking over the top of the menu, mostly, thought Ros, at her tits.

'Incidentally, Inspector . . .' began Nick.

'No please call me Raymond. I feel we are almost like old friends by now.'

Sure! One old friend suspecting the other of murder,

thought Nick. He continued, 'Incidentally, *Raymond,* how come you're allowed to walk around with clothes on, flagrantly breaking the rules of Le Paradis?'

'That's terribly simple to answer. It's because I'm an officer of the law.'

Nick was certain Lagardère had pronounced "law" with an exaggerated French accent mimicking Peter Sellers as Inspector Clouseau. He looked at him, but Lagardère was giving nothing away.

'It wouldn't do to have pictures of French policemen in the nude appearing in newspapers. It wouldn't exactly be the best career move for me,' Lagardère continued.

The waitress came to take their orders. Salades for Nick and Ros, moules et frites for the Inspector. A further bottle of rosé was ordered as Nick topped up their glasses.

'I propose another toast,' said Lagardère, 'A successful conclusion to the investigation.' He raised his glass. Nick and Ros did likewise.

For a while they sipped their wine in silence, gazing out at the peaceful lake glittering in the heat, dots of windsurfers here and there, to-ing and fro-ing.

Nick followed up Lagardère's toast. 'So how *is* the investigation coming along?' Seemed a shame not to find out, while they had Lagardère captive, so to speak. 'Any sign of a successful conclusion?'

'Or any conclusion?' added a disgruntled Ros.

Before addressing Nick's question, Lagardère looked at Ros and smiled, 'I think we are making progress.'

'You do know that Giles Curtis was a retired Customs Investigator, don't you?' said Nick.

'Yes, we were aware of that fact.'

'Did you know that one of the cases he investigated many years ago was the so-called Heathrow Heist bullion robbery?'

Lagardère looked slightly surprised at Nick's knowledge of this. 'Yes we also knew that.'

'Wasn't that the same case Charles was sent down for? You know, receiving a small amount of bullion.'

'If it is the same case, then so what?' asked Lagardère.

Nick's reply was interrupted by the arrival of their food. Lagardère almost disappeared behind a "poof" of steam as the waitress opened his enormous bowl of mussels.

Nick continued. 'Well, let's say that Charles was more involved in the robbery than mere receiving. Let's assume he has some of the bullion stashed away somewhere, maybe in Portugal.'

Lagardère seemed to be more interested in prising one moule from its shell, using one of its empty companions as an eating implement, than listening to Nick. But Nick felt he was paying attention, so he carried on.

'Then if Giles Curtis knew about this . . .'

'And could prove it.' Lagardère interrupted.

That was a slight drawback to Nick's theory. He carried on regardless. '. . . and could prove it, then there really could be a blackmail motive to the murder.'

'So you're saying that Giles Curtis threatened to reveal Charles's true role in the bullion robbery to the authorities unless he handed over a portion of the loot? Charles agreed, lured him out and battered him to death?' Lagardère had to stop eating to deliver this little speech but quickly turned back to the moules.

'Exactly!' said Nick. But even as Lagardère had been summing it up, the theory sounded a bit far-fetched.

'Did you know also that Charles and Jack go back a long way? Almost to the time of the robbery?' Ros decided to impart the information she'd picked up at the barbecue.

Again, Lagardère looked interested. 'Tell me more.'

'I think Jack told me he'd bought this place in 1983 — something like that, I can't be sure.' She remembered being more interested in watching Nick check out Janet's boobs at the time. 'And Charles bought his caravan here, what, around the same time.'

'You didn't tell me that,' said Nick to Ros.

Ros shrugged, an action which raised her breasts attractively, thought Nick as, he also noticed, did Lagardère. 'I have had a lot of other things on my mind since then.'

Nick decided not to press the point.

For a while they all munched in silence, if you can munch a salad in silence. Lagardère then asked. 'Where did you find out the information on Giles Curtis?'

Some detective, thought Nick again. 'It was in the newspaper. The Daily Telegraph.' Nick explained about Phillip reading it to him. He also remembered Camilla complaining that there were no English papers in the resort that morning. The morning the very Telegraph should have arrived bearing the story of Curtis's untimely demise. He also mentioned this to Lagardère.

'Now that *is* interesting. A bit similar to the case of the dog that barked, or rather didn't bark, in the night,' said Lagardère.

What was he going on about now, thought Nick. 'Care to elaborate?'

Lagardère had now finished demolishing the pile of mussels and was wiping his mouth with his napkin. 'Sherlock Holmes. It's sometimes the things that don't happen that are more instructive than those that do.'

Lagardère clearly wasn't going to say any more about this. He promptly changed the subject. 'So how many people in Le Paradis now know that Giles Curtis was a senior investigator and involved in the bullion case?'

Nick tried to remember who he'd told. 'Well, there's Ros and me, obviously. Then Garry . . .'

'Ah yes, our Mr Hollins,' the inspector interjected, un-necessarily thought Nick.

'. . . and, well, that's about it. I think. Can't be sure. Why? Are you telling me I shouldn't mention the fact to anyone else?'

'On the contrary, Nick, I think you should tell everyone you meet in Le Paradis about it,' said Lagardère, taking a sip of wine.

Coffees arrived. Conversation continued in desultory fashion.

Nick decided to bring up the other ''suspects'' in the case. 'You do know that Hamish, Jack and Charles all know one another, don't you? And that Hamish lives on one of the Spanish Costas?'

'Living on one of the Costas? Is that a reason to arrest someone?' enquired Lagardère.

Some might think so, thought Nick. Instead he said, 'No, I mean, connections with crime and so on. Perhaps Hamish was also involved.'

'Any other theories?' Lagardère looked slightly amused. The professional listening to the rank amateur.

'Well, Janet and John. Have you spoken to them?'

'Ah yes,' the inspector sounded almost wistful, 'Extraordinary breasts!' He glanced at Ros's as if making a mental comparison. She crossed her arms for protection.

'I get the feeling they know more than they're letting on. And they did know Giles Curtis, er, fairly intimately.'

'I gathered from the appearance of, what are their names, Janet and John, that they are probably into sado-masochism. Are you saying Giles Curtis was also a devotee?'

'Well, yes,' said Nick, although he felt a bit disloyal towards Janet and John by mentioning it.

'That also is interesting,' said Lagardère, although Nick

didn't know whether that was from a professional or personal point of view.

Ros decided to ask a question. The one most important to her: 'So how close are you to finding the murderer?' Sub-text, so we can all get the fuck out of here!

Lagardère seemed to think seriously about this. 'Not much longer, I shouldn't think. In any case, I'm not sure that we can hold everyone here after the weekend. They won't put up with it.'

'The weekend!' It was Tuesday today. That would mean another three to four days imprisoned without clothes.

'And then remember that Nick here is still a suspect. So . . .' Lagardère shrugged. Ros went into a sulk.

The bill arrived and Lagardère picked up the tab. 'I will pay for this. It's been a most enlightening lunch. And thank you for your time.' So saying, he got to his feet, took another peek at Ros's breasts, did his Casablanca-style salute and was off.

'Bloody man!' said Ros. 'Did you notice he kept looking at my tits?'

'That's because they're very attractive. You should take it as a compliment.'

'Huh!' Any good mood Ros had harboured had evaporated with the lunch and Lagardère's news that they could be here for the rest of the week. 'And tell me. What did we learn from lunch with the inspector? I'll tell you what. Nothing! Absolutely nothing! He picked our brains as cleanly as he did his moules!'

Nick thought over the conversation. Ros was right. Whatever information Lagardère had he kept safely filed away. As safely filed away as the inhabitants of Le Paradis. Filed under P for private; P for prisoners.

31

Ros and Nick left the restaurant as waitresses were clearing the tables, getting ready to close. They stood in the shade of the awning and debated what to do with the rest of the afternoon.

Given the choice, Ros would probably liked to have retire to her free ''with the compliments of the management'' sun-lounger. She doubted Jean-Luc would be back, but she knew Sam almost certainly would be. She'd now added Sam to the growing list of women suspicious of her involvement with Jean-Luc. Great!

One other option was to go back to the cabin for an afternoon of passion with Nick. Given the events of last night, that activity looked like it was on hold for the time being. Until the ankle-binder issue, as Nick might have called it, was resolved.

Ros sighed. There was nothing for it but to fulfil her Hippocratic oath. 'I think I'd better go and see Lynne.'

'Er, do you think I should come with you?' Nick asked.

'Would you like that?' Ros knew she was being bitchy but couldn't stop herself.

'Not if you don't want me to,' Nick said contritely.

'I think I would like the chance to see Mrs Russell on her own. We may have a few words to say to each other that you may find disturbing.'

'Right,' said Nick, adding, 'Look remember we still have to live virtually next door to them when we get back to London. Er, don't go too mad, will you? I mean, no harm was done. She was just a bit pissed, is all. And it's best for Geoff not to know.' He wasn't sure how Geoff would react and didn't want to find out.

'Don't worry. I'll be the soul of discretion – as far as Geoff's concerned,' were Ros's less than reassuring words. 'What are you going to do?'

'I don't know.' That was a good question. What was he going to do?

'Why don't you take over my sun-lounger for the afternoon. It's paid for.' She didn't think it was quite the time or place to elaborate on precisely how she had paid for it.

'That's not a bad idea. I think I will,' said Nick.

Having shown him the lounger, noting that Sam and the kids had yet to return from lunch, she kissed Nick on the cheek and set off for the Russells' luxurious holiday home.

Following Nick's directions, Ros found Avenue D with no problems. Even she couldn't get lost in Le Paradis – geographically at least. The residents of this part of the site mainly occupied tents, motor homes or caravans of the towable variety. It was a distant cry from the tidy lawn, clipped hedges and large plot that Camilla and Charles inhabited.

Walking down the Avenue, light dappling through shading trees, Ros soon spotted the Russells' van, parked back from the roadway. Attached to the front was a large white tent extension, which must have doubled the living space provided by the vehicle itself. The white space had a zip-up central section, zipped shut.

Coming level with the ensemble, the first thing she noticed was a large brown roundish shape lying on a lounger. It was Geoff. On his back. Snoring. Not one of the seven wonders of the world, that was for sure. But, as she'd previously noted – with some exceptions, of course – not much that Le Paradis had to offer in the way of naked flesh was.

Many of Le Paradis' inhabitants suffered from that most common of western ailments. Overweight. But they didn't seem to mind very much, happily parading their trophy rolls of fat to all around, with seeming impunity.

Others decided that the world needed to view their assorted piercings. Ros thought of John's alleged hidden heavy metal and involuntarily shuddered. She wondered just how many people she passed on the streets of Stoke Newington had hidden piercings through their privates, meant only for the eyes of their partners. If Le Paradis was anything to go by, more than she cared to think about.

And why had the world suddenly gone tattoo-crazy? Even the naturists here in Le Paradis, who you thought wouldn't want to swap their clothes for inked skin, sported them. The only one Ros had seen that she'd quite taken to was one on the right hand buttock of a young man she was fairly sure was gay. Designed and shaped like a manufacturers' round stamp, it simply read 'Made in Holland'.

No, there was a lot to be said for wearing clothes. Clothes hid a variety of skins. And body shapes. And sizes. Getting dressed had its attractions. When she got back home, if they ever got back home, she was determined to make just a bit more effort with her wardrobe. She now appreciated that clothes weren't just for warmth or comfort, they disguised, cajolled and flattered, improving on the basic and imperfect package beneath.

Take Geoff, for example, he looked far better in his usual dirty blue jeans, trainers and shirt than he did at this moment. Mind you he'd also look more attractive in sackcloth and ashes.

Ros walked over to him. She bent down and said gently, 'Geoff. Wake Up. It's me, Ros.'

He opened his eyes and looked at her. 'Oh, hi Ros.' Geoff struggled to his feet and blearily looked around, whilst involuntarily scratching his balls. Another unappealing feature Ros had noticed about the male inhabitants of Le Paradis. 'No Nick?'

'No, he's working on his tan down by the pool. How's the invalid?' Ros whispered, though why she was whispering she didn't quite know.

'Oh, a bit better.' He looked towards the white, tented structure. 'We take her temperature every hour.'

'And how is it?'

'Almost back to normal, we think,' Geoff said.

'No more vomiting?'

'No.'

That's a pity, thought Ros. 'I'd better go in and see her. You wait here and catch up on your beauty sleep.'

'Right. And thanks Ros.' Geoff sat back on the lounger, which creaked complainingly under the stresses being imposed on it. Geoff settled down into his impression of a large brown hairy molehill.

Ros unzipped enough of the white cover to slip into the tent. Lynne was lying in the middle of what was she supposed was the marital holiday double airbed. A vision came to Ros of Geoff getting into his side of the bed and propelling Lynne out her side, so great was the weight differential between the two of them.

Lynne was lying on her back, naked but for a covering sheet

– which didn't cover that much, as it was pulled right down to just above Lynne's crotch. In fact, Ros could see a wisp of pubic hair just showing above the sheet edge.

The fact that Lynne also seemed to be asleep gave Ros the opportunity to examine her body, visually not physically. Come to think of it, even as a doctor she didn't get to look at a complete totally naked body at such close quarters very often. Just the individual parts that patients felt were troubling them.

Although she was quite thin, Lynne had very good muscle tone, thought Ros. Bitch! She probably worked out at some Women's Only gym every day. And while she was a few years older than Ros, her breasts remained nicely shaped and were still quite firm. Double bitch!!

Lynne opened her eyes and looked at her. 'Oh, hi Ros.' She looked a bit guilty – as well she might. 'You needn't have come across. I told Geoff I thought I'd be OK. You know, just with a bit of rest.'

Ros sat down carefully on the side of the airbed and took hold of Lynne's wrist to take her pulse. Whilst looking at her watch, Ros had a sudden vision of Florence Nightingale, administering to the troops in the Crimea. Must be the tent that did it. And the stifling heat.

'That seems quite normal,' said Ros releasing her hand. 'Now where's the thermometer?' Just like a member of the Health Police to have their own personal thermometer.

Ros took Lynne's temperature. It was slightly high, but then again it was very hot in the tent. 'I think you may well be over the worst. So how are you feeling today?' Ros asked, pointedly.

'You know. A bit dehydrated.' Not surprising the amount you put away last night, thought Ros. 'I've been drinking a lot of water. That seems to be helping.'

'Well, you do need to rehydrate the system.' In Doctor Ros

starring role, last performed in Frenchman's bedroom. 'Have you been taking paracetomol?'

'Yes, but not too many though,' said Lynne. 'You do read how they can cause liver damage.' Not as much as you inflicted on yours last night, thought Ros.

'Well, keep taking the tablets,' Ros couldn't resist saying, 'and you'll be as right as rain in no time.' She couldn't help noticing she'd morphed into Dr Finlay.

Lynne raised herself into more of an upright position which, Ros saw, left her body totally exposed. Lynne didn't seem to notice. Or probably care. Lynne looked towards the tent flap. 'Thanks Ros. Er, you haven't mentioned to Geoff last night's, well, little indiscretion have you?' So that's the term she applied to flinging her nude body at an ineligible male.

'No I haven't Lynne. And I don't intend to.' Ros kept her voice low so Geoff, even if he was awake, wouldn't hear. She paused for dramatic effect and added, 'But what the fuck did you think you were playing at!?'

Lynne involuntarily moved her head back as if slapped. She looked shocked. Ros rarely swore – out loud, anyway. 'I don't know. It must have been the heat and the booze. Sometimes you can get carried away. It was most unlike me. I just don't know what I was thinking of. I really am terribly ashamed. I'm so sorry, Ros. I really am.'

Ros had thought Lynne had grovelled enough. After all, Ros wouldn't be automatic first choice at the head of the queue in the stone-throwing event. 'OK. I know what you mean. I suppose it is easy to get carried away, sometimes.'

'And sometimes, you know, things can look worse than they are. Innocent actions seem much more suspicious.'

Hang on, thought Ros. This was a bit below the belt. Lynne was in danger of spoiling a perfectly good apology.

Ros remembered that, whilst Geoff and Lynne had been

playing tennis, Lynne had seen Ros and Jean-Luc together going down to the boathouse. Was she referring to that? Shit! She'd added yet another woman to the ''Ros is a guilty slut'' list.

Ros decided to back off. 'Yeah, well I suppose we've all done things we regret at some time or another.'

Lynne changed the subject. 'I've noticed that you don't seem to be happy about being nude lately, Ros,' looking down at her covering wrap. 'You were fine when we first met you here. Remember?'

'That was then. Now is now. It's really getting to me.' Why was Ros sharing this information with the bitch? A woman to talk to perhaps? It seemed that since she'd been here, she was missing female conversation.

'I quite like life in the nude.'

'I think I've noticed that,' Ros just had to add.

Lynne ignored the comment and continued, 'I think it's probably the sun and fresh air. And, of course, the sense of freedom.'

'Sometimes I think you can have just a little too much freedom.'

They both thought about that for a while, in silence.

'I've got an idea,' Lynne said. 'Why don't we all have a totally textile night? Get dressed up for the evening.'

'Who's all?'

'You know, you, me, Geoff and Nick. We could go for dinner in the restaurant.'

'If you're well enough, of course.' Lynne seemed to have made a remarkable recovery in a very short time, thought Ros. One to write up for The Lancet.

'Well, yes, I should be all right by then,' Lynne continued. 'And let's go down the night club afterwards. Again, clothed. How about it?'

Ros looked doubtful. 'Are you sure there's no rule we

haven't heard about yet, like obligatory nudity every third Tuesday in the month? Something like that?'

Lynne smiled. 'No. I can promise you Ros that you can keep your clothes on and everyone else will be dressed as well. Apart from Janet and John, of course.'

At that moment, the idea of spending a civilized evening with clothed people in convivial surroundings was one which appealed greatly to Ros. 'All right! You're on! What time do you want to meet?

Lynne said, 'In the restaurant. About eight?'

'I'll have to check with Nick, of course, but I'm sure he'll agree.'

I'm sure he will, thought Lynne. After all he'd never had the chance to turn down her invitation to visit one of the lower private rooms in the basement of the night club. And, in her mind, it was an invitation that was still well and truly open.

32

Ros had been gone less than five minutes. Nick had just made himself comfortable, sitting up on the lounger enjoying the sun, when Sam re-appeared, accompanied by ankle-binders – but no Garry.

'Oh, hello, Nick,' said Sam. 'Didn't expect to see you down here. No Ros again, then?'

Nick thought he sensed that look of pity once more. 'No. Gone off to see Lynne. She's not feeling too good after last night.'

Sam spread her towel out over her lounger and sat sturdily on the side of it looking over at Nick. 'Don't see you two together very much.' It was part-question, part-statement.

'Not this holiday. No. Doesn't seem to have worked out that way.' Nick replied. Mind you, he was thinking, I haven't noticed you and Garry playing inseparable bosom buddies, either.

'You do need to be together, as a couple I mean. To look after each of you's. Keep an eye out for one another.'

This was a strange conversation, thought Nick, though in all truth he ought to have been used to the concept by now. Every casual chat he had with anyone in Le Paradis seemed slightly out of kilter, off balance. Agreeing was easily the line of least resistance. 'You're right Sam. Absolutely right.'

She turned away from him to lie on her lounger. For want of something to do, Nick picked up Ros's paperback. Its cover showed a swashbuckling, handsome Cavalier-type character on horseback, fighting a Roundhead. In the background, a winsome maid in long dress and revealing cleavage looked fearfully on at the action. As he had nothing better to occupy his time, he opened it at the beginning and began to read.

'These were difficult days at Hawksworth Manor in the year of our lord sixteen hundred and fifty one . . .'

'That doesn't look the sort of book a grown-man should be reading.' He agreed. Just a minute who was it that had said that?

He looked up. Standing by the lounger, looking down at him was none other than Shareen. His view was exactly the same as his view of Lynne last night. Crotch-level. It was a viewpoint one could easily get used to.

Nick quickly raised his eyes and smiled at her. He looked at the cover and said, 'No it's Ros's book. I was a bit bored so decided to give it a try.'

'I'm glad you're bored.'

'Sorry? Why?'

'Because I am as well. I thought we could go for a bit of a walk?'

'Who's looking after the bar?'

'Oh, Garry's volunteered to hold the fort for a while. There aren't usually many customers this time of the afternoon. Though what the French ones will make of him I don't know.'

Nick looked across to Sam to see how she was taking this conversation. She appeared to have dozed off.

'OK. Why not,' said Nick getting to his feet and putting his towel over his shoulder.

They set off towards the lake. In fact, Sam wasn't asleep and was thinking that it hadn't been like this in her day, when she was the same age as Nick and Ros. I don't know. Couples going off willy-nilly with each other's partners. And the day that she was remembering as "her day" was only ten years' earlier, she thought, somewhat ruefully.

As they walked towards the lake, Nick remembered Shareen "cuddling up" to him on the jetty, presumably to make Jean-Luc jealous. Trying to keep the suspicion out of his voice, he casually enquired, 'Jean-Luc about, is he?'

Shareen looked at him. 'Oh, so Ros told you about him?'

'Well, told me you're an item.'

'Sometimes. Trouble with Jean-Luc is that he has a wandering eye. And that's not all that wanders, if you know what I mean,' said Shareen, looking at him.

'I do,' said Nick. Agreeing with people in Le Paradis seemed so much less of a problem. 'Where are we going?'

Shareen brightened up. 'I thought we'd walk over to the old summer house? Have you seen it?'

'Can't say I have. Is it far?'

'It's on the far side of the boules court. You wouldn't notice it if it you didn't know it was there. There's a little path leading to it. Bit overgrown, but it's a nice secluded place to sit and think.'

Nick wondered why Shareen had asked him to go for a walk. He had the distinct impression this morning that she had something on her mind, something she wanted to tell him. Perhaps that was it. He'd see how it went.

'How's the investigation going? I saw you guys having lunch with the inspector,' Shareen said.

'Didn't really find out much. He plays his cards close to his chest.' Almost as a Pavlovian reaction, Nick glanced down at Shareen's breasts. Looking her in the eye, he said, 'Lagardère thinks, or rather hopes, he may have the murderer before the week's out. But then again . . .'

To pass the time, and deflect his attention from the fact that he was walking along with a naked attractive woman in an increasingly under-populated part of the resort, Nick brought Shareen up to speed with his theory about the murder. But to be honest, she seemed a touch distracted.

'Here we are,' she said brightly. The boules area was deserted. Numerous dog-ends left by Garry around the bench were the only sign they'd been here this morning. And a litter bin full of empties.

Nick followed Shareen towards the back of the court. At the far end were trees and an overgrown hedge. Nick had thought there was nothing beyond it except more of the same. He was wrong.

Leading the way, Shareen pushed aside a branch and exposed a small low gate, rotten and barely clinging onto rusted hinges. Passing through this gate, a narrow overgrown path led between the bushes. Nick noted that it had seen some recent use, as the grass appeared trodden down. Maybe worn down by Shareen and Jean-Luc? Nick didn't like to think about that.

The path turned a corner and there, at the end of a small clearing, was a five-sided wooden gazebo, such as you might find in the garden of an old Victorian house. The front two sides were open to the elements and were facing towards them. The whole had a pointed roof. It was in bad repair with creepers up one side and holes in the roof which let in shafts of sunlight. It looked to have been built roughly the same time as the cabin in which Nick and Ros was staying, but in far worse condition.

'Voila!' Shareen indicated the ruin. 'Great isn't it?'

Great wasn't the word Nick would have chosen. 'You just wouldn't know it was here.'

'It's like a secret garden. Did you ever read that book as a kid, Nick?' Shareen asked and carried on before he had a chance to answer. 'It was about a hidden place that could take you away from the boring and mundane. To somewhere anything was possible.'

The clearing and summer house had clearly lightened Shareen's mood. 'Hey. Let's go and sit down.'

She walked over to the gazebo. Just inside was a bench which looked the twin to the one that the lads had sat on this morning. Nick guessed that it had been carried over here some time recently. It was like a plain park bench, with wooden slatted back and seat. The bench faced outwards into the clearing and towards where the boules court was, albeit hidden in greenery.

Nick automatically put his towel down on the bench, noticing as he did so that Shareen didn't have a towel about her person, nor in fact, anything else other than her flip-flops. Thongs, he thought they were called in Australia.

'Mind if I share your towel?' asked Shareen, sitting down. 'Remember, splinters in the bum can be painful.'

Both sat together and looked out. Bees buzzed. Flies hummed in the roof of the gazebo. Sun rays shone through the branches of trees round the clearing.

Nick couldn't help but notice that Shareen was uncomfortably close to him. It was about to get even less comfortable. Shareen took his hand and looked up into his eyes. 'Hey, Nick, you're a good looking guy you know?' Beat. 'For an older man.' She laughed. 'Only teasing.' Adding 'About the older bit, that is.'

She wasn't only teasing when she moved her mouth towards

his. He'd begun to notice that this was something else that seemed to happen a lot in Le Paradis. Leave him with a woman on his own and she wanted to kiss him. So who's complaining?

As he hovered between deciding to move his own lips down to hers, it flashed across Nick's mind that this could potentially be a lot more embarrassing than last night's clinch with Lynne. On that occasion he'd been wearing clothes. Today he was nude, with no boxers or trousers to conceal any possible movement that may arise.

Fuck that! Nick thought. So what if it did? What did she expect? He returned her kiss. Shareen put her arms around his neck and pressed the top of her body against him. The casual observer might have detected the faintest similarity with the pose in Rodin's ''Kiss''.

Nick could feel a hard nipple against his chest. It wasn't the only thing that was hard. He couldn't look down at the moment to check the evidence but experience told him that he had a substantial erection. It wasn't in contact with Shareen's body at the moment, but it was only a matter of time until she noticed.

She pulled back from the kiss and looked at him. 'That was nice. Do you think we should do that again.'

Nick managed a husky 'Sounds like a good idea,' before re-engaging her mouth. This time Nick found his hand creeping up, like something with a mind of its own, to Shareen's left breast. She gave a little moan as his palm rubbed over her nipple. Nick noticed they were both breathing heavily at this point. He then found himself kissing her neck and shoulders and she had her hand round his back.

He suddenly thought of kissing Ros's neck last night, which gave him brief pause. Guilt kicked in. He rapidly kicked it out again.

Christ! Give him a break! He was only flesh and blood after

all. How likely was it that a chance like this would present itself
ever again? By this time he was sucking one of Shareen's breasts
and enjoying it enormously.

Nick suddenly felt a hand round his cock. And it wasn't his
own. It was Nick's turn to groan.

Shareen looked down. 'You're a big boy when aroused,
aren't you? It excites me to see my hand down there.' Nick
could not but agree.

There was an extra frisson about outdoor sex, Nick had
always found. Although it was fraught with danger of discovery. Which was perhaps what made it so sexy. He
remembered one memorable occasion when he'd been making
love to an old girlfriend in a secluded part of the Black Forest,
when a German scout troop appeared just five minutes after the
act had been consummated. Ten minutes earlier and the troop
would have been able to add a further fieldcraft spotters badge
to their sleeves. One that even Baden Powell would have had
difficulty imagining.

Back at the gazebo, and some time later, Nick removed
fingers and face from an intimate part of Shareen's anatomy and
just couldn't wait any longer. Shareen was sitting, legs apart on
the bench at the time, head back and Nick thought this would
be as good a position as any to take her.

As he was just about to put this into practice, Shareen
suddenly looked up and shouted, 'Stop! No!' Which he did. He
looked at her with he hoped not such a pleading expression on
his face as he suspected he had.

'What? What's the problem?' asked Nick.

'I'm not on the pill.' It was a piece of information Ros could
have supplied, if Nick had thought to have asked. 'You're
gonna have to use a preservatif.'

There was that bloody word again. This time he knew what
it meant. Courtesy of Ros. But it didn't help much.

What was going on here? Last night Ros wouldn't fuck *if* he wore a preservatif. This afternoon Shareen wouldn't *unless* he wore one. Life could be very trying at times.

'But, I don't have any.' Which was pretty obvious really, given that skin, for all its advantages, didn't run to built-in pockets. 'And I can see you don't. Don't worry. I can always pull out before I come.'

'Too risky, Nick, can't do it.' Shareen panted. 'But I think I have an alternative idea you might quite enjoy. Come and sit here.'

They changed places. Nick sat on the bench and Shareen knelt down in front of him. And well, not to put too fine a point on it, gave him a totally satisfying and, some might say, extremely efficient and almost professional blow job.

When he'd come, very noisily as it happened – out of sheer relief – Shareen rose from her knees and sat back beside him on the bench. Nick put his arm round her, bathed in a post-climactic glow. She snuggled her head against him. 'There, how was that?'

'Fantastic.'

'I bet old hoity toity Ros couldn't give you so much pleasure?' said Shareen.

She could actually, thought Nick, but silence in some instances really is the best policy. Ignoring her somewhat strange remark, he remembered that she seemed to have something on her mind this morning when she visited him. He decided it'd be safe to ask now. 'Shareen?'

'Yes, Nick.' She turned her blue eyes up at him.

'This morning? When you came round to the cabin? I had the feeling you wanted to say something to me. To tell me something. What was it?'

Shareen looked forwards, still nestled against Nick's shoulder. 'Oh, it was nothing. It's irrelevant now, anyway.'

Nick looked down at her, not quite understanding what she was talking about, but not really wanting to pry too much. Just enjoying the sight and feel of her naked body pressed against him. A more worrying thought occurred to him. 'Er, Shareen?'

'Yes, Nick?'

'Er, you're not going to mention this to anyone, are you? I mean, it was something just between ourselves, right?'

Once again she turned those blue eyes on him. And smiled. 'No, Nick. I'm satisfied now. My lips are sealed.'

He took her in his arms again and they kissed gently. Shareen broke off and looked at her watch. 'Gotta shoot. Before Garry drinks the bar dry.' She got to her feet and bent to give him a final kiss. 'Been a great afternoon.' As if he'd taken her to the movies.

Shareen walked away from him, her rear doing its usual thing. A rear that he'd become intimately acquainted as he'd been holding those very same buttocks in both hands not ten minutes earlier.

She disappeared from view. There was silence in the clearing. Nick was left to reflect on what had happened. He first checked to see if he felt guilty. Did he? Well of course he did! After all, it was the first time he'd been unfaithful to Ros.

Hang on, though! He hadn't actually fucked Shareen. But he was honest enough to admit that he would have done if he'd had a preservatif about his person. And who in his position wouldn't, he reasoned? You'd have to be a saint off the Mother Theresa scale not to have succumbed to Shareen.

But why had *she* done it? This was his next thought. Was it to make Jean-Luc jealous? It was one thing making your partner jealous, quite another having oral sex with another man.

Maybe, just maybe, it was Nick's after-shave. No. Didn't wear any. All right, his animal magnetism. Erm? In the end he thought it would have to go down as one of those unexplained miraculous occurrences that only happen when you venture, on a sunny summer afternoon, into a secret garden.

Nick didn't leave the clearing immediately after Shareen. He'd learned his lesson the other day when Shareen had been spotted by Ros returning from the jetty, closely followed by Nick giving a fair impression of one man and his dog. What also delayed his departure was the need to replay some of the highlights of the recent encounter in his brain, committing them to memory.

Eventually, Nick felt he could get up without knees buckling weakly under him. He gazed idly around the clearing and, for something to do, walked round the boundaries. And nearly fell into a large hole, partly covered by twigs and branches.

It was in the far corner. He stood back and looked at it. Someone had dug this relatively recently, he thought. It hadn't filled with leaves or detritus. A fresh mound of earth stood under the hedge, difficult for the casual observer to see. And next to it lay a shovel.

The most notable thing about this particular hole was its shape. It was just the right length, width and depth to accommodate a human body. In fact, it bore an uncanny resemblance to a grave. A grave waiting to receive an occupant.

33

Not having a great deal to get back to, except her lounger and bonkbuster, Ros had taken up Lynne's invitation of tea and jaffa cakes from home. Now they'd cleared the air and had their "little chat", Lynne and Ros spent some time building bridges, while Geoff did his Rip Van Winkle impression.

It was some time later when Ros arrived back at the pool. The talk with Lynne hadn't gone too badly, she felt. Sure, Lynne didn't seem as repentant as she should, but Ros was certain that her attempted seduction of Nick was an aberration – a one-off. Ros had made that perfectly clear to her. The message, in country and western parlance, was "don't mess with my man."

Where was her man, by the way? She'd now reached the lounger and he was nowhere to be seen. Nick seemed to have made a habit of going absent in Le Paradis. Probably the lure of the bar called. Hang on. The lure of the bar included a certain

Aussie slut. Should she check? No, come on Ros, that really would be pathetic. So she went to check anyway.

She looked in at the entrance and there was Shareen, behind the bar, chatting to Garry. Laughing at something he was saying whilst drying glasses with a tea towel. No sign of Nick in the place. Shareen saw Ros and waved to her. Didn't seem to have taken this morning too seriously then, thought Ros as she raised her hand in acknowledgement.

Ros walked slowly back to the lounger. Nick was lying on it, reading her book. 'Hi there.'

'I was here a minute ago. Where were you?'

Nick indicated the toilet block behind them. 'In the bog. Then I took a shower. It's very hot this afternoon.'

If anything, it seemed to be even hotter than yesterday. So hot that there was hardly anyone around, or in, the pool. Not even Mason, Gareth and Sam.

'How about a swim?' Nick suggested, getting up from the lounger. 'Cool you off.'

'Why not?' Ros smiled, shed her wrap and dived into the pool. The water felt good on her naked body. Nick joined her, doing his normal impersonation of the shark from ''Jaws'', humming the theme tune as he pretended to move in for the kill. A laugh a decade.

They splashed about a bit and relaxed. As if re-connecting after the nightmare events of the past few days, Nick also seemed in good form, thought Ros.

He was now lying back against the poolside, arms along the pool edge, floating, legs making water-treading movements, seeming content and at one with the naked world of Le Paradis. Ros was floating on her back, looking at her breasts and pubic hair which seemed to be the main things breaking the water line, like islands in a tropical sea. She spotted Nick watching as well. 'Lagardère has good taste, I think.' said Nick. 'In women, if not murder suspects.'

Ros turned on her front and swam across to him. She adopted a similar position to Nick, by his side.

'How did it go with Lynne?' he asked. She detected a slight worry in his voice.

'Gave the bitch a good kicking and told her not to touch my man again.'

Nick stopped swishing his legs and looked at her. 'Please tell me you didn't really do that?'

'No, I just told her that I'd appreciate it if she wouldn't pay so much sexual attention to you in future.' Which, for Nick's consumption, was Ros's spin on ''What the fuck were you playing at?!''

'And how did she take it?' asked Nick.

'She apologized and promised not to do it again. Said she didn't know what came over her. That she'd had a lot to drink. Etcetera. Etctetera. Grovelled quite a bit actually.'

'Er, and Geoff?'

'Knows nothing about it. You'll still be able to go and get pissed with him down the Prince of Wales.' Nick looked relieved. 'Incidentally, Lynne suggested we all go to the restaurant for dinner tonight. The four of us.'

'I thought you'd had enough of the Russells?'

'That was this morning. Now we've made our peace, so to speak, I thought it would be rather nice.' Especially the getting dressed bit, thought Ros.

'Well, we've got nothing else on. Literally.' Nick agreed.

'That's partly the point. We will have something on if we go to dinner. Clothes.' said Ros, looking down at her body. Whatever her increasing problems with nudity, she did enjoy swimming naked. 'Lynne also suggested we go on to the night club afterwards, if she feels up to it, of course.'

The night club. Nick remembered a very drunken Lynne making a rather improper suggestion to him about the night club. Still, she had been pissed at the time. And, if he remembered rightly, the night club was also a textile area. Lynne would be wearing clothes, which would automatically cushion and damp down any contact. In fact, he couldn't see what could possibly go wrong.

'Yeah, that would be nice,' Nick agreed, paddling his feet up and down in the cooling waters of the pool.

34

Once they'd dried off and left the pool area to walk back, it was gone six. Both Nick and Ros had taken quite a lot of sun that day and their tans were coming along well.

The cabin of evil sweltered as Ros eventually salvaged the door key from her bag. Sometimes, Nick thought, it would be easier getting stuff out of the Titanic. They left the door open to let in some air.

'Do you want first shower?' asked Nick.

'Don't mind. You go first if you like,' said Ros, taking her wrap off and draping it over the dressing table chair, examining her tan in the mirror. 'I really am looking forward to getting dressed this evening. It'll be such a relief.'

'Well, it'll be different,' said Nick, getting into the shower.

Under the spray, Nick pondered on the afternoon's main event. Now that he could think about the whole thing dispassionately, it seemed even more unlikely. Shareen had left the bar, come down to find him and taken him to the summer house with a sexual encounter on her mind. But if she really had wanted to have full sex, surely she would have brought some condoms with her? It could hardly have been an oversight.

He hoped to fuck she wouldn't tell Ros. His number one concern at this moment. Women! He really would never understand them. And that worried him even more.

As he was drying himself, Nick also thought of the empty grave he'd come close to accidentally occupying. Who had dug it? And, more pertinently, why? Had it been intended as the last resting place of Giles Curtis? He kind of thought it might. Or had it been dug since his death for a victim as yet still alive? Or, here's a scary thought, one that was already dead but yet to be interred?

Nick would have liked to discuss this with Ros but thought it might be difficult explaining how he'd found such a remote spot. Particularly when he was supposed to be lying on a lounger by the pool. He knew, though, that when he next saw Lagardère he would have to mention it to him.

Nick returned to the bedroom, drying his hair, saying rather unnecessarily, 'Shower's free.'

'Thanks,' said Ros and headed past him, giving him a swift peck on the cheek as she did so.

Nick decided to dry his hair on the verandah. Pausing only to grab a beer from the fridge, he headed outdoors. Martin Pike was sitting outside his own cabin. He had in front of him his evening glass of ''urine'' and a notebook and pen. He was staring into the middle distance and not looking too jolly.

By contrast, Nick felt in sociable mood. Funny how a blow job can make even Pike seem more bearable. 'Hi Martin!'

'Oh, hello Nick.'

'How's the book going?' Nick indicated the fat notebook on the table.

'Not too badly. I'm just researching a piece about Nudity and the Finnish Sauna. It's interesting, you know, how communal life revolves around mixed nude use of the sauna in Finnish society.'

Nick didn't say anything, content to stand there and drink his beer. He waited for Pike to continue with his dissertation. He didn't. His heart really wasn't in it today.

Pike spoke again. 'Actually, Giles's murder has depressed me quite a bit. It really is a wretched business. Very unsettling as well. "In the midst of life there's death", you know, all that. "Naked we come into the world, naked we leave it".'

And in Le Paradis, naked for the bit in between as well, thought Nick. Pike was clearly in philosophising mode.

Pike continued. 'Then there's Hamish. Wife not long deceased. Lives all alone in a huge house near Malaga. Poor chap. Trying hard to come to terms with it all. He's invited me to go down and stay with him.'

For want of something to say, Nick asked, 'And are you going?'

'I think I might. Be company for him.' And you as well, thought Nick. 'Be good to investigate the naturist clubs down there for the book.' Pike seemed to cheer up slightly at this thought. 'And, of course, it's a great place for watching migratory birds, across the Straits of Gibraltar.'

Nick had forgotten Pike's extensive list of hobbies. Given a decimal point of a chance, Nick expected that Pike could be just as boring on many other subjects than naturism. Before he could continue, Nick asked 'So what are you doing tonight?'

'Staying in probably. Getting a bit behind on the book. May pop down for a "swift half" at the bar.'

'Nick?' Ros called from inside. 'You dressed yet?'

'Just coming!' Nick called over his shoulder, and in explanation to Pike. 'We're going out for dinner tonight. Chance for Ros to get some clothes on.'

'Oh. Well, have a nice time,' said Pike, giving his own unwitting impersonation of Marvin the Paranoid Android.

Nick went back inside. Ros was sitting at the dressing table, paying attention to her make-up and looking rather sexy, thought Nick. She was wearing white brief panties and nothing else. They looked even whiter against her tan.

'Is that what you call getting dressed?' Nick asked, hand on the back of her neck. She smiled and moved away from his touch, not out of protest but because it was not helping her eyeliner application.

'I thought I'd wear that little white number you like so much. You know, the low cut one with those narrow straps.'

He did like it, he remembered, not only because it was quite short and clingy, but because Ros normally wore it without a bra. Which seemed to be her intention tonight.

She turned to look at him. 'And what are you wearing? Don't even think of going out like that.' Indicating his naked body.

Nick sighed, dragged out his case and considered its limited contents. He guessed the pale chinos and white short-sleeved shirt would complement Ros's outfit so he lugged these out, together with a clean pair of white Calvin Kleins.

Ros looked at his selection. 'We're going to look like a washing powder commercial,' she smiled. Nick noticed that Ros had perked up considerably at the prospect of being clothed.

He got dressed and combed his hair. By that time, Ros had completed her make-up and slipped into, that was the only way to describe it, her skimpy dress. Putting on a pair of white strappy shoes with stacked heels, she turned to Nick. 'There. How do I look?'

She did look pretty gorgeous, Nick had to concede. 'Good enough to eat.'

Ros almost blushed, remembering Jean-Luc's efforts in that direction. 'Well, let's not go too far.'

*　　　*　　　*

As they approached the front entrance of the restaurant, Ros recalled their first night-time visit. She could still feel the acute embarrassment of the sudden realisation that they were virtually the only nude people in sight.

'Bon soir, Madame, M'sieur.'

Ros replied to the Maitre D'. 'Pour quatre personnes. Le nom est Russell.'

The Maitre D scanned the reservations, spotting the booking. 'Oui. Russell. Mais pour six personnes.'

He picked up menus and they followed him, back down to a table at the front of the restaurant. They were the first to arrive. After consulting Ros, Nick ordered a couple of kirs from the waiter.

'Did I hear him say it's for six people?' Nick asked, picking up his napkin and placing it over his chinos. Three coverings of cloth, rather than none. It felt strange.

'Yes. Lynne didn't mention that she was inviting anybody else.' Ros shrugged, just hoping the other couple weren't Janet and John. She wouldn't fancy Nick trying to look down Janet's cleavage all night. That is, if she was wearing anything with a cleavage to look down.

In any case, Ros wasn't going to let anything spoil this evening for her. Here they were sitting in a civilized restaurant, fairy lights strung and reflected in the waters of the lake. About to have dinner and pleasant conversation. And wearing clothes, just like a normal holiday dinner, or meal back home.

The waiter brought their drinks and they clinked glasses. As they did so, Lynne and Geoff arrived.

Lynne, Ros thought, looked remarkably well for someone who'd been literally flat out this afternoon. Her hair was freshly washed and groomed, almost shiny, like in those shampoo ads. And, my God! Not only was she made-up, she was also wearing a pale lipstick! In clear contravention and wilful flouting of Health Police rules. If this ever got back to the sisterhood in Stoke Newington, well . . .

Ros and Nick got up to greet them. 'Hi Ros.' Lynne and Ros exchanged kisses on cheeks as did Ros with Geoff and, a tentative Nick with Lynne. Once that was all over with, they resumed their places.

Ros noted, with some irritation, that Lynne had applied her own liberal interpretation to the words ''get'' and ''dressed''. In contrast to Ros, she was wearing black. She had on a silky top which, whilst not as low cut as Ros's dress, made up for it by being transparent. As anyone but a registered blind person could see, Lynne wasn't wearing a bra. Her brown nipples, well, and everything else were clearly visible below the top. And there wasn't much of that to start with, ending almost as soon as it began, just above her midriff. Exposing, Ros noted with some annoyance, the well-toned, tanned stomach and slim waist she'd examined that afternoon.

Below the waist Lynne had on a short clingy spandex or lurex skirt – the sort that somehow appears to stay up without any visible means of support. Ros unkindly, but as it happens correctly, suspected that Lynne wasn't wearing knickers underneath it. Well, they'd spoil the line, wouldn't they?

Completing the slut look, thought Ros, were those strappy fuck-me shoes, getting another airing from last night. Back by popular demand.

'You look great, Ros!' said Lynne, picking up her napkin, and smiling at her. 'The white really shows off your tan. Doesn't it, Geoff.'

'Ermmmm?' Geoff looked up from the menu, seemingly noticing Ros for the first time. 'Yes it does.' Before returning to the list of tonight's specials.

Even Geoff seemed to have made a bit of an effort. He was wearing light-coloured slacks and, like Nick, a short-sleeved shirt. Unlike Nick's, it was loose fitting to accommodate Geoff's large girth.

Ros acknowledged Lynne's compliment. 'Thanks, Lynne. You look really good yourself.' Forgetting to add ''that is if you were venturing out for a night's soliciting on the Reeperbahn''. Instead she asked, 'How are you feeling now?'

'Oh, much better thanks. Although I think I'll take it easy on the alcohol tonight. Must have used up all my units for the week in one go yesterday.' She did have the decency to look a bit sheepish when delivering this, Nick noticed, but kept his head down in the menu.

It didn't take a pupil of Einstein to notice that there were two empty seats at their table. Nick mentioned the fact.

Geoff replied. 'They're for Charles and Camilla. We went for a late swim and bumped into them by the pool. They weren't doing anything so we asked them along. You don't mind, do you? '

'No. Just thought they'd be for Janet and John,' said Nick.

Did Ros detect a slight wistful note in Nick's voice? Geoff laughed. 'No, I think they've reverted to their blood-sucking diet tonight.' Quite witty – for Geoff. 'Here they are now.'

He was, of course, referring to Camilla and Charles. They turned just in time to view Camilla sweeping towards their table, Maitre D' trying valiantly to keep up, Charles some way behind.

'Terribly sorry we're late,' said Camilla, exchanging air kisses with each of them in turn, before taking her seat.

Camilla was wearing a classically styled, expensive dark sleeveless dress, modestly scooped at the neck. She had a black belt around the waist and a pair of those black low-heeled shoes with gold chains round the back – the hallmark of the Sloane clan. Plus, of course, the usual assortment of thousands of pounds' worth of jewellery. She had also taken the opportunity to display a large jewel-encrusted brooch, something she obviously couldn't wear when naked. Well, not without a fair amount of pain.

Charles was also conservatively dressed in open necked long-sleeved shirt, well-cut pleated trousers and black Gucci slip-ons. Unlike Camilla, his only accessories were a large gold Rolex watch and a slim gold chain around his neck.

Ros noticed Nick looking at Charles, no doubt remembering the theory he'd expounded about him to Lagardère this morning. Ros found it hard to believe that Charles could be Giles Curtis's killer. Sure, he looked as if he could have been quite hard in his youth. He still looked fairly tough, but capable of murder? She didn't think so.

Camilla took up her menu, and looked over it. 'Now, what's everyone having? I'm absolutely famished!'

The dinner progressed smoothly. There were no major rows or incidents. Camilla was entertaining, if monopolising, company. Charles was his usual monosyllabic self. Geoff was amiable. Nick seemed pre-occupied. Lynne was easy on the wine – and, thought Nick, on the eye. And Ros was just enjoying the simple sensation of wearing clothes.

As the coffee arrived, conversation fragmented and Nick found himself talking to Charles, who had the seat at the head of the table beside him.

'I was talking to Garry today and he tells me that, way back, you both come from Islington?' said Nick. And, as way of explanation, 'Ros and I live in Stoke Newington.' Taking care not to add Garry's view of the borough as 'poncey'.

'Originally. Yes. But a long time ago.' Over those inter-vening years Charles had mislaid any hint he may have had of a North London accent. He sounded more like the Chief Executive of a retail store group.

'In the 'eighties, wasn't it?' asked Nick.

'Yes, before we moved to Portugal.'

By way of Wormwood Scrubs, or wherever, thought Nick. 'Do you remember him from those days?'

'Can't say I do. But he's a good bit younger than me. I have the feeling that he could have been something of a tearaway,' said Charles, conveniently forgetting his own sojourn in one of Her Majesty's free hotels.

Before Nick could say any more, he was interrupted by Camilla. 'Nick, sorry to interrupt but I wondered, did you tell Jack about the papers not arriving this morning?'

Nick turned towards her. 'I did. He told me he'd look out for them. Probably a strike or something. That's why they hadn't turned up.'

'Well, it's just not good enough.' She turned to the others. 'I can usually breeze through the crossword, but there were two clues I really couldn't get the previous day. Unusual for me, I know. I'll probably go to my grave wondering.' Understatement was not her style.

Nick remembered what Lagardère said about letting people know about Giles Curtis's previous status in life. This seemed as good a time as any to impart the tidings to Charles and Camilla – although, if Nick's theory was right, this would be very old news to Charles.

'Actually we spoke to some friends on the phone who did manage to get a Telegraph today and there was a short news piece on Giles' murder.'

'Oh really! What did it say? Do tell!' Said Camilla.

Nick looked at Camilla whilst trying to keep an eye on Charles for a reaction. 'It said that he was a senior Customs and Excise Investigator.'

'A VAT-man!' Camilla couldn't stop herself from saying, in a tone of voice she might easily have reserved to describe an Afghan refugee seeking asylum in Sloane Square.

'Well, yes, but not one who checks your duty-frees. It says that he was involved many years ago in investigating a bullion robbery at Heathrow. It was quite famous at the time. Think it was nicknamed the Heathrow Heist.' Nick casually turned to Charles, including him in the conversation to see how he was taking this news. Nick did have the feeling that Charles looked a bit grimmer than previously but it was hard to tell.

Geoff and Lynne seemed to take the news neutrally. So what if Giles had worked for Customs and Excise? He had to do something when he was working.

It was Charles who now spoke. 'Does Lagardère know about this?' Directed at Nick.

'Yes he does. We were speaking to him only at lunch-time,' Nick replied.

'You wouldn't know where he is at the moment, would you?' Charles politely enquired, taking a sip of coffee.

'Not precisely,' said Nick. 'He could be anywhere. But I do know that when he's on-site he lives in the next cabin to us in Avenue A. Cabin number 14.'

'Well, you'd never have guessed it would you darling?' said Camilla, vaguely in Charles's direction.

Charles looked thoughtful. 'No, you certainly wouldn't.'

The conversation seemed to have passed out. It was Lynne that revived it. 'We were thinking of going to the night club now. Would you both like to come along? It should be fun?'

'That would be super, wouldn't it darling?' No reply from Charles who seemed to have reverted to strong silent status.

'Let's pay the bill and go, then,' Lynne said, a bit too keenly for Ros's liking. 'I could do with a bit of exercise.' Nick hoped she was just thinking of the dance floor.

35

The night club was a large single-storey building at the far end of the lake. To reach it you had to go clockwise around the lake, as opposed to anti-clockwise to reach the boathouse. A concrete path, lit by low lights at regular intervals, took you right to the door.

Nick and Ros held hands as they walked under a starry sky. The moon was yet to rise. Cicadas were doing what cicadas do. And it was even just a touch cooler. A perfect August summer night.

Geoff and Lynne were ahead of them and Nick couldn't help but notice, from an academic point of view, how nice Lynne's rear appeared in that skirt. Set off perfectly by her tarty shoes.

Others were also making their way along the path. Other couples, that is. The club was "couples only", so there was no admittance for the like of Pike and Hamish. Although some might unkindly put them in the couples category. Or may in the near future. Nick suspected that the only reason Charles was accompanying Camilla is that she couldn't have got in on her own. He didn't look in the mood for an evening out.

Nick wondered vaguely what the significance of the "couples only" rule was. He guessed it was to keep out drunken yobbish single men, but he hadn't seen any of them around Le Paradis. Naturist resorts somehow seemed not to appeal to young singles of either sex. After all, where's the fun in trying to get each other's kit off if you're already naked?

As they approached the building, Nick noted the red neon sign, companion to the one that had led them into the resort. It read "Le Club Paradis", above a double set of doors.

Below this, outside steps led downwards to a separate entrance. This had a black door on which were painted, in red, the words "Le Dungeon", each letter looking like it was dripping blood. Little devils with pitchforks and hobgoblins had been added to complete the effect.

Having decided to go up to Paradise, rather than down to Hell, the party headed for the main club's double doors.

In the small inner lobby a large man dressed in white shirt and dark trousers greeted them with a 'Bon Soir' and took their ten euros per person entrance fee – which included a free drink. Nick thought the man probably doubled as a bouncer in case of trouble.

From here, they pushed through a sort of hinged saloon door and into the air-conditioned night club.

On the right hand side was a long zinc-topped bar with high wooden stools, such as you'd find in trendy London bistros. Nick checked behind the bar. No Shareen. Nick guessed even she had to take time off occasionally, apart that is from the odd afternoon break. The bartender was Jack, helped by a young woman who Nick didn't recognize. The night shift at Le Paradis.

To the left were collections of leather sofas and leather easy chairs around low tables, again a look favoured by fashionable Islington bars. There were low voltage lights embedded in the ceilings above the furnishings.

The sofas and tables also stretched around part of the third side of the rectangular space of the club. Then there was a dj booth. It was clear this was going to be no Ibiza rave – or whatever the kids called it today, thought Nick.

The person "mixing on the decks", or more accurately, selecting the cd tracks, made Jimmy Saville look scarcely out of short trousers. Bald with a paunch, and a Gitanes hanging from mouth, he looked as if he'd be happier sanding the dance floor than filling it.

Abba were playing as they walked in – well not literally, you understand – and Nick surmised that this was probably the most recent record he'd hear that evening.

The area prepared for dancing was in the centre of the club. A few couples gyrated self-consciously on a reasonably sized dance floor below the coloured spots and obligatory, slowly rotating, mirror ball.

At the far end of the club, a staircase led down, presumably to the toilets. And perhaps to the private rooms Lynne had mentioned last night.

Whilst Nick was taking all this in, Camilla had taken charge of the party. She found a vacant table in the left hand corner, which offered an excellent view of the dance floor. She'd also organized Geoff to get the drinks and got Charles to help her re-arrange sofa and chairs in an arrangement that probably matched closely her sitting room in Sloane Square.

Nick went with Geoff to order and collect the drinks. This gave him an opportunity to study their fellow boppers. Teeny they weren't, the couples ranging in age from late twenties to late fifties. An audience unlikely to indulge in ecstasy or class A drugs, thought Nick. But you never could tell. Nothing would surprise him in Le Paradis.

There were not that many people in the club. Perhaps thirty or forty. It was still early. What came as something of a shock to Nick, once his eyes had acclimatised to the general low level of lighting, was that most of the women in the club made those out on the town in Newcastle look completely over-dressed. In itself, some achievement.

While the men were mainly wearing, what could probably be termed, ''smart casual'' clothes, their partners were, well, Nick could only describe them as ''half-naked''. And which half clearly depended on individual preference.

As he wandered across with Geoff, he noticed an attractive woman in her thirties dancing in a short lace dress ending just below crotch level. And nothing else. Close to the bar he saw another woman wearing something that looked so much like a translucent black slip that it must have been just that, over a black suspender belt, stockings and high heels. Inadvisable really in that she must have been a good couple of stone overweight. A third woman at the bar was wearing a dress so low cut that her nipples were clearly visible peeking over the neckline.

Compared with their female compatriots, Lynne was on the conservative end of the scale, Ros a Sunday school teacher and Camilla a dowager duchess.

As they waited to be served at the bar, Nick mentioned this to Geoff. 'Er, Geoff. Have you noticed the women here?'

'Yes. Great isn't it. Thought you might like it.'

'But why are they all, well, wearing so little?'

Geoff removed his eyes, reluctantly it seemed, from the virtually topless woman waiting for her drink at the bar, and turned back to Nick. 'If you look at it in a slightly different way, approach it from the other direction if you like, they may see it as wearing a lot. Let's not forget that everyone here has been nude all day. From their point of view, they are actually wearing perfectly respectable outfits.'

'Oh come on!' said Nick, as a woman walked past with literally a dress that ended halfway up her hips, exposing shaven crotch totally to everyone who cared to glance in that direction. 'It's just sheer exhibitionism. I didn't think that had anything to do with true naturism?'

If Martin Pike had been allowed into Le Club Paradis Nick could have asked him his opinion on the subject. As he wasn't, and he couldn't, we'll have to turn to the Naked Guide for enlightenment:

> Exhibitionism has been defined by one dictionary as 'a perversion involving the public exposure of one's sexual organs.' If we accept this limited definition, does it follow that ALL naturists, male and female, are exhibitionists? After all, being naked in public automatically means exposing sexual organs to general gaze.
>
> No, I think we must look further at the definition. From the naturist point of view, exhibitionism only becomes a perversion if the person doing the exposing is carrying it out purely to achieve sexual excitement or gratification. In the case of the male, it could be said for obvious reasons to be easy to spot, and to control! But what about the female exhibitionist?
>
> Some experts say that exhibitionism is seldom evident, if it exists at all, in women. Others say that it is not uncommon, but is not usually identified as deviant behaviour because there are many more socially acceptable ways for women to display their bodies.
>
> So are the women who wear scanty clothing in places such as naturist, or clothing optional, resort night clubs displaying exhibitionist tendencies? The writer is of the opinion, and it is a personal opinion, that they are. This is reinforced by the general feeling that women wearing some clothes are seen to be more sexually arousing than thos who are completely nude – viz the success of Ann Summers retail outlets.
>
> In this writer's view, exhibitionism in either sex has no place in the naturist canon. And, with the increasing popularity of clothing optional resorts (see separate entry) worldwide, it's a dilemma that's going to continue

Before Geoff could say any more, Jack turned up to take their order.

'Hello Nick. Hi Geoff. Nice to see you both down here. What can I get you?'

They placed their order, gave Jack their free drink vouchers and off he went to get them.

Nick resumed his cross-examination of Geoff. 'OK. If you think that all the women here, or the majority of them anyway, are – what did you call it – ''wearing respectable outfits'', then how come none of the men are doing an impression of the Full Monty. You know, parading round in see-through trousers, leather thongs or vest and pants?'

'Well, it would just look silly, wouldn't it? I mean, can you imagine me walking round here in a jock strap?'

Unfortunately Nick could. 'You've proved my point. It's OK for the women because it's erotic and tantalising, but not for the men. It means the women are dressed to thrill. Simple.'

Geoff appeared to change the subject but it was related. 'If you think this is revealing, then you should pop downstairs later.'

Nick looked at Geoff, as this was precisely the suggestion Lynne had made to him last night. 'Why?'

'Well, when we were here last, I was going to the bog and took a wrong turning. It *is* very dark down there. I ended up in a room full of couples shagging.'

'And?'

'And? Isn't that enough? I mean it was like an orgy.'

'So you made your excuses and left?'

'I got out a.s.a.p, I can tell you. Well, after stopping to watch for awhile.'

'Didn't have you down as a voyeur?'

'No more than the next man.' Geoff looked furtively around, as if afraid someone might be listening into the conversation. 'Tell you what, if you can slip away later we can pop down and . . .'

The sentence remained unfinished as Jack returned with the drinks. 'There you go. Enjoy!' He then bustled off as the bar was beginning to get busy.

As Nick tried not to spill the drinks he was carrying, nor mix the contents, he couldn't help but reflect on his conversation with Geoff.

It appeared to him that many of the men were parading their women as if exhibiting the goods. Waiting for an offer. Which is, of course, what many of them *were* doing. Like Le Paradis itself, what you saw wasn't what you necessarily got.

To the casual observer, Le Club Paradis was just a 'disco', albeit one where the women were a trifle under-dressed. Dive below the surface and you had a different proposition. Couples who were after the sort of evening you just wouldn't get down your local working men's institute.

They returned to the table and drinks were distributed. The sound level of the music wasn't too loud to prevent conversation, although Charles didn't seem in a very talkative mood. No change there. He kept staring at the bar, presumably at Jack.

Ros raised her glass to Nick in toast. He wondered if she'd noticed the way the women were undressed in the place but didn't want to point this out lest it ruined her good mood.

'Nick, have you noticed that some of the women aren't wearing very much?' asked Ros. 'Sort of fancy undress?'

'Er, yes, I had noticed.' Nick replied, as a woman wearing a negligee type top over a thong walked past. 'Does it bother you?'

Ros smiled. 'No, not at all. Although I do think Lynne was slightly bending the truth telling me it was textile.'

Nick said, 'Apparently other things go on down here as well. Couples swap partners. Downstairs, I'm told.'

'Who told you that?' asked Ros, suspiciously.

Nick thought quickly. 'Geoff. Apparently, last time he was here he took a wrong turn downstairs and ended up at an orgy.'

Ros laughed. 'There's an improbable image. He didn't, you know . . . join in?'

'No. He left. Eventually.'

Just at this moment, as he knew it would, the unmistakeable opening bars of "Brown Sugar" broke through the speakers. Off they, and virtually everyone else, went to dance. Even Camilla dragged Charles out to shuffle around.

Whilst doing his normal impersonation of a headless constipated chicken, Nick caught Lynne smiling across at him. She had that look which Nick interpreted as "I haven't finished with you yet." Lynne also managed to look cool and sexy, jiving with Geoff, who was, surprisingly, an extremely good dancer.

Ros and Nick stayed on the dance floor longer than the others. Ros couldn't remember the last time they'd had a really good dance. Probably at various friends' weddings. There seemed to have been quite a few of those in the past few years. Yes, and divorces as well. But nobody celebrated those.

Eventually they returned, slightly sweaty, to their armchairs. Whilst they'd been away, the party had been swelled by the arrival of Garry and Sam. There was something strange about them, thought Ros. She realized what it was. It was the first time she'd ever seen them anything but naked. Garry was wearing shorts and a t-shirt, whilst Sam was wearing a low cut, loose white dress, which did a lot for her figure. That is, it totally disguised it.

'Watcha Nick. Ros.' Garry kissed Ros and hugged Nick. Sam stayed where she was in her seat, sipping what could have been a small port and lemon.

Ros and Nick sat down with them. 'Nippers were asleep so

we thought we'd pop across.' Sam explained.

Garry was lighting a cigarette. 'And, before you report us to the Social, the people next door are going to look in on them from time to time.'

'What you drinking?' Garry asked.

'No. Let me,' said Nick. He took orders all round and he, Garry and Geoff left to go and buy the drinks. The music was now louder, making anything bar a two-way conversation impossible. It was also getting very crowded.

'It's nice to see you two together,' said Sam to Ros. 'Saw you on the dance floor. You make a nice couple.'

Ros smiled. 'Thanks. We do enjoy a bit of a bop every now and again.'

'Getting Garry out there is like winkling cockles.' Sam looked round and said to Ros. 'Here you don't go in for all that couples lark, you know, downstairs, do you?'

Ros looked surprised. 'No. Why do you ask?'

'Well I got the impression that you and Nick, well, you know, had a sort of open arrangement. See other people, that sort of thing. "Swingers" is what we used to call it.'

'What on earth gave you that idea?' asked Ros, knowing full well what had given Sam that idea about her. But Nick?

'Oh, nothing really.' Sam quickly back-tracked.

Ros had another thought. 'You and Garry, I mean, do you, you know, indulge in that sort of thing.'

Sam laughed. 'Don't be silly. It would take up to much of Garry's valuable drinking time.' She seemed much amused by the suggestion.

Ros was thoughtful. Had their relationship come to such a sad state that even casual observers like Sam believed that they could have sex with other people? Or, indeed, were actually doing so?

36

Nick set off to the toilets, with the express purpose *not* to take any wrong turnings and end up in a room with a bunch of heavy-breathing strangers. Ignoring the darker reaches of the basement, which seemed to have little light but a lot of people milling around, he took care in the general gloom to follow the little matchstick men and women signs for the lavatories.

Doing what he'd come to do, he left and was still on course for a safe re-entry to the club when he bumped, literally, into a tall female figure.

'Oh! Sorry!' It was Janet. One quick glance told him it could be nobody else. She was wearing a black leather zip-up jacket, which could have featured in an early James Dean or Marlon Brando movie. Zipped up half-way, it gave the casual observer a very good view of most of her breasts beneath. Over the top of her arm was coiled, Indiana Jones fashion, a black leather whip. Around her waist was a wide leather belt from which hung a pair of handcuffs, what looked improbably like a coiled leather dog leash and other unidentified implements, which wouldn't have appeared out of place on a prison warder in Alcatraz. And on her legs were a pair of thigh-length boots straight out of Barbarella. Studded neck and wrist bands completed the ensemble.

Janet had either decided not to, or had clean forgotten to – that memory again! – wear anything below the belt other than the boots.

'Nick! Lovely to see you,' she said, and this time gave him a peck on both cheeks. An action which pressed her chest up against his.

They were standing to one side of the stairs going back up to the club's main area. 'Er, what are you doing here? I thought you were going to the Dungeon tonight?'

'I did, silly!' Treating him to that giggle again.

'Well, did you get bored and come here instead?' Although she was wearing very few clothes, she wouldn't have looked totally out of place upstairs.

Janet giggled again. 'No, the Dungeon shares toilets with the Club. You get a pass to get out of the Dungeon when you want to use the loos.'

Nick suddenly had an image of relieving himself while standing next to a naked, pierced John in the Gents. It wasn't one he found very comforting.

She indicated a black door behind her, hard to see if you weren't looking for it. 'Want to come in for a quick look round? I could sneak you in.' Like a boarding school girl inviting you for a midnight tuck feast.

'Er, well.' Janet was now standing very close to him, her breasts still in close contact with the thin cotton of Nick's shirt. Mind you, that still meant that the rest of her was a fair distance away.

Nick couldn't carry on standing here with Janet for much

longer. Already she'd got some very strange looks. Some were hostile (mainly the women) and some lustful (mainly the men). And Nick didn't want to be in this position, both literally and metaphorically, when Ros eventually decided to use the facilities.

Janet looked him in the eyes. In her high heeled boots, she was as tall as he was. She moved the whip from her shoulder and put it round his neck, holding both ends and pulling his head even closer towards her. 'Come on. I promise I won't do anything you won't like.'

Nick gulped. He seemed to do that quite a lot when Janice was around. He was, he told himself, curious to see the inside of the Dungeon. And this may be the only chance he'd get to visit an S and M club. Be silly not too, really. And he and Ros could have a good old laugh about it when he told her.

'Oh all right then. But just for five minutes. Or Ros will come looking for me. Then you'll be in trouble.'

Janet smiled, removed the whip from his neck, re-coiled it over the top of her arm and turned towards the door. His research brief didn't include the need to study and admire Janet's very fine rounded buttocks, but he decided to do so anyway. Just for the completeness of his findings.

He thought her rear looked particularly attractive framed by the black belt round her waist and the line of the thigh-high boots, literally at the bottom. It took monumental will-power to stop him reaching out and putting both hands round her buttocks. Something which he felt Janet wouldn't have minded but for which he would be expected to pay with a fair amount of pain.

She went through the first door, which was a kind of airlock. If the casual Le Club person had stepped through it they would have been confronted by a similar, but locked, door and presumably have gone back to the Club. Instead, Janet touched a piece of plastic hanging from her belt to a magnetic strip reader in the wall and the door in front clicked open. She stepped through. Nick, with some trepidation, followed her.

It was quite dark in the Dungeon. What light there was came from groups of candles, or imitation candles, little islands of illumination in a general gloom. There was also low level ethereal music playing in the background. Probably from the "Top Tunes To Torture By" cd.

When his eyes had adjusted to the dark, Nick could see that the Dungeon was about half the size of the Club upstairs. From which he could hear the strains, appropriately, of the bald dj's current selection, "You keep me hanging on". An apt choice in the light of what he was about to see.

The ceiling was painted black, giving the room a strange feeling of infinite height. The walls were painted trompe l'oeil fashion so at first glance you thought the Dungeon was built of roughly hewn stones. Some mildewed, some covered in mould, some in blood. Well, he hoped that the blood stains were simply painted on.

At the far end, near what he surmised to be the actual main entrance to the Dungeon, it was lighter and he could see a roughly hewn wooden bar. Large crates were placed round primitive wooden tables. The crates, even from this distance, looked capable of delivering painful splinters to anyone sitting on them. But then again, that may just have been the idea. The decor of this area was so far removed from that of the club upstairs as to make chalk and cheese appear identical twins.

Nick now turned his attention to his immediate surroundings. John had said that the Dungeon was very well-equipped. Nick could now check that claim for himself. Although not cognisant with the niceties of torture and submission, to Nick's amateur gaze it did seem fairly comprehensive.

There was a pillory that you could lock somebody's head and arms into, whilst somebody presumably whipped you – probably Janet. Iron rings were set in the walls with shackles and chains nearby. Whips, canes and even a cat o' nine tails sat in iron baskets ready for use. In fact, if Torquemada had time-machined forward, there was much that would have kept him both entertained and industrious.

Whilst taking a cursory glance around, Nick's attention was distracted by a figure that crawled out of the darkness. From what he could see, it was a man, naked save for a studded collar much like the one Janet was wearing. He was on all fours, Nick noted, because his arms and legs were shackled in such a way as to make standing impossible.

This man looked at Janet from his position on the floor, which, thought Nick, in itself must be a pretty awesome sight. 'Bitte, Janet?' the man said, rather pathetically, holding onto one of her boots with his hands.

Nick correctly presumed that the man wasn't asking Janet for a glass of beer, but was pleading with her in German.

Janet looked down at him, much as you would if you found dog dirt on your shoe, and crunched her high heel into his back pushing him to the ground. The man groaned. Whether from pain or joy Nick didn't know – and was not sure that he wanted to.

'This is Herman the German. He's an alsatian. Aren't you, Herman?' Herman looked up and nodded. Janet bent down, detached the dog leash from her belt and attached it expertly to Herman's collar. 'Let's go walkies, Herman.' So saying she walked on slowly, Herman at heel, crawling behind.

Janet said to Nick, in way of explanation, 'He's a bit of a sour kraut tonight.' And giggled. Nick had inadvertently walked onto the set of "Carry On Sadist".

At this moment, the power of speech seemed to have eluded

Nick. It was all just too bizarre. Like those tacky programmes he sometimes used to catch by accident on Channel Five when arriving home late from the Prince of Wales.

A few steps further on, Nick and Janet came upon another naked man. This one was wearing a hood over his head and was chained against, and facing, the "stone block" wall.

Stopping in front of the man. Janet handed the leash to Nick. 'Hold my dog for me a moment, would you?' Nick looked down at Herman, who seemed quite content to look up at his mistress. Janet uncoiled her whip and casually gave the hooded man three lashes. He writhed as each stroke of the whip lashed his flesh. It was not enough to draw blood – thank God for that, thought Nick, as he may have fainted – but enough to raise three welts across his back.

Despite himself, Nick was impressed. It must have taken great skill to exert the exact level of force to achieve that effect. It was as if Janet had read his mind. As she re-coiled the whip she said to him. 'I took lessons from a circus ring-master.' Adding 'Are you happy with Herman or would you like me to. look after him?'

Nick hastily gave her back the leash. 'Let's go and get you a drink. I'm sure Herman would like one as well.' She looked down at him and, almost imperceptibly, he nodded his head.

As they went towards the bar, Nick noticed in the general gloom other men and women. Leather seemed to be the chosen "à la mode" this year. The most popular garments seemed to be waistcoats, bodices, thongs and boots – mainly in red or black. Nick thought it would be impolite to look too closely at what they were all up to, but a lot of it seemed to involve chains, handcuffs, rope and such like.

Nick wondered where John was. He soon found out. In an alcove next to the bar was a wall-mounted wooden St Andrew's Cross, the diagonal X-shaped one. Four rings were bolted to the cross, one at each corner. And chained to these four rings was a spread-eagled John. He was naked apart from his leather waistcoat and Timberland boots. It didn't look the most comfortable of positions, as John's boots barely touched the floor. It must have been an excellent stretching exercise. Good for the posture.

John had a strained expression on his face and eyes closed. This may have been a result of the discomfort of the position on the cross or from the effect of the rather dumpy looking homely woman, wearing nothing but a mask, basque and stockings, kneeling in front of him and giving him head. The woman was being helped in this venture by a man standing behind her – presumably her husband, but one can never tell, can one? – who was pushing her head backwards and forwards.

Nick actually was quite shocked by this sight. It was the first time he'd ever seen, in the flesh, something so sexually explicit which he hadn't personally been involved in. He looked at Janet, who seemed totally unconcerned. 'Looks a bit amateurish to me. Still it seems he's having fun.' Were the only words she offered.

At this point, John looked up and saw them. She smiled and waved at him. He grimaced back. Hard to wave when you're chained to a cross.

They reached the bar and were served red wines and a half of lager by a young woman. Totally clad in leather, she had piercings through ears, brow, eyebrows, nose and cheeks. In fact, she had so many holes in her face that it would make drinking a cup of tea something of an achievement.

They carried their drinks to one of the primitive tables and sat on the crates. Janet didn't have a towel noted Nick. Not very hygienic, he thought. Pike would not have approved.

Janet bent and fished out a dog bowl from under the table. She poured the beer into it and put it down on the floor.

'There, mummy's bought you a nice drinkies.' This addressed to Herman who gratefully stuck his face in the bowl to lap up his drink. Perhaps his initial assumption about Herman was incorrect and he had wanted Janet to buy him a beer all along.

Janet was sitting opposite him, with the table to one side, so he had a full frontal view of her sitting on the crate. 'Cheers!' she said, raising her wine glass. Nick raised his glass in response. She took a sip and put the glass on the table. She looked down at Herman who was once again looking up at her. Nick had to hand it to Herman, being Janet's dog wasn't the worst job you could possibly have. It did have significant fringe benefits.

Janet looked at Nick and deliberately totally unzipped her leather jacket, moving the two halves away so as to expose her breasts to Nick – who could but stare. Herman groaned. And was rewarded for his pains, well, with pain, as Janet kicked him in the groin. Nick winced in sympathy. Herman seemed to take it all in a day's work. It really is a dog's life.

'It's hot in here,' Janet said once again looking him in the eyes. As she said this, she slowly and deliberately opened her legs. Nick used all his will power to stop himself looking. But he just didn't have a large enough supply. He was able to confirm what Lynne had mentioned at dinner the other day. In the perfectly smooth and shaved lower regions of Janet's pubis glinted a ring that could have been either silver or gold. Nick dragged his eyes back to Janet's face.

'And what can I do for you, Nick?' Janet stuck her tongue out and deliberately wet her lips. As she did so Nick noticed that she had a stud through her tongue. It wasn't there yesterday. Maybe, like a best suit, it was only worn on special occasions. He wondered what it would feel like if . . . No, best not to think about it. Janet leaned forward.

Nick thought he heard the very faintest of groans from

Herman. Janet didn't seem to have noticed, as Herman's balls remained unattacked. Nick considered the question. He doubted Janet could do anything for him that did not involve a great deal of physical discomfort.

He looked her in the eye. A difficult enough feat in itself. 'Yes, there is something you can do for me.'

Janet gave him a small smile. 'Yes, Nick. What would you like me to do?'

'You can tell me what happened the night Giles Curtis died.'

'What do you mean?' said Janet, moving her legs together as she did so.

'Just that I know you saw Giles on the night, or should that be morning, of his murder.' He didn't, of course, but was bluffing. 'And Lagardère knows as well,' he added just for the hell of it.

Janet reverted to prim primary school teacher, even drawing her jacket round her as she would a cardigan on a cold day teaching Class 1b. 'That's ridiculous. It's just not true. We had nothing to do with his murder.'

'But you do know more than you're letting on about, don't you?' Nick pressed.

'We didn't kill him.'

'No, I don't think you did, either.' Nick agreed.

'It was just as much a shock to us when we heard he'd been battered to death.'

'Would you care to tell me more?'

Even in the gloom of the candle-lit room, a shadow fell across the table. Nick looked up and wished he hadn't as he got a close-up view of a pair of testicles which, judging by the number of studs and chains through them, could only have belonged to one person. He checked out also the ring through the end of his penis and the totally shaved muscular body.

John looked down at him, a little aggressively. He must have heard some of what Janet had been saying. Nick became suddenly aware that he could be in acute personal danger. And not just of the incidental pain variety.

John pulled up a crate and joined them, making room by casually pushing Herman to one side with his boot. Not that Herman seemed to mind.

'Let me,' said John, turning to Nick. Nick inadvertently flinched. He needn't have. John was in a talkative mood. 'It started out as a bit of harmless fun.'

This was their story. When Giles had finished dinner and left Camilla and Charles that night, he had decided not to go straight home, but to visit Le Dungeon. He'd enjoyed, if that was the word, some bondage – hence the marks on wrists and ankles – and a jolly time was had by all.

When the Dungeon closed, Giles came back with Janet and John to their caravan. They decided to indulge in a little sex with asphyxiation on the side. This involved cord and a plastic bag over Giles's head.

'We've done it many times before, without anything going wrong,' John explained, 'But this time, well . . .'

Janet took up the tale. 'Giles passed out and we couldn't seem to revive him.'

Janet and John thought Giles was dead. They couldn't detect a pulse. They really believed they'd killed him.

'We panicked,' said John. 'We thought the best thing to do was get him back to his cabin. It was late and dark. Nobody about. So we decided to carry him back and put him in his bed.'

They'd nearly managed this and were almost at the cabin, when Giles miraculously revived.

'We heard a groan,' said Janet, 'and nearly dropped him in fright.'

'We were so relieved.' John said. 'We propped him up

against a tree and he began to come round. He was a bit confused but definitely alive.'

'We stayed with him for ten minutes or so, and eventually he was able to stand up. We offered to take him back to his cabin, but he insisted he was all right,' Janet said. 'And off he walked. That was the last we saw of him.'

Janet looked at Nick, wanting him to believe the story. 'That's the truth, I swear. We were totally shocked when we heard he'd been killed. If only we had taken him all the way back to his cabin, he might be alive now.' She looked serious.

'So why didn't you tell Lagardère all this?' Nick asked.

'We didn't think he'd believe us. We thought he might think we did it,' said Janet. 'Anyway, you said that he knows we saw Giles that night.'

'It would be good if he heard it from you personally,' Nick said.

Janet and John looked at one another. 'Well, we'll think about it,' said John.

Nick looked at his watch. Shit! He'd been down here for half an hour or more. What would Ros be thinking? He got up. 'I've got to go. Do I need a pass to get out?'

'No, you just push the door,' said Janet.

He left them looking very thoughtful and worried. Just an ordinary couple enjoying a quiet drink, faithful dog at their feet.

37

Nick shouldn't have worried about how long he'd been away. Ros wasn't missing him a great deal. She was having a good time and maybe a few too many drinks.

'No, Garry, Stoke Newington isn't poncey. You see there's a great community element around the place,' she was explaining.

'More like "Care in the Community", with all those social workers and therapists infesting the place.' Garry gave one of his half-laughs, half-coughs. 'And you can't throw a pig's trotter without hitting a health food shop or vegetarian restaurant.'

'Garry's idea of a healthy meal is a fry-up with a bit of lettuce on the side,' explained Sam.

'But it's good to eat healthily,' Ros said, clearly side-tracked by Garry's last comment, and not really minding. It was one of those conversations. 'If you saw the number of people I get in my surgery, problems caused by unhealthy lifestyles including eating the wrong sort of food and too much of it.'

Garry put out his cigarette and took another swig of lager. 'We all got to go sometime, Ros. So I'm enjoying myself while I'm here. Come on let's dance.' The last remark aimed at Sam.

Off they went to the dance floor, where an old Tamla Motown number was playing, leaving Ros with the others. She wondered vaguely what was taking Nick so long. Instinctively she checked to see if Lynne was still about. She was. And was talking to Camilla. Ros also hadn't seen Shareen, the other nude female Nick seemed so keen to be around. Ros relaxed. Wherever he is, he's not with some naked woman, she reasoned, as it happens, totally incorrectly.

As she gazed around the Club, sipping a red wine, Ros noticed a figure at the bar dressed in a white t-shirt and jeans. He looked vaguely familiar. Ros eventually put a name to the face. It was Jean-Luc. And as with Garry and Sam, it was the first time she'd seen him with clothes on. He caught her looking at him and raised a glass to her. Oh, no! He was coming across the floor to talk to her, squeezing between couples to reach her.

Jean-Luc came over and sat next to her. Ros hoped Nick wouldn't come back at this stage. But wait a minute! There was absolutely no problem with this. They were both fully dressed for a start – a major achievement in itself – and in a public place. It was all quite harmless.

'Hello Ros.' Jean-Luc gave her chaste kisses on both cheeks.

Lynne noticed that Ros now had male French company and smiled knowingly across at her. Cow! Ros pretended not to see.

'Hi Jean-Luc.'

'You look good in that dress. It really suits you.'

Ros realized with something of a shock that this was also the first occasion that Jean-Luc had seen her wearing anything but a smile, frown, ecstatic expression or look of total panic.

374 • A W Palmer

'Thank you. About today. I really meant it when I said it's all finished,' she said to Jean-Luc.

He gave a good-natured shrug as if to say "you can't win them all." 'That's OK. I understand.'

'Is Shareen with you?' Ros thought she'd use the opportunity to double-check that Nick hadn't gone off with Aussie slut.

'No, she's had an early night,' Jean-Luc smiled.

'Then who are you here with? Don't you have to be in a couple to get in?'

'Not if you know Robert.' He pronounced this the French way. 'He's the man on the door. Bob the Bouncer we call him. And once you're inside, you know, there's no need to have your own woman. There are many to choose from. Down-stairs.'

Ros wasn't sure whether he was boasting. She suspected he was just telling the truth. Hang on! Hadn't Nick gone down-stairs and not re-appeared since? No, she was being just too distrusting.

Jean-Luc continued. 'Would you like to come . . .' for one second she thought he was going to ask her to go downstairs with him '. . . for a dance.' He indicated the dance floor. 'For old time's sake.'

'Yes, I would.' Ros said, and Jean-Luc led her onto the dance floor.

As the DJ was still playing records you could leap about to if you were so inclined, dancing didn't involve getting into a clinch with Jean-Luc. Although, having only held each other nude, it might have been an interesting experience to do so with clothes on. Sort of living a relationship backwards.

Jean-Luc was quite a good dancer in a very laid-back cool way, occasionally using a hand to push back the lock of hair that fell over his eyes.

As they danced, Ros found herself next to Garry and Sam.

Sam smiled at her and then noticed who her dance partner was and involuntarily lifted her eyes to the ceiling. Ros wasn't doing her slut reputation much good, she thought, but at that precise moment didn't care. Making the most of dancing with this good-looking young Frenchman.

After three or four records, the DJ put on a slow number. Jean-Luc looked queryingly at Ros. She smiled, but shook her head. They left the dance floor and went back to Ros's group.

Jean-Luc took her hand raised it to his lips, rather theatrically, thought Ros, and kissed it. 'Goodbye then Ros.'

He smiled and was off, disappearing into the crowd.

Ros watched him go and now realized that Sam, now sitting down, had been watching all this. 'That was Jean-Luc you was dancing with, wasn't it?'

Ros sat down next to Sam. 'Yes it was. He is hard to resist,' Ros said lightly.

'Well at least you had your clothes on this time,' said Sam.

What could she mean? Ros decided to ignore this last comment. Instead she took drink orders for Camilla, Garry, Geoff and herself. Lynne had already used up her units apparently and Sam was "taking it easy". There was no sign of Charles. As Geoff accompanied her to the bar to help with the order, Ros saw why.

Charles was at the far end of the bar and was having an argument with Jack. It looked as if Charles was extremely angry indeed. He was leaning across the bar and Jack was putting as much distance as possible between them, holding up one hand as if to stop the flow of words coming his way.

Geoff noticed the argument as well. 'Looks like we'll have to wait a bit for our drinks.'

Just then, Charles, having used up his store of invective, turned away and marched towards them. He bumped into Ros

376 • A W Palmer

and apologized when he saw who it was. He was clearly very
agitated.

'Charles, can I get you a drink?' asked Ros.

'What? Oh yes. I mean, thank you. A whisky and soda
please.'

He seemed to calm down slightly and went back to the table.

'What was all that about?' asked Geoff, not expecting an
answer.

A pale-looking Jack came and took their orders. He looked
as if he'd had a bit of a shock. 'No pleasing some customers,' he
said, shaking his head.

Having got the drinks and having returned to the group, Ros
found herself sitting next to Lynne and Geoff. Lynne seemed to
be behaving herself tonight, thought Ros. Their chat that
afternoon had seemed to work in that she was not throwing
herself at Nick. In fact, where was Nick?

'Have you seen Nick about?' asked Ros.

'No I haven't,' Lynne replied, a touch defensively.

'Maybe he's downstairs organising, or participating in, an
orgy,' said Geoff, grinning.

Ros thought that most unlikely. Then again, he had been
acting strangely since they'd been trapped in Le Paradis. 'I'm
sure he'll turn up.'

'Anyone fancy a dance?' enquired Geoff. 'Lynne?'

'Not at the moment.'

'How about you Ros? Come on. Won't do you any harm.'

'All right.' Ros put her drink down. 'Why not?'

Lynne thought that Nick may just be in the basement,
waiting for her to turn up. So as soon as Geoff and Ros were on
the dance floor, she made her way to the stairs.

38

Nick stumbled out of the Dungeon "airlock" with a lot to think about. Janet and John seemed to be telling the truth about the night of the murder – finally. They had left Giles Curtis close to the cabins and that was the last time he'd been seen alive.

Nick thought of the people who had cabins in the vicinity. There was Ros and himself, of course, the odds-on favourites. Then there was the High Court judge, Parker, who checked out in the night. At a time, he remembered, when Giles Curtis may or may not have been alive. And let's not forget Martin Pike, friend of Giles Curtis, who also lived very close to where the body was found.

What he now knew was that somebody had attacked Giles Curtis in the very short distance he'd had to travel between where Janet and John had left him and his cabin. Then maybe dragged round the back of Nick and Ros's cabin, out of the way of prying eyes. But who?

The Charles blackmail theory still seemed a reasonable one

to Nick. He could have come late to Giles Curtis's cabin, lured him out and killed him. As in fact could any of the others.

Nick emerged into the gloom of Le Club's basement. He'd already seen his first S and M club – and he suspected his last – so why not complete his sex-spotters badge by just having a quick peep into the gloomy space opposite. It would only take a few extra minutes, he reasoned.

He crossed the space to the rooms. It was very dark in there, with the odd coloured bulb throwing out light. In front of him were a couple of men and women who appeared to be looking into a mirror on the wall. He wondered what they were doing so went up behind them.

When his eyes had adjusted to the darkness, he could see that the mirror was in fact a window into a room beyond. What the spectators were watching was a naked couple having sex.

Nick was once again shocked. Unlike pornographic videos or dvds, this was immediate and live. He decided to watch a while anyway. Just out of academic interest.

'Hi Nick!' A voice in his ear made him jump. He turned. It was Lynne. 'I didn't take you for a voyeur?'

'No I'm not. I was just looking.' Sounding as if he was browsing for new shirts in Paul Smith.

Lynne replied, as a shop assistant might. 'Seen anything you like?' Looking over his shoulder at the action. 'To try on yourself, that is?'

'Er, no,' said Nick, and took a couple of steps away from the viewing window towards the exit. He didn't want to go further into the rooms, fearing what else might be in there. 'Look, about last night . . .'

'Yes?' Lynne, as usual, was standing quite close to him.

'Well, we got a bit carried away. That's all. Had a narrow escape. So no more, eh?'

Lynne appeared not to have heard. 'I investigated earlier,

when the place was empty. There's a small private room further back. Without a viewing window.' She took his hand and tried to pull him along with her.

Nick resisted. 'No, Lynne. Look I'm Geoff's mate, for God's sake! Not to mention the fact that we're practically neighbours!'

'Come on Nick. Just the once. It can't do any harm.' Still the pull towards the inner recesses of the basement.

Nick managed to get his hand free. 'No Lynne. It's totally out of the question.'

'Am I really so unattractive?' She was now pressing herself against him, her arms had switched to round his neck. Her face was inches from his own. He had the feeling she might make a move to kiss him any second.

Gently he moved her hands from round his neck and held them down at her side. 'On the contrary, you are incredibly attractive and sexy. But you have to see this is a very bad idea.'

Lynne seemed to be deflated by this speech. She looked down. 'Geoff and I rarely have sex these days. It doesn't do a lot for my confidence.'

Nick was embarrassed. This was too much information. It also rather guiltily reminded him of the infrequency of Ros and his own sexual activity.

Lynne continued. 'I put it down to the strain of the IVF treatment.'

This was news to Nick, and he was sure to Ros. 'IVF?'

'Yes. Fertility treatment. We didn't like to tell anyone, well you don't do you, but we tried to have a baby for years. We went through all the procedures. Nothing worked. There's nothing physically wrong. It just wasn't for us, I guess. And it turned sex from a pleasure into a chore. We've given up now. The treatment that is. But I sometimes think sex, as well. It's too late.'

She looked up at Nick. 'Are you and Ros trying to have kids?'

'No, not really the right time for me at the moment. Perhaps later.'

'Well don't leave it too late. Like Geoff and me. You'll regret it I'm sure.' And with this Lynne burst into tears. Nick held her against him. It seemed that if he wasn't holding naked women, he was holding weeping ones. No half measures with Nick.

They were standing right in the entrance of the rooms and in full view of anybody coming down to use the toilets. Nick was concerned that someone would see them there. He was right. At that very moment Sam walked down the stairs. She spotted Nick and noticed that the woman he was holding wasn't Ros. Was everybody at it? She thought, raising her eyes and toddling into the Ladies.

It was past midnight. Nick had left Lynne downstairs to refresh her make-up and joined the others upstairs. The crowd had thinned. It seemed the naturists of Le Paradis weren't all-night ravers.

When Nick returned, Geoff was jiving with Ros giving a very good impression of an overweight Teddy Boy. Ros saw Nick and smiled. At least she seemed to be having a good time.

Their party too was breaking up. Sam returned from the Ladies and she left with Garry, giving him what his mother might have termed ''an old-fashioned look''.

Lynne came back, slightly red-eyed. She sat next to Nick. They watched Geoff and Ros dancing, not saying anything.

Geoff and Ros finally left the dance floor. Geoff looking a trifle sweaty; Ros a bit puffed.

'I've been exercising your husband for you,' Ros said to Lynne, who gave her a tiny smile. That's exactly what Lynne had had in mind for Ros's partner. Ros gave Nick a peck on the cheek. She didn't even ask him where he'd been. Which was unusual.

Lynne decided she'd had enough of the evening and both she

and Geoff readied themselves to leave. Camilla got up to join them.

'Come on Charles. Are you ready to go home?' Camilla asked.

Nick noticed that Charles was nursing what looked like a large Scotch. He didn't seem too happy. Positively grim, in fact. 'No, you go on with Geoff and Lynne.'

'We'll drop you off at your place,' Geoff said to Camilla. 'It's on our way.'

Charles indicated his drink. 'I won't be long. Just got some unfinished business to attend to.'

Lots of goodbyes followed and Geoff and Lynne left with Camilla.

Then there were three. 'How about a dance before we go?' Ros suggested to Nick.

'Why not.' Nick joined Ros for a smooch to a slow number which could have been Barry White – and probably was.

On top of everything else that he'd seen and heard this evening, the conversation with Lynne had really shaken him up. He hadn't known that Geoff and Lynne had been trying for children. What did she mean by the fact that it was too late for her. She was only thirty-nine. Surely there was still the chance of a baby? Lynne didn't seem to think so. And Ros wasn't many years behind her.

Nick didn't want Ros *never* to have a baby. It just wasn't convenient at the moment. But would there ever be a convenient time? He suspected not. And he knew that he didn't want to lose her. These few days in Le Paradis had been filled with temptation and while it was good to give into it at times, he knew that it just wasn't the life for him.

Sacrifices would have to be made somewhere and he knew who would have to make them. He held Ros against him as they danced. And knew she was the only one for him.

By the time they'd finished their dance, Charles had disappeared as well. Time for them to seek their beds.

39

It was quite dark when they came out of the club. If there was a moon, and Nick hadn't noticed one since they'd been here, it was extremely late rising. The only light was provided by the stars and by the lamps set at regular intervals along the path back round the lake.

Ros and Nick strolled arm in arm, enjoying for a change the warm air after the cool of the Club. Ros seemed to be pleasantly relaxed and didn't appear worried about his prolonged absence that evening. He'd tell her all about it tomorrow – well, perhaps not the bit about Lynne. He didn't want to get Lynne into further trouble.

As they turned the corner that led to the now-darkened restaurant, Nick heard noises. Looking more closely he could see two human shapes in what he initially thought was a strange dance. His brain slowly realized what he was actually seeing.

A man seemed to be attacking another. As he watched, one of the human shapes was pushed to the ground. Nick saw a shadowy form lying on the ground, hands up to protect himself, while the person above was wielding a long implement, hitting the person on the ground. He could hear sickening thuds of, what he presumed was, wood or metal on flesh and bone.

Nick would never have put himself in the "have a go hero" category and could never later explain why he immediately rushed over, shouting as he went.

The standing figure turned as Nick got close and swung the implement at him. Nick ducked out of the way. His momentum carried him into the attacking figure and Nick instinctively grabbed at the weapon. He experienced a blinding pain above his left eye as the man swung a fist at him, trying to get Nick's hand free of what, Nick could now tell, was a rounded wooden club.

Nick clung on, as he felt something running down into his eye, presumably his blood, making it even more difficult to see anything. Despite feeling sick at this realisation, he still managed to hold onto the club. With his other hand he tried to reach up into the attacker's face.

The attacker's free hand pushed Nick backwards. As Nick did so he fell over the prone body on the ground, losing his grip on the club. As he lay there, Nick looked up at the figure. Silhouetted against the stars of the Milky Way, the figure raised the club above its head. Nick raised his hands to protect himself against the impending blow.

At this moment, another shadowy figure sprang into the scene, as if catapulted. It was shouting and screaming. It leaped on the attacker clawing his face, biting and pulling his hair. It was Ros.

The attacker was so surprised at this interruption and pain, that he turned away from Nick. Nick got up, and this time managed to grab the club again. The man was so pre-occupied with trying to protect his eyes and face that he let it go suddenly.

Realising that he may be outnumbered, the attacker shook off Ros and bolted away, disappearing behind the restaurant block and into the trees of the resort site proper.

Ros dropped to her knees. 'Nick are you all right?' In a tremulous voice.

'Yes. I think I'm bleeding but not too badly.'

He got to his feet holding the club in his hand. It was as if this was the cue in a theatre for the lights to go up.

Suddenly the whole scene was illuminated by what seemed to be a dazzling white light. In reality it was only a very powerful torch. Nick and Ros raised hands to shield their eyes. A voice behind the light said 'So, what have we here?' It was Lagardère.

'Thank God!' Nick said, even though, seen through the eyes of the inspector, the scene was less than helpful to Nick's pleas of innocence.

Lagardère's torch showed a bloody-faced Nick, holding a baseball bat and standing over a figure on the ground, head covered in blood.

It was Ros who reacted first. She immediately went over to the prone body. 'Quick! Throw some light over here!'

Lagardère complied. The head was covered in blood but the attacked man was instantly recognisable to them all. It was Charles.

Ros bent down to examine him more closely. Nick looked away. 'He's still alive. There's a faint pulse. Call an ambulance. And quickly!'

Lagardère gave the torch to Nick to hold while he called out rapid instructions in French on what, Nick presumed, was a short-wave radio handset.

'Nick. Give me your shirt. Quick,' said Ros.

Nick took his shirt off and handed it to Ros who instantly tore it into pieces, using the teeth and hands that had come to his rescue, to stem blood flow or compress the skull, or whatever she needed to do. Nick again couldn't really watch that closely.

'I think he may have a fractured skull,' Ros said.

Lagardère had finished calling on his hand-set. 'Will he live?'

'I can't say. He's unconscious and lost a lot of blood. You can never tell how badly this will affect his brain. He could have a blood clot developing. Anything is possible. But it's important to move him carefully. How long is that ambulance going to take?'

'Half hour. Maybe slightly longer,' replied a concerned Lagardère.

The scene in front of Nick, coupled with the blood that he kept trying to stem from the cut above his eye with a bit of his shirt handed up to him by Ros, was too much. Nick handed the torch back to Lagardère as he sunk to his knees and was violently sick.

They were finally alone in their cabin. It was half past one in the morning. Almost three days to the hour since they'd first arrived at Le Paradis. It may as well have been a century ago.

The ambulance had eventually turned up and Charles, still unconscious, had been loaded in. The gendarmes had roused Camilla from her bed and she'd followed Charles into the ambulance – which then set off at speed for the emergency facilities at Perpignan. Ros had done what she could but the injuries were so serious she had her doubts whether Charles would regain consciousness, let alone survive.

Ros turned her attention to Nick's injury. It looked much worse than it was. A nasty cut but requiring no stitches. She cleaned the wound, with much flinching by Nick, and dressed it with some butterfly clip dressings.

She stood back to admire the results. 'There. Shouldn't leave a scar or spoil your boyish good looks. Here, take a couple of these as well.' Ros gave him a glass of water and some strong prescription painkillers. One of the benefits of living with a doctor.

Ros then turned her attention to her own appearance. Her slinky white dress had become covered in blood. And she had dried blood on her face. Looking in the mirror, Ros resembled a wife who'd been with her statesman husband at the time of his assassination.

'Not sure this dress could ever be rescued again.' Ros said, turning her back to Nick. Nick unzipped it for her and she stepped out to go to shower.

While she was in the bathroom, Nick got into bed under the thin sheet. As he lay down, he felt slightly dizzy. So who was it that had attacked Charles? It had all happened so quickly and it was very dark.

The would-be or, if Charles failed to pull through, actual murderer was of medium height and strong. Strong enough to overpower Charles. He was wearing clothes, which must have been covered in blood by the time he left the scene. He couldn't be that hard to trace. Could he?

Nick's brain began to wander. The drugs kicked in to soporific effect. By the time Ros returned from the bathroom, Nick was asleep. Ros looked down at him tenderly. He had, after all, possibly helped save Charles's life. She never thought he could do something like that.

Forgetting that her actions had probably saved Nick's life.

DAY FOUR

'The body says what words cannot'
Martha Graham

40

Nick came to, with a start. Bright daylight shone through the flimsy net curtains. The cut above his eye was throbbing and his head was banging. No, it wasn't his head. It was coming from outside. Someone was knocking repeatedly on the door of the cabin.

He checked Ros. She was immobile beside him in the bed, hair over her face. Reluctantly, Nick got out of bed. He felt stiff, probably the result of last night's exertions. Going through the bead curtains, he part-staggered, part-walked into the kitchen and opened the door. And instantly wished he hadn't.

Standing on the verandah, confronting a naked Nick, was Lagardère flanked by two uniformed gendarmes. They looked very serious. Whilst Nick had recently been at ease with his own nudity, he suddenly discovered this did not hold true when confronted by policemen. Images of morning visits by the gestapo or stasi arrived unbidden into his head. He felt uneasy and was about to feel even more so.

'Nicholas Boughton,' said Lagardère. 'I am placing you under arrrest for the murder of Giles Curtis and the attempted murder of Charles Jameson. I must warn you . . .'

Nick didn't hear the rest of what Lagardère was saying. He could only stand there mouth wide open in a state of shock and disbelief. Then he noticed that Lagardère had stopped talking, and that one of the gendarmes – make that both – were trying unsuccessfully not to smile.

Lagardère joined them in this activity. 'No. Just joking. We've come to tell you we've apprehended, I think that's the word your "boys in blue" usually use, the actual murderer. And that you are free to go.'

Dismissing the gendarmes, who went off with broad grins on their faces, Lagardère continued. 'I'm making some coffee next door. When you're ready, why don't you and Ros come over and I'll tell you about it. You may want to get dressed first.' Once again indicating Nick's naked body. 'But then again, you do seem to have adapted well to life in the nude.'

Nick regained the power of speech, just, as he replied 'Er, right. Say in about fifteen minutes?'

Lagardère nodded, turned and walked down the steps. Nick walked back into the cabin. It was finally sinking in. They were free to leave. At last, they really could go on holiday.

They sat on Lagardère's verandah in his canvas director-style chairs, steaming coffee cups in front of them. Ros was dressed, probably much to Lagardère's regret, in shorts and t-shirt. Sod the rules, thought Ros. We're leaving anyway. Nick was wearing just a pair of shorts, in deference to the semi-formality of the occasion.

'How is Charles?' Ros enquired of Lagardère.

'He's out of immediate danger. He has a fractured skull but

is conscious. Both your actions saved his life,' said Lagardère. 'I must congratulate you.'

They pondered on this for a while. Nick spoke next. 'So what's happened? Who was the murderer?'

'All in good time, Nick,' said Lagardère, taking a sip of his coffee. 'I must say that your theory was on the right lines. You had the right motive but wrong man. We now have a confession and, as far as we can tell, the facts are these.

'Unlike many of the English at Le Paradis, Giles Curtis was a first time visitor. A bit like yourselves.' Lagardère couldn't resist adding. 'When he arrived, he thought he recognized someone in the resort. Somebody from his investigations into the Heathrow Heist. The brains behind the job. Someone he'd even issued an arrest warrant for all those years ago.

'At the time, the police had been ready to take him into custody but he disappeared. Into thin air. Just like your Lord Lucan. Never to be seen again. Some surmised that he was dead. He wasn't. Curtis had found him. By pure chance. Unluckily, both for Curtis and his murderer.'

Lagardère poured more coffee into his cup and topped up Nick and Ros. He continued. 'Curtis was now retired and, while he may have got enormous kudos for eventually capturing the mastermind behind the bullion robbery, money was far more useful to him. So, he approached the man and threatened to expose him to the police unless he paid him a sum of money. Pure blackmail, as you surmised Nick.

'At first the killer went along with the suggestion, promising Curtis a significant part of the bullion horde which, he said, he still had in his possession.'

'And the killer – whose name you seem determined to keep to yourself – had he still got the bullion?' Nick asked.

Lagardère smiled, clearly enjoying his Poirot moment. 'We questioned him about this, but he denies having anything left.

From what he told us, though, we now have a good idea what happened that last night – the night of the murder. Curtis was late back to his cabin . . .'

'That's because he'd been down to Le Dungeon,' Nick interrupted. 'You know, the S and M club in the resort?'

Ros looked at him as if this was news to her, which, of course it was. 'I'll explain later,' said Nick.

Lagardère said. 'We didn't know that. But I guess it's irrelevant now.' Nick thought Janet and John were safe. Even if they did confess to Lagardère.

'The killer waited for Curtis in his cabin,' Lagardère continued. 'When he returned, under the pretext of showing him where the mythical gold was, he led him away from the cabin. He passed right by your cabin, and the murderer indicated for him to go down the narrow space between the cabins. Curtis stumbled over something . . .'

'That will be the bloody dustbin I fell over as well,' said Nick rubbing the still-bruised part of his shin.

Lagardère smiled. 'He fell over the dustbin and that must be when he grabbed, unluckily for you, one of your business cards that must have fallen from your bag. Before he could get up, the killer thought this might be a good time to strike. Risking the noise, he struck Curtis a heavy blow with, what we now think was, a shovel. He went down. The killer dragged him to the back of the empty cabin – the one vacated by the judge, this very one,' Lagardère indicated his cabin behind them. 'And finished him off with three or four heavy blows.'

Ros had a question. 'But why leave the body there, where it could be easily found?'

'Not so easily found. Remember, the judge leaving meant there was nobody in this cabin. And you would be vacating your cabin that morning. It was very unlikely that the body would have been found before the killer could dispose of it the following night. It was sheer bad luck that you discovered it,' said Lagardère.

'Hang on!' said Nick. 'You say that the killer knew this cabin would be empty? And that our cabin would be empty the next day? Only one person could know that.'

'Exactly!' Lagardère smiled.

'Jack? The owner of Le Paradis? Are you saying he's the missing bullion mastermind? The man who killed Giles Curtis?'

'The very same,' said Lagardère.

Nick and Ros sat quietly trying to get a grip on this piece of information.

'But how did you find out?' asked Ros, at last.

'It was something that Nick said at lunch yesterday that raised my suspicions. Remember, the fact that the English newspapers hadn't arrived that day? The very day when details of what Curtis used to do for a living appeared in the Daily Telegraph. Only one person could have ensured that the papers were not on the supermarket shelves. That was Jack.'

Nick remembered Jack reading a French newspaper that morning. Nick had assumed it was an old one. In fact, it could have been one that had been part of the batch Jack had confiscated and, presumably, later destroyed.

Lagardère continued. 'I figured that Jack didn't want one particular person in the resort to know the previous status of Curtis. We decided to keep Jack under closer surveillance after that, but we were too late last night to prevent him attacking Charles.'

This was the part of any explanation by a police inspector where one of those listening says "but what I don't understand is".

That role fell to Nick. 'But what I don't understand is Charles's involvement. After all, he and Camilla were friendly with Giles Curtis. They had dinner with him the night of his murder?'

'Well, according to Jack, Charles didn't recognize Giles Curtis, his name or previous occupation. It seems that Charles had been arrested and sent down for his part in the Heist very early on. Long before Curtis was appointed to the investigation. Because of that, Curtis didn't recognize Charles. It was a long time ago, after all.'

'But Jack and Charles knew one another, didn't they?' Ros asked.

'They did. We can't prove it yet, until we talk to Charles, but Jack tells us that Charles wasn't as straight as he seems. Over the years, Charles, on a commission basis, has been helping Jack find new homes for the odd gold bar. They were, in a legal sense, partners in crime.

'And that was at the heart of the problem. Jack didn't tell Charles about Curtis's blackmail, figuring he'd handle it himself. He knew that Charles would want nothing to do with murder. Jack figured that he'd get away with it just as long as Charles didn't think that Jack had been the killer. Unfortunately, if Charles had seen the story in the Telegraph, linking Curtis to the Heathrow Heist, he would have put two and two together. He would then have known that Jack had killed him to keep his secret safe.'

Nick took up the story. 'So when I mentioned Giles Curtis's previous occupation to Charles, he worked out that it must have been Jack that killed Curtis.'

'I saw Jack and Charles having a furious row in the Club last night,' Ros added. Now it was Nick's turn to look surprised.

'Charles didn't want to be an accomplice to murder, which he technically might be, so told Jack that he was going to turn him in. Hence, Jack tried to kill him as well. The attack last night. And he very nearly succeeded,' Lagardère said.

They all sat on the terrace absorbing the information so far. Nick asked. 'So did you go to Reception and arrest Jack?'

'We went to the office, yes. But there was nobody there. We searched his living quarters. We found bloodstained clothing but no Jack. It was just as if, yet again, he'd disappeared.

'Making sure Le Paradis and surrounding roads were sealed, I set off for the hospital to see how Charles was and whether he was fit for questioning. When I arrived, I asked directions to the intensive care private room where Charles had been taken.

'As I got there, I saw Camilla dozing on a bench outside and a figure just entering the room. It was none other than our friend Jack. There to finish off the job, before Charles could regain consciousness and tell all.'

Lagardère shrugged modestly. 'There was a brief struggle and voilà, he was in our custody.'

'So what will happen to Charles?' asked Ros.

'Well, if Jack is telling the truth, and Charles has been involved in a little receiving, I would think he may spend some more time in prison.'

'And will Charles be tried as an accomplice to murder?' Nick asked.

'I very much doubt it. I think Charles is in the clear – on the murder front at least.'

Silence again fell over the table, well, not literally of course. 'So that's it?' asked Nick. 'We're free to leave?'

'Absolutely. You are now no longer helping police with their enquiries.' Lagardère smiled. He pulled back his chair and stood up. 'I have a lot to do today. Reports to write and so on.'

Nick and Ros got up as well and Lagardère shook both their hands. He left the verandah first, turning as he reached the bottom to deliver his Casablanca salute and he was off. Looking, Nick thought, pretty pleased with himself – as well he might.

There were a couple of pieces of information, though, that

the good inspector didn't have, thought Nick. He turned to Ros. 'Could you bear being here for a few more hours?'

'As long as I can sit quietly somewhere with my clothes on. Why?'

'I've got a couple of things I need to check out.'

Ros was instantly suspicious. 'That doesn't involve any women, naked or otherwise, does it?'

Nick smiled and kissed her cheek. 'No. But I think it might, once we reach Phillip and Kathy's.'

What Nick had in mind was an outing with a certain well-equipped naked man. And it had nothing to do with sex.

41

A relieved Ros was inside the cabin packing and looking forward to a clothed existence, as Nick, nude once more, set off with the naked man in question. Martin Pike.

They set off from Pike's cabin. Pike was carrying a strange device. He was explaining it to Nick. 'They are so sophisticated these days. Up to about ten years or so ago, you couldn't differentiate between different sized and different composition objects at varying depths. Today, this latest state of the art MDE 4000 is mind-bogglingly accurate. Tells you whether you've found a penny or a horseshoe. And how deeply it's buried. Remarkably versatile as well.'

The sky was its usual azure. Birds were doing what birds do. The temperature was climbing nicely. It was the perfect day to be off prospecting.

Reaching the boules court, Nick led the way through to the clearing beyond. The summer house and bench drowsed in the sunshine.

'Here we are,' said Nick.

'What exactly are we looking for?' asked Pike, as he switched on the metal detector and adjusted his earphones.

'You won't be able to miss it, if and when we find it,' Nick replied. 'Let's just say we're looking for oblong objects, maybe a foot or so long.' He suddenly realized he'd no idea how big a gold ingot was. Nor how much it weighed. After all, he'd only seen them in Bond movies and the Italian Job. 'Let's start over by the boundary behind the summer house.'

Nick and Pike went across to where the hole had been dug. It was still as he'd seen it yesterday afternoon. Nick now concluded that this was destined to be the last resting place of Giles Curtis. In his imagination, he saw Jack sweating, digging the hole in the dark of the night, while Giles Curtis's body lay at the back of their cabin ready to occupy the space.

Nick thought it would have been the perfect crime — if he hadn't discovered the body. If Giles Curtis suddenly disappeared from the resort, Jack could field any enquiries by saying he'd checked out. Nobody would ever have known.

Giles Curtis also lived alone in London. By the time anybody had noticed him missing, the trail would be so cold that the likelihood of tracing him back to Le Paradis would be as slim as a fashion model with acute anorexia.

'Why this looks much like a grave,' said Pike.

'It does, doesn't it,' Nick agreed. Now wasn't the time to explain the whole thing to Pike. 'Can you start around here. See if anything is buried.'

Pike methodically started sweeping the ground with his metal detector. 'There are a few pieces of metal, probably nails or maybe coins. Nothing big though.' He reported to Nick.

'Keep going.' Nick sat down on the bench, remembering yesterday's tryst with Shareen with some guilt — and a fair amount of pleasure. He promised himself that would be the last time he'd ever be unfaithful to Ros.

He looked behind him into the summer house. It had a hard dirt floor, partly covered with leaves and detritus. It was just possible, he supposed.

He stood up and called to Pike. 'Martin? Can you bring that thing over here?'

When Pike made his first sweep of the summer house floor he leaped back seizing the earphones as if stung by a thousand hornets. 'My God! There's something huge down there!'

Nick took Martin's hand and shook it. In what he imagined to be a true Klondyke accent, he said, 'Well done partner. I think we've just struck gold.'

'Whatever it is, it's about three feet below the surface and takes up an area of a couple of square metres. It's a dense metal. You say it's gold?' Pike was incredulous.

'Unless it's a lead septic tank, I think we've discovered what remains of the famous Heathrow Heist bullion.'

Nick went outside and grabbed the shovel over by the fence. He felt peculiar picking it up, suspecting that it could be the very implement that had crushed in the skull of poor Giles Curtis.

'Right. Where do you think we should start?' Nick asked.

Pike indicated a spot and Nick started digging.

It was hot work under the enclosed roof. Flies buzzed into his eyes. Sweat ran down his face and body. His head hurt from last night. Pike and Nick took it in turns to dig.

After half an hour, when the hole was big enough to stand in, Nick, who was digging at the time, hit something hard.

Pike was looking at him from above, himself covered in sweat and dirt from the excavation, specs glittering in the light.

Nick bent to shovel dirt away from the object with his hand. He reached in and lifted with both hands – and that took some doing — an ingot of pure gold. Measuring about the size of a small house brick, he reckoned it weighed something in the region of twenty to thirty pounds. And he could see that it was not alone. It seemed to have a great many companions.

It was midday. Nick and Ros were now, at last, ready to leave. Well, almost ready. Nick had just taken a shower to wash off the dirt from the dig and was drying himself with his towel. He reflected back on the morning's events.

Having informed Lagardère of the find, a grubby and naked Nick and Pike, with a clothed Ros by their side, had looked on as two burly gendarmes had taken the best part of an hour to dig up the rest of the bullion.

Each ingot weighed, in fact, twenty seven and a half pounds.

Lagardère had estimated that at the current gold price of around $400 dollars an ounce, each bar was worth around 160,000 euros, or £117,000 in real money. The total number of ingots recovered was 48, making the haul worth a staggering five and a half million pounds.

Lagardère had told Pike and Nick that they could expect a substantial reward from an extremely grateful insurance company.

Nick was elated by the discovery. He still couldn't quite believe it had all happened. 'Can we do just one more thing before we leave?' Nick asked Ros, drying his hair.

With the prospect of at last escaping Le Paradis and the further bonus of a cash windfall, Ros was in accommodating mood. 'Yes, what?'

'Can we go via the bar? Drive down there and say goodbye to our fellow inmates. Buy them a drink to celebrate. Before getting dressed and getting back to reality. What do you say? We won't stay long.'

Ros remembered that the Aussie bitch might be about, but

then so what? There wasn't much Nick could do in a crowded bar, except ogle, of course. She thought the hell with it! Why not? It'd be nice to say goodbye to Geoff and Lynne, if they were about. And the others. And spread the news of the events of this morning.

'Yes, of course we can. Why don't we take Pike with us as well.' Ros lifted her t-shirt up and pulled it over her head, revealing her breasts. 'And just this once, mind.' She unzipped and stripped off her shorts and pants and stood naked in front of Nick as she had on that first morning in Le Paradis. 'Just to be sociable. And for the last time ever in public. That's a promise.'

Despite her Tahitian cover-up, Ros now had quite a good all-over tan, she thought, looking in the mirror to straighten her hair. She caught Nick smiling at her in the mirror and turned to kiss him briefly.

They packed up the car and put their clothes, ready to change into, on the back seat. Ros, armed only with her towel, sat in the front seat while Nick, towel round neck, went to the next-door cabin to knock up Pike.

Pike, evidently thinking a small celebratory shandy was in order, returned with Nick and got into the back seat, keeping their clothes company. Nick got behind the wheel. Here was another first for him. Nude motoring.

It felt strange driving the car again, let alone shorn of clothes. It was the first time he'd been in it since that first morning when he'd arrived at the cabin with a naked Shareen in the front. Who'd now been replaced by a naked Ros.

Arriving at the bar, they parked and Nick led the way inside. Although it was just gone midday, the bar contained a number of familiar faces. Garry, Hamish and Geoff were sitting at the bar, behind which was Shareen. They were, of course, all nude and all deep in conversation as Nick, Ros and Pike arrived.

Garry noticed them first. ' 'old up! It's the 'ave a go' hero!'

Garry got to his feet, with difficulty, shook Nick's hand and put his arm round his shoulders, cigarette in hand. 'Well done, my son! I hear Charlie's going to be all right.'

'Don't thank me. It was Ros here who made sure I didn't end up the same way as Giles,' said Nick.

'Well done Ros as well, then!' Garry said, giving Ros a peck on both cheeks, making her blush slightly.

'You could have knocked me down with a dingo's dongler. Pardon my French. Jack a murderer? Just couldn't be right?' said Shareen. 'All the staff are in a state of shock. I can tell you.'

'What's going to happen to the place?' Ros asked Shareen.

'Pasquale, you know, Jack's wife? She's returning today to take charge of the resort. I don't think she knew about any of this. She's just as shocked as the rest of us.'

Pike went over to Hamish and sat down next to him. Pike was definitely looking perkier this morning. As he should be with the possibility of a pension-increasing lump sum shortly to hit his bank account. They were having their own private conversation. No doubt Pike was filling Hamish in on the details of this morning's excavations.

'Shareen, how about some drinks? A bottle of champagne, glasses for everyone. And best put another bottle on ice please,' said Nick.

She smiled at him and went out the back to fetch the ice and ice bucket.

'What are we celebrating?' asked Geoff, draining his half of lager to make room for the unexpected bubbly. Nick wondered if Geoff's "beer before wine, fine" mantra applied to "lager before champagne".

'Well, Pike and I have just discovered £5 million of gold bullion.'

Now this was news that hadn't travelled round the resort. Nick had to explain how they'd found and dug up the gold.

By this time glasses had arrived and champagne had been poured. Nick and Ros had pulled up stools in a widening circle at the bar, joining the others. Pike chipped into the conversation with the odd, less than fascinating, factoid about the capabilities of his MDE 4000 metal detector.

'So how did you guess where the gold was?' asked Geoff, when Nick had finished his story.

This was a tricky one. Shareen had been listening and knew bloody well what had given Nick the idea. He looked at her. She had a small smile on her face, which you wouldn't have noticed unless you were looking. 'Yeah, Nick. How did you guess?'

'It was the other day. When we were playing boules. I hit a stray shot over there and discovered the clearing behind.'

Garry looked at Geoff, as if to say "I don't remember that happening" but merely shrugged. 'What I want to know is, did you keep a spare gold bar for me? You know, as a souvenir.'

Nick smiled. The thought had occurred to him, but he wondered what Customs and Excise at Dover might have said if they'd found a gold ingot with one of their stamps on it in the boot of his car.

At Nick's request Geoff went off to get Lynne and Sam, from their places by the pool, to join them for a drink.

Lynne looked as if she'd recovered from last night. She took her glass of champagne and clinked glasses with Nick and Ros. Sam also came in and gave Nick a peck on the cheek.

The second bottle arrived and the gathering fragmented into individual conversations. Ros was talking to Geoff and Lynne.

'So you're off today, are you?' said Geoff, taking a last opportunity, thought Ros, to study her nude form.

'Yes, in a minute. Provided Nick hasn't drunk too much, that is.'

'Well, it'll be a shame to see you go,' said Geoff, turning to Lynne. 'Won't it love?'

'Yes, it will,' Lynne replied. 'But let's all get together in London for dinner or something.'

Ros agreed, though she wondered if she'd ever be able to see the Russells again without the image of them naked coming into her mind. 'We'd love to. Only on one condition.'

'Which is?' asked Geoff.

'That we all keep our clothes fairly and squarely on,' said Ros.

Nick was talking to Pike, who was still sitting next to Hamish. 'We're going now, Martin,' said Nick. 'Thanks for the use of the trusty MDE 4000.'

'Still can't get over it,' Pike said. 'The most I've ever detected before today was a Georgian sovereign. Quite remarkable.' He seemed in a state of stunned shock, which he had every right to be.

'And the best of luck with the book. I hope someone takes it up. It's such a good idea,' said Nick, shaking Pike's hand in farewell.

He also said goodbye to Hamish, who grunted something unintelligible which Nick took to be Scottish for "take care".

Ros found herself talking to Sam, who was even browner than when they'd arrived. And perhaps a touch plumper. Ros had got used to the nipple rings by now but still couldn't ever think of having it done to her own body.

'So you're off then?' asked Sam rhetorically. 'Have you enjoyed yourself?'

'It's certainly been an experience,' said Ros, ignoring the

undertones of Sam's question. 'But not one I'd like to repeat. Naturism is not for me. Too much freedom can bring its own problems.'

'Didn't seem to bring you many problems, Ros. From what I saw, you seemed to have quite a time.' That suspicion again.

'It had its moments. But for the rest of the holiday, you'll be pleased to hear, I'm keeping my clothes firmly on.'

Sam gave her a farewell peck on both cheeks. 'Well, look after yourself. And that Nick of yours. Make sure you look after him as well.'

'Bye then Nick.' Garry was shaking Nick's hand and holding his shoulder at the same time. 'So what's the name of this boozer you go to?'

'What the one in poncey Stoke Newington?' Nick smiled.

'The very same. Thought I might come down there one night and give you and Geoff a thrashing on the dart board.'

'That would be great. The game that is. We'll see about the thrashing. It's the Prince of Wales. But remember you'll have to get used to organic crisps.'

Garry laughed. 'Yeah, most likely only sell real ale and meat-free pork pies as well. Bastards.'

They were finally ready to leave. Having said all their good-byes, Nick went to the bar to pay for the champagne. Shareen turned to put the money in the till, giving Nick his last full-length view of her body. Ros noticed him looking but she honestly couldn't blame him.

'There you go, Nick. Ten euros change.' Shareen handed him the note. This reminded Nick that they hadn't paid for the cabin. But, then again, they hadn't been there by choice for more than the one night. He didn't think Jack would miss the money where he was going.

'Good luck with the therapy and everything,' Nick said. 'I hope it all goes well for you.' And he genuinely hoped it would.

'Yeah, well, we can only hope,' Shareen said. She bent forward to kiss Nick on both cheeks, making sure her breasts didn't brush his chest. 'You take care as well, Ros.' Shareen kissed her cheeks as well.' If only Ros had known where those lips had been yesterday, thought Nick, guiltily.

They left the others in the bar and walked the short distance to the car. The sun still beat down. The sky was still blue. It was still well over thirty degrees.

Ros had got through to Phillip and Kathy earlier to tell them they'd been released. They had been promised a salad lunch with cold wine whenever they arrived. Phillip had checked on the location of Le Paradis and it seemed it was only 35 minutes away from the gite. He'd also given detailed instructions of how to find them.

As Ros and Nick got dressed, standing by the car, Nick took one last look around. At the restaurant, where diners were having lunch. At the naked sunbathers round the pool. At people just enjoying themselves on holiday.

They got into the car and drove slowly up the Champs. The gates of Le Paradis were open. So Nick and Ros went through them, from Paradise back into the mundane world of textiles.

42

Nick and Ros were taking all their clothes off again. But this time for bed. In the guest cottage, close to the pool. It was as quiet as their cabin at Le Paradis but slightly cooler.

They'd arrived at Phillip and Kathy's early afternoon and had been welcomed like long-lost friends, which is exactly what they were. A leisurely lunch in the shade was followed by lazing in and by the pool, in conventional swimwear, of course. A delicious dinner had been prepared by Kathy, accompanied by excellent wine and conversation.

As Nick was undressing, he couldn't help but think of their incarceration in Le Paradis. Of the strange sensation of going naked in public for the first time; of the seemingly placid surface of normality below which lurked murder, vice, secrets and strange sexual practices; of the attack on Charles; the discovery of the gold; and the illicit, but not wholly unwelcome, attentions of Lynne, Shareen and Janet.

Even at this short distance in time and geography, the whole experience seemed totally unreal. The one thing that did seem tangible was Ros. She had probably saved his life but it wasn't just that.

Le Paradis had acted as a wake-up call, jolting him from his complacency. Showing him that there were other ways to live; that freedom could often be an illusion; that time really was in limited supply. Simply, he realized that he wanted to spend the rest of his life with Ros, whatever the effect on his own personal freedom of choice.

As Ros brushed her hair in the mirror, she was musing on how pleased she was to be out of Le Paradis. To be able to wear clothes again. Removing clothes for Ros meant removing her inhibitions. Maybe there was too much temptation in nudity. At least as far as she was concerned. She was shocked by the whole episode with Jean-Luc. How on earth could she have done something like that? It had just been too easy. She couldn't see that happening again.

She also thought that she and Nick had some unfinished business to discuss. The baby issue. It would have to be mentioned. But she dreaded where it might lead.

Ros turned to look at Nick as he got into bed. 'What's the bed like, super sleuth?'

'Very comfortable. Crisp cotton sheets. Firm mattress.' Nick sat up in bed, sheet pulled to waist level, exposing a surprisingly brown chest.

Ros finished brushing her hair and slid into bed beside him. He put his arm round her shoulders and she snuggled into his chest.

'I also think I'd like to investigate your body, doctor. More thoroughly than in the past few days.'

'You've seen a lot of it.'

'But not sampled it, so to speak.'

Ros looked up seriously at him. 'What about preservatifs?'

'Never heard of them.'

Ros double-checked. 'So no preservatifs tonight?'

Nick looked at her with a serious expression. 'Or any other night. No, no preservatifs.'